the girl in the tangerine scarf

A NOVEL

Mohja Kahf

CARROLL & GRAF PUBLISHERS
NEW YORK

THE GIRL IN THE TANGERINE SCARF

Carroll & Graf Publishers
An Imprint of Avalon Publishing Group, Inc.
245 West 17th Street, 11th Floor
New York, NY 10011

AVALON
publishing group incorporated

First Carroll & Graf edition 2006

Library of Congress Cataloging-in-Publication Data is available.

ISBN-13: 978-0-78671-519-0
ISBN-10: 0-7867-1519-7

9 8 7 6 5 4 3 2 1

Interior design by Maria E. Torres
Printed in the United States of America
Distributed by Publishers Group West

Acknowledgments

Many people have read and responded helpfully to the manuscript since it began in 2001 as a thirty-page piece called *Henna'd Hoosiers,* and then became *Greetings from Islamistan, Indiana,* before getting its present title. I am grateful to my daughters, Weyam and Banah, who are my finest and most hard-to-please critics, for whom the original vignette was written, and to Iffat Renae Quraishi, Dr. Asifa Quraishi, Zeynab Ahmed, Dr. Yemisi Jimoh, Abdal-Hayy and Malika Moore, Patricia Dunn, Michael Muhammad Knight, Pamela Taylor, Ginny Masullo, Brenda Moossy, Alison Moore and my classmates in her 2002 writing workshop, Molly Giles, Freda Shamma, Afeefa Syeed, Nadifa Abdi, Dr. Fatima AbuGideiri, my brother Usama Kahf, Carmen and Darrel Davis, Kristi Arford, Cherri Randall, all the students in my Muslim American Literature course of Fall 2005, Leslie Berman Oelsner, Rachel Stubblefield, Rahat Kurd, and Z.S., who does not want to be named. *Merci à* Dr. Nancy Arenberg *et* Louise Rozier, and to Judith Levine. I am grateful to Patty Lebbing, Chad Andrews, and Sheila Nance for office help, and to the folks at Postal Center Plus, whence I have good luck mailing manuscripts. Thanks also to the myriad people of goodwill whom I plied for information about life in Bloomington, Turkish cigarettes, entomology labs, and tons of other things I had fun researching. Loving thanks, always, to Najib for holding down the fort so I can pursue the muse. The women who cared for my baby while I wrote have my tender gratitude: Kate Conway, Carmen Davis, Joy Caffrey, Hamsa Newmark, Kelley O'Callaghan. To the editor, Michele Slung, I owe enormous thanks for finding the story amid the clutter, and to Adelaide Docx at Carroll & Graf for her work in the final stages. The flaws that remain are due to my inordinate failings and not for lack of good help.

I am grateful, also, to the beautiful crowd of authors, living and long gone, whose points of inspiration to me may, if I am lucky, be discerned here.

. . . my creative life is my deepest prayer. . . .

—Sue Monk Kidd, *The Dance of the Dissident Daughter*

"Liar," she says to the highway sign that claims "The People of Indiana Welcome You." The olive-skinned, dark-haired young woman drives west on the old National Road. A small zippered Quran and a camera are on the hatchback's passenger seat in easy reach, covered by an open map—*States of the Heartland*. Khadra Shamy spent most of her growing-up years in Indiana. She knows better than the sign.

She passes over the Whitewater River, bracing herself. Here comes the unbearable flatness of central Indiana. She has the feeling that the world's been left behind her somewhere, in the final stretches of Pennsylvania, maybe, where the land had comforting curves. Out here there seems to be nothing for the eye to see. Strip mall, cornfield, small town main street, Kmart, Kroger, Kraft's, gas station, strip mall, soybean field, small town main street, Kmart, Kroger, Kraft's, strip mall. All blending into one flat sameness.

There are silver silos and pole barns, tufts of goldthread on the meridian, and the blue day beginning to pour into the dark sky. But it is not mine, she thinks, this blue and gold Indiana morning. None of it is for me. Between the flat land and the broad sky, she feels ground down to the grain, erased. She feels as if, were she to scream in this place, some Indiana mute button would be on, and no one would hear.

And the smell, she thinks, getting out at Glen Miller Park to pray *fajr* on the grass near a statue labeled *Madonna of the Trail*. God, what is it? She has forgotten it, living for years away. There is a definite smell to the air in Indiana. It's not pollution; not a bad odor, really—nor a good one; just *there*. Silage, soybeans, Hoosier hay, what? she asks the Madonna after *salah*. The stone Madonna in a bonnet, holding a baby in her right arm, a little boy clinging to her skirts, peers stonily into the distance.

"No checks no credit no credit cards." Khadra buys antacid and a postcard of the *Madonna of the Trail*: *Greetings from Richmond*. Eyeing the postcard, she thinks: sloppy work. I could do better. Peering into the tarnished restroom mirror, she examines her face. Her forehead is high, with a Dracula's peak, and a bit of grass has matted to it from prostration. She brushes it off.

Gray-black pieces of a busted tire flap in the lane in front of her as she gets back on the road. A faded woman in a backyard adjacent to the highway hangs a large braided rug on a rope. Khadra sees a sign for the "Centerville Christian Church." Isn't that redundant? she wonders. Like "Muslim Mosque?" *". . . of Bosnian leader Alija Izetbegović, in war-torn former Yugoslavia. . . ." ". . . traffic heats up as racecar fans converge on Indianapolis this weekend. . . ."* And then, finally, some music: Sade pouring out "Bullet Proof Soul."

Khadra glances sideways at fields of glossy black cows. A sign flashes, "Mary Lou and Mother, Rabbit Foot Crafts," but Khadra does not slow. Stimpson Grain Drying Corp. "100% American," a sign advertises—what, she doesn't know. Burly beardless white men in denim and work shirts sit in front of a burned-out storefront. The giant charred store sign, Marsh's, leans against a telephone pole. Possibly their only grocery for miles. The men's loose jowls have the cast of a toad's underbelly. She feels them screw their eyes at her as she drives past, her headscarf flapping from the crosscurrent inside the car. She rolls the windows up, tamps her scarf down on her crinkly dark hair, and tries to calm the panic that coming back to Indiana brings to her gut.

A little girl's face appeared, a girl with dark hair and a high forehead. She peeked out from between the swaying bed linens—vined, striped, and flowered—alive on clotheslines. Tucked in the elbow between two buildings in the Fallen Timbers Townhouse Complex, the laundry corner was little Khadra's hideout. Ruffled home-sewn nightgowns became Laura and Mary Ingalls racing Khadra along the banks of a prairie creek. Quivering calico blouse sleeves brushed against her as train brakes whinnied in the distance. Daddy longlegs moved from crevice to crevice in the bricks of the bordering buildings. *Old Father Long-legs, wouldn't say his prayers, take him by the left leg, and throw him down the stairs.* Khadra followed them, fascinated. Picked up fat jewel-box caterpillars with white, yellow, and black stripes. Touched a potato bug, which cringed and curled into a ball, world within worlds.

Her mother always ran the laundry twice in the Fallen Timbers basement laundry room with the coin machines. Because what if the person who used the washer before you had a dog? You never knew with Americans. Pee, poop, vomit, dog spit, and beer were impurities. Americans didn't care about impurities. They let their dogs rub their balls on the couches they sit on and drool on the beds they sleep in and lick the mouths of their children. How Americans tolerate living in such filth is beyond me, her mother said. You come straight home.

Sunshine filtered through the fabric forest. Khadra thrilled to its flutter of secrets and light, its shuttering and opening motions. Suddenly it revealed a boy with heavy pink flushed cheeks on a dirt bike, tearing through the hung laundry, pulling down rope, soiling sheets with his tire tread. Khadra ran. Screamed and ran. Fell, scraped her cheekbone on the cracked asphalt. He wheeled and turned. Gunning for her.

"Stop it! Stop! You leave me alone, Brian Lott!" She scrambled to her feet. The back of her head was still ridged from where he'd knocked her against the brick of the apartment wall last time. She'd kicked him in the shin then, and she would do it again, even if it was a fight she must lose. She braced now for the next blow coming at her from Brian and the snout of his bike.

"Khadra!" Three more kids on bikes wheeled around the corner of the building. Her assailant paused to look over his shoulder and she dodged out from where he had her cornered. O thank God. It was Eyad her brother, and his best friend Hakim, and her own friend Hanifa.

"Come on!" Hakim called, slowing for her to get on. Khadra hopped onto his banana-seat and held on to the chrome back as he lifted his bottom up off the seat to boost his pedaling momentum. And they were off.

They were four Muslim children of the heartland—two Arab, two black—flying in the blue-and-gold world on their bikes, right through the middle of the 1970s. Khadra flung her arms out in exultation and Hanifa, whizzing past her at high speed, had a beatific smile on her face from the thrill of the ride.

"Brian Lott, whyn't you go pick on someone your own size?" Eyad yelled at the boy on the dirt bike.

"Fuck you, raghead!" Brian shouted back. "We're gonna get all you fuckers!" He wheelied on "fuckers."

Before they got to Khadra's street her brother Eyad skidded to a halt and said, "Get off Hakim's bike and get on mine. 'Cause he's a boy and Mama might see you."

Hakim used to give her handlebar rides all the time, but she was getting older now, and her mother said she shouldn't ride with boys anymore.

The Lott boys had been the bane of Khadra and her family since day one. The day years ago when the Shamys moved in to number 1492 Tecumseh Drive, Fallen Timbers Townhouse Complex, Indianapolis, Indiana, on the southern city limits where the sprawling city almost met up with the small adjoining town of Simmonsville. Little Khadra had got out of the wide station wagon, blinking in the sunlight, a pudgy, shortwaisted girl wearing an elastic friendship bracelet.

There was her father, wiry and olive-complexioned, with glasses. He wore a short beard on a thin pointy chin. Her mother was green-eyed and ivory-skinned and lovely. She wore a white wimple on her head, and a long blue robe. The color of sky, it swept the earth. A boy with short, smooth chestnut-brown hair got out last, stretching. Khadra's brother Eyad was ivory-colored like the mother, with the high contrast between dark hair and pale skin that many Syrians have.

Khadra and Eyad were unloading the U-Haul when they heard taunts behind them. Two boys with coarse pink faces, noses broadened in sneers. What they saw spilling out of the station wagon with its fake wood panel was a bunch of foreigners. Dark and wrong. Dressed funny. Their talk was gross sounds, like someone throwing up.

"Hey, Allison-Bone!" one of them called. "Get a load of this."

A thickwaisted white girl with a bowl haircut peered over their shoulders.

Khadra and Eyad were inside calling dibs on bedrooms when they heard the crash of glass. Beer bottles, a pile of brown and gold shards at their doorstep.

Their father went up to the door across the street and knocked. Khadra and her brother sat on the curb, watching as their mother swept up the glass bits with a plastic yellow broom. Skinny little white woman answered the door. Yellow hair like the broom bristles.

"Yeah, that's Vaughn's boys."

Sound of their father saying something. Stiff British textbook English, in an Arabic rhythm. Back of his head bobbing. He believed, he believed in the innate goodness of people, and in the power and sweetness of communicating with them.

"Vaughn!" the yellow-haired woman called over her shoulder.

Burly man at the door now. "—ACCUSING MY CHILDREN

—OFF MY PORCH—BACK WHERE YOU PEOPLE CAME FROM!"

The neighbors on the other side were as nice as the Lotts were mean. They were a young couple and each had long hair and wore loose clothes and lots of necklaces. Lindsey and Leslie bewildered the Shamys, because you couldn't tell which of them was the woman and which the man.

"Miso soup for our new neighbors!" one of them said at the door, holding a bowl of something with a potholder under it. If male, he had very cleanshaven soft skin. If female, she had big knuckles and a very flat chest. This unnerved Khadra's mother. If she could be sure it was the woman, she'd invite her in, but if it was the man, she'd stay behind the screen door and be careful not to touch his hand when she took the bowl. What was she supposed to do? In the end, she smiled politely and thanked him or her, wondering what on earth was in the soup.

Khadra peers up now at the passing signs on the highway. "Home of James Whitcomb Riley." "Pecans, We Buy and Sell" (hand-lettered on rough boards). "Merchants and Farmers Bank, your neighbors who care." "Indianapolis Motor Speedway, use 465 to 65." Her family had always avoided that route this time of year, and she now does the same. No sense getting pulled into Indy 500 traffic. "New Palestine Jct. 74." And finally, "Welcome to Indianapolis—City at the Crossroads." Here we go. Looking for the exit sign that will lead her back to horrible little Simmonsville.

Back where you came from.

How shall we sing the Lord's song in a strange land?

—Psalm 137

The first world Khadra remembered was Square One. This was before Indiana, when they lived in the Rocky Mountains. Four buildings faced a center playground, and around the playground lay a swath of green grass, dandelion dotted. Forming a ring around the grass was a sidewalk wide enough for hopscotch and Big Wheel drag racing. There was a willow tree on the lawn, which her mother called "the Shy Tree," its Arabic name (because look how it's tucking its head down shyly). The lawn was watered by wonderful spigots that made a musical sound as they inched around, chica-chica, chica-chica, chica chica. Then up swept an arc of water going back to the beginning, chica-chooooo.

"Mama, what's heaven?"

"Heaven is where you have all your heart desires."

Khadra figured that meant heaven was Square One. There were swings on long silver chains. You wriggled your butt into the seat and you got pushed up-up-up and you learned the lines of the *Fatiha:*

"Bismillah arrahmani 'rahim!" Khadra sang as her father pushed her up. Green grass full of dandelions fell away beneath her.

"Alhamdu lilahi rabil alamin," Eyad yelled on the next swing. He knew how to pump for himself.

"Arrahmani 'rahim!" Khadra called as she climbed into the blue atmosphere like an astronaut.

Her father, pushing her one day, said, "Lift your legs hard going up. Push them down hard going down."

Suddenly Khadra could do it. "I can swing! By myself, I can swing!" Treetops flashed beneath her feet. "See me, Mama, see me, Baba!" And they saw.

In Square One, their mother used to be willing to wash Eyad and Khadra's bottoms. Your butt hung in the bowl, chin to knees, legs dangling down the white porcelain, you called, loud's you could, 'Mamaaaaa! Pleeease wash my boootom!" And she came hustling. The big fat water tin was too heavy; a grown-up had to lift it.

One day she got a pink plastic watering can. It was small and light. "Look. You pour the water with your right hand like this, and you reach down with your left hand like this, and while the water runs over your pee-pee or your poo-poo place, you wipe and wipe and clean yourself."

"Ew."

"No ew and no phew about it, young lady. Everybody has to clean their own bottom in this world."

Alessandra-called-Sandra was from Mexico and spoke only Spanish until day before yesterday. A lot of the children in Square One were from other countries besides America. The American kids in Square One didn't seem to know yet that they were supposed to be better than the rest because it was their country. Their parents were all students at the same university.

Khadra and Eyad spoke only Arabic at first. You didn't need to speak the same language to exchange friendship bracelets, and this Khadra and her Spanish-speaking friend did. Khadra couldn't remember how she learned the new language, only that she opened her mouth one day and English came out. Pretty soon after Khadra and Alessandra-called-Sandra could talk to each other in English, they started making fun of the little Japanese boy in South Building for saying "I sreep in my loom."

"Chinese, Japanese, dirty knees, look at these!" Khadra and Sandra taunted, pointing to their non-existent breasts at the last line. The boy cried and went whimpering home.

"You be'd mean to that boy," Eyad said to her. He was two and a half years older than Khadra.

"You're not the boss of me!" She stamped her foot.

Her parents called her and her brother in: prayer time. "Hafta go," she said under the Shy Tree to Alessandra-called-Sandra.

"Why?"

"Hafta pray."

"Can I come?"

Khadra made her wait at the door, by the tin box where the milkman left cold bottles of milk at fajr time. "Mama, can Alessandra-called-Sandra watch us pray?"

"Welcome, welcome to the guest," Mama said, sitting the little girl on a slatted wooden chair. "The guest is always welcome." There wasn't much furniture yet. America put wardrobes right into the walls, saved you having to buy them.

Her father was calling the *qad qamat*. Eyad spread the prayer rugs. Khadra ran to splash her ablutions fast-fast so she wouldn't miss the bow and have to do the whole ralat over.

"Elbows, please," her father said gently, when she skidded into her place on the prayer rug, dripping water.

She stuck her elbows out for inspection.

"Dry elbows," he said, shaking his head. "Do over."

"What if I just wet my elbows?" Khadra said.

"That's not ablution," her mother said. "Ablution goes together, can't be separated. It's all one thing. Like prayer."

May my hands be instruments of peace, may my mouth speak only truth, may this nose smell the fragrance of holiness, may this face shine with the light of compassion, may these ears hear the Word of God, may this neck bend in humility to the One, may these feet walk in paradise.

Alessandra-called-Sandra swung her little ashy legs against the chair, bumpity-bump, while the family whispered the Fatiha, arms folded across chests. When they all knelt down-down-down, and put their faces on the floor for the *sajda,* her legs went still and her eyes got round as saucers.

In Square One, Khadra and her brother didn't notice how, near the end of each month, their mother measured out the cups of rice smaller and cooked a little less every day. They did notice marvelous snow-covered days, when she'd scoop the fresh fall into a bowl and sprinkle sugar on it and hand them spoons. Snowcones from God.

The family's first winter in the new land was a season of wonder. Khadra's parents took the children for a drive up a Rocky Mountain ridge. The snow gave a halo to everything.

"Look! Up there!" her father said as they turned a corner. Tall grand houses were padded with white down and outlined in colored lights, gable and turret and door.

"And—look down!" her mother cried, pointing.

There, spread below them, was the city, pinwheel after pinwheel of light. Spinning gears of light. This was amazing. This was America. The children marveled, but the parents were young themselves, and could hardly believe they were looking upon the world from these dizzying heights. They were a galaxy away from home, for the first time in sober young lives spent mostly within a small radius around Damascus.

Danger abounded. Pork was everywhere. At first the young couple thought it was merely a matter of avoiding the meat of the pig. Soon their eyes were opened to the fact that pig meat came under other names and guises in this strange country. Sometimes it was called bacon, other times it was called sausage, or bologna, or ham. Its fat was called lard and even in a loaf of Wonder Bread it could be lurking. Bits of pig might appear in salad—imagine, in salad! Jell-O had pig. Hostess Twinkies had pig. Even candy could have pig.

Pig meat was filthy. It had bugs in it, Khadra's father said. That's why God made it *haram,* her mother said. If you ate pig, bugs would grow and grow inside your stomach and eat your guts out. Always ask if there is pig in something before you eat anything from *kuffar* hands.

Mrs. Brown the kindergarten teacher poured the candy corn into a little flowered plastic cup on Khadra's desk.

Khadra said, "I can't eat this," her round, baby-fat face grave.

"Why not, sweetie?" Mrs. Brown said, bending low so her white face was next to Khadra's.

"There's a pig in it."

Mrs. Brown laughed a pretty laugh and said, "Nooo, there isn't a pig in it, dear!"

"Are you sure?"

"I'm positive."

She was so pretty and so nice and so sure. Khadra ate the candy corn and put some in her pocket. But when Eyad saw the candy corn on the bus he said, "Ommm, you ate candy corn. Candy corn has pig!"

"Nuh uh!"

But it did. And it was too late to throw it up. Khadra was tainted forever. If she lived, that is. Too ashamed to tell her parents, she waited in horror for the bugs to grow in her stomach and eat her guts out.

Go forth lightly and heavily and strive with your wealth and your selves in the path of God, that is best for you, if you but knew.

—Quran 9:41

One day Khadra's father heard a call in the land and, the love of God his steps controlling, decided to take his family to a place in the middle of the country called Indiana, "The Crossroads of America." He had discovered the Dawah Center.

His wife said that a Dawah worker's job was to go wherever in the country there were Muslims who wanted to learn Islam better, to teach it to their children, to build mosques, to help suffering Muslims in other countries, and to find solutions to the ways in which living in a kuffar land made practicing Islam hard. This was a noble jihad.

"Position open: Chapter Coordinator, Dawah Center. Develop Islamic education programs via logical Islamic methodology. Requirements: Practicing Islamic lifestyle, sound Islamic belief, college degree. Contact: Br. Omar Nabolsy or Br. Kuldip Khan, Indianapolis Home Office, 1867 New Harmony Drive, Simmonsville, Indiana." (Classified in *The Islamic Forerunner*)

So they loaded up everything they owned on the luggage rack of the station wagon and set off over prairie and dale like pioneers. Tall tall mountains shining in their eyes. Immaculate lakes like God's polished tables. Rivers that churned and frothed. Forests, high-treed and terrifying, and then land so wide and flat it made you lonely.

"Where's Syria?" Khadra asked Eyad, staring at her stubby toes on the back window of the station wagon where they lay on a Navajo blanket. Khadra couldn't remember Syria, although she thought of it whenever she rubbed a little boomerang-shaped scar on her right knee that had been made on a broken tile in Syria. Red blood running down a white stone step. *Walay himmek. Ey na'am.* Sometimes she had a vague memory of having been on a mountain. Dry sunny days that had a certain smell made her think of Syria, and when she bit into a tart plum or a dark cherry, her mouth felt like Syria.

Eyad, with his serious gray-green eyes, remembered Syria in complete sentences, not flashes of words and tastes. Life there had Aunt Razanne and Uncle Mazen. And their kids, cousin Reem and cousin Roddy, drinking powdered milk from a big tin that said NEEDO. Syria was Mama's daddy called Jiddo Candyman, with his tuft of thick white hair like cotton candy, throwing you up-up while you screamed with delight. The *adhan* floating down from up in the air.

Streets busy with people who spoke Arabic in the same rhythms as his mother and father, *ey wallah,* people whose faces bore his parents' features. Here in 'Mreeka, no one looked like them and they looked like no one.

"Far away," Eyad said gravely. "Syria's far, far away."

"Where? Point. Where the sky touches the ground, is that Syria?"

"No," he said, with authority. "Farther."

"Like a star?" She squinted at the street lamps, making them send rays of light to her eyes.

The little frontier family trekked the Oregon Trail in reverse, with as much wonder in their hearts as the pioneers of an earlier century heading the other way. Square One itself had been strange enough and new, and now they were going further, over the edge of the known world. At the start of every day, their mother recited the Throne of the Heavens and the Earth Verse, the three "I seek refuge" chapters from the Quran, and her favorite travel prayer: *O Thou My God: I seek refuge in Thee from humiliation or humiliating, from being astray or leading others astray, from wronging or being wronged, from ignorance or having ignorance perpetrated upon me.*

It has been seven years since the adult Khadra had set foot in Indiananapolis. She'd left in the middle of a college degree, in the middle of a marriage to a nice Muslim guy, in the middle of community ties she cauterized abruptly. The Fallen Timbers Townhouses are coming up on the right and, on a whim, she turns off on General Wayne Drive toward it: the old homestead.

There are laundry lines by the corner wall. There's number 1492 Tecumseh Drive. A caramel-colored girl comes out the door swinging a brown shopping bag full of fancy ladies' shoes. *"¡A la casa de Simona!"* she shouts over her shoulder.

Khadra, returning to this ground that didn't love her, tries to stave the panic in her gut that is entirely the fault of the state of Indiana and the lay of its flat, flat land, to which she had never asked to be brought. She repeats the favorite prayer of her mother aloud to the windshield of her little car and grips the steering wheel a little tighter, like someone holding a small lantern and going out to investigate, a little afraid of what she might find.

Hoosier \'hü-zhər/ a native or resident of Indiana — used as a nickname.

—Merriam-Webster

. . . in the eighteenth century, Hoosier was used generally to describe a backwoods-man, especially an ignorant boaster, with an overtone of crudeness and even lawlessness.

—Howard H. Peckham, *Indiana, A History*

The Shamy family had come to Indiana for God. It wasn't much pay.

"It doesn't matter," Khadra's mother said. "We are not in love with the glitter of this world." But oh, Khadra loved the glitter of the purple banana seat bike at the garage sale. Her father haggled the price down to four dollars.

"How come 'Nifa and them get new bikes, Baba?" she asked, skittering to keep up with her father as he maneuvered the bike to the station wagon.

"When I was your age back in Syria, my folks were so poor I had to work after school till dark. Days we had nothing in the house but bread and olives."

"Yeah, but how come Hanifa and them get new bikes?"

"Say *al-hamdu-lilah,* Khadra." He hoisted the bike into the cargo space of the station wagon. "Give thanks for what you have."

"*Hamdilah*. But how come—"

His mother's mother had been a seamstress. In the days of privation and cholera epidemic in Damascus, when menfolk were drafted by the Turks and forced to fight the Safar Barlek, she scraped through by sewing for the neighbors. She pedaled that kettle-black Singer to success. By the 1920s, ladies from all over Damascus would come to her with fashion magazines, point at an outfit, and she'd custom tailor it for them, or delegate it to one of her apprentices—young women vied to be trained by her.

"Like, a fashion designer?" Khadra said, looking at the woman with the arching brows and upswept hair in the faded photo, one of the few pictures the Shamys packed with them from Syria. Her father's grandma eyeballed you, looking kind of magnificent and cheekbony, not like the pictures of Mama's mother, which showed a plump, sweet-faced woman looking like she was about to give you a big cozy hug in shades of black and white.

The Shamy side tended to look heroic and solemn in photographs. Khadra's dad, Wajdy, had a picture of his father, Jiddo Abu Shakker, in his youth, standing at attention in a military uniform. His mother, Sitto Um Shakker, is seated next to him in her bridal dress. Both look brave and sad and serious. Of course they wouldn't have been called Um Shakker and Abu Shakker then, because they hadn't had the first baby, Shakker, yet.

Jiddo the Soldier-Man had died the year before they came to

America. It happened when her father's big brother Shakker got put in jail for saying things against the Syrian government. Her father said Syria was a mean government, and that Shakker had told the truth to its face and that's called standing witness and that's what a good Muslim should do. Shakker died a hero. A martyr. In Syria, everyone in the Shamy neighborhood called Wajdy "Shakker's little brother."

The last picture they had of Jiddo Abu Shakker is of him in a fez and a full gray beard, smiling sadly. Baby Khadra is in his lap and little tyke Eyad in a sailor suit at his knee.

"They didn't have such fancy titles as 'fashion designer' in Syria then," her father answered Khadra. "Seamstress is what she called it." He had learned to sew almost by osmosis. *"Burdas"*—that's what Wajdy called sewing patterns—"burdas are for beginners."

Little Khadra had only to point to a dress in her *Sleeping Beauty* Golden Book and her father would whip it up for her on the secondhand Singer. Her friends may have flaunted gorgeous new ghararas from Hyderabad on Eid, with gold-on-red and silver-on-green *chumki*-bordered brocade and matching depattas thrown over their shoulders like glamorous boas. But they had nothing on the fairy-tale gown Khadra's father made for her. It boasted five—count 'em, five—tiers of ruffles on the full-length violet skirt, and a petal collar with rickrack trim.

Their mother was getting fat. Soon the children were told—it wasn't fat, it was a new baby on the way. Khadra and Eyad got it then—the worry about money. They clipped coupons for double coupon day and saved pennies for baby-food jars and diapers and plastic panties.

In brother-sister huddles, Eyad and Khadra discussed getting jobs that would help the family budget. "Paper route?" Eyad whispered. "How much money do they make?" Khadra whispered back.

Their mother didn't work. At least, not outside the home. Inside she worked plenty, scrubbing things clean, getting spots out, refolding aluminum foil, deboning chicken to make it last several meals, stretching things out until the next paycheck. Making sure filth did not seep underfoot from the trickle around the toilet bowl and get carried to the rest of the house by the wet squishing soles of plastic bathroom slippers. *Don't wear the bathroom slippers outside the bathroom. Leave them at the door—you're tracking impurities—now we can't pray there until the carpet's shampooed and purified!* Making sure the kids did chores and didn't turn into lazy American children. *But Mama—Hanifa and Hakim are waiting for us to ride our bikes to the candy store!*

Hanifa and Hakim al-Deen lived in the Fallen Timbers. Their dad, Uncle Jamal, worked at a big pharmaceutical company but their mom, Aunt Khadija, was a secretary at the Dawah Center so they played with the Shamy kids nearabout every day.

"I have a college degree, like Wajdy," Khadra's mother said to Aunt Khadija. At one time, she thought she might go to medical school. "But after I graduated, I chose to stay home. For the children." She patted her belly, which globed firm and round in front of her.

"That is her most important work: making more Muslims," Khadra's father liked to say jovially. "Good-quality Muslims, that is. An educated mother is the child's first school!"

Ebtehaj Qadry-Agha had a good-quality Muslim baby at the

hospital. A beaming Wajdy Shamy pointed him out to Khadra and Eyad through the nursery window, a red, squinting, mewling bundle that turned out to be a boy named Jihad. Khadra and Eyad spent the night at Hakim and Hanifa's.

The al-Deen townhouse was a mirror image of the Shamys'. Where the Shamys' entrance and hallway were to the left of the dinette, kitchen, and living room, the al-Deen hallway was to the right. Instead of a matching country plaid couch set in harvest gold and hunter green, the al-Deens had a beige overstuffed sectional that overfilled the living room. Instead of the Shamys' big wooden TV with the rabbit ears (on which they'd all watched Nixon's big square head say "I am resigning the office of the presidency effective at noon tomorrow"), the Al-Deens had a hi-fi stereo system and stacks of records and eight-tracks by K-tel, from Al Green to the Valadiers. Khadra's parents ignored this wall of music when visiting Uncle Jamal and Aunt Khadija and didn't understand why they kept this monument to their pre-Muslim years.

. . . the Honorable Elijah Muhammad's teaching . . . is part of Islamic tradition, not an isolated, unique invention of half-baked negro theology. . . . Arabs have no monopoly on Islam.

—Marvin X, *In the Crazy House called America*

Aunt Khadija's name used to be Kacey. Kacey Thompson, then she changed it to Kacey X, then Khadija X, then Khadija Kareem when she became a Bilalian, then Khadija Al-Deen when she married Uncle Jamal.

"Was that when you finally became a real Muslim?" Khadra asked, licking powdered Tang out of a paper cup, a habit for which Aunt Khadija said she'd lose all her teeth before the age of twenty. "Or were you still that Elijah thing. The fake Muslims where it's only for black people?" Khadra was perched on the side of Aunt Khadija's desk in the secretarial pool at the Dawah Center, swinging her short legs. It was the room that used to be the front parlor when the house had been a family home.

Aunt Khadija didn't answer right off. She turned her face away and filed some papers in a metal cabinet. Things were busy because it was almost Memorial Day, the time of year when the Dawah Center held its annual conference.

"What is a real Muslim, Khadra?" Aunt Khadija said finally.

"When you do the Five Pillars," Khadra shrugged, "you know, and follow the Quran and the Prophet and wear *hijab* and follow the Islamic way of life and—"

Aunt Khadija said gently, "Shahada. That's all. Belief that God is One. When that enters your heart and you surrender to it, you are a Muslim."

Khadra felt alarm. It wasn't that simple. Her parents said so. You have to *practice* Islam to be a real Muslim.

"Remember," Aunt Khadija said, "I was born a Muslim, Khadra. Just like you." "But—you converted," Khadra protested. She had seen Aunt Khadija's yearbook. She used to be a regular American girl with beehive hair, wearing a miniskirt, having a boyfriend. That's not Living the Islamic Lifestyle. She peered wonderingly up at Aunt Khadija's face, her rounded cheeks like dark red apples. Khadra's father said all that Elijah Mohammad business was nonsense. He said it was a good thing Black Muslims like Aunt Khadija and Uncle Jamal converted to real Islam or they would be wandering astray.

"I don't say I 'converted,'" Aunt Khadija said gently. "I say I *'reverted.'* Everyone is born in a state of surrender to God. That's what the word 'muslim' means, really. I rediscovered my natural state, that's all. Surrender is—"

"Khadra, Khadra, let Aunty do her work," Khadra's father said. Hundreds of mailed-in conference registration forms needed to be sorted.

Aunt Khadija helped Khadra tie on her scarf for prayer. "Imagine being made to stand naked in front of a whole bunch of people," Aunt Khadija murmured.

Khadra drew back with a look of horror.

"Mmm hmm. That's how it was," Aunt Khadija said, her face framed in a plum-colored scarf. "That's how it was for black women back in slavery times. Up on the auction block. Covering up is a strong thing." Khadra hopped off the desk and followed the back of Auntie Khadija's dark rose thobe as it trailed, dignified, up the stairs to the prayer room.

One time in fourth grade, Khadra thought she might start wearing hijab like the big girls, but then Hanifa had called to say "let's go swimming!" so she'd put it off and run to meet her friend at the Fallen Timbers pool. The two girls cannonballed and butterflied, and raced squealing to the finish line in the water, basking in sun and air.

After hijab, she'd still be able to swim in private pools, such as at the home of the Sudanese doctor's family up in Meridian Hills. Dr. Abdul-Kadir's elegant, *tobe*-clad wife sometimes invited all the girls to a women-only pool party, and Khadra and Hanifa got into splash fights with Maha, the doctor's daughter.

The Abdul-Kadir family and the other Northern Indy Muslims were rich. They didn't work for the cause of Islam full-time like Dawah people but were doctors, lawyers, engineers. Khadra's mother said somebody had to do those important jobs. "I used to dream I would be a doctor one day, and open a free clinic for poor people," she said. And Khadra's dad said it was okay to be rich, but it was a trial from God. What would you do with it?

The Abdul-Kadirs did good things with it. Like, a lot of Muslims were being killed in Cambodia, and the Dawah Center wanted to help Cambodian Muslims get to a safe haven in America, but raising enough money was hard. Khadra and Hanifa baked tray after tray of brownies, and Aunt Trish made her carrot cake, and Aunt Dilshad fried her samosas (Too hot! They made your eyes water). Eyad and Hakim and Malik Jefferson and the Haqiqat sisters pitched in to sell it all for weeks and weeks after *juma* at Masjid Salam. Still, it wasn't enough. Then the Abdul-Kadirs wrote a big check, as much as had been raised in weeks of bake sales, and boom, just like that, there was enough to bring over the Cambodian family, Sufiya and Ali and their baby Hassan. Only Uncle Kuldip said to call them Cham, not Cambodian.

"They're here, they're here!" Uncle Kuldip was bringing the Chams from the airport. The "auntie crew" was stocking the cabinets with groceries. Eyad and Hakim and Danny Nabolsy had to shovel the walk to the guest house and, since it was the kind of snow that had sat and iced over for days and came off only in chunks, they had a job of it. Danny's big brother Sammy sat on the back porch with his feet up on the rail, laughing at them. Nilofar Haqiqat and Hanifa al-Deen hustled to put the vacuum cleaner away. Khadra, at the window with Insaf Haqiqat, stared curiously as Uncle Kuldip drove up with the newcomers.

They'd never seen Cham people before. The Cham lady was Khadra's height and the man was not much taller and so slight of build he looked like an Indiana winter wind could knock him flat. In his arms was the tiny, fragile, wrinkled Cham baby.

Dr. Abdul-Kadir examined the baby with a stethoscope from his black bag. He didn't say anything. He then took out an ear doogiemabob and looked in baby's ears and nose and throat. Aunt Trish was holding her breath the whole time. When the doctor said the baby was "*alhamdulilah* okay," she let out a little laugh and blew her nose. Not just Aunt Trish.

When Tayiba Thoreau moved into Fallen Timbers, there was quite a stir. For one thing, her family had a dog. They were Muslim and they had a big blond hairy dog named Custer. What's more, her father was a white man, a white American man who was a Muslim.

"Nuh-uh," Khadra said, jealous that Hanifa saw the new girl first. She had floor-scrubbing chores. But at least her friend had raced right over to give her the scoop.

Who had ever heard of such a thing: a white American man, Muslim? "CIA plant?" some of the grown-ups whispered. "FBI?"

The four kids rode their bikes over to see the new family. They ogled: Tayiba was mod. They had never seen a mod Muslim girl before. She wore platform shoes with holes through the heels, bell-bottom jeans, a breezy peasant blouse and large sunglasses that rested atop her hijab—a jaunty little kerchief tied at the side of her head. A hijab with a *side* tie? Hanifa and Khadra looked at each other.

Tayiba was three years older than Khadra, plus she came from Chicago. So, of course, she was loads more sophisticated than any of them. Her father was from Nebraska and her mother from Kenya.

"It's haram to have a dog, you know," Khadra lost no time telling Tayiba.

"Is not," Tayiba said, scratching behind Custer's ears.

"Is too." The animal was jumping around Tayiba's knees and Khadra eyed the interaction closely for signs of dog drool. "And you better wash your hands seven times."

Tayiba turned away, bristling at Khadra's know-it-all airs about religion.

Her dad was a very pale white man with almost white-blond hair. Khadra did not know hair could be that blond for real. He was the Dawah Center accountant. He also gave "Why I Embraced Islam" lectures regularly at mosques across the nation.

Tayiba's mom, Aunt Ayesha, did secretarial work at the Center part-time. She was thin-lipped, pointy-nosed, and sharp-tongued. Her oval, upwardly slanted face with aristocratic features was as darkest blue-black as her husband was palest white. She came from a family of schoolteachers in Mombasa. If she fixed a certain look on you through her turquoise cat's-eye glasses that were studded with tiny rhinestones, you were pinned to the spot and forgot whatever foolish thing you were going to say.

Tayiba's sister, Zuhura, was a lot older, practically a grown-up to Khadra and them. She went to Indiana University, Bloomington. A well-spoken girl, she had adult conversations about social justice in Islam with the learned Uncle Kuldip and with Khadra's father and the other uncles and aunties. Aunt Ayesha, standing next to her husband, managed to maintain a stern gaze even as you could see she was beaming at her daughter's eloquence. Zuhura looked like a taller, plumper version of her mom, not like her dad at all.

"She's full Kenyan," Tayiba said. "My mom's first marriage."

It took two people to handle Tayiba's hair, which bulged enormously under her headwrap. When she let it out of its bundle, it bounded out, with a span nearly a yard wide. Khadra couldn't even believe how big it was.

When Tayiba had to wash her hair, everything came to a screeching halt. "I can't go biking with you today, I have to wash my hair."

"So? Wash it and get your booty out here," Khadra called up to Tayiba's window, annoyed. What a blow-off. "Wash my hair" —like that takes all day.

Tayiba rolled her eyes. "You don't understand. I have to WASH my HAIR," she said. "It's not like washing your little ole hair, girl. It is a whole THING of its OWN."

It felt weird calling Tayiba's dad "Uncle Joe," the way the kids in the community called all the Muslim grown-ups "aunt" and "uncle." "Joe Thoreau" just did not seem like a proper Muslim name. Uncle Joe was so white he had that blotchy pink type of face that white men had. The kind that, when it loosened and got jowly on older men like the school principal, made Khadra's mom shudder because she said it looked like the underneath parts of a man's body that should be covered. Why didn't American men grow beards like decent folk?

After a while, Tayiba's dad changed his name from Joe to Yusuf. Then he grew a beard. And sent the dog away, to his brother in Chicago. He started to fit in at the Center much better.

. . . the presence of the heart with God, always or most of the time, certainly has primacy over the ritual acts of worship. . . . Indeed, the rest of the realm of worship is sanctified by this conscious remembrance, which is itself the ultimate aim of the practical act of worship. . . .

—al-Ghazali

Hanifa cartwheeled across the *masallah*—the prayer space—of Salam Mosque.

"Betcha won't!" Khadra had dared, and that was all it took —Hanifa was off, a flash of arms and legs. She was like that, a daredevil.

"You too!" she said to Khadra, flushed and laughing.

Khadra, after looking over her shoulder, had just lifted her arms high in the air when an uncle walked in. She stopped short, and then she and her friend dissolved in giggles, and couldn't help having intermittent giggle fits all the rest of that day in Sunday school.

Masjid Salam Alaikum, or Salam Mosque, was a storefront space in the black part of Indianapolis and had served the local Muslim community before the Dawah Center was a gleam in a bearded engineering student's eye. The Salam community welcomed the influx of immigrant Muslims in a cautious embrace, only to find the Center siphon off some of its members toward the (very white) south side of the city to work at the Dawah office. Meanwhile, earnest young Dawah members like the Shamys attended juma at Masjid Salam and felt free to tell the Afro-American brethren how to run things, despite the fact that, as far as the number of years in Islam went, many of the birth-Muslims hadn't been awakened to their Islamic consciousness any earlier than the converts had converted.

Masjid Salam was where Khadra and the other Dawah children went for weekend Islamic school. The name of the mosque was taped in homemade lettering across the big front window. Black-eyed Susans and spindly Queen Anne's lace grew up to the windowsill in summer. It used to be a travel agency and there was still a poster of a spinning globe in one corner of the window. A faded calico curtain was pinned up across the window.

There was a new-carpet smell to the flat, cheap office carpet in the masallah, where masking tape marked prayer lines for men and women, with open space between them that got filled up only on Fridays. A cubby shelf for shoes stood in the foyer. At the rear of the prayer area was a little hallway that led to a small dim bathroom, freshly painted white to cover up graffiti and grease stains from previous renters. Spray cans of cleanser stood under the chipped porcelain sink and on the floor next to the toilet was a plastic jug for washing yourself. The jug looked like it might have been red once but was faded to a dusty salmon color. Taped up by the scratched mirror was a piece of notebook paper with "Cleanliness, is part of *iman!"* scrawled earnestly in black magic marker, the letters blurry where water from somebody's elbow-rinsing had splashed them.

In the narrow back hallway was a map captioned "The Muslim World." The countries that were mostly Muslim were dark green. Light green meant they had a lot of Muslims, yellow-green and yellow meant they had some, and the pink and dark pink countries had next to none. The U.S.S.R., Khadra was surprised to see, was light green. China was yellow. The U.S. was only pink. Muslims didn't count for much here.

That's all there was to the mosque: the open masallah area and the back bathroom and hallway. The prayer space was where everyone sat: men, women, children, and where everything happened: lessons, meetings, elections, dinners. And of course, prayers.

First position, *qiyam.* Standing, feet planted hip-distance apart for balance, focus, before you raise your arms in *allahu.* "Straighten your lines, close the gaps—stand shoulder to shoulder and foot to foot," the imam at Salam Mosque said before he called the first allahu. "Shaytan gets between you if you leave a gap." Like one of the pushy boys in the lunch line at school, Khadra imagined. She squinched close up against Tayiba and tugged Hanifa's arm to pull her into line. "No pushy Shaytan gonna get between us, hunh."

"Wala addaleeeeen," called the imam.

"Aaaahmeeeen," the congregation responded. Khadra loved the 'ameens.' The strong vibrations of the men's voices and the murmurs

of the women made her feel safe. Sandwiched between them, she was right where she belonged. Everyone knew her, and who her mother and father were; little Jihad whimpering down the prayer line was as likely to get picked up by Aunt Fatma or Aunt Khadija as by his mother.

You went into *ruku,* the bow, with your knees locked and back straight as a table—someone should be able to put a full glass on your back without spilling. You whispered your *subhana-rabial-atheems,* looking down at your toes in their own little lines. Here comes the signal to rise—

"Sami allahu li man hamida," everyone rose from ruku. Khadra's father and all the uncles in Western pants had to pick wedgies out of their butts at this point. But those who wore loose shalvars or dashikis were good to go.

"Rabbana wa laka alhamd," one congregant responded loudly.

Now you dropped into sajda, prostration. No flopping elbows on the floor, because that's a dog posture and Muslims don't do dog. Humility yes, dog no. Seven surfaces only touch the mat during sajda: Palm, palm, knee, knee, foot, foot, forehead. There, after three *subhanas,* you whispered your private prayers, nose brushing the bumpity carpet. You left room for a baby. If Khadra's brother Jihad was lying there, say, she should be able to make the sajda over him. (And maybe give him a little belly tickle along the way).

When the portly Uncle Abdulla imamed, his curly-haired little girl Sabriya giggled and threw herself on the round mound of his back and clambered up for a piggyback ride. He let her play, just like the Prophet Muhammad let his granddaughter play on his back when he led the entire Muslim *umma* in Medina. Khadra sneaked a peek to see why the sajda was so long. Uncle Abdulla waited until the girl had a good grip on his neck, then said *"allahu akbar"* in a slightly choked voice, and rose, lifting her up-up-up on his back. She squealed with such delight that some people in the prayer lines tried to suppress smiles and think of God. Others managed to smile *and* think of God at the same time.

American converts found the *juloos* posture hard. You sat with legs folded under you, thighs pressed against calves. "Americans hardly ever sit on the floor," Khadra's mother observed. "Their bodies forget how to pray after sitting up stiffly at tables and desks, working to gain the wealth and glitter of this world."

"You forgot to fold your hands, Auntie Dilshad. Mama, why did Auntie Dilshad forget to fold her hands?" Khadra had never seen anyone put their hands down by their sides after the first *allahu akbar*. "And why is there a piece of rock in front of her?"

Her mother said "Hush."

Dilshad Haqiqat *salaam'd* out of prayer mode and said, 'It's okay, *beti,* it's how Shias pray."

The Shia members of the congregation were the Haqiqat family from Hyderabad, Uncle Zeeshan and Auntie Dilshad and their girls, Insaf and Nilofar. "The rock is from Karbala," she went on. "Where the evil caliph of Syria killed the grandson of the Prophet."

Her mother steered Khadra away. "We need to go get our shoes," she said.

All the Sunnis knew the Shias had wrong beliefs but tried to be polite and not talk about it. At least, not in front of them.

* * *

For Sunday school each class took a corner of the mosque and sat on the floor around the teacher. The children were taught by a rotating roster of aunties and uncles anchored by Uncle Taher, who was black and round and immense, with a large, mournful face. He was like a mountain that moved. Khadra used to be scared of him when she was a very little girl, newly arrived, and would run to her seat, heart pounding, when he lumbered around the corner.

Uncle Taher taught them the Five Pillars. *"Tawhid,"* he said on the first day. "One God. *La ilaha ila allah.* That's it. That's Islam—learning to surrender to Oneness. Learn that and you can go home." Tawhid took up half the year. Even after the Tawhid unit, it seemed like every other lesson went back to Tawhid some way or another.

"God don't look at your skin color. How come?"

Hakim's hand shot up out of his heavy parka. "Because it's only one God created everyone, so all men are equal."

"That's right," Uncle Taher said. He blew on his fingers and rubbed his hands together. Outside, the snow was falling. The mosque heater was on the fritz. Four portable space heaters glowed red in the masallah.

Tayiba raised a mittened hand. "What about women?"

"'Man' include women," Uncle Taher said. "It's just the way we talk."

"So men and women are equal too?" she said.

"God don't care whether you a man or woman, anymore than He look at black or white," Uncle Taher said. "The Quran says, 'God don't suffer the reward of *anyone's* deeds to be lost, male or female.' None of that matters with God."

Tayiba slid back onto her bottom, satisfied.

"And who was the first Muslim?" Uncle Taher went on.

"Abu Bakr," Eyad said. He wore a blue woolen cap with a big yellow puffball.

"Nah," Uncle Taher said. "Not the first Muslim." Eyad was crestfallen. His puffball fell to one side.

"Ali," Danny Nabolsy said. His little brother Ramsey fidgeted beside him.

"No." Uncle Taher paused for effect. "Abu Bakr was the first *man,"* he said, and Eyad's cloud lifted a little—vindication. "And Ali was the first child. Ten years old—and doesn't that show a child can do something important?" he said, and they all sat up taller on their ankles. "But what I asked you was, who was the first *person* to become Muslim, the very first?"

"Oh—I know!" Hanifa raised her hand so high that she needed to hold it up with the other hand. Uncle Taher called on her. "Khadija!" she fairly sang.

"That's right!" Uncle Taher boomed, and she beamed with the glory of it. "The Prophet's wife, Lady Khadija. And who was number one in the *deen* after the Prophet's death, that everyone went to with their how-come questions?"

"Aisha!" Khadra said, with a triumphal glance at Hakim.

"That's right. And who was the person closest to the Prophet's heart?"

This time Hakim's hand went up first. "Fatima," he said, without so much as a sideways look at Khadra.

"Show me how you pray," Uncle Taher said, sitting cross-legged in the masallah with a brown leather *kufi* on his head. The kids lined up, girls on one side, boys on the other. Malik Jefferson started to raise his hands for the first "allahu."

"Hang on," Uncle Taher said. "It's not the hundred-yard dash. You want to focus. You want to hold on to your *nia*—your purpose and intent."

Khadra, Hanifa, and Tayiba gave Uncle Taher a workout with their questions. *Are birthdays haram? Mama said birthday parties are vainglorious. What is vainglorious? How come the Islamic year is only 1398? How come Muslim men can marry non-Muslim women but Muslim women can't marry non-Muslim men? Will all non-Muslims go to hell?* He called them the "How Come Girls."

"Do everything with nia," he admonished, as the children filed out.

As far as they could see, to the east and to the south and to the west, nothing was moving on all the vastness of the High Prairie. Only the green grass was rippling in the wind, and white clouds drifted in the high, clear sky.

"It's a great country, Caroline," Pa said. "But there will be wild Indians and wolves here for many a long day."

—Laura Ingalls Wilder, *Little House on the Prairie*

Zuhura stood on the porch of the Dawah Center Home Office in a full skirt, one hand on her hip, the other shading her eyes from the sun as she looked out across the street at a red pick-up truck, around which a klatch of locals hostile to the Dawah was gathering. The Center was only a mile from the Fallen Timbers Townhouses at the edge of Indianapolis, but technically lay within the city limits of Simmonsville, a small, economically depressed town. Many of its residents were not so happy about the Muslims doing God's work there, and some of these were the men Zuhura was watching.

The Dawah Center was not a mosque like Salam, but a nonprofit outreach office, a dream begun by devout but impoverished Arab and Indo-Pakistani graduate students in the mid-1960s and run from filing cabinets in the home of one or the other of its board members. Until recently, that is. The Center only had a shoestring budget and was lucky to have found a Victorian fixer-upper on this quiet, old-fashioned street lined with maple, black walnut, and elm trees. It had a big backyard with three crabapple trees and one mulberry that the Dawah children picked bare in June. A large side yard spread with gravel served as the parking lot; a freestanding garage served as a garden shed. A flagstone path led to a charming outbuilding behind the house. This had been insulated and converted into small guest quarters. There was a root cellar, used mainly as a warehouse for Dawah literature.

Dutchman's breeches, Johnny-jump-ups, and wild violets crept here and there over the flagstones. A deep bank of tiger lilies camouflaged the chain-link fence on one side of the yard. Tall lilacs grew along the fence shared with the back neighbor, and a pussy willow bush filled one corner.

On the oaken front door was a small placard of Quranic calligraphy:

Let there arise from among you
a band of people,
inviting to all that is good,
enjoining what is right,
and forbidding what is wrong.
They are the ones to attain felicity

Thumbtacked underneath it was a framed postcard picture of an oil lamp glowing in a niche. Rather than quaint old oil lamps, of course, fluorescent tubes were the actual source of light in the house—there was an energy crisis, after all.

The Dawah Center officers, including Khadra's father, worked long hours for low salaries. Denied themselves other careers where they could have made more money. Got home haircuts from their wives, lived simple and frugal lives. Yusuf Thoreau, the office accountant, was so scrupulous with Dawah money that if he accidentally took a pen home he charged himself for it. The Center wives took turns cleaning house, right down to the toilet bowls, to save on cleaning bills, and the Dawah men mowed the lawn and did the maintenance work themselves. Service for the sake of the On-High.

On the other side of the chainlink fence in the Center yard, an elderly white woman could often be found working in her vegetable garden. This morning, she marched with spry step to the Dawah Center door, ignoring the men around the red pick-up, and announced to Zuhura and to Kuldip Khan, who had joined her on the porch, "I am Mrs. Moore. I am a Friend. Here is some rhubarb." She presented long reddish stalks that mystified Kuldip, the one-armed Pakistani editor of the Dawah newsletter, *The Islamic Forerunner.* He'd lost his right arm in a printing-press accident in Rawalpindi and wore a prosthetic one, most days.

He thanked her profusely.

"Salam alaykom," Mrs. Moore said.

"Wa alaikum assalam, wa rahmatulla!" Zuhura responded, beaming at her.

"You speak Arabic, then?" Kuldip said, surprised. He spoke Urdu but, of course, read Arabic.

"Bits and pieces," the woman said, her face half hidden under her voluminous straw hat. "Just enough to get around when I lived in Syria, you know."

"You've lived in the Middle East?"

"Although you could get around just as well with French in those days," Mrs. Moore went on. "But I prided myself on learning a bit of the language wherever I was. Unlike Agatha, who never bothered."

Kuldip, who had never been able to cure himself of being an Agatha Christie reader, despite discovering, in secondary school, that her writing reeked of Orientalism, was going to ask, his voice squeaking excitedly, "*the* Agatha?" but Mrs. Moore was already pottering down the sidewalk, getting baleful stares from the crowd at the pick-up.

"Where did this wonderful rhubarb come from?" Trish Nabolsy asked, coming out of the front door as Zuhura stepped in to put the stalks in the fridge. Kuldip explained the unexpected gift of the morning as Mrs. Moore waved good-bye.

"Well, praise be," Trish said. Like Kuldip, she'd come out to keep an eye on the worrisome situation across the street. Trish was an American convert with bright red hair, eyelashes so pale she seemed to have none, and freckles all over her face. Her husband, Omar, was the Dawah general director and looked like an Arab Marlboro Man, rugged and mustached. He and Trish and their four sons lived in a notoriously messy white clapboard house. Khadra and Eyad rode to many a Dawah youth camp in the Nabolsys' muddy Volkswagen. The Shamy kids loved going to Aunt Trish's: the Nabolsy house was messy, but you could *do* stuff there—finger paint and rock polish and wood burn, or feed Ramsey's iguana or the hamster that belonged to little Jalaludin (called JD). "As long as you don't feed the hamster to the iguana," Sammy, the oldest boy, joked. And Danny, the nicest brother, would push you on the tire swing that hung off a fat four-trunked cottonwood tree in the front yard. Or all the kids together could play air hockey or ping-pong in the basement, amid the beat-up armchairs and cobwebby signs that said "McGovern" and "My Mercy Prevaileth over My Wrath."

Trish didn't like it when people assumed she became a Muslim for her husband. "I was Muslim for years before I met Omar," she'd bristle. She'd been in the peace movement in the 1960s at a place called Haight-Asbury in San Francisco. She was unique in the Dawah Center community because she was the only woman who didn't cover her hair, except during prayers. It was the special project of Khadra's mother to persuade Trish to "perfect her Islam," as she put it, by covering that red hair with hijab.

The group across the street was the doing of a man named Orvil Hubbard. Hubbard was a tall, gaunt man with a crew cut and a limp, who liked to wear his old army uniform with the Congressional Medal of Honor pinned on whenever he protested against the Muslim presence. He'd announced at a city council meeting that, due to the incursions of "certain parties" on the character of their town, he and other private citizens were forming the American Protectors of the Environs of Simmonsville, and whoever wanted to join was welcome. "I'm not speaking from ignorance," he'd said quietly. "I've lived in their countries, and I know. They *will* destroy the character of our town."

The first act of the Protectors, as they came to be known, was to call Immigration and Naturalization authorities, charging that the Center harbored illegal immigrants. Hubbard had paced across the street, hoping to see someone hauled off and arrested. The INS raid yielded no illegals. But they did find Sammy Nabolsy's secret BB gun, which he'd hidden in the garden shed of the Dawah Center, and which got him in tons of trouble with his father.

Hubbard was disappointed, but not ready to give up. His next move was to invoke zoning ordinances. Today he was waiting across the street for the zoning inspector, who arrived shortly and began his tour of the Victorian house, with Wajdy Shamy at his side. Zuhura followed them. While the building inspector was measuring the shutters, she looked over his shoulder and said, "Did you know that zoning law has often been used as a tool to keep people of other races out?"

Jotting things on his clipboard, the white man nodded politely but paid no attention to her.

"I was going to say—I just wanted to know if you intend—" she pressed, dogging his steps, and he scowled slightly. Wajdy gently but firmly signaled for her to go back into the house.

Zuhura was not accustomed to being brushed aside. She did not have the habits and mein of most of the Indiana black women the building inspector would have come across in his life, or their understanding of the unspoken rules of "getting along" in this place where they lived. She was likely to accost and question you, man or woman, even if you had an air of authority, and she did so with an attitude that assumed her objections would be addressed. Fully. Her mother was the same.

These were good skills for a lawyer, as Zuhura hoped one day to be. Like the sharp rational faculties of Aisha, the early Muslim woman beloved of Sunnis, they were good skills for the propagation of Islam, and the Dawah culture encouraged them, in girls as well as in boys. They were not, however, the best skills for getting along as a foreign newcomer in Simmonsville, or as black woman in the social landscape of central Indiana. Zuhura didn't fit into this landscape. She didn't fit what the locals thought they knew about someone who looked like her as they saw her approaching. And so there was always a sense of something off-kilter, a bristle in the air that went around with her. It was as if her physical presence was a challenge to knowledge held dear, to some core that made them who they were, and so the hair on the back of their sun-reddened necks stood on end at the sight of her, without them even being aware of it, necessarily. At the sound of her voice, something went "click" and disconnected between them and her. Both sides might continue speaking, but the line between them was dead.

It wasn't just Zuhura. The Dawah people as a whole didn't know much about the character of their new environs. In grad school carrels, they'd put their heads together over a map and said, "There! That's the middle of the country, so Muslims in all parts of the land can find us." That Indianapolis, besides being centrally located, had an international airport, low crime rates, and affordable land, was enough, to their minds. None of them had ties to the people there, not even Trish—she was from California. Some, like Aunt Khadija, did come from the black Muslim population native to northern Indianapolis. About the lives of the small-town residents of Simmonsville and southern Indianapolis, however, the shopkeepers and schoolteachers, the beer-and-peanuts crowd and the country club set, much less the outlying landscape of central Indiana with its farmers in crisis, many facing foreclosure in the 1970s, the Dawah folk knew next to nothing, and didn't care to know. They bent their heads to their task.

Ayesha didn't know why, but there was something slightly familiar about the figure of Hubbard limping beside his truck, suspiciously watching the exchange between her inquisitive daughter and the building inspector. She couldn't put her finger on it. Her step crunched over the gravel as she went to her car in the driveway of the Victorian house. She knew one thing: she was already tired of Hubbard and his plots. They were draining precious energy, the Center's and hers.

"Klansmen without sheets," Ayesha sniffed to Kuldip, who had followed her out with a box of bulk mail, holding it rather awkwardly to his chest.

"He has a prosthetic leg from stepping on a mine in Korea," Mrs. Moore said quietly, over the chain-link fence. Ayesha jumped, not expecting anyone to have overheard her comment.

"Really?" Kuldip said. He found this interesting, as someone who wore a prosthetic limb himself. He did not ask how she knew. Americans knew things about each other. They learned them in places mysterious to Kuldip, such as golf courses and bars and, naturally, in their own homes, where he rarely had reason to go.

Indianapolis is not so bad—not unpleasing in places, really.

—Theodore Dreiser, *A Hoosier Holiday*

Crunching over gravel, Khadra pulls the hatchback into the driveway of the blue Victorian house, almost expecting to see Mr. Hubbard and his truck across the street, even after all these years. She wonders if the old coot is still alive. She pulls her tangerine scarf, which has slipped down to her shoulders, back up around her face. This was going to be the Dawah Center's last summer in the old house. Staffers were preparing to move the offices into a glass-and-concrete box off the interstate.

This summer of 1992 is a crossroads for the Dawah Center. Until now, it's run on donations scrounged from its own hard-up membership. But bigger donors have begun to take interest: wealthy Muslim businessmen and bankers from Saudi Arabia, Brunei, Pakistan, Nigeria, and Malaysia. At the same time, there are those who want the organization to outgrow its immigrant founders and their "back-home" concerns, and to become more American. To face squarely the needs of those Muslims permanently settled in America. The American-bred children of immigrants are clamoring for more say. So are indigenous American Muslims, who until now have been the neglected stepchildren of Dawah. The move to corporate-style offices will begin a new phase of Dawah. Already its flyers look slicker.

Khadra isn't sure how she feels about the change. It's nice to see the upgrading to the same level of professionalism many American churches and nonprofits already enjoy. At the same time, there was something so homey about the earnest pamphlets with bad English, and she will miss all that. She will miss the house most of all, the aging blue Victorian with its cream-colored shutters and misshapen crabapple trees.

Khadra takes a canvas tarp from the car. Dufflebag of workout clothes, an old self-help book with a torn cover *(Recovery for Adult Children of Missionaries)*—she pushes those aside and yanks out the ice chest that holds her film. Strapping her Pentax manual over her shoulder, she loads it and snaps a few shots of the gnarled crab apples, the old mulberry, the one she and her brothers and their friends used to climb and pick clean and hang upside down from. Every kid should have a mulberry tree.

A smooth 'fro'd head, then a whole man, comes out of the earth behind the tree and appears in Khadra's viewfinder. Handsome, broad-shouldered. It's been ages since she's seen him. "Hey, Hakim," she says lightly, but with pleasure.

"Khadra!" Hakim has emerged fully from the cellar carrying a crate of pamphlets. "Hey, *assalamu alaikum.* So it's true you're back." He has a beard now, and his hairline is higher, but Hakim she'd know in any guise. He drops a yellowed pamphlet and she picks it up, glancing at the familiar typeface. It's from the '70s and announces a program theme of "Preserving Our Islamic Identity in the Midwest."

"Only for a visit," Khadra replies as she hands it to him.

She is, in fact, back in Indiana on assignment. The news desk of a Philadelphia- based magazine, *Alternative Americas,* for which she works, is doing a feature on minority religious communities in Middle America and has decided to feature the Indianapolis Muslims among them—to Khadra's dismay. She cringes at the thought of putting her own community in the spotlight. She doesn't think she herself can take one more of those shots of masses of Muslim butts up in the air during prayer or the clichéd Muslim woman looking inscrutable and oppressed in a voluminous veil.

When her boss, Sterling Ross, himself a globetrotting photojournalist, had learned of her connection to the Indianapolis Muslim community, that she'd actually grown up in it, he'd been ecstatic. "Behind the veil! Wow! A keyhole view of the hidden, inside world of Muslims." He was impossible to discourage, since it seemed like a hard-to-top scoop to him. He walked away, leaving Khadra still uncertain.

"I don't think so," she muttered, and exchanged looks that said volumes about the limits of white liberalism with Ernesto, the photo editor.

"You'll have creative control, Khadra," Ernesto told her soothingly. "You're the one behind the lens."

Khadra fiddled with a dusty stack of issues of *Photo District News* on a damaged wooden end table. Ernesto seemed to know where he was going in the field. Herself, she'd stumbled from job to job, unsure of her direction. She knew what she loved doing—social photography, and nature—bugs, mainly—yeah, and also architectural. This last came from loving the space inside mosques. She knew what she didn't want—corporate work, advertising, being around people focused on the surfaces of things. Hard news photojournalism? Too fast and furious. Then there was art photography, like her friend Blu produced, but that didn't seem to be Khadra's thing either. Meantime, she had to pay the rent.

She'd been thrilled when she got the job with *Alternative Americas,* after having spent a number of years doing morgue photography and selling photos to stock houses. It gave her the creative leeway she wanted, the right pace. It's just lately she'd been growing impatient. Then this assignment came along and, even though her stomach sank at the thought of Indiana, she knew she had to do it. Thinking about her career direction would have to wait.

So here she is. Back in Indiana. *Back to India-aana*—yeah okay. Hakim loads the crate of pamphlets in the bed of his pick-up. He moves effortlessly, as if holding back his strength for bigger things. It's "Imam Hakim" now, of course. His star had risen during his grad school years at Harvard Divinity, where he'd been a campus Muslim leader. He'd done summer Arabic in Cairo and Islamic sciences stints in Medina and Damascus. When he'd come back, he had a wife, Mahasen, a fourth-generation African American Muslim whose grandparents had been with Elijah, peace be upon him, and whose great-grandparents had followed Noble Drew Ali. Khadra could only imagine the dinner-table discussion between generations in that family. From Moorish Science to Nation doctrine to the brief Bilalian phase, now capped by Mahasen the conservo-neo-traditional orthodox-with-a-twist-of-Wahhabi! But what about Hakim, where's his thinking "at" these days, she wonders. She knows him well enough not to try to pin a label on him. There are layers to Hakim.

"Need a ride?" the man in question asks awkwardly.

"I have to drive my own car," Khadra says, gratified at this sign that his characteristic kindness toward her is as ever. "But mind if I—?" she holds up her camera, and he waves permission. Behind him, the gnarly trees—click-shee, click-shee—the open cellar door, the blue-and-white home office of Islam in America—click-shee click-shee click-shee—Hakim's deep amber face with the Indiana sunshine full on him, bringing out the coppery undertones. His arms bared to the elbow, the glint of his silver wristwatch. Something missing. She looks again through the viewfinder, because in there she can zoom in without him noticing her gaze. The ring. Where is his silver wedding ring?

Hakim disappears into the house for a moment, leaving Khadra to head for the backyard. The crab apples are still green and small. The mulberries are closer to ripeness. She spies a large straw hat bobbing amid the greenery across the back fence. "Mrs. Moore!"

"Why, Khadra!" The familiar neighbor makes her way over to the fence. Khadra can feel her frail tremulous bones as she hugs her.

"How have you been? How's life in Philadelphia?"

"Fine, it's fine. I went to the Quaker Meeting Hall like you suggested."

"Yes?"

"It was the strangest thing."

Mrs. Moore raises an eyebrow.

"Silence. The prayer was—silence. I mean, that was the whole service. Someone leading the people through a whole hour of silence. I've never seen anything like it."

Mrs. Moore smiles.

"That's how Quakers pray, then, through silence?"

Mrs. Moore looks at Khadra as though she has already said too many words. "You *have* grown," she says, and goes back to her garden.

Khadra follows Hakim's pick-up, with its tattered green "As for me and my house, we serve Allah" bumper sticker, south out of Simmonsville into hill country. But what did "his house" consist of? Last she'd heard, he and Mahasen were doing fine, although no kids. He'd always had a restless edge, an unsatisfied seeker in him. It was not just career ambition, the kind that got him to Harvard, although it could manifest that way; it was more. It was a search for something underlying, a quest for what is real. Is he satisfied now?

Beanblossom, Helmsburg, Needmore—passing the turn-off for Hindustan, a blink-in-the-road whose name Uncle Kuldip used to find enormously funny, stopping to take a picture of himself next to the highway sign. The road to B-town had eaten part of her foot, as the Arabic saying goes, or, in the American idiom, she knew it like the back of her hand. The last time she'd been in Bloomington, she'd lived in the Tulip Tree Apartments, whose hallways smelled of curry and *kabsa* all afternoon, so thick that a mile away you could tell what was cooking and who was doing the cooking—Saudis, was it today? Or, at the other end of Muslim sectarian politics, Iranians? Or were the Malaysians frying squid?

Before the garment industry emerged, introducing its ready-made sizes—clothes that do not know a body, do not acknowledge each body's distinctiveness . . . we in the East . . . were making fabrics that were increasing in beauty . . . refining [our] expression of the unique relationship between the cloth and the body. . . . Who, these days, sees in a length of cloth its origin, its place of birth, the caravans' voyages?

—Hoda Barakat, *The Tiller of Waters*

Here is something new. On Old State Road 37 near Bloomington, a placard at a construction site says "Coming soon: Dagom Gaden Tensung Ling Monastery." Khadra does a double take. She gets a mental image of Hubbard hobbling angrily across the street from a colony of tiny men in orange robes. But no, times have changed. Haven't they? As if to prove it, a car whizzes by her, its bumper sticker proclaiming "Visualize whirled peas."

Khadra arrives on the IU campus knee-deep in the golden Indiana day, time for *duhr* prayer. It has been transformed into Muslim Land for the weekend. Thousands of Muslims fill Assembly

Hall, the great basketball stadium where the Hoosiers practice, turning the Big Ten bastion into a high-raftered mosque. Khadra enters the arena just as the imam calls the first "allahu akbar." She steps out of her cute strappy sandals and slips into a prayer line next to a woman whose petite body, a presence of bone and flesh under the fabric, brushes against her.

Several hundred Muslim foreheads touch the arena floor in unison, her own widow's-peaked one among them. Only a thin bedsheet between the forehead and the hardwood. Palm, palm, knee, knee, points of contact with the ground. Campus staffers in Go Big Red T-shirts watch the Muslims pray, their eyes widening when everyone goes down in prostration.

"Here is the way Muslims touch the ground," Khadra thinks in sajda. "Here is the way we shift our bodies daily, and alter our angle of looking." In prostration, you see the underbelly of things. Daddy longlegs moving carefully side to side. Old gum underneath a bleacher plank. Hems, sari edges, purse buckles beside your eye. Feet. Long bony toes of tall skinny women and little cushiony ones of short round women, the littlest toe barely there, tucked sideways shyly. In the rising posture, she looks down at her long tissuey skirt with its Mayan temple images in blue and bronze. Her mother's voice in her head tsk-tsks her bare feet. In response, she wriggles her stubby toes.

After the salam, Khadra decides she will try low camera angles. It is not the prayer she will photograph, not from the outside, but: what does the world look like from *inside* this prayer?

She helps fold the dormitory sheets that have served as prayer rugs. She picks up one end and someone picks up the other, a young woman who is perhaps Bosnian or East European, wearing a floral *écharpe*. Khadra loves being in this forest of women in hijab, their *khimars* and saris and *jilbabs* and *thobes* and *depattas* fluttering and sweeping the floor and reaching out to everything. Compact Western clothing doesn't rustle, or float, or reach out to anything.

Khadra spots a familiar figure across the prayer hall. Stray red hairs are sticking out from under a calico prayer wrap. "Aunt Trish!" She is bent over someone in a wheelchair. She turns, pushing the wheelchair. It is Uncle Omar—Khadra gasps softly. She'd heard he had developed multiple sclerosis, but never dreamed it had gone this far so quickly. She remembers how he'd gone after Ramsey with a strap after catching him with Insaf Haqiqat when they were teens; he'd been powerful as an ox.

"Khadra Shamy?" Uncle Omar says through his big mustache. "I haven't seen you since you were this high! Where have you been hiding all these years?"

"Oh," she says brightly, "I'm in Philadelphia now."

"Why don't you have a baby in your hands and three more behind you?" he demands gruffly—winking.

"I—well—how are *you?*" Khadra says. "I was so sorry to hear—"

"It's stage three progressive," Aunt Trish explains. "He had to go to a wheelchair within a year of diagnosis." She is matter-of-fact about it, although he seems to slump at her words.

Khadra is about to add a word of condolence for Ramsey, but she doesn't have the heart to bring up another sorrow just then.

On her way to check in at the Union Hotel, Khadra picks up a bright green flyer.

FIRST TIME EVER AT THE DAWAH CONFERENCE—ISLAMIC ENTERTAINMENT CONCERTS FOR MUSLIM YOUTH!

- *Nasheeds* by Phat in the Phaith!
- Hijab Hip-Hop by Nia Group!
- Spoken Word to Your Mother, then Your Mother, then Your Mother—with Brother Bilal!
- Special Performance by The Clash of Civilizations! (Islamic behavior and attire required of all youth attending. Responsible adult chaperones to supervise. Concerts strictly in accordance with *shariah* restrictions as per Dawah Conference Committee Guidebook on Islamic Rules for Entertainment Programs.)

Was Hijab Hip-Hop a *girl* group? Hunh. The Dawah has evolved, Khadra muses, stuffing the flyer in her bag.

The Clash of Civilizations is her brother's band—her little brother Jihad. It's an eclectic group of boys. Sort of a Muslim John Cougar Mellencamp meets Wes Montgomery, with a Donny Osmond twist. There's Jihad and an African American Muslim teen from Gary named, coincidentally, Garry, but with two *r*s. Garry Abdullah. The Osmond twist is the Mormon component, Brig and Riley Whitcomb. They're leaving out the instruments this gig, singing a capella, so it will be acceptable to conservative Muslims who have issues with musical instruments.

Of the thousands of people at the conference, she keeps running into Hakim. Here he is at the Union café.

"Good to see you again, Sister Khadra," he says stiffly. An invisible veil falls over his face now, a curtain that keeps her out.

Sister? He never called her that before. It seems to be for the benefit of a cluster of conference brothers ordering coffee ahead of them, who recognize him and nod.

"You know what, I think I'm going to go ahead and get coffee, Sister," he says, edging away from her.

"You know what, Hakim, me too." She steps right next to him, directly behind the group of bearded brothers.

"How's your mother?" she says sweetly. The brothers in front of them glance around at Imam Hakim, then back at Khadra.

"Fine, praise God," he mumbles. Khadra remembers that she heard his wife had gone heavy traditional on him during their latest stint in Mecca, and taken to *niqab* and black gloves, even back in the States. Did Mahasen go full-steam Wahhabi?

"And how's your wife? Any little ones on the way?" Khadra presses on, knowing she's being just as obnoxious as the aunties who used to pry into whether or not she was pregnant during her brief marriage.

"We—we—" He has a look of extreme discomfort on his face.

Khadra is immediately sorry. She only meant to be a little pushy. "Never mind," she says hastily. "That was forward of me."

His expression shifts, as if he's undecided, weighing, and then he shrugs and says, "I might as well tell you. I was just talking about it with your brother this morning. I'm ready to tell friends," he says. Now his tone of voice is normal. He orders coffee.

It's nice to be acknowledged as a friend, Khadra thinks, even if you can't shake hands or hug. "House coffee please," she says.

"Goodness, no, just the small size. Thanks." They walk to a table and set the cups down. Khadra sits but Hakim stays standing awkwardly.

"We've divorced," Hakim says. "Mahasen and I got a divorce about seven months ago." A brother in the group of beards who are now clustered at a nearby table shoots a sideways glance at him.

"I'm sorry," Khadra says. Imam Hakim with those famous *khutba*s on marriage! 'The couple that reads Quran together, stays together!' She used to listen to the tapes during her own marriage troubles. "Is it—is it final, then?"

"Yeah. The *iddah* is over and all. We tried to get back but it didn't work." Hakim pulls out a chair across from her and sits down, ignoring the curious brothers at the next table. Khadra hopes that means he will spill the beans. What was his divorce about?

"Mahasen and I were going in different directions," he begins carefully.

"Really?" Khadra says with equal care. Did Mahasen leave him or did he leave her?

"Alhamdulilah," Hakim says. Khadra hates when people say that as a replacement for specific information.

"It—it must be painful. I'm sorry." What do you say? There were set phrases for marriages, births, deaths, but not for divorce.

"After the hard time, there is the easing," he says, after a minute. So it was she who left him, Khadra speculates. His face smoothes out. "After the hard time, there is the easing."

There is no single word in English that conveys the scope of the Arabic word Salat. *'Prayer,' 'blessings,' 'supplication,' and 'grace' are implied, but all fail to convey the Salat's marvelous integration of devotional heart-surrender with physical motion.*

—Coleman Barks and Michael Green, *The Illuminated Prayer*

Zuhura led the three "Little Sisters"—that was what she called Khadra, Hanifa, and Tayiba—in duhr prayer. It was a quiet Saturday at the Thoreau home in the Fallen Timbers. They stood in line next to her tall plump form in her two-piece patterned prayer wraps of *leso* cloth. Khadra hastily took her half-chewed gob of bubble gum out of her mouth and stuck it on the coffee table. She nestled into Zuhura's side, shadowing her every motion as Zuhura imamed them through the four *rakats* of duhr prayer.

After the salam, before the girls made to dash off, Zuhura held them back. "Say after me," she said. "My dear God, you are Peace."

It was only by comparison with Zuhura that some aunties called Tayiba "the quiet one" of the two sisters. Tayiba wasn't that quiet; she just didn't have the leadership energy that fired Zuhura, her easy command of speech, her forward drive. In any environment, but especially in a small community, Zuhura would stand head and shoulders above not only her peers, but her elder and younger cohorts. It was natural for the three younger girls to follow her lead, not because they were docile—they were not—but because she had presence, and they felt it.

"My dear God, you are Peace," the younger girls now said in unison. Khadra had already stuffed the wad of gum back into her mouth.

"And from you cometh Peace," she chanted.

"And from you cometh Peace," they said, Khadra through bubble gum.

"And to you belongeth Peace."

"And to you belongeth Peace."

"Blessed be You and All-high."

"Blessed be You and All-high."

"You of the Majesty and the Welcome."

"You of the Majesty and the Welcome."

Zuhura wiped her face with the cupped hands of prayer and the girls all wiped their faces likewise, and were indeed at peace, for one microsecond, before they ran noisily out to the porch and clambered onto their bikes, speeding off into the sunny, littered streets. Leaving her swathed in her prayer clothes and the noontime calm. But no—she ran out after them to call, "Don't forget—dinner at Uncle Abdulla's!" Khadra groaned. Uncle Abdulla made you eat too much. Zuhura went back inside to work on a paper about colonialism in Kenya.

There had always been murmurs of disapproval about the amount of latitude Zuhura's parents gave her in allowing her to commute to the Bloomington campus. Khadra's parents, for their part, believed a Muslim girl should go to college close to home. What was wrong with the Indianapolis branch of IU? Zuhura was going farther afield than a Muslim girl ought to be, especially when it entailed driving home late at night by herself.

"She's a smart girl," Aunt Ayesha said firmly."She can take care of herself."

Zuhura knew better than to stop in Martinsville, at any rate. She may not have had many of the other survival skills developed over generations by American blacks, but everyone in Indiana knew that Martinsville was no place to be unless you were white.

True to her mother's expectations, Zuhura began to be active in the Campus Muslim Council. A dean's list student, she helped lobby the university administration to recognize Muslim holidays, and organized speaking events on "Islam, the Misunderstood Religion" and on social justice issues. Sudan, Uganda, Palestine, Iran, Cambodia, Kashmir: everywhere, Muslims were being persecuted, it seemed. She was the first Muslim to write for the IU paper and get a front-page—above the fold—byline. Her op-ed supporting the Islamic dissent in Iran caused a campus stir.

It was agreed that the Shah was a tyrant. Iranian Muslims were rallying for change and being persecuted for rallying. *The Islamic Forerunner* tried to keep Muslims in America up to date on events there, the exciting stirrings toward, possibly, the first Islamic state in the modern world since the destruction of the Ottoman caliphate in 1924. Most people who read *The Forerunner,* and certainly all who worked for the Dawah Center, believed that an Islamic state and an Islamic society was, or should be, the hope of every believing Muslim today. In it, everyone would be good and God-fearing and decent and hardworking; there would be no corruption or bribes; the rich would help the poor; and all would have work and food and live cleanly, because an Islamic state would provide the solution for every social ill.

"But if Iranian Muslims made an Islamic state, would that count, being Shia?" This was Khadra's father asking the question as he spread newspapers on the carpet in Abdulla's Fallen Timbers living room.

The answer came from Zeeshan, Brother Zeeshan Haqiqat, a favorite sparring partner. "In Hyderabad, Hindu fanatics didn't stop to ask my brother if he was Shia or Sunni before they beat him to death."

Zeeshan's point stopped Wajdy cold. Like the first Pilgrims, the immigrants of the Dawah Center came to America with persecution and suffering at their backs. Sunni or Shia, they had too much in common not to work together.

The tensions between the sects in the Dawah organization would not explode until a few years later, when funding from wealthy private donors abroad started to come in. Powerful Sunni donors made exclusion of Shia elements a condition of the money, some said. Others said no, it was the Shia members who had a problem taking money from Sunnis. The donors had attached no strings. There would be shouting matches in the blue Victorian house, at the annual Bloomington conferences, and even in the little apartments at Fallen Timbers. Uncle Zeeshan would eventually leave the Dawah staff and Khadra would no longer see his daughters, Nilofar and Insaf, every Eid in their gorgeous ghararas, and Auntie Dilshad's fried samosas would no longer be on the potluck table at the women's weekly Quranic study (hot! run for a glass of water! mouth on fire!)

"Wajdy! Zeeshan! We'll have none of your Sunni-Shia arguments tonight," Uncle Abdulla called out, his face jovial. "Tonight for eating only!" This hospitable Egyptian and his wife, Aunt Fatma, brought out platter after platter to set on the newspapers before the men. The women at at the table in the dinette; the kids ran amok everywhere.

"Eat, eat!" Uncle Abdulla bellowed, grabbing Khadra's paper plate and heaping greasy rice and slabs of fatty meat onto it. She didn't know how to fend off his generosity. Between that, and your parents telling you it was haram to waste food, you were stuck, and had to eat it all.

Uncle Abdulla had spent five years in the concentration camps of Gamal Abdul Nasser for belonging to the Muslim Strivers, an Islamic movement that strove to reform Egyptian society along Islamic lines. Starvation for days at a time was one of the punishments the wardens had inflicted on Abdulla in the prison camp. The poorest man in the little neighborhood of Muslims in the Fallen Timbers, he wanted everyone to be well fed in his home.

After dinner Zuhura cheerfully volunteered to do the dishes. Luqman, Fatma's handsome younger brother newly arrived from

Egypt, carried armfuls of crusted casserole pans and blackened-bottom aluminum pots to her into the kitchen. The older kids had to watch the younger kids out on the playground. They were glad to get out of the overfull apartment.

When only Khadra, Eyad, Hakim, and Hanifa were left outside, they took turns putting pennies on the train tracks that ran behind the fence at one end of the apartment complex. Leaving their bikes in a heap in the high-grown weeds, they crawled through the tunnel made by thickets of wild raspberry bushes. They went down one as far as they could, to where it bent in the undergrowth. They scrabbled for sweet dark berries, getting stabbed by thorns in their fingertips, knuckles, knees, palms, feet, and smudged faces. The last sunlight filtered through the raspberry bushes as the children crawled through flickering light and shadow within.

I reckon—When I count at all—
First Poets—Then the Sun—
Then Summer—Then the Heaven of God—
And then—the List is done—

—Emily Dickinson

The four children Lewis and Clarked over a lush summer carpet of fallen berries. They emerged, mouths and knees berry-stained, at the edge of a cornfield bordered by shagbark hickory and silver wattle trees. There they forded a yard-wide creek. Its dark shimmering banks crawled with frogs and crawdads and other small rustling life, forms, fully deserving the total surrender of their attention. The mud that oozed between their toes soothed their feet. Upon crossing the creek, leaving their shoes behind, they found a dead possum. It was crawling with maggots. Hakim and Eyad wanted to dissect it. Hanifa and Khadra wanted to bury it. They didn't have the tools for either. Then Khadra yelped. She had stepped on a crawdad and its pincers grabbed her toe. "Get it off, get it OFF!" she screamed, hopping around, and Hanifa laughed, and kept going "Ew, *ewww*," but Hakim helped her get it off, and Eyad said now she would need a "tetmas" shot. It was only after the crisis passed that they began to notice that the darkness had thickened to a rich eggplant hue.

By the time they recrossed the creek, collected their shoes, crawled back through the raspberry tunnel, jumped the tracks, hopped on their bikes, and pedaled homeward, their parents had begun combing the streets and parking lots of the apartment complex. Having had no luck locating the children, Khadra's father was about to call the police.

Their father dragged Khadra and Eyad by their ears to the door, flung open by their mother, a cranky and tired baby Jihad straddling her hip. They were mudspattered, tufts of cobwebs and twigs clinging to their hair, covered very likely with impurities that would require washing seven times. Ebtehaj was trembling all over, her pale ivory face ashen.

She looked like she was about to cry, but what she did was scream. "Do you think we are Americans? Do you think we have no limits? Do you think we leave our children wandering in the streets? Is that what you think we are? Is it?" Then she burst into sobs.

She marched Khadra up the stairs and pushed her into the bathtub ("Don't go anywhere!" she yelled at Eyad, "You're next!"). With the water running hot and hard even though their father always said "The Prophet teaches us not to waste, even if we are taking water from a river," she scrubbed and scrubbed her daughter with an enormous loofah from Syria. "We are not Americans!" she sobbed, her face twisted in grief. "We are not Americans!"

Who were the Americans? The Americans were the white people who surrounded them, a crashing sea of unbelief in which the Dawah Center bobbed, a brave boat. (There were black people who were Americans, but that was different.) You had your nice Americans and your nasty Americans. And then there was the majority of Americans; the best that could be said about them was that they were ignorant.

White-haired Mrs. Moore was a nice American. She belonged to a church called the Friends and they invited the Muslims over for a pancake breakfast. Which was a very American thing to eat, and which was nice of them.

Nasty Americans: You had Orvil Hubbard and his cronies, Vaughn Lott, his sons Brian and Brent, and Mindy Oberholtzer and Curt Stephenson and all the other kids at school who tormented the Muslim kids daily while the teachers looked the other way.

Regarding ignorant Americans, "Well, just look at how nine hundred commited suicide in Jonestown, Guyana, with Jim Jones." Khadra's father remarked when that story broke on their old shadowy TV. "Following false prophets."

"Wasn't he from Indiana?" someone said.

Allison, the girl down the street who was nicknamed the Bone, was a typical American. "That's a lost girl," Khadra's mother observed. "Look how she is allowed to roam the street, no one caring for her." Allison had run away from home three times. She hated her stepfather. She got into fights. She kicked and cussed.

Generally speaking, Americans cussed, smoke, and drank, and the Shamys had it on good authority that a fair number of them used drugs. Americans dated and fornicated and committed adultery. They had broken families and lots of divorces. Americans were not generous or hospitable like Uncle Abdulla and Aunt Fatma; they invited people to their houses only a few at a time, and didn't even let them bring their children, and only fed them little tiny portions of food they called courses on big empty plates they called good china. Plus, Americans ate out wastefully often. Khadra's family ate at home (except once a year on the Eid holiday, when they went to the all-you-can-eat-for-$2.95 steakhouse).

Americans believed the individual was more important than the family, and money was more important than anything. Khadra's dad said Americans threw out their sons and daughters when they turned eighteen unless they could pay rent—to their own parents! And, at the other end, they threw their parents into nursing homes when they got old. This, although they took slavish care of mere dogs. All in all, Americans led shallow, wasteful, materialistic lives. Islam could solve many of their social ills, if they but knew.

Also, Americans did not wash their buttholes with water when they pooped. This was a very big difference between them and Muslims.

"It's appalling. Because no matter how much toilet paper you use," Wajdy said, stirring three teaspoons of sugar into a small glass of mint tea for Téta, "you cannot remove all traces. Water is a must."

Téta couldn't agree more. They called her 'Téta' even though she was not Wajdy's mother but his aunt. She had raised him after his mother's early death and he loved her like a mother. Her visit brought the scent of laurel soap, *sabun ghaar,* into the house. A greeny, tree-bark smell. She stacked the bathroom with the cakes stamped *"Made in Aleppo."*

"But can it really be true?" she asked, her plump frame comfortably settled on the faded couch in Khadra's little living room. Above her, a green crushed-pile prayer rug thumbtacked to the wall featured a threadbare image of the Ka'ba on one half and the Prophet's mosque on the other. "How can they stand to go around with a smear of shit in their crack all day?"

"Believe me, it's true," Khadra's father said. "One of the Dawah workers used to work in the laundry of a big hotel. Big fancy executives stayed there. What do you think he found on their underwear?" He sipped his tea.

Téta grimaced. "No!"

"Yes!"

"If that is how it is with their high classes, their common people must be even filthier!" she retorted.

"And they think they are more civilized than us, and tell us how to run our countries." Wajdy shook his head. The Western imperialism and high-handedness endured by the far-flung Muslim peoples of the world were that much more outrageous in light of the fact that its perpetrators did not even know how to properly clean their bottoms. Khadra's father got up to close the curtains, or else the Shamy family, sitting in the energy-saving fluorescent lights of the living room as night came on, would soon be exposed to the eyes of the Americans.

Treasure of Shaam, O,
Treasure of Damascus,
Treasure that cannot be
altered by time

No matter how far you go
No matter how long ago
Come to me, my love will be
unchanged by time

—"Ya Mal al-Shaam," Damascene folk song

When Téta visited, she opened her suitcases and out poured Ali Baba's treasure, gifts from Syria without measure. Red roasted Iranian watermelon seeds in striped paper sacks, "birdnests" and sesame cookies in oval wooden boxes. Little mechanical eggs that whirled open to reveal a baby chick if you kept pushing the lever. Aleppan woolens for Jihad, Chinese pajamas for Eyad, and cotton nightgowns for Khadra. Embroidered with little cherry clusters, they made her dream of reaching up-up-up to pick plump fruit from a tree spread against a turquoise sky.

Téta also passed on to them the gifts sent by others. Aunt Razanne, Ebtehaj's elder sister, always sent updated photos of her children, while they, in turn, sent little tokens to their American counterparts, a cartoon Roddy cut out of *Tintin* or *Osama* comics for Eyad, a red red rose on adhesive paper from Reem for Khadra's dresser mirror. And letters to Ebtehaj on crinkly sky-blue airmail paper, fat ones from Aunt Razanne, skinny ones from her father.

Jiddo Candyman, Ebtehaj's father, sent candy-coated chickpeas and rock candy, smelling of rose water. They were from his candy factory. "So you won't forget in America what sweetness there is in Syria!" he scribbled on the brown paper bag. But when he sent a picture of himself with a skinny, elegantly coiffed and made-up woman, the two of them sitting in faded Louis XIV armchairs with gilded edges, Ebtehaj snatched the photo from her daughter. Later, Khadra found the skinny lady's side of the photo snipped to pieces in the wastebasket.

"That's Sibelle," Téta whispered to Khadra. "Your mother's Turkish stepmother."

Wajdy took Téta downtown to see the sights.

"I have seen the capitals of Europe, the palaces of Topkapi and Versailles," she said, "and you want to show me *this*—?" she pointed to the Merchant's Bank Clock at the corner of Meridian and Washington, with its nifty digital display of time and temperature. She sniffed.

"Fine," Wajdy said. He took her to Monument Circle to see the great suspended pendulum at the State Museum. The pendulum she found mesmerizing. They stood in the circle for over half an hour watching it swing, almost reach, swing, almost reach. Wajdy had to pry her hands off the circular railing and gently pull her out of the pendulum's sway. Her scarf, which she wore old Damascene style, pulled back so the crown of her head showed, had slipped even farther back on her glossy black hair.

Téta was tenaciously raven-haired. When silver roots started to come in, it was time for a trip to Kmart and a box of Miss Clairol. She emerged, fierce and sleek and black-haired again, and singing. *"I'll be buried with my hair as black as coal, When I go down, I will go down beautiful!"*

Inanna opened the door for him
Inside the house she shone before him
Like the light of the moon
Dumuzi looked at her joyously

—Diane Wolkstein & Samuel Kramer,
Inanna, Queen of Heaven and Earth

Zuhura was getting engaged to Aunt Fatma's brother Luqman. They had first met at Uncle Abdulla's dinner. Luqman had then sent his sister Fatma to inquire with Zuhura's family. A meeting had been arranged that had begun with each looking shyly at the other and had ended with them talking animatedly, ignoring the other family members in the room, who, in any case, slipped out quietly during the interview.

First there would be an engagement party, to be held in the Fallen Timbers community room. There would be a wedding after the academic year finished. Luqman attended the city branch of IU.

He was trying to persuade Zuhura to transfer to the city campus; she was trying to get him to transfer to Bloomington, but nothing was decided yet.

Zuhura was featured in the college paper for being the first Muslim woman to head the African Students Organization at IU. Her mother proudly showed Luqman the article. "The first Muslim woman *in hijab,*" Ayesha said, tapping the photo.

"You're going to drop that African student group when we're married, right?" Zuhura's fiancé said.

"What?" She drew her hand out of his. She was living on coffee and No-Doz tablets—she had to, to keep up with as many classes as she was taking this semester—and everything made her tense.

"Isn't that rich pampered Nigerian athlete in it?" Luqman said. "It's all men. Why you want to hang around men?"

Zuhura's brow furrowed. She had a good answer, almost as scathing as one of her mother's reproofs, but she was beginning to see that her argumentation talents, while they suited her career ambitions, were not the skills needed for becoming Luqman's wife.

Bolts of patterned cloth that Aunt Ayesha called leso arrived. Aunt Ayesha would write, on the edges of the cloth, secret messages in Swahili meant only for Zuhura, to be read on her wedding night. Zuhura's darkest ebony skin was soon flawless, softened and cleansed by the special baths her mother drew for her using ingredients sent by Kenyan relatives.

"I'm going to get my hair braided," Tayiba said, her nostrils flaring with excitement. "Zuhura's having hers done, and my mother said I could do it too."

"So?" Khadra shrugged. "I braid my hair all the time. You don't need a hair stylist for that."

"Not braided like your hair," Hanifa said impatiently. "Braided like *our* hair. Tayiba—can I do it too?" Her eyes lit up, catching the sunlight. She was tired of the way she usually wore her hair, drawn into a poof on top her head. That was the style she'd graduated to after the multiple pigtails of childhood held with gumball hair holders that bounced this and thataway as she and Khadra had raced for the ice cream truck.

"It's expensive," Tayiba said importantly. "You got to get permission."

Hanifa ran home to do that, and her mother said yes, and she came back jubilant, the red sashes of her sundress fluttering behind her like pennants.

"Can I watch?" Khadra asked Tayiba.

"Sure," Tayiba said magnanimously.

Khadra sat and watched Tayiba's enormous untrammeled hair go down into orderly braided rows for about half an hour before she started to get restless.

"Why can't I braid my hair too?" she whined when she got home. Her mother had vetoed it. Eyad was pushing Jihad in his plastic Big Wheel on the tiny back patio.

"What, like the tribe of Zunuj?" Téta said from her lawn chair. Eyad looked up at the odd word, *Zunuj.* Téta stroked Khadra's coarse brown hair. "Such pretty hair, not like that repulsive hair of *Abeed,* all kinky and unnatural."

Khadra pushed her hand away angrily. "You can't say that."

"Say what?"

"Abeed," Eyad chimed in. "That's haram."

"Again with the haram, this child. What did I do that's haram this time, hmm, *te'eburni?"*

"It's haram to be racist," Khadra protested. "Eyad! Isn't it haram to be racist?"

"Yeah. You can't say *'abeed.'*" He gave Téta a look that reminded her rather of his father in his teenaged years, when he started getting religion.

Téta looked bewildered. Hurt. "What? That's just what we say in Syria. I am not a racist."

It had been Téta who first noticed Khadra's breast buds coming in. She shared Khadra's bedroom during her visits.

"You're going to have magnificent boobs, just like mine," Téta told her.

"I am?" Khadra looked uncertainly at Téta's sagging bazoomies. She knew their dimensions well, from when Téta called her in to scrub her back during her weekly bath. Although Téta's back was turned, a modesty cloth on her lap, Khadra could see her heavy breasts hanging down her sides. They were monuments of Khadra's childhood.

"Like me in my prime," Téta amended, straightening her posture. "Women in my family have always had good ones. Not itty bitty almonds like your mother." She broke into song:

I can see into your heart, and it's a beautiful green place
You are connected to my heart, can you follow the trace?
God is beautiful, loves beauty, loves the heart you cultivate

Téta had a song for everything and loved music. But Khadra's parents felt that music, while not outright haram, tended toward frivolity and the forgetfulness of God. Instead of music, they listened to tapes of melodious Quranic recital and nasheeds—songs with voice only, no musical instruments whose permissibility was questionable. Songs in male voices celebrating the Islamic resistance movement of Syria on cassette—Abu Mazen crooning sadly for Muslims to "awake at last from their long night, and make again the world right" and Abu Rateb lamenting the suffering soul in prison:

Like a candle, like a candle burning in the night crying, melting itself down to its heart of light.

Nonetheless, Khadra's father kept a small stash of Um Kulsoum and Fayruz and Abdo and Nazem cassettes.

"From my *jahiliya* days," he confessed, "my time of ignorance, before I woke up to Islamic consciousness."

"Why don't you throw them away?" Khadra's mother said.

But he couldn't bring himself to put them in the trash. In moments of weakness he would still turn them on and put his hands to his forehead and go "Ah, ah" in delight, and dance with arms outstretched, in spite of himself. *For in song lies the mystery of Being.* Even Ebtehaj had been known to smile at moments like these and sway in Wajdy's open arms, in spite of herself.

I was a hidden treasure, and I loved to be known.

—attributed to God in a Hadith Qudsi

Zuhura's henna was to be held in the community room of the Fallen Timbers Townhouse Complex. An engagement party was women-only, of course. So they could remove their headscarves and cover-ups at the door and enjoy an evening dressed as they were within the home, with their hair out and their bodies as attractively clothed as they wished. However, an obstacle to this was discovered the morning of the party: there were no drapes on the large picture windows of the community room. To solve this problem, Uncle Yusuf bought plastic tablecloths—Aunt Ayesha made him get them in colors that coordinated with the decorations. Khadra, Hanifa, Hakim, and Eyad worked to tape them up on the glass. Hanifa switched on the radio while they worked and Kool and the Gang sang "Ladies' Night" Then the Commodores came on.

"My grandmother's a cousin of one of the Commodores," Hanifa boasted.

"Nuh uh," Khadra challenged.

"Yeah huh, she is too. She's Lionel Ritchie's cousin. He grew up right in her hometown, Tuskegee, Alabama. She's known him since he was a baby."

After which Khadra ran home to get dressed.

She was thrilled when Ebtehaj seated her at her own dresser mirror, where she made up her face every day before Wajdy got home. Then he'd lift her hand to his lips and say, "Thank God for the blessing of Islam!" Little compacts of make-up and circles of blue eye shadow and small plush jewelry cases stood in neat rows. The kohl came in a brass vial with a filigreed stopper. It had been a gift from her own mother, who had died when Ebtehaj was fifteen.

"Like this," her mother said, sliding the metal applicator into the vial. It came out with a fine dusting of kohl. "Khadra, what are you doing?" Ebtehaj giggled. Her daughter was blinking rapidly and trying to roll her eyes backward into their whites. "You don't have to do that to put on kohl, Doora."

Khadra basked in her mother calling her by her baby nickname.

"Just—here, you hold the kohl rod—now slide it through so it touches the rim of your eye. There."

She looked at herself in the mirror. She saw a magical creature, something from the stars, a Princess Leia.

"And what about earrings?" Ebtehaj said, stepping back and surveying her handiwork.

"Gold hoops," Téta, who'd been overseeing, said. And stepping up, she opened her palm and supplied them.

"Téta! They're perfect!" Khadra cried when she put them on, turning her head to see in the mirror. Time to move up from turquoise babygirl studs!

Hanifa wore gold hoops too, and a long poly-orlon dress like Khadra's, with bottom ruffles and yoke ruffles and eyelet and rick-rack, only she filled out her dress more—she was already wearing a bra. The Haqiqat sisters, Insaf and Nilofar, came paisleyed and bangled and bespangled in ghararas of green and saffron, tangerine and purple. Tayiba arrived as Khadra and Hanifa had never seen her before, elegant from her silver beaded hair to her feet in blue satin pumps. She looked like a model.

But Zuhura—Zuhura was stunning. Her braids, gold-beaded in dazzling constellations, clicked pleasantly when she turned her head. Her lower lip had a mauve sheen that matched her eye-shadow. Her body was plump and glowing with health, as if she'd just stepped out of a sauna. Her gown was cobalt blue woven with bronze so that it seemed to be a different color with every shift of light, like a night sea with schools of fish under the surface.

Flowers arrived from the fiancé, deep red coxcomb and fragrant tuberoses, and were set around Zuhura's seat. Tall vases of pussy willow cut from the Dawah Center backyard graced the guest tables. Rose petals were scattered in the bride's path by well-wishers, Aunt Khadija's idea.

"Bismillah, bismillah," Aunt Fatma said, kissing her fingers and waving them in a circle around the bride-to-be to ward off the evil eye. Ebtehaj and other ladies kept on the look out for grown-up girls

who might make good matches for the bachelors they knew, friends of their husbands and such.

Khadra was glad she'd brought her camera, her first, a cheap 110mm she got for Eid. She snapped pictures of Hanifa and Insaf and Nilofar and was about to take one of the bride but Aunt Ayesha shook her head.

"Here," Aunt Ayesha said. She handed Khadra a chunky black box. It was one of the new instant cameras! "This way, no film clerk sees us without hijab." Giving Khadra a packet of instant film, too, she said "You figure it out for us." She did, excited at the chance to use this new kind of camera.

"Dag!" Hanifa exclaimed, peering over Khadra's shoulder at the first picture as it developed before their eyes.

The henna artist knelt upon a carpet of rose petals at Zuhura's feet, drawing the arabesques on her palms and soles that gave the party its name. Guests sipping sugarcane juice clustered around to get a look at the emerging designs. Tayiba henna'd after the bride, followed by their Kenyan cousins from Chicago, and then Khadra and Hanifa were permitted to henna their hands.

Hanifa's design smeared because all she wanted to do was dance. She whirled like she was melting down to her "heart of light." "Come on!" she called to her friend, laughing, out of breath, but Khadra shook her head and was careful with her hands.

At prayer time, the women rustled back into their headscarves, the hairdos giving them funny shapes. First, though, there was a bit of a shuffle at the bathroom, those whose ablutions were broken hastily remembering to renew them and emerging with wet elbows, dabbing with paper towels at mascara slightly running. Tayiba made the call to prayer in a strong and tender voice.

Tayiba's mother graciously invited Khadra's mother to lead. Ebtehaj declined three times, inviting Ayesha to do it, and then finally accepted and stepped into the middle of the line of women standing pressed into each other's sides. "Allahu akbar," she began.

Khadra, wedged between bony Aunt Ayesha and plump Aunt Fatma, knelt as they knelt and went down with them into prostration on the floor, her nose and forehead pressed into the clean bedsheets. Around her were the overlapping rhythms of women's whispered glorias to the Lord on High . . . and something else, a jarring noise, coming from outside. Slurb! Thwack! Plshshst! They might not have heard, if not for the quiet of prayer.

No one broke prayer. Ebtehaj continued in her imaming, as if oblivious, and even after she salam'd there was no indication on her face of having been disturbed in her glorifications. She had this: the ability to block out the assault of the world while engaged in prayer. But Khadra, as soon as she salam'd, ran to the window and lifted up a corner of the taped-up vinyl and pressed her hands around her face so she could see out into the night.

"Mama! Aunt Ayesha!" she cried. And everybody ran outside. Including Zuhura, who immediately transformed from a henna'd bride to a pre-law student activist, taking charge and calling out directions: "Don't touch anything! Don't step in the footprints!"

The struggling boxwood hedge at the entrance was slimed with rotten eggs and tomatoes. Toilet paper was everywhere. Markings in white spray paint were blazoned across the windowpanes of the clubhouse. Aghast, Khadra snapped pictures of them: FUCK YOU, RAGHEADS. DIE. They were signed: KKK, 100% USA.

The energy that was buried with the rise of the Christian nations must come back into the world; nothing can prevent it. Many of us, I think, both long to see this happen and are terrified of it. . . .

—James Baldwin, *The Fire Next Time*

The only Muslims on television were Arab oil-sheiks, who were supposedly bad because they made America have an energy crisis. Teachers at Khadra's school had to pass out purple-ink mimeographed worksheets that said "Switch off the lights when you leave the room!" And President Carter pleaded with Americans to use less gas. Nasty Arab sheiks appeared on *Charlie's Angels,* forcing the shy angel, Kelly, to bellydance.

"As if the oil in Arab ground wasn't our own national treasure, to use to develop our own countries," Wajdy harumphed. He got up to adjust the strip of aluminum foil coiled around the rabbit-ear antennae, then sat back on the couch in his checkered double-knit polyester pants.

"Not that they will, those degenerate Saudi princes," Ebtehaj said.

"Whoremongering on the French Riviera," Wajdy agreed.

Ebtehaj nudged him and said, "Language, Wajdy—the children" and then she got up and switched the channel to *Carol Burnett and Friends.*

Charlie's Angels was not appropriate viewing for Muslims even though Khadra watched it on the sly at Hanifa's. Khadra liked Sabrina best because she never wore bikinis but dressed modestly, and was serious and smart and respected herself. Sabrina was almost the Muslim Charlie's Angel, she and Hanifa agreed.

All the Muslims in the Timbers were glued to their televisions when *Roots*, the miniseries, came out.

When Umaru, Kunte Kinte's father, came on screen, Wajdy cried, "You see? They're Muslims! Umaru is 'Umar.' It's Arabic!"

"Africanized Arabic," Jamal said, leaning back on the couch in his dashiki shirt.

"Yes, Arabic!" Wajdy repeated, not really listening to him.

Khadra hated Miss Ann the most. Because she was supposed to be Kizzy's *friend*. That girl refused to help Kizzy at *all* when she was dragged away to be sold. All Miss Ann would've had to do was say something to her daddy, the plantation owner. Stick up for Kizzy. Instead, she frowned and turned away. Some friend! When old lady Kizzy spit in old Miss Ann's cup? She deserved it.

The Lott boys started mocking Hakim and Hanifa as "Kunte" and "Kizzy." Khadra would've liked to spit in *their* cup.

The Lott boys were not the only kids in the neighborhood, of course. There were plenty of other kids. There was Ginny Debs, a white girl with bottle glasses who invited Khadra for a sleepover. Khadra was not allowed to go to sleepovers.

"Girls whose parents care anything about their well-being do not allow them to spend the night at someone else's house," her father said firmly. "It's depraved indifference," a phrase he'd picked up from *Streets of San Francisco,* a program he enjoyed now and then after the kids were asleep.

"Does she have a brother? How old? What is her father like?" her mother said. "Does he drink alcohol? Will he walk around drunk in his undershirt and try to touch you? No? How do we know he won't? We don't know, do we? We don't know anything about these people." Khadra was allowed to go to the party, but not to sleep over.

"Be careful of impurities!" her mother called after her in Arabic from the door of the Debs' house. Ebtehaj was leaving her daughter at an American house for the first time. She took one last sizing-up look around the living room, yesterday's *Indianapolis Star* headlines ("Drunken boyfriend rapes woman's daughter, 12." "Junkie mother passed out while ten-year-old starts house fire") flashing through her head.

Ebtehaj whispered three *Kursis* for her daughter's safety as she slipped behind the wheel of the station wagon. The thought of staying parked outside the kuffar house until pick-up time crossed Ebtehaj's mind, but she cast a final doubtful glance at the door and pulled away.

Just as she did, Ginny Debs's mother was picking up the phone.

Her neighbor on the line said, "You know what you have in your driveway?"

Mrs. Debs looked out the window. "It's just one of the mothers dropping off her kid," she said.

"Hmmph," the neighbor said, and then hung up.

Livvy Morton, with her bangs rolled into a Lincoln Log across her forehead, was the next experiment in having American friends.

"Does she have a religion, this Libby, Liddy—what is her name?" Ebtehaj said, looking up from her leatherbound Volume Four of al-Ghazali's *Revival of Religious Knowledge*.

"Livvy. Oh yes, her parents are real strick." Khadra said. "They're, um . . . a type of Christian, she told me but I forget. It starts with a P."

"Protestant?" her father said, pronouncing it *protesTANT*.

That wasn't it. "It rhymes with *librarian.*"

"Does she have any morals?" her mother said.

"Oh yeah, definitely," Khadra said. "Her parents don't drink or smoke. They don't approve of dancing or rock music. And Livvy and her sister—she only has a sister, no brothers in the house—are not allowed to date. Not till they're seniors."

And so that was why Livvy wasn't popular and why she would hang with Khadra. She was not bottom-of-the-barrel untouchable like Khadra but uninviteable-to-parties unpopular. Mindy and JoBeth called Livvy a "virgin" and snickered whenever she passed them in the hall, pasty-faced and bewildered.

"Hmmph," Wajdy said, his head bent intently to his task of regluing the buckle onto his old black briefcase from Syria, using the nifty new super-strong glue. That Americans allowed their kids to do this thing they called "dating" boggled his mind. How could any decent father hand his daughter over to a boy and tell them, go on, go out into the night, hold hands, touch each other? Some profound perversion of the soul made American men accept this pimpery.

Livvy taught Khadra how to sing "Jeremiah Was a Bullfrog." See, first you turned your back to your audience, knees bent, hands on your thighs, beating time. Then you jumped around facing your audience and sang the first line, the title line, at the top of your lungs. Then you broke into dancing for *"Was a mighty good friend of mine!"* Both Livvy and Khadra came from no-drinking families, so they skipped the line about the bullfrog always having some "mighty fine wine" for his friend. At the last, jubilant *"Joy to you and me!"* Livvy and Khadra would point to each other and shimmy their shoulders.

Out of breath from the dance and sweating, Livvy and Khadra went to the kitchen for cold water. Khadra banged the metal ice-cube tray on the counter. Ebtehaj, making fish sticks like she did when she was too busy preparing for Quran study to cook, right away set to offering Livvy food and drink. Khadra noticed her mother noticing how short Livvy's shorts were and how skimpy her halter-top. Wajdy came in from fixing the station wagon engine and washed his hands at the sink, nodding hello at Livvy and frowning slightly and tucking his head down.

Suddenly poor virginal Livvy, standing there on the mustard-yellow diamond patterned linoleum of the Shamy kitchen, seemed very naked to Khadra. She was all thin bare legs and shivering goose-pimply arms. Like you wanted to wrap a warm blanket around her. Did Livvy feel it too? She crossed her skinny arms across her bare midriff awkwardly. Her mousy hair fell forward over her pointy shoulderbones.

"Let's go play chess," Khadra said. "It's in the living room."

"I don't know how to play chest," Livvy said.

This kind of surprised Khadra. She thought everybody played chess. Her father had taught her and Eyad when they were five or six.

"Do you have Monopoly?" Livvy asked.

"We're not allowed to have Monopoly," Khadra said. But she knew how to play; she played it over Hakim and Hanifa's house. Her father said it taught greed. Monopolies were haram in real life, and so was interest, so why play at them?

"Checkers?" Livvy suggested.

"Jihad lost three of the pieces. What about cards?"

"Okay! What card games you know?"

Khadra's mother didn't approve of playing cards but they were in the house because Téta brought them and, as she was an elder, Ebtehaj couldn't say anything.

"Not haram if we're not gambling," Téta had crowed triumphantly, shuffling the halves of the deck with expert fingers.

More so than perhaps any other state, Indiana's population was native born, white, and Protestant. . . . This population homogeneity was . . . so significant that it is perhaps best to seek an understanding of it . . . by considering first the people . . . that partly contradicted the images of sameness.

—James H. Madison, *The Indiana Way*

Zuhura called her mother from Bloomington to say she was heading home right after the African Students' meeting. Luqman told her not to travel so late, because the Klansmen were returning from Skokie, where they'd not been allowed to have the big rally they had planned. Simmonsville, Martinsville, Greenwood, Plainfield, not to mention Indianapolis—all these towns had sent out truckloads of bigots to the march, and they'd be pulling into the last stretch of home right about then, mad as hornets.

"Christian terrorists on the loose," Luqman said. "Skip the stupid meeting." Then he complained to her parents about her stubbornness.

"Maybe Luqman's right," Uncle Yusuf told Aunt Ayesha. "I'll go get her." They phoned Zuhura to tell her this, but she'd already left.

Four hours later Aunt Ayesha started to pace. She figured two hours for the meeting and an hour, tops, for the drive home. By one a.m. she was frantic. Uncle Yusuf went to the police, but they said you had to wait forty-eight hours because she was an adult. They were maddening.

"College girl, Friday night? Probably at a party," they said.

Party? They didn't know Zuhura. They didn't know who she was. All they knew were typical American girls.

Yusuf took his wide-bodied Impala and went out with Abdulla and Luqman to look for his stepdaughter, since the police were refusing to help. Wajdy took two other Dawah men and went out in his station wagon. While Yusuf sped to Bloomington, Wajdy's search team drove slowly over the route Zuhura usually took, stopping at filling stations to show Zuhura's picture. Ayesha was persuaded to stay home only when her husband pointed out that they needed someone by the phone in case she called. Ebtehaj went to be with her, putting the kids to bed over at Khadija's.

"She's stalled somewhere and walking to a phone, that's all," Ebtehaj said to Ayesha. *"Inshallah."*

There was no sign of her. The men found a tall young man in the Eigenmann Dorm lounge, where foreign students hung out. He recognized her picture.

"Sure, everybody knows the Big Z," the student said, looking at the photo. Luqman frowned. "We all have a great deal of respect for her," the student added hastily.

He dropped a bombshell. She hadn't been at the African Students meeting.

"That's not possible," Yusuf said. Luqman narrowed his eyes and exchanged a look with Abdulla.

"She could have come late," the student said doubtfully. "I left early."

Where had she been? Why had she said she was going to the meeting, and then not gone? A small cleft opened between Zuhura's stated plans and her actions. And a gap of doubt in the minds of those who knew her.

Morning broke with no Zuhura. The Dawah men went back and covered the same stretch of road in daylight. By now they knew they were searching for something bad—a car that had veered off the road into some ditch where she lay, bled out. Or worse. They feared what they might find.

Yusuf went back and forth to the police station in Indianapolis and the Monroe County Sheriff's Department. The police search finally began. But two, three, four days passed and she was still nowhere to be found. Hope sputtered out. Except in Ayesha, who was fierce.

The women took turns going over to her apartment to pray with her, and to make her tea and see that she ate something, and to cook for Yusuf and Tayiba. Ebtehaj, on her shift, cleaned the kitchen, Ayesha being too preoccuppied to notice the dirty cups piling up in dangerously teetering towers. Looking over her shoulder at Ayesha, Ebtehaj also took the opportunity to toothbrush-scrub her base-boards, the dust on which always bothered her when she came for dinner. Ayesha sat hunched on the couch, her eyes bloodshot through the fierce pointy glasses. Every time the phone rang she jumped. She didn't like to be seen crying, but these women wouldn't leave her alone, so instead of crying, she shouted.

"Leave my baseboards alone! I clean my own kitchen!"

"No—of course—but—just a little grime—you might have missed it, sister—" Ebtehaj said, with the foaming toothbrush in her yellow-latex-gloved hand, hoping while the argument went on to tackle just one more gritty corner.

They found Zuhura's car. It had a flat tire. The spare and jack were still in the trunk. There was no evidence of a struggle. Just the usual Zuhura props: her dog-eared LSAT prep book and a paper sack with her prescription migraine medicine and her over-the-counter caffeine pills. Her backpack was on the seat, heavy with textbooks. Her macramé purse was there too, with her wallet in it. That didn't bode well.

"Martinsville? How did her car get to Martinsville?" No one knew. A little ways down the road from her car there were skid marks. Nothing else.

The scene at the Dawah Center was subdued. People lowered their voices when Yusuf entered the room, and stole looks at Ayesha's empty desk.

"Even if she is found alive now, she is ruined," Abdulla said in a low voice.

"No," Ebtehaj said flatly to her daughter. "You can't go on a field trip." She pushed away the permission slip that would allow Khadra to go with her classmates to Conner Prairie, the historical village.

"But, Mama! Everyone's going! The whole school'll be empty."

"Good. Then you can stay home. Right here next to me. You can help me scrub baseboards."

"Great."

"And go take a shower. You're filthy."

"I am not."

Ebtehaj slammed a jar of dried mint on the kitchen table and Khadra jumped. "BATH!" she yelled. *"Now."*

Days later, Zuhura's body was found in a ravine near Beanblossom Bridge. Murdered. Raped. Cuts on her hands, her hijab and clothes in shreds—the grown-ups didn't want to give details in front of the children, but it was in the news.

Some aunties said someone may have given Zuhura the evil eye, maybe someone who saw her radiant at the henna party and did not praise God. Such forgetting unleashed evil forces, and you never knew what form they would take. A fire, a crash, or maybe what had happened to Zuhura. When they heard, Khadra and Hanifa and Tayiba each had unvoiced fears that she could have been the one. You could give someone the eye even if you didn't mean to. Just by forgetting the Divine Name. And who, who lived in a state of constant mindfulness?

Some folks at the Dawah Center didn't believe in the evil eye. The erudite Kuldip said it was superstition, and superstition was close to idolatry. How could it be idoloatry, Wajdy argued, when it was right there in the Quran? Ebtehaj said, of course the eye was real. The Prophet had said so.

Poor Aunt Ayesha. No one had ever seen her like this. She insisted with her usual forcefulness on going to the morgue, even though Uncle Yusuf told her it would be better not to.

"What if it's not true?" she said. "Only I can tell for sure if it's my daughter! What if it's all a mistake?"

When she saw the body she froze. What if God was tricking her senses? All she really knew was it *seemed* to be Zuhura. What did the Queen of Sheba say in the Quran? When Solomon showed her the impossible sight of her own throne in his polished court where it couldn't, simply couldn't, be—she wisely said "This *seems* to be it." Your senses can trick you. They are not the final arbiter. Only God, the Unseen, is the final arbiter.

Ayesha trembled. She took off her rhinestone-studded turquoise cat's eye glasses and wiped them. *And they did not crucify him, but it was made to seem to them as if they did.* The Quran said that. The Quran said that about Jesus, peace be upon him. *It was made to seem to them.*

Sometimes God did things like that. Made things seem what they were not. But why? But why? It was a test. It was a test. A test for the believers. *For men who believe and women who believe.* Ayesha peered through the morgue window again. Her glasses clattered to the floor. She didn't bother to retrieve them. What was the point? Why was God making her see this? Yusuf bent and picked up her glasses and tried to give them to her; she pushed them away. Her eyes were too bleary to see clearly, and she didn't want to look anymore, anyway.

Without the familiar glasses, she looked naked, broken. All her fierceness gone. Yusuf had to keep his arms around her shoulders to hold her up. Her body was so small suddenly. Who knew she was so petite under the voluminous robes she liked to wear? Whereas before, you couldn't be in a room with Aunt Ayesha without being intensely aware of her presence, now she came and left all crumpled, like nothing. People tried not to look at Ayesha because it was so hard to see her like that, and there were many men and women alike, and even a few bewildered children, who almost wished she would fix them with one of her famous unnerving stares.

Clearly it was religious bigotry, the Muslims said. Salam Mosque and Dawah people agreed. It was related to her vocal espousal of Muslim causes on campus, it was political. The *Indianapolis Freeman*—Uncle Jamal brought over a copy—said it was about race, said how could it not be, in light of the Skokie affair and recent area rumblings from the Klan? It called Zuhura "a young black woman" and didn't mention that she was Muslim at all. On the other hand, the *Indianapolis Star* pretended like race wasn't there at all, calling Zuhura a "foreign woman" and "an IU international student," as if her family didn't live right there in town. The *Indianapolis News* article treated it like just some random crime, giving it one tiny paragraph in the back pages. The front-page news was about a march. A photo that showed a group of white women yelling "Take Back the Night!"

"We liked her to pieces, but she was an opinionated little bit," a student council rep said in the college newspaper, and a classmate described her as "a little black spitfire." Tayiba passed the article to Khadra without comment.

"But that makes no sense," Khadra said, reading it. "Zuhura was big and tall." How could anyone call her "little?"

"She should not have been traipsing about the highways at midnight alone," Wajdy and Ebtehaj agreed in late-night kitchen-table voices. And the whispers and undertones around the water cooler at the Dawah Center agreed: She had been asking for trouble. Sad as it made them to say it. And her family should've given her more guidance. You protected your daughters.

"Women wash the body of a woman and men wash a man. It is a service incumbent upon members of the faith. Seven pieces of shroud for a woman; three for a man." Ebtehaj reviewed the janaza chapter in her tattered *Fiqh al-Sunnah* book and went out to take part in the washing of Zuhura. When she came home afterward she unwound her headscarf silently, shaking her head. She unzipped her long jilbab and folded it over her arm and went upstairs to take *"the purification bath required of those who wash the dead."*

And what of the dead, where do they lie in a non-Muslim land? Next to kuffar graves whose graven images may deter visiting angels? And what do you do if a country's laws require burial in a box, when a Muslim should be buried with nothing but a seamless shroud between her and the receiving earth?

These were some of the questions of adjustment that the Dawah Center was created to address. In America, you could not be passive about enacting your faith; you had to "Do for Self." No one was there to do it for you, like in the Old Country. There were hardly any Muslim institutions yet in this wilderness. You had to study your faith, dig out the core principles from underneath all the customs that may have accrued around them in the old Muslim world, and find a way to act on those principles in the present conditions. The spring after Zuhura's funeral, the Dawah Center would print up a pamphlet giving all the answers in easy-to-follow directives based on sound shariah research. Wajdy Shamy was one of the authors. Untold numbers of the U.S. faithful appreciated *How to Be Buried as a Muslim in America.*

Maybe we don't *belong here,* Khadra thought, standing next to Hanifa in the crowd at Zuhura's graveside. Maybe she belonged in a place where she would not get shoved and called "raghead" every other day in the school hallway. Teachers, classmates—no one ever caught her assailants. They always melted into the crowd behind her.

The whole Indianapolis Muslim community came out for the funeral—they were all family—and a lot of students from Bloomington, even some non-Muslims. There was a Nigerian athlete, and another young black man who cried hard and left quickly, mystifying the Dawah folk. But he exchanged a few quiet words with Zuhura's mother, and she nodded, seeming satisfied.

Instead of looking for the killers, or rounding up any of the APES (American Protectors of the Environs of Simmonsville) for questioning, the police handcuffed Luqman and threw him in the back of a car. Where was he that night? they asked. Was Zuhura seeing someone on the side? they asked, maligning her morals with horrible questions. "No!" he shouted, "She was an *honorable* girl!" The *Indianapolis Star* reported on him being a suspect: *Murder Possible Honor Killing—Middle Eastern Connection,* they said, with a sidebar on "the oppression of women in Islam."

No charge of murder was brought against Luqman. He was deported anyway, on a technical visa violation.

Zuhura's murderer was never caught. The Dawah community labored on with its godly task, if a little heavier of heart. "Just like the early Muslims," Khadra's mother said. "When one fell, another one picked up the banner and struggled on."

If there were no eternal consciousness in a man, if at the foundation of all there lay only a wildly seething power which writhing with obscure passions produced everything that is great and everything that is insignificant, if a bottomless void never satiated lay hidden beneath it all—what then would life be but despair?

—Søren Kierkegaard, *Fear and Trembling*

Khadra's father and the other Center workers took the Dawah on the road. They drove to chapters across the country, developing Islamic awareness. Ebtehaj was just as involved in organizing local Muslim women's groups, although she was not a salaried Center employee like Wajdy. So the whole family piled into the station wagon for these mission trips.

In this way, Khadra and Eyad got to see more of America than most of their American classmates. They made ablutions in the Great Salt Lake (it really *was* that salty!) and prayed duhr at Mount Rushmore with the giant faces of the presidents gazing down upon them ("Carved by a Klansman," Wajdy said). They uttered the journey blessing in unison as they went up the Gateway Arch in St. Louis, and they pushed Jihad's stroller between the Lincoln Memorial and the Washington Monument.

One of the road trips took the Shamys to the Grand Canyon. The family stood at the top of a lookout point on the South Rim. Jihad was on his mother's hip. Her sky blue jilbab swept the ground and her white crepe wimple outlined her head against the sky. Khadra's father stood next to her in his double-stitched tan leisure suit, his arm around Eyad. Khadra brought them into focus and snapped the picture.

An elderly white-haired man in an old-fashioned suit coming up the stairs stopped short before this family scene. *"Santa Maria!"* he murmured. He came up the rest of the stairs without taking his eyes off Khadra's mother. "Beautiful, beautiful," he said, to himself—or to her, it wasn't clear. He had some kind of European accent.

Ebtehaj looked flustered, and shifted Jihad from one hip to the other. Wajdy seemed amused.

Later in the day, the family was walking along Hermit's Road, the sunset painting thick magenta and turquoise streaks across the sky above the deepening indigo and saffron of the canyon, when a siren wailed behind them. They scurried to the side of the road to let the police car pass; instead, the officer waved them down.

An elderly man had climbed out to a ledge and was poised to jump. He kept calling for "Madonna in the blue robe. Madonna with the angelic child! Madonna of the mountain!" Would Ebtehaj talk to him?

It ended well. Afterward, before she could stop him, the old gentleman lifted her hand to his lips and kissed it. "God sent Beauty to save me!" he said.

Khadra's mother got all flustered again. She didn't even shake hands with men, and now her ablution had to be remade, of course. "It was not me—it was God's will," she said sternly, but not without compassion.

"What happened up there?" Wajdy asked, back at the Motel 6. The children were piled into one of the two double beds with chintz coverlets, asleep, except for Khadra, who heard her parents talking as she drifted to sleep.

"He said he just loved God and wanted to be with Him," Ebtehaj said, taking her hair out of the clip at the nape of her neck. "He said the world was too ugly. He wanted to see God's Beauty.'" Her chestnut hair fell down her shoulders, curvy from where it had been held back all day.

"And then?"

Ebtehaj made an impatient noise. "I said you can't do that, that's haram, of course! In your religion like in ours. If you love Him, you must obey Him." That was love, she felt. Not following your own desires, willy-nilly. The sun was setting and she'd said to the man, My God isn't this enough beauty for you, Mister? She now dabbed a bit of night cream on her face and smoothed it. "Wajdy, do you think," she said, considering a brand-new problem, "their prayers are counted by God?"

"They're People of the Book; of course their prayers count," Wajdy said, yawning. "Though not like ours," he added, before he fell into the silence toward sleep, leaving Ebtehaj staring absently at the hairpins on the chipped veneer of the nightstand and behind it, the grubby hotel drape.

Beyond that lay the striped asphalt road with its caravans of people and the immense gaping canyon and the question of what does it all mean, the question which, if not answered by faith, is answered by what? Then what railing would hold us from falling into the great gulch? No. The sure footing is the straight path, the rock-solid first ground of faith, where she was. She settled into the thin pillow.

Returning, there was always that funny Indiana smell. A sign of home.

"What is that smell, do you think?" Ebtehaj asked. "That Indiana smell?"

"Gas," Wajdy said.

"Who farted?" Khadra wondered, joining the conversation from the sleeping-bag-padded cargo area, and Eyad guffawed.

"No really, the smell of the state comes from natural gas," Wajdy insisted. Everyone in the car was laughing now. "All these towns in Indiana used to sit on top of natural gas reserves."

"Indiana has to make *wudu!*" Eyad hooted.

"Gas used to be the basis of the whole state economy," Wajdy went on, but it was no use. Even their mother gasped that she was going to have to renew her wudu at the next rest stop, as she had laughed so hard she may have broken her ablutions and impaired the purity of her underwear. That set off a new wave of laughter in the back seat.

They purified for God in foul-smelling rest-area bathrooms. They prayed by the side of an Amish country road in the dirt and ironweed, in the shade of a shagbark hickory tree. They made symbolic ablution by striking their hands against a rock in the Painted Desert. They prostrated in a windy corner of the observation deck of the Sears Tower in Chicago ("Built by a Muslim engineer, you know!" Wajdy told them). Once, lost trying to get to Mishawaka, they even prayed next to a giant roadside egg. Twelve foot high, made of concrete. The lettering beneath it declared, "Greetings from Mentone, Indiana—the egg basket of the Midwest."

"Don't worry about people looking at us," Khadra's father said. "Focus on the patch of earth in front of you." He pointed to the place where the forehead would touch the ground. They had pit-stopped at a Dairy Queen outside Kokomo, on the way back from visiting the Mishawaka community.

The Shamys had been scandalized by the Mishawaka Muslims. They had one of the oldest mosques in America up there, founded by Arab Muslims who had come to America as far back as the 1870s. But slowly, over generations, they had mixed American things in with real Islam, Wajdy explained, so that now they needed a refresher course in real Islam from the Dawah Center. None of the women up there wore hijab and none of the men had beards—they didn't even look like Muslims. And they did shocking things in the mosque, like play volleyball with men and women together, *in shorts.* And they had dances for the Muslim boys and girls—dances! "Mishawaka Muslims" became a byword for "lost Muslims" in *The Islamic Forerunner*.

At the Kokomo Dairy Queen, Ebtehaj got out of the big clunky station wagon in her tan double-knit polyester jilbab and a beige headcover. With a fussing Jihad in tow, she headed for the restroom, people's stares following her. Her washing-up cup was in her handbag. She was always looking for handy personal hygiene cups, and this one had a collapsible design that folded into the shape of a compact.

Their father spread the Navajo blanket as a prayer rug for Khadra and unrolled a narrow woven mat for Eyad.

"But you don't have a rug," Eyad said.

"I don't need a rug, son." Wajdy said. They were on a patch of weedy dirt at the rear of the DQ.

"What if the ground is impure?" Khadra said, remembering Islamic school lessons: purity of place required for salah.

"The earth itself is considered pure, *binti,*" he said. "All the world is a prayer mat." Even central Indiana Dairy Queen backlots were okay with God. So Khadra and Eyad knelt on the knobby ground behind their father. A blue beetle started picking its way up and down a pile of broken bricks near Khadra's head during the first rakat and made it over by the end of prayer. Palm, palm, knee, knee, foot, foot, forehead. Rising, her father brushed off bits of gravel that had embedded in his forehead.

"A whole family assembling regularly for the purpose of prayer is fine!"

—Fanny, in Jane Austen, *Mansfield Park*

From when Khadra first became aware of Ramadan, she begged to be allowed to fast. Because you got to wake up in the dark dewy pre-dawn, part of a secret club. The rest of the human world was asleep. No faint whoosh of cars from the main road, and the parking lots of the Timbers were absolutely still. Even the crickets, even the birds, were asleep. The milkman hadn't come yet to take the empties left in the tin box on the porch and replace them with full bottles of milk. Khadra's mother and father padded around in the little kitchen, bleary-eyed, setting out *suhoor* food on the chipped Formica table. Sometimes little Jihad woke up from hearing the unaccustomed noise at this hour—they'd look up and find him standing there in his PJs, casting at the family a look of such accusation for leaving him out, such a baleful *"et tu?"* glare that, young as he was, he was soon a participant in the ritual.

"Lentil soup, eat," Wajdy said, as Ebtehaj ladled it. "Protein. It will stick to your belly, binti. It's a long fasting day." The clink of spoons in soup bowls were the only sounds in the whole black universe. An alarm clock sat on the kitchen table tick-tick-tick is there time for one more bite tick-tick-tick is there time for a long cool gulp of water tick-tick-tick.

"Khadra ate past Time!" Eyad said, pointing at the clock.

"I did not!" Khadra said, horrified.

"Did too!" The clock hands were incontrovertible. One minute past the correct time to stop eating.

"It wasn't Time when I started the bite!"

"It's okay, Khadra. What's already in your mouth can be swallowed," her father said.

"Yeah, Eyad!" Khadra said. She hadn't known this before. "Back off, boy!" she added, snapping her fingers at him.

"Enough!" her mother said. "The two of you clear the table and then go make wudu."

Each of them slipped away to make ablutions and came back, face wet and fresh from the washing. They spread the prayer rugs and prayed fajr together on the floor between the threadbare couch and sunken armchair. After the salam, Eyad lay his sleepy head in his mother's lap while she counted out Glory Be's on her fingers. When she finished, she smoothed his hair back from his forehead.

After everyone went back to bed, Khadra stepped out on the patio. She felt the first stirring of birds and other things that lived in the earth and trees and skies. And those that lived in the Fallen Timbers Townhouse Complex stirred too, here and there a window filling with yellow light in the dimness. It was a whole other world Ramadan gave you, eerie and dreamlike. The faint sound of a train grew closer. Then the filmy glow in the sky spread into pink streaks that got wider and wider and became daylight, and things slowly took their ordinary shape.

"Khadra?"

She whirled around. Jihad was standing behind her. She put an arm around him.

When Téta's visits coincided with Ramadan, there was always a tug of war at *maghreb* between her and Ebtehaj: Eat first or pray first? Ebtehaj said pray first. Téta said eat first. She quoted the Prophet, and she always won. As soon as the meal was over, Ebtehaj clapped her hands and said "Prayer! Prayer time!"

"For goodness' sake, give us time to fart!" Téta protested as she got up to make ablutions.

Ebtehaj gave her a look as the children giggled. Wajdy hid his mouth behind his hand.

"What?" Téta said innocently. "If you don't fart first, then all you're thinking about in prostration is how not to let it fly."

When your daughter's menarche comes, cook sweet wheat-bean pudding and distribute it to your neighbors in celebration!

—Damascene custom of unknown origin (now nearly defunct)

Khadra finally got it in the middle of Ramadan—her period. Her mother had prepared her. Ebtehaj, having been pre-med once, pulled out full-color anatomical diagrams with fallopian tubes and all sorts of things labeled. She went over it scientifically—the descent of the egg, and so on, and also Islamically—the requirements of the purification bath, the excused prayers and fast days. "My mother never told us," Ebtehaj said. "She was very traditional. But that's unIslamic, see?"

Ebtehaj and Wajdy and the Dawah-style Muslims were very dubious about popular Islam, Islam as practiced by the regular believing masses. It had heaps of wrongheaded customs substituting for real religious knowledge and mixed in with modern shortcuts. They were out to purify it. Not telling your kids about puberty when they were close to it was one of the legacies of prior generation of Muslims that they felt was not in tune with authentic Islam, the Islam of the Prophet's time.

"You should know, because puberty makes your Islamic duties fully incumbent on you," Ebtehaj said. "Now you are of age. Now sins count."

"They didn't count before?" Khadra said. Nobody'd mentioned that! So—eating the pig candy corn didn't hurt?

"Mama, is this my period?" she said, passing her underwear to her mom from behind the bathroom door. "I thought it would be red. This is brown. How does this belt contraption work?" The belt held the big fat pads in place. "Mama, what are tampons?"

"Virgins mustn't use tampons," her mother replied. "They're for married women. And even then—" Ebtehaj, who had distinct views on many health issues, felt tampons were unhealthy. "How healthy can it be to keep waste stuffed inside your body instead of letting it drain out?"

"But Livvy said they're more comf—"

"American girls don't care if they're open down there!"

The big bonus from getting her period, of course, was that Khadra got to break her fast. She pulled her fist toward her in triumph: Yessss! She made a triple-decker beef salami sandwich on sesame-seed bread with tomato, lettuce, mushrooms, mayo, ketchup of course, and beet pickles.

"Periods rock," she mumbled with her mouth full.

Eyad walked in and did a double take. "You're cheating?" he said. "You're cheating in Ramadan!"

"Nah, I ain't cheatin'," his sister crowed. She chomped down on another fat bite. He eyed her sandwich, mouth watering. "Tell him, Mama."

Eyad knew about periods too, for the same reason Khadra did; he'd learned it as part of shariah studies.

"Young lady, you might be more discreet about it," Ebtehaj said. "And more considerate than eating in front of a fasting person," she added, looking sideways at Khadra's chunky sandwich dripping its tomato juices.

Ebtehaj sneaked a peek at her watch. It was still hours to *iftar* time. She went back to marking a passage in her book very lightly and carefully with pencil. She was reading Zamakhshari on Aisha's contention with the scholars and enjoying it tremendously. How could you not admire Aisha, the courageous daughter of Abu Bakr? So full of intellect and activism, so well studied, not only in Islam but also in medicine and history. Even her mistakes only revealed her love of the faith and zeal to protect it, Ebtehaj felt.

Khadra's father took her to pick material for her first real hijabs at Philpot's Fabric Emporium. "You want a fabric that breathes and has good drape, binti," he said.

He knew his fabrics. After the jilbabs Ebtehaj brought with her from Syria began to get threadbare, even her favorite sky-blue summer linen one, it was Wajdy who made new ones for her. He made Ebtehaj a winter jilbab out of a nubby polyester double knit. He cut it fashionably on the warp so the cross-hatching went diagonally, and gave it a big pointy collar right off the pages of a fashion magazine. It was Ebtehaj's first American jilbab. "This will never need ironing!" Wajdy had exclaimed as he guided the wondrous newfangled synthetic under the sewing machine arm.

For her headscarves, Ebtehaj used only ultralightweight crepe georgette, fine as onionskin and supple as a living membrane. This she wrapped around her head with a precision that made the other Dawah women marvel. Never a hair out of place, that was Ebtehaj's hijab. You could tell if Ebtehaj had been in a town on one of her Dawah trips with Wajdy by the fact that, in her wake, women would try to imitate her scarf style. Ebtehaj influenced hijab fashions from Fort Collins to Cleveland.

Ebtehaj hand-washed her scarves. She sang softly to herself while she worked up a lather:

Ghazaleh ghaza-a-aleh, tab jurhi tab
Gazelle, gazeh-eh-elle, now my wound is healed

Then there was the grand and wonderful shaking out of the scarves, for she never wrung or twisted them to dry. Ebtehaj lifted the wet lump of delicate fabric out of the basin. She held one dripping end and the son or daughter helping her held the other. They backed away from each other until the crepe opened to its magnificent full length between them, a gossamer bridge.

"Hold it from the corners. Don't let it fall to the floor. One—two—three—SHAKE! And one—two—three—AGAIN!" and then Ebtehaj gathered up the ends of her scarf from her daughter or son and neatly brought each corner to corresponding corner and hung it on the shower curtain rack to drip dry. *Gazelle, gazeh-eh-elle, healed, my wound is healed.*

Jihad loved to run underneath the gauzy canopy and get a soft rain on his face. The space under the gently rising, gently descending parachute was curved and graceful. You could be Sinbad under the wing of an enormous bird. You could be anything anywhere.

At the Washington Square Shopping Center looking for the cloth of her first hijabs, Khadra could not find crepe georgette as fine and lightweight as the fabric her mother treasured from Syria. She found instead lightweight seersucker in cornflower blue with yellow daisies, a white cotton eyelet that would go with anything, and a jade jacquard in sophisticated chiffon. And a warm woolen paisley for winter. Buying all this at one go was a breathtaking splurge.

"This is a special day, Doora," Ebtehaj said, using Khadra's baby nickname. "You pick whatever you want."

Wajdy gave her scarf edges a rolled-edge finish using the zigzag stitch feature on the sewing machine. And then Aunt Khadija gave her a sparkly topaz brooch she had been saving for her—she'd bought two at Montgomery Ward's, one for Khadra and one for Hanifa. The topper came from Ebtehaj: she had Wajdy make a tan, polyester double-knit jilbab for Khadra, out of the same fabric as her own, so they could have matching mother-daughter jilbabs to wear on Eid!

The sensation of being hijabed was a thrill. Khadra had acquired vestments of a higher order. Hijab was a crown on her head. She went forth lightly and went forth heavily into the world, carrying the weight of a new grace. Even though it went off and on at the door several times a day, hung on a hook marking the threshold between inner and outer worlds, hijab soon grew to feel as natural to her as a second skin, without which if she ventured into the outside world she felt naked.

"Aren't you hot?" Khadra and all the other hijab'd girls and women often got asked by Americans.

"Even if I am hot, same as anyone on a hot day, I'd no sooner take off my hijab than you'd take off your blouse in the middle of the street, Livvy," she said to her American friend.

Tayiba, ever one step ahead in hijabi fashion, had silkscreened a T-shirt that explained it all. "You think I'm hot?" it said across the front. Danny Nabolsy's jaw dropped when he saw her wearing this bit of sass. Then she turned around, and on the back it said, "It's hotter in hellfire—lower your gaze!" and his ears turned red.

If there was a common thread, when our better writers took a hard look at Hoosier living, they seemed to find a tight-lipped people, afraid to take risks but longing to leave, just trying to hang on in a tough world. Trucks didn't run well and neighbors were as likely to shoot you as lend you a cup of sugar.

—Michael Wilkerson, "Indiana Origin Stories,"
Where We Live: Essays About Indiana

At first, Téta just observed Mrs. Moore gardening. She was absorbed in her task. She wore a big straw hat and canvas gloves, and carried a pad for her knees.

"You've got a fallen tomato branch," Téta called to her in Arabic, pointing to the branch which had fallen in an area visible to Téta but not to Mrs. Moore. Mrs. Moore came around to where Téta was pointing and plucked the red tomato off the ground-lying vine.

"Thank you," Mrs. Moore replied in English, propping the fallen stalk.

"Your lilacs are doing very well," Téta said in Arabic, indicating the tall bushes. "Lilac" was recognizable; it was the same word in Arabic, *"leylak."*

"El-hamdo-leelah," Mrs. Moore said, spreading her palms open heavenward.

Téta was pleased with Mrs. Moore's Arabic and didn't bat an eye. "I have lilacs too," she said. "In Syria."

"Vous êtes Syrienne?" Mrs. Moore said. *"Quelle belle terre—de civilizations très anciennes, n'est-ce pas?"*

"Bien sûr," Téta said. *"Damas est la plus ancienne ville du monde."*

And away they went, throwing in Arabic or English whenever they got stuck in French, and hoping the gist came through. They discussed the merits of honeysuckle and cyclamen and the multitude of medicinal benefits of sweet bay laurel. As a treatment for arthritis, rashes, stomachache, female troubles, there was no end to its uses. And it warded off evil eye. Téta had a bay laurel tree at home in Syria that she would have loved to show Mrs. Moore.

Mrs. Moore's yard had a large weeping willow and a walnut tree, recognizable to Téta because both species also grew in Syria. She also had a ten-foot shrub with round leaves that she called a Wayfaring tree.

"But every garden should have a fruit-bearing tree," Téta suggested. "Fig? Or perhaps cherry."

Mrs. Moore shook her head. "Wouldn't grow here. Wrong climate."

True. Téta mostly came in the warm weather; she had never wintered in Indiana, but she knew it was much harder than the Syrian winter, where they might get a dusting or two of snow but never the knee-deep drifts the Shamys told her about.

"But then, the lilac grows here and there, both," Téta said. They pondered different plants and their adaptability. When Ebtehaj came looking for Téta, she was wondering what might happen if she could manage to bring a cutting of her cyclamen.

"Ça depend," Mrs Moore replied.

"À quoi?"

"Le genre de temps." If the plant could weather the first few seasons, if you avoided planting it in the high heat of summer, and protected it well the first winters, it might catch on and thrive, they concluded.

"I am going to visit this Madame Moore in her home," Téta said magnanimously the next morning over breakfast, with its little plates of olives and cheese. "Wajdy, when you go in to work today, would you please ask her when her reception days are?"

Ladies in Damascus had standing 'reception days' when you could pay a formal visit and sip Turkish coffee and leave your calling card and be visited back in your home on your own reception days. Téta's days, for example, were second Mondays and first Saturdays.

Mrs. Moore made high tea for Téta. Then Téta invited her to the Shamy house for Turkish coffee, which, Mrs. Moore cried, she hadn't had in ages, simply ages.

And so their mutual visits became an essential part of Téta's every trip to Indiana. Mrs. Moore introduced her to her garden club, and Téta crossed the threshold of sweet little southern Indianapolis and Simmonsville homes that the Shamys would never have thought to enter. Téta brought Mrs. Moore cakes of laurel soap and ground laurel bark hair balsalm, and oval wooden boxes of birdnests, a treat that featured pistachios arranged in the middle of tiny shredded-pastry nests drizzled with syrup.

"There was a family lived in that house, you know." Téta liked to pass on tidbits of Mrs. Moore's stories. "Where you work, Wajdy." She was squatting in the tiny patio out back, pulling a few weeds from around the spearmint in Ebtehaj's little herb patch. "A nice big Catholic family," Téta continued. "Nine children at the turn of the century. They gave them such a hard time, though."

"Who?"

"The Protestants. They don't even consider the Catholics real Christians, imagine."

Wajdy hadn't realized the gulf was so huge. They were all Christian to him. "Like the Sunnis and the Shias, I suppose," he said.

"In the twenties, they tried to run them out of town," Téta went on, shifting her knee pad under her. She had taken a cue from Mrs. Moore's nifty gardening knee pad—with a vinyl casing, it was sturdier than a folded up old towel—she made Wajdy sew up one like it for her to take back to Syria. "Terrorists wearing white masks," she said.

"Them I know," Wajdy said.

"They killed Zuhura," Khadra informed Téta solemnly.

"We don't know that for sure," her father corrected her.

"Them, or people like them," she said.

The American Negro has the great advantage of having never believed that collection of myths to which white Americans cling: that their ancestors were all freedom-loving heroes . . . invincible in battle and wise in peace . . . dealt honorably with Mexicans and Indians and all other neighbors or inferiors . . .

—James Baldwin

That November, revolutionaries in Iran blindfolded American embassy workers and took them hostage. They let the women go. They knew women didn't run America. Then they let the black men go, because blacks were oppressed by America just like Third World peoples. That left fifty-two white American men hostage.

"A taste of their own medicine," Wajdy said. "They make everyone else in the world suffer while they live like lords. They create terror in other people's countries while they live in safety and luxury. Let them see how it is to have to worry."

Kuldip said, "Anyway, they're not tourists. Half of them are CIA. They knew the risks."

"Acting the innocent victims now, Americans," Omar Nabolsy, the Palestinian Dawah director, said.

Everyone at the Center agreed that under normal circumstances, hostage taking was bad. But they could understand why the Iranian students did it. The Iranians had suffered under the Shah, who imprisoned protestors, tortured prisoners, encouraged booze and corruption, and tried to eliminate Islamic identity in his country. All with America's blessings and weapons.

For the first time, the Iranian people called the shots. Now the tables were turned and the powerless were powerful. Fifty-two white American men, used to having the final authority over any situation, had to sit helplessly at the other end of the guns of young bearded men (and one scarf-wearing woman!).

This made America hopping mad. America was mad at Khadra personally, thc Shamy family, and all the other Muslims of Indianapolis. Simmonsville residents who didn't know the Shah of Iran from Joe Schmoe yelled "Long live the Shah!" as their Muslim neighbors got out of their cars and went into the blue house on New Harmony Drive. Vandalism of the Dawah Center with soap and white spray paint was something the police couldn't seem to stop; they only came and took pictures every time it happened.

Khadra took pictures too, with her own camera. She showed them to her father, and he showed them to Uncle Kuldip and Uncle Omar, and they actually used one of them under *The Islamic Forerunner*'s article "Hostage Incident Sparks Increased Vandalism of U.S. Islamic Centers."

* * *

Even if the schoolbooks didn't say so, Islamic civilization was responsible for most of the good scientific inventions of the world, up until the last hundred years or so. The clock. Eyeglasses. "I thought Benjamin Franklin invented them," Khadra said.

"He may have, I don't know this Ben-Yameen," her father said. "But if he did invent them, it's because Ibn Sina advanced the science of optics in the eleventh century."

There was a picture in the ninth-grade social studies book of an Arab with an unkempt beard standing in a dirty caftan next to a camel, and a picture of an African bushman with no clothes and a bracelet threaded through his nose that made Khadra wince.

"Islam is scientific," Ebtehaj said, in English because Hanifa was there with Khadra. "Not like Christianity. Islam, it encourages us to learn science. In history, Christianity killed the scientists."

"It was an Arab who discovered the world was round," Wajdy said. "This is why Christopher Columbus came to America."

But Tayiba's parents said it was an African scientist who discovered the world was round. So which was it, an African or an Arab? It was a Muslim named al-Idrisi. He was African and wrote in Arabic. Aunt Ayesha spoke of the great empires of Mali and Ghana and the glories of Timbuktu and Benin, while Ebtehaj told of the glories of Al-Andalus and the beauties of Baghdad and Cairo in their prime.

None of this information was in any book Khadra could find at the school library. Sometimes she wondered if maybe a little bit of Muslim pride made them exaggerate.

One time her father told her Shakespeare was really an Arab.

"Just look at his name: It's an Anglicization of Sheikh Zubayr," he said, with a straight face.

She insisted on it for fifteen minutes to her language-arts teacher the next day. When she got home and related the story, her father threw his head back and laughed, and only then told her he'd been joking.

To back her claims about Islam and science before her doubting daughter, Ebtehaj showed Khadra one of her old Damascus University books on Muslim contributions to medicine. But it was too hard to read, in close Arabic print with no pictures.

Khadra and Eyad could just about manage the little Arabic readers that their parents made relatives send from Syria every year. "See Mazen run. Rabab goes to market. See Father and Mother. Father is brave. Mother reads a letter from Father at the front." Father wore a Syrian Army uniform and Mother never wore hijab. They were secular Baathist textbooks, with a picture of the Syrian president, Hafez Asad, in the front. The first thing Khadra's parents did was tear that page out and throw it away. Then they set to teaching the children Arabic, and gathered them on the prayer rugs to recite the Quranic *suras* they worked hard to memorize. Eyad was working on *The Cave*, an ambitious project. Khadra was all the way up to *Surat al-Fajr,* the "O Soul made Peaceful" section: *Come in among My worshipers, and in My Garden, enter*.

No matter how hard they worked, however, the children could never keep up with their cousins in Syria, whose always exemplary Arabic composition was pointed out to them whenever the featherweight bluepaper letters arrived by airmail. Khadra harbored a secret loathing for Reem and Roddy.

By the rivers dark, I wandered on
I lived my life in Babylon
. . . . .
By the rivers dark, where I could not see
Who was waiting there, who was hunting me

—Leonard Cohen, "By the Rivers Dark"

Where was the soul at peace? Somalis were in the grip of a terrible famine. There was fighting in Western Sahara. Afghans filled refugee camps in Iran and Pakistan. Patani Muslims were being persecuted in their Buddhist-dominated country. Life in Lebanon was a hell of shelling and death. None of this was an important part of the news in America. Whereas the minute details of the lives of the American men held hostage, and the tears and hopes of their mothers, fathers, grandparents, and second cousins in Kissamee made news every day. Only they were human, had faces, had mothers. People wore yellow ribbons for these fifty-two privileged white men who now were, if the American news was to be believed, the most wretchedly oppressed of the earth. Anchorman Walter Cronkite counted out the days of their captivity at the end of each news broadcast.

Khadra counted out her days in George Rogers Clark High School where, for four hundred and forty-four days, she was a hostage to the rage the hostage crisis produced in Americans. It was a battle zone. Her job was to get through the day dodging verbal blows—and sometimes physical ones. By the time she got home, she was ready to be crabby and mean to anyone in her way.

"Why are you such a sourpuss?" her mother asked sharply, when Khadra snapped at Jihad.

"And what's wrong with your grades?" Wajdy demanded. "A C in English composition? You used to get As."

"She's prejadess," Khadra retorted.

It sounded like an excuse, but the comp teacher was prejudiced for real. Whenever Khadra wrote an essay about how hypocritical America was to say it was democratic while it propped dictators like the Shah and supported Israel's domination of Lebanon, "and then they wonder why people over there hate them," she got big red D's and Mrs. Tarkington found a reason to circle every other word with red ink. As soon as she turned in a composition on a neutral topic, no politics or religion, the Tark gave her a big fat A. It was that black-and-white.

Khadra felt a jab between her shoulder blades. Her books slipped to the floor—*An American Tragedy* by Theodore Dreiser, and *The Autobiography of Malcolm X.*

"Oops," said a voice behind her. She whirled. Brent Lott and Curtis Stephenson. She was cornered. The whole school was at the rally in the gym. She could hear the pep squad's war whoops in the distance.

Curtis grabbed *Malcolm X* off the pukey green floor.

"Give me that." Khadra glared.

"Take off your towel first, raghead."

"Give it!"

"Why don't we take it off for her?" Brent Lott's hammy hand clamped on the nape of her neck, yanking her backward. The scarf went down around her shoulders. If Mindy Oberholtzer's little pleated cheerleader skirt had been ripped off, so that she'd been rendered half-naked right in the middle of school where people could see her, she might have felt as mortified as Khadra did then.

"Look, raghead's got hair under that piece a shit," Curtis crowed.

Brent yanked again.

"Cut it out, jerkoff!" Khadra yelled, swiping uselessly at his arm behind her back. Ow—the topaz scarf brooch opened, poking her skin, drawing blood.

"Want me to hold her down for you?" Curtis grabbed one of her flailing arms.

"Stop it!"

A ripping sound. Brent stepped back, waving a piece of scarf. Khadra lunged—tried to grab it—her scarf was torn in two, one strip in Brent's hand, the other wound tightly around her neck.

"I hate you!" she screamed.

"I hate you!" Brent mimicked in falsetto. "It's just *hair,* you psycho!"

"What a psycho," Curtis echoed. The two boys ran down the hall, the thump of their Adidas'd feet merging with the clatter of the pep rally.

Khadra knelt and started collecting her things. *Algebra*, *Hola Amigos II,* her binder with all the papers falling out of it on the floor, *My Antonía* crumpled on its face.

"I hate you! I hate you! I HATE you!" she screamed at their receding figures.

Mr. Eggleston came out of his room down the hall. Silhouetted by the daylight streaming from the double doors at the end of the hallway, he shook his head, gave her a look of mild disapproval, and went back inside.

Mama was going to freak out, Khadra knew. "Where is your scarf? Why did you take it off?" Her father would say gravely, "But why were you talking to a boy anyway?" They didn't get it, they didn't get *anything.* She slid to the floor, her back against the cinder blocks. After her breathing got back to normal, she shoved her stuff into her locker and kicked it shut, wiping her face with the back of her hand. She would not cry in this hateful school. She never should have let them get to her. Hated herself for that.

The scarf. It was a mess. She didn't want to give anyone in this building the satisfaction of seeing her bareheaded. She shoved her disheveled hair under it. The brooch from Aunt Khadija was broken. Great. There was a smear of blood on the folds of the scarf where the brooch had poked her. Just great. That'd never come out.

She needn't have worried about her mother's reaction—when she got home, Ebtehaj was in another world. She and Aunt Trish were focused intently on the news of the day: ". . . massacre . . . Sabra and

Shatila . . . allege that Israelis allowed Phalangist forces to enter the camps at . . . Red Cross estimates . . . death toll rising . . . . "

"Omar heard from his cousin in Tripoli it was several thousand," Aunt Trish said, worried. Her husband's brother Muhammad lived in Sabra. Was he among the massacred, or just temporarily unreachable because of all the terror?

All of Omar Nabolsy's brothers had been named Muhammad, out of some fancy of their slightly unhinged mother, whom their father indulged. There was Muhammad Ali, Muhammad Taha, Muhammad Khair, and plain Muhammad. When things started to get confusing in the household crowded with Muhammads, he'd put his foot down and named the last boy Omar. But since the Nabolsys had been thrown to the four directions by the Palestinian diaspora, and there seemed little chance of the Muhammads ever reuiniting in their city again, it didn't matter so much anymore.

Nothing mattered to Khadra, except surviving the minefield of each day.

"Why can't we be friends now? . . . It's what I want. It's what you want." But the horses didn't want it—they swerved apart; the earth didn't want it, sending up rocks . . . the temples, the tank, the jail, the palace, the birds . . . they said in their hundred voices, "No, not yet," and the sky said, "No, not there."

—E. M. Forster, *A Passage to India*

Livvy and Khadra could no longer meet each other's eyes. Not since the Hellfire Showdown. It was after Livvy's Christian youth-camp revival where she rededicated herself to Jesus. Livvy was sharing the experience with Khadra as they lay on their stomachs across Livvy's purple checkered bedspread, twirling their ankles in the air, Debby Boone playing faintly on the bedside radio. Livvy kept saying "God's Son this" and "God's Son that." Each time she said it, fingernails scraped against a blackboard in Khadra's head.

She finally put her hands to her ears and said, "Stop!"

"Stop what?" Livvy said.

"You don't understand. That's the worst possible sin in my religion, okay?" Khadra said. "That whole son of God thing. I can't listen to that anymore. Even listening to it is, like, a really big sin."

The conversation deteriorated from there to:

"Am I going to hell? According to what you believe, am I going to hell?"

And each one had to admit to the other: Yes.

"Because you're not Saved," Livvy said tearfully. "You haven't accepted Jesus as your Savior. The best I can tell you is, some Christians believe in limbo, but that's really only for children who die young. Like, unbaptized babies. I'm not sure how old the cut-off is. Maybe you'll die young?"

"You want me to die young? Well, guess what, Livvy, you're going to hell too," Khadra said in a quavering voice.

She wasn't sure on this point. Sometimes her mother and father said Christians and Jews could possibly make it to heaven. It was in the Quran. But on the other hand, the Quran was also pretty clear that you couldn't go but to hell if you associated a partner or son with God. That was idolatry. Denying God's oneness. The biggest sin.

Livvy put her head down on her Paddington Bear and cried. Khadra went home feeling miserable. After that, Livvy and Khadra could only look at each other across the lunchroom with big sad eyes and weren't friends anymore.

She missed Hanifa, but they'd grown apart this new school year. All Hanifa did in her spare time these days was take apart and put back together the engine of a junked Ford Pinto she'd found behind the train tracks, sometimes with the Jefferson boys, Malik and Marcus.

And get in trouble with her parents for taking the family car on joyrides—she didn't even have a license! Last summer, Khadra'd caught her friend in some unIslamic behavior on the back seat of the wrecked car, and gave her a good talking-to for it.

"What was she doing?" Tayiba had wanted to know, when she heard about Khadra's tirade.

"I'm not at liberty to say," Khadra'd said primly. "That would be tale-bearing." Of course, her vagueness only made worse the whispers in the community.

And now Hanifa had been absent from school for a while. Khadra and Tayiba heard a rumor that she was getting ready to go live with her non-Muslim grandmother in Alabama. Hanifa looked sullen when she answered the door. Khadra followed her to the threshold of the living room. "What's going on?"

"I don't want to talk about it," Hanifa said. "I want to lie down."

Khadra was hurt. Hanifa closed her eyes. Fingers of afternoon light filtered in, but Hanifa lay in shadow, her face smooth and not giving up secrets, her legs stretched out on the sectional sofa. In shorts. She was listening to music. UnIslamic music.

Well, she was related to non-Muslims, wasn't she? She was related to this music, to Lionel Ritchie, to some old non-Muslim grandmother in Alabama. She could just up and leave this life she had where Khadra was her friend, where you abided by the Total Islamic Lifestyle, and go off somewhere else. Be some other person. Leave Khadra in the lurch.

Something snapped in Khadra and she raged at her friend, "You're going astray, you know. Soon you'll be just like any American. You're going to hell, you know!"

Khadra didn't really know how she walked home. She just remembered her outburst, Hanifa's blank face, and then being exhausted, sobbing, in her bed at home.

Then, one day, she heard Hanifa was gone. Khadra's already tight world was one person smaller.

Aunt Khadija teared up when Khadra asked about her. Folded a fitted bedsheet—struggled with the corners—"I just can't figure out how to fold these anymore," she said, her voice getting stuck in her throat, the sheet in a heap in her lap. Khadra, sitting cross-legged on the Al-Deens' sectional sofa, rolled a pair of tube socks together and absently reached into the basket for more.

"But where did she go, Aunt Khadija? Why did she leave?"

Aunt Khadija murmured something about Hanifa going to stay with her grandmother in Alabama, and didn't want to say any more. Khadra smoothed out a cotton crewneck undershirt and picked up a pair of shorts, then realized they must be Hakim's, and quickly put them down.

"Never speak her name again," Ebtehaj said when Khadra said how strange it was about Hanifa.

"She's having a baby," Eyad said to his sister, later, in private. He had information from Hakim.

Khadra's jaw dropped.

They are a people who take the earth for a carpet, its dust for a bed, and its water for perfume; they take the Quran for a watchword and prayer for a covering

—Ali ibn Abi Talib, *The Peak of Eloquence*

Wajdy and Ebtehaj always viewed their stay in America as temporary. That was part of the reason they were always reluctant to buy many things; they'd just be more attachments to leave behind when the time came. Money saved buying beat-up furniture in America was money that could be spent back home in Syria one day. Who cares what you sat on if this was not home? If your walls were white and bare, or had only a tacky prayer rug with some faded image of mosques pinned up, and your children craved beauty and form, let it be a lesson to them on the value of plainness and the fleeting nature of the life of this world compared to the next. The plan was to return to the House of Islam, ramshackle as it was.

But the return kept getting postponed. First there'd been college degrees to be earned, for learning was a virtue for man and woman, and to travel in search of learning, yea even unto the West, was loved by God. Then there was Islamic work to be done in the Dawah. Wajdy's idea had been to set things on a good course, train his replacement, and leave. But year piled on top of year, and soon two whole children, Khadra and Eyad, had practically grown up, with Eyad in college and Khadra in high school. And Jihad was halfway through a childhood spent in America only by default.

Meanwhile, things were on fire in Syria. *"Islamists and Freemasons, landlords, shopkeepers, workers, and peasants, conservatives and revolutionaries, Syrians and Palestinians—nearly all opposed the regime."* The Islamic movement was getting stronger all the time, by word-jihad and deed-jihad, by peaceful means and by the taking up of arms. By any means necessary. The government was punishing those who opposed it—and even those who didn't, since whatever flimsy rules of evidence and legality had existed before were jettisoned in the face of this onslaught—by means of sweeps, mass arrests, executions, rape, and torture.

Wajdy attacked the Syrian dictator constantly in *The Islamic Forerunner* and urged support for the Islamic movement that sought to overthrow him. Just to express this opinion privately, much less to publish it, was a capital crime in Syria, so this exercise of freedom of speech made Wajdy a "terrorist." If he were ever caught in Syria, he'd be sent to the reeducation camps in the desert.

Whenever Téta got home from one of her American trips, the *mukhabarat*—horrible men with enormous power, loathed by everyone—hauled her in to question her about Wajdy. *When did you see him? Where? Why?* He's my nephew, for heaven's sake, a nephew I raised, like a son to me. *Who are his associates? What are his activities? Who else did you see in America? What are their political beliefs?* For hours and hours they kept Téta sitting in their office, talking to her roughly, as if she were a criminal. They even threatened to put her in Mazzé Prison to try to coerce Wajdy to come to Syria.

"Trying to intimidate me," she said to Khadra when she told the story the next year. "But they don't know me! I am one tough cookie. I know no fear. *I am the salt of the earth, I am,*" she sang, dropping her voice to a macho baritone and thumping her abundant bosom. But she looked tired. What indignities they really put her through, she never hinted at. And she never once reproached Wajdy. "My dissident boy," she called him proudly, over the kitchen table in Fallen Timbers.

Then the Hama massacre happened. Twenty thousand Syrians were killed, thousands dragged off to prison, thousands more wounded, and seventy thousand left homeless because the government razed half the city. Even though the resistance was beaten down in the first ten days of fighting, the government forces kept pounding and pounding the city as collective punishment for its rebellion. The wound was deep, and affected everyone in Syria, no matter if they were pro-government, pro-opposition, or neutral. Fear was in the air, and explosive anger. In *The Islamic Forerunner,* Wajdy let loose with fiery op-eds condemning the Asad regime.

Téta decided not to risk travel abroad that summer, and that was the end of her long lovely stays with Khadra and her family. "I'm too tuckered out for this," Téta told them over the phone. "*Te'ebruni*, such a long journey, and the stress. . . . *And you will ever be at sea, no harbor in your destiny,*" she said, and started singing Abdul Halim's Nizar poem, "The Palm Reader." Here Hayat Um Abdo, her neighbor and best friend, tried to take the phone from her, but Téta yanked it back and finished the song:

Grieve not, my son—Love is our fate
And whoso dies on the path of love,
lives forever, like the saints.

After that there was only the telephone. *May you bury me, lovesies, may you bury my bones, call me.*

The spirit is truly "at home with itself" when it can confront the world that is opened up to it, give itself to the world, and redeem it and, through the world, also itself. But the spirituality that represents the spirit nowadays is so scattered, weakened, degenerate . . . that it could not possibly do this until it had first returned to the essence of the spirit: being able to say You.

—Martin Buber, *I and Thou*

There had always been the telephone, providing its staticky line to Syria. Such communication, however, was rare and extremely expensive. If Eyad and Khadra came home from school and their mother was shouting at the top of her lungs "WE'RE FINE, FINE! THANKING GOD! MISSING YOU!" then they knew there was a phone call to Damascus going on. You had to talk real loud on an overseas call. And you took the phone call standing on edge. You couldn't read a book or eat a snack while a phone call to Syria was in progress. Everyone stood at attention. It was a major family event, like a childbirth or a hospitalization. And indeed, aside from the two Eids, you mostly only phoned Syria when events like that happened, like Jihad's birth the year after they moved to Indianapolis, Wajdy's appendectomy and, on the other end, the births of Mafaz, Muhsin, and Misbah, the younger siblings of Reem and Roddy, those model Muslim children.

The phone call to Syria followed almost exactly the same script year after year, except instead of bulletins like "JIHAD'S TEETHING!" they began to say things like "KHADRA'S IN HIGH SCHOOL NOW!" and "EYAD GOT A SCHOLARSHIP TO COLLEGE!"

"We don't have that," Hakim said one day to Khadra, when she spoke of having to hurry home because there was a phone call to Syria.

"Huh?" she said.

"We can't phone home like you all," he said. A dog-eared book of poems by Marvin X was under his arm, a black book with a star and crescent on the cover. *Fly to Allah,* the title said. Ever since Hanifa'd dropped out of sight, Hakim had acquired kind of a hard edge, read militant black authors, and talked tough about "self-discipline," as if to distance himself from what she'd done, an undisciplined thing. "This stuff's for real," he liked to say of his new reading matter. That was what he was after, whatever the latest book in his hand: what was for real. Where was it to be found?

"Who? What are you talking about? Who's 'we?' and who's 'you all?'" Khadra thought his quest and even his newfound fierceness noble, but was frustrated by how it locked her out. Not that they saw much of eath other, other than in the context of time their families spent together. Past a certain age, girls in their community didn't hang out with boys. This sometimes had the effect of lending a mystique to the few interactions they did have, whereas constant familiarity might have dulled down their views of each other to a sisterly-brotherly boredom.

"You all is, immigrant brothers and sisters. 'We' is, black people. I mean, African people. African people in the North American wilderness."

"You're not African," Khadra retorted. "Aunt Ayesha's African. And 'we' are all one thing: Muslim." This was the Dawah Center line: No racism in Islam. Meaning, none is allowed; a commendable ideal. But it was also a smokescreen of denial that retarded any real attempt to deal with the prejudices that existed among Muslims.

"Oh yeah?" Hakim shot back. "Then how many Dawah Center officers are black? How many immigrants do you know who've married African American? Be for real! Immigrant white-pleasers'll marry white Americans, Muslim or not, but they won't marry black people."

"Yeah well that cuts both ways," Khadra countered. "I don't see the proposals rolling in from the African Americans to the immigrants, either." She bit her lip, knowing he was right. Syrian Arabs like her parents sure didn't think black was beautiful.

They pretended it was about language, not color. Losing Arabic was tantamount to losing the religion, so "You have to marry a native Arabic speaker" made sense.

Then, one day, Eyad worked up the nerve to enlist his parents' help in asking for the hand of the Sudanese doctor's daughter, Maha Abdul-Kadir, a regal beauty whose color was rich and dark. Her family lived far and high above the Dawah Center Muslims in a

Meridian Hills mansion, and the only problem he could foresee was his lack of means, especially compared to what she was used to. But maybe religious ideals—that material wealth matters little compared to piety and character in a spouse, and so forth—could overcome any qualms she or her family might have about the economic gap? And maybe they could be persuaded to bear in mind that he was pre-med, so that, even if he was poor now, he had good prospects?

Khadra had noticed Eyad mooning over Maha at the massive Muslim Eid prayer at Eagle Creek Park. That is, he seemed to be trying a little extra hard to lower his gaze when he found himself in her vicinity. She was an usher, responsible for passing the *zakat* alms box up and down the women's rows. He lit up when she tapped him on the shoulder, even though it was only to hand him the box and ask him to see that Brother Derek, the men's usher, got it, because Brother Derek was too deep into the men's crowd for her to proceed to him modestly.

The girl had impeccable character, was active at the mosque, and wore flawless hijab with not a hair showing. And, definitely, she was a native speaker of Arabic, with a pure accent, and a fluency aided by the private Arabic tutors her father had hired. She was splendidly qualified to teach their future children the language of the Quran. Piety, character, beauty, brains, the right language, the right home culture—what more to ask in a bride?

"So . . . I was wondering what you would think about the idea of proposing to Dr. Abdul-Kadir's daughter Maha," he began timidly one evening in the kitchen.

His father stopped deboning the chicken, mid-breast, and blurted, "But for heaven's sake, she's black as coal!"

So there it was. Out in the open.

As soon as he'd said it, Wajdy looked queasy, and seemed almost taken aback that such a thing had come out of his own mouth. He lowered his eyes to the chicken bones and made no further comment. Ebtehaj was silent, but it was clear that black grandchildren were not what she had in mind, either. She concentrated on drawing out a slippery crescent of meat hidden between the bones of a chicken wing.

Eyad seemed dazed, even paralyzed. The gulf between what they'd taught him and what was happening—and his not wanting to face that gulf even in light of what his father had just said—was overhelming. All of a sudden, his thought processes slowed down and he could only stare blankly.

"But more importantly, she's older than you," Ebtehaj jumped in after the long awkward pause. "The woman should always be younger, because girls are more mature than boys and women go downhill faster in old age."

"She's only older by a few months," Eyad said weakly. He was never going to marry anyone to whom his parents' first reaction was so negative. So that was that. He lowered his gaze to what would please his parents, believing their approval to be next to God's.

Like many religious 'radicals' they were persecuted, to the point of being executed for heresy. Finding no safe haven in other surrounding countries . . . a conservative faction . . . took the name of its leader, Jacob Amman, adopted his severe social and familial code, and looked for a better life across the sea. . . . The Amish follow an oft-misunderstood idea called gelassenheit, *loosely translated as . . . submission . . . one must strictly adhere to or risk being shunned . . .*

—Thomas Huhti, *The Great Indiana Touring Book*

"We have no passports," Wajdy told Ebtehaj. Their old raggedy green ones had expired, and the Syrian embassy was not about to renew the passports of dissidents and their children. So now they were paperless in America. Stuck. Plans to go on Haj had to be put on hold. But it was worse than that—their American residency papers, their green cards, depended on having valid passports to back them up. Remaining in this situation was not an option. Next they would become undocumented aliens, a precarious limbo status.

"We're going to court to become U.S. citizens," Wajdy said one morning over his small cup of Turkish coffee. "Pick you up after school."

Eyad guffawed and Khadra laughed. Surely their father wasn't serious. Becoming citizens had never been part of the picture.

But he was. Very serious. It was a cloudy and confusing day. Ebtehaj looked as if she had been crying all the wounded afternoon.

The five of them walked into the Marion County Courthouse in Indianapolis like a family in mourning, the wiry, olive-skinned father with the short beard and crinkly brown-black hair, the ivory-skinned, green-eyed mother in a blue georgette wimple; handsome grown-up Eyad with his mother's coloring; Khadra, now a young lady with her father's coarse hair peeking out of her scarf at the forehead; and seven-year-old Jihad, who was fair enough to have freckles across his nose.

What did it matter to Jihad, Khadra thought, he was born here. He's American, anyway. To her, taking citizenship felt like giving up, giving in. After all she'd been through at school, defending her identity against the jeering kids who vaunted America's superiority as the clincher put-down to everything she said, everything she was. Wasn't she supposed to be an Islamic warrior woman, a Nusayba, a Sumaya, an Um Salamah in exile, by the waters dark, of Babylon? Wasn't she supposed to remember always the children in Syria who had to scour toilets on their knees at her age? For whom her tongue cleaved to the roof of her mouth, hamburgerless, with the guilt of one who got away? It was an ache that had gnawed her gut for years. What was all that, a big fat lie? She seethed. Land where my fathers died, hunh.

There was no courtroom drama to it, like on TV. It took place in a room with the fancy name of "judge's chambers." It looked like any small, generic office, with a metal filing cabinet and framed photographs of bare-shaven American politicians. The Shamys sat in chrome-and-orange-vinyl chairs. Jihad, looking shy, leaned against his father's knee. The judge was a middle-aged white man with silver hair and the look of a pink-gilled fish around the eyes and jowls. He asked them to raise their right hands. *For they required of us a song.*

They'd studied the citizenship booklet. Wajdy and Ebtehaj had memorized things like "Thomas Jefferson" and "judicial, executive, and legislative branches," things Khadra and Eyad already knew from school. They'd studied the booklet all right, but still it was startling when the judge asked if they renounced polygamy, drugs, and crime. None of the Shamys in that room countenanced polygamy personally, but it was still an honorable Islamic institution, not something dirty like drugs or crime. It was insulting, somehow.

Then he asked if any of them were, or had ever been, members of the Communist Party. For a second it reminded Khadra of how Téta described the questions of the Syrian mukhabarat—*and who are his associates? What are their political beliefs?* But the kicker came when he said they had to swear to defend the U.S. in war when and if called upon to do so. Eyad made an involuntary motion and Khadra rolled her eyes—like she was ever going to help the U.S. and its buddy Israel kill more Palestinians and Lebanese! *Remember O Lord the day of our destruction at Deir Yassin, at Sabra and Shatila, and even now they continue to destroy Palestinian homes, the children of Israel, with American guns, and they say 'raze them, raze them, even to the foundations thereof.' Happy shall he be, who rewardeth them as they have served us.*

The judge hadn't even looked up, but Wajdy saw their facial expressions, and shot Khadra and Eyad a terrible, stern look. Khadra's face froze, and her heart sank. How could her father and mother be doing this, how, and how could they be asking her to say these things? *And her tongue clove to the roof of her mouth, yea, and her brother the same.*

"You could have jeopardized everything," Wajdy snapped, once they were back in the car. By the rivers dark, he panicked on.

"It's just a piece of paper," Eyad muttered.

"This is serious," Wajdy yelled. He hardly ever yelled. "Our futures are at stake."

Ebtehaj sniffled and blew her nose. She did not have a cold.

"What happened?" Jihad asked. He'd missed the glance in the judge's chambers and the whole drama.

"Nothing," Khadra answered angrily. "Just me practicing my First Amendment right to freedom of expression," she added, under her breath.

"What?" Jihad pressed.

"Shut up," Khadra said.

"Don't tell your brother to shut up," Ebtehaj said. And blew her nose again.

By the waters of Indianapolis, everyone withdrew into sullen silence the rest of the way home.

"In many ways, my brothers, America is more Islamic than the countries of the Muslim world. There is no widespread corruption. You can enter a judge's offices and not need to bribe his secretary for the simple basic services." It was Wajdy's turn to give the khutba at the Dawah Center's small juma service. He always said "brothers" even though Sisters Khadija and Ayesha and Ebtehaj and lots of other women attended. He said it was okay, sisters were included in brotherhood, that's just how language was.

"Brothers, do not for a minute think that we will stop protesting against the immoral and unfair policies of America outside, in the Muslim world. May my tongue be cut off if I forget Jerusalem. But let's face it: here *inside* America, there are many good qualities. Law and order, cleanliness, democracy, freedom to work and honestly seek the provision of the Lord"—heads nodded among the immigrants—"freedom to practice religion. These are Islamic qualities. America," he concluded, "is like Islam without Muslims. And our sick and corrupt Muslim home countries—they are Muslims without Islam."

He began the prayer, reciting from the Quran, *"He who forsakes his home for the sake of God finds in the earth many a refuge, and abundance; should he die as a refugee from home for God and his Messenger, his reward becomes due and certain with God, and God is oft-forgiving, most Merciful."*

Wajdy's citizenship khutba was not received as warmly when he was invited to lead the juma prayer at the predominantly Afro-American Salam Mosque.

"You're just discovering that you're American and you want to wave a flag now?" Brother Taher said over a paper plate of whiting fish bought from a Muslim pushcart vendor in the parking lot after juma. "Brother Wajdy, I've been American all my life. And I still don't want to wave no flag."

Wajdy was uncomprehending.

"You immigrant brothers come in yesterday, and suddenly you

white," Brother Derek chimed in. "We been here longer and this country was built on our backs. I don't see nobody trying to give us a silver platter."

Anyway, it was done. The Shamys—on paper, anyway—were now American.

Whoso believeth in God and the Last Day, let them be generous to the guest, and whoso believeth in God and the Last Day, let them be generous to the neighbor, and whoso believeth in God and the Last Day, let them speak kindly or keep silent.

—Prophet Muhammad, peace and blessings be upon him

The androgynous couple next door was moving away. "We'll miss you!" Lindsey, or maybe it was Leslie, said, waving at the Shamys. They were headed for someplace called Fayetteville, Arkansas. They'd found what they were looking for, something called "an intentional community." Did that mean group sex? Wajdy wondered, but tried to put out of mind and think better of them. He and Ebtehaj nodded and waved. They hoped wherever it was they were going, it would help man-woman-Leslie-Lindsey sort themselves out.

New neighbors moved in. They seemed like a regular family, thank God—the man was a man and the woman was a woman.

They had twin boys Jihad's age, and a little girl. Ebtehaj knocked on their door with a "welcome, neighbor" tray of goodies and invited them for coffee. The Whitcombs said they didn't drink coffee, but would like to come anyway. Coffee and tea were against their religion.

"How does one socialize without coffee *or* tea?" Ebtehaj murmured.

At the same time, she and her husband were impressed. Especially when they realized the Whitcombs didn't smoke, either, or drink alcohol. There were Americans who observed religious prescriptions for halal and haram in their diet?

As it turned out, the Whitcombs and the Shamys seemed to have many values in common. John Whitcomb was a hard-working family man who stayed close to home in the evenings. Norma Whitcomb had married young, just like Ebtehaj, and dressed modestly, often in long denim jumpers and spotless white blouses.

"Her kitchen is so clean, it sparkles like snow!" Ebtehaj exclaimed after a visit. For Ebtehaj to be moved to remark on the cleanliness of another woman's kitchen, much less that of an American woman, was a historical moment, Khadra drily noted to her brother.

The two women began to exchange recipes while Jihad Shamy played outside with Brig and Riley Whitcomb and their little sister Sariah. Ebtehaj taught Norma to bake pita bread, which Norma always called "Bible bread," and Norma taught Ebtehaj to make an important American dish called tuna casserole.

Norma was quite the artist with Jell-O. One day she brought over a marvelous mold of lime green striped with cherry red.

"You're very kind," Ebtehaj said, but she had to explain to her that they couldn't eat it. "It's the gelatin," she said. "It's made with enzymes from animal fat. Could be pork."

"Oh, dear," Norma said. Far from poo-pooing Ebtehaj's concern, she, putting herself in her neighbor's place for a moment, was almost as chagrined at the Muslim woman's close brush with pork as she would've been had she herself been offered a food prohibited by her church or her personal views. After that, whenever the two women wheeled their carts side by side at the Safeway, she was anxious lest her friend pick up something with pork and, if Ebtehaj had any doubt about a word on the nutritional label, Norma double-checked it.

So the Shamys' sojourn in the land grew long and, although there was danger in it still, there was also relief from danger and, beyond even that, moments of unexpected grace.

And you put on the ugly mask
and try to smash through
. . . You don't care who you offend
. . .
the teacups shatter,
and you bash into the barrier
again and again.

—Starhawk, *Truth or Dare*

That was the year Khadra donned black headscarves with a surge of righteous austerity that startled her parents. They thought a young girl should be wearing lighter colors. Stern in dress and gaze, she descended the stairs. She wore a no-nonsense black scarf and a navy-blue jilbab her father had sewn at her request.

"Going to a funeral today?" Ebtehaj asked sharply.

A scathing look was all she received in response from her sixteen-year-old daughter.

Khadra and her friends were impatient with traditional Islamic scholarship, with its tedious, plodding chapters on categories of water purity and how to determine the exact end of menses.

"Islam is action in the world!" Khadra said. "Not studying the various levels of water purity for ablution."

Agreed, her parents would have said, given half a chance. But their moderate Islamic revival movement she now scorned, for it did not go far enough down the revolutionary path.

Wajdy and Ebtehaj exchanged looks but didn't say anything. What could they say? They were the ones who had introduced Khadra to the works of Islamist revolutionary Sayid Qutb, after all, and his multivolume *tafsir* of the Quran sat on their rickety bookshelf in the living room. She seemed only to be taking his rhetoric a step or two further along the path of its own logic.

It had begun with an argument some of the Dawah teens had about Iran when they were leaving a Muslim youth camp up in Lafayette. At first the kids had stared out the van windows at the Hoosier horizon rolling out flatly unto forever. Then, with the earnestness of Dawah teens, they began discussing the disappointment of Iran's Islamic revolution. It had seemed to be the beginning of truly moral Islamic government in the whole Muslim world. Then the leaders of Iran had become power-and-politics obsessed, no better than any other regime.

"Yeah, it's just like early Islamic history," said Ramsey—he was the third Nabolsy brother, the redhaired one. He tossed a miniature foam football up in the air and caught it again and again. "It was all spiritual for, like, five minutes and then as soon as the Prophet died, it all went to crap."

"That's not true, Islam wasn't all downhill after the Prophet"

Eyad said gravely. "Peace be upon him. You had the four rightly guided caliphs. May God be pleased with them."

"Who were followed by Muawiya," Ramsey said sardonically, as if it were a punch line to something. Danny Nabolsy did not look up from the Rubik's Cube he was twiddling.

"Yeah, so?" Eyad said.

"Whose son had the Prophet's grandson *killed?* Who had the Prophet's entire *family* killed?" Ramsey was like someone waiting for a reason to explode.

"Muawiya didn't mean it to happen that way. It was just a tragedy—"

"Bullshit!" Ramsey said. Khadra did a double take.

"Don't use that language!" Eyad said, batting the football away. "And don't badmouth a Companion of the Prophet! Muawiya's still a Companion, no matter what mistakes he made."

"*Mistakes?* It's all a lie, don't you *get* it?" Ramsey said as they pulled through Zionsville. "I don't get how anyone could even *be* Sunni after finding out about Karbala."

Khadra struggled to remember what she'd learned about the Sunni-Shia thing from Sunday school. The Sunni-Shia split had by now rent the Dawah Center. No one talked about it anymore.

"Sunni Islam is just a sellout," Ramsey went on, his voice rising. "It's just a load of compromises and lies told by *cowards* too *cowardly* to fight for what they believe in."

"Keep it down!" Uncle Omar yelled from the driver's seat. They froze, because he could get a little scary sometimes.

Aunt Trish turned and smiled lamely. "Everything okay back there?"

The argument petered out.

* * *

Later, Khadra asked her father if it was true.

"Is what true?" he said.

"That Yazid killed the Prophet's grandson, and no one did anything about it?"

It was true. "Why didn't everyone rebel? Why didn't they all go Shia?"

"To avoid further bloodshed and strife," her father said. He tried to put a good face on it, just like he had about becoming citizens. It was his nature to see things in the best light, the kindest interpretation, rather than the worst. But that just confirmed Khadra's fears. The bottom fell out. The whole rest of early Islam after the life of the Prophet—including all the scholarship—had been formed under the government of a dynasty that had mercilessly slaughtered the Prophet's own grandson and most of his remaining kin.

Led by the boozing, whoring Yazid—and the Sunni scholars *knew* how corrupt he was—the whole thing had been a travesty of the faith. It was awful, just awful. How had this been glossed over in Sunday school?

Radical action was required to redress all this, Khadra felt. The Haqiqat sisters, Nilofar and Insaf, agreed. She deliberately hung out with them, knowing that, as Shia, they were now *persona non grata* in the Dawah circle. Radical Islam was her James Dean.

Khadra and her friends applauded the assassination of Sadat and wished Saddam had met the same fate before he'd crushed the Shia Islamic resurgence in Iraq. They cheered the growing anti-Israeli resistance of the Shia Amal militia in the south of Lebanon. Insaf now liked to wear men's shalvar-qamises in stern plain grays and browns. She "liberated" them from her father's closet.

"If I were an Amal girl," Khadra said, on purpose choosing to identify with the sect opposite her Sunni background, "they'd have to torture me to try and make me tell them anything. Uh-huh. They'd have to kill me, like Sumaya." Sumaya, the first Muslim martyr, died under torture, killed horribly—with a spear thrust upward through her—by her master, an enemy of Islam.

Eyad found Khadra's radicalism bewildering. He was in the swing of an Islamic modernism phase. Earlier, he had gone through a yearning-for-traditional-Islam phase, when he'd felt that there was something missing in his life which learning classical Islamic scholarship and classical Arabic beyond the Muslim Sunday school level would set right. His parents were glad to oblige. He had been sent to seminars in D.C. and a two-month summer shariah program at Al-Azhar University, Cairo. However, Khadra hadn't had the opportunities afforded Eyad. Travel abroad, a girl alone? For the Shamys, it was out of the question.

Khadra went on a regime of dates and water to emulate the diet of the Prophet.

"That is ENOUGH," her mother said on the fourth day. "You will eat my cooking!" And she slammed the pot of okra on the kitchen table so hard it splashed Jihad with hot tomato sauce so he screamed. "Look what you made me do!" her mother shouted.

The next morning Wajdy came and leaned on the edge of Khadra's desk and said quietly, "Do you know how much we spend weekly for groceries? You mother cuts coupons till her hands blister.

Do you know how much dates cost? Five or six dollars for a small package that lasts one day with you eating nothing else. *Binti*, the Prophet ate dates because they were the most abundant food of his land. You can emulate him by analogy. Not by being ridiculous."

"Soybeans," Eyad said to her. "That's what Shafie would have said." The ninth-century scholar he'd studied had pioneered the idea that local conditions of different lands should be taken into account when crafting Islamic laws.

"Say what?"

"Soybeans are to Indiana what dates are to Arabia. The most important crop."

"Yeah, we're surrounded by soybeans. So?"

"So, eat soy-based foods. If you want to emulate the Prophet by analogy, in Indiana, you eat soybeans."

"Soybeans?" Insaf hooted.

"I know! Can you *believe* him?" Khadra said. Her goal of *doing* something to further the cause of Islam in the world was being realized already: She and the Haqiqat sisters were making buttons that said "Islam Rules!" to sell at Islamic conferences. To fundraise for—well, for future projects that would raise the glorious banner of pure, revolutionary Islam in the world; they just weren't sure what.

Then Nilofar got a marriage proposal from a handsome young Delhi-born doctor interning in Chicago. Khadra was shocked when she accepted. They had passionately discussed not getting married young but going to college first and becoming Islamic activists.

"He's really into Islam and all," Nilofar insisted to a dubious

Khadra. She showed her the velvet box with the wedding jewelry. "Look—he had it specially made—it's a star-and-crescent pattern."

Insaf exchanged dark looks with Khadra behind Nilofar's back. "But I'm still going to be an Islamic activist," Nilofar exclaimed. "You'll see, I'm going to start a *halaqa* that will revolutionize Chicago!" She got pregnant the first month.

"Well, really, the best contribution to an Islamic revolution for a woman is to educate her children in the true Islamic values," she said plaintively on a visit home in her first trimester, dressed in a becoming, pale pink *shalvar-qamis*. Then she ran to the hall bathroom to puke. Khadra and Insaf, lying on their sides looking at each other across Nilofar's old bed and several shoeboxes full of "Islam Rules!" buttons, mourned the death of another Muslim warrior woman.

But there is a oneness of the self, an integrity or internal harmony that holds together the multiplicity and continual transformations of being, and it is not an "imitation" of the unity of the Logos, nor is it the individual's "piece" of the Logos. In every individual . . . the whole principle and essence of the Logos is wholly present. . . .

—James Olney, *Metaphors of the Self*

Haj! Their parents announced it. They were going this year! "Mecca—be square or be there," Wajdy said, in a valiant attempt to use the hip youthful language he was picking up from the new American secretaries at the Center. Khadra and Eyad were so astounded by the news, they forgot to roll their eyes.

"Wash your hair several times," Ebtehaj called from outside the bathroom door. Khadra could tell she had her mouth pressed right up to the door by how loud her voice was even over the running water.

It was bath night before the Haj trip. They were going to don *ihram* on the plane midway to Saudi Arabia, and wouldn't be able to bathe after that until their pilgrimage was over.

"Do any personal shaving you need to do now, Khadra," Ebtehaj called again. As if she was standing and waiting at the door. "You need a clean razor?"

"No, Mama! Leave me alone. I can bathe myself!" Khadra muttered the last bit to herself.

Instead of using a razor, Khadra leaned dripping out of the shower, pulled open a drawer, and fumbled for the hair scissors. She pulled a clump of hair and clipped, clumsily. *Ow.* Cut into some labia. *Ow!* Carefully washed and dried off the scissors and stuck it back deep in the drawer.

"Give your hair three rounds. Did you give your hair three rounds of shampoo?" Ebtehaj called from the doorframe.

"LEAVE ME ALONE!" Khadra shouted, smarting from her cut.

Khadra pasted her face to the airplane window. There was Indianapolis, laid out like patchwork. That splotch to the south had to be Simmonsville, and beyond it the squarish outlines of farms and then—gone, under the clouds. Khadra felt funny. The phrase "leaving home" came into her head. But Indianapolis is not my home, she thought indignantly. Catchphrases from Islamic revival nasheeds flashed in her head—how a true Muslim feels at home wherever the call to prayer is sung, how a true Muslim feels no attachment to one nation or tribe over another. I don't even care if I never see the Fallen Timbers Complex again, Khadra thought. Over the lump in her throat.

Ebtehaj had a tear in her eye as the plane rose over the city of Indianapolis. "Our community is the best ever," she sighed, leaning her head on her husband's shoulder. "Those sisters are my best friends in the world."

In Amsterdam, the tone of the plane changed. From white to brown. From the Shamys being almost the only Muslims on board, to a scene in which the white middle-aged American couple whom Khadra had spied in first class, the only people left over from the Indianapolis leg of the journey, now looked distinctly out of place among the mostly Muslim, mostly darker folk that boarded the Amsterdam-Jeddah connection, some of them already in their pilgrim whites. The American woman, a blonde who had those tanned, speckled arms that American women get when they age because of the careless way they expose their bodies in youth, slipped on a long-sleeved white blouse.

That's right, you cover yourself up, Khadra thought, catching a glimpse of her through the curtain that marked off first class. We're the majority now.

A funny thing happened in the airspace over Jeddah. The Arab women who had boarded in Western clothing, black hair splayed down their shoulders, suddenly covered up in black *abayas* and turned into picture-postcard Saudis dotting the airplane rows. Ebtehaj, who was sitting at a distance from Khadra, shook her head and said loudly, "As if God sees them only in one country and not in the other."

Ihram time. Wajdy, Eyad, and Jihad emerged from the bathroom in their white towel sarongs and white towel shoulder scarf. Eyad was self-consciously trying to tie his shoulder piece so his bare white chest would not show, seeming to feel the eyes of all the women on the plane upon him. It was the sensation of being underwearless in public that was doing that to him. Underwearless beneath the *ihram,* due to the rule barring clothing with seams—for male pilgrims only, not women. Ihram, the great equalizer—making men feel the nakedness and vulnerability of their bodies the way women more often did, in the usual run of things.

Jihad thought the ihram outfit was the coolest thing. "Where's yours?" he asked Khadra. She and her mother had already changed into simple cotton caftans and white wimples.

"*We* don't go topless for Haj, kiddo," Khadra said, tickling him under his now bare arms. He squirmed and almost mooned the entire left wing passenger section when his bottom towel wriggled half-off.

They landed. At last, Khadra thought, *someplace where we really belong*. It's the land of the Prophet. The land of all Muslims.

Three lanes separated people for visa processing: Saudi and Gulf nationals, U.S. and European passport holders, and "Other." Khadra was dismayed to find that she and her family fell in behind the American couple in the U.S. line.

The American couple sailed through the entry gate and headed toward baggage claim. A Saudi clerk was leading them looking eager to please, Khadra noted.

"Gimme a break," she said, rolling her eyes at their receding figures.

Wajdy followed her gaze. "Yes, did you notice them?" he said, smiling.

"Why are they even here?" Khadra said. "To prey on Saudi oil?"

"To do Haj," her father said quietly.

"But—they're not even—are they even Muslim?" Eyad objected. He'd noticed them too.

"They are Muslim," Wajdy said.

"Converts?" Khadra asked sharply. If so, why weren't they practicing Islam? Which she could tell they weren't, by the way they dressed.

"No," her father said. He seemed to be enjoying her confusion. "Born Muslim."

"Well, obviously they know nothing about Islam," Khadra huffed. "They don't even know enough to be wearing ihram."

"I would be surprised if they did," Wajdy said. "It's an amazing story, really. The man told me—I chatted with him in the bathroom at Amsterdam—I was making wudu and he asked me how."

"He's a Muslim and he doesn't know how to make wudu?" Eyad scoffed, holding the knot of his shoulder piece tightly.

"He wasn't allowed to learn. They're Albanian. Did you know Albania is a Muslim country? The only Muslim country in Europe. When he was a child, there was a communist takeover. They didn't let Muslims practice. They forbade them to learn Quran or go to the mosque. His family and his wife's both managed to come to America."

"Glory be to God," Ebtahaj said. Maybe it was the tiredness, but she was moved almost to tears. "And yet they want to make Haj."

"They don't remember very much about Islam," Wajdy said, matching her feeling. "But they want to learn. They didn't have anything in English with the prayers in it. So I gave them our guidebook. I gave them the Dawah phone number and invited them to visit after we get back home. Imagine, Ebtehaj, they live only two hours away from Indianapolis, yet they've never heard of the Dawah

Center." You could see it in his face, how the story of the Albanian couple had renewed his sense of mission already.

The Shamys rode into Mecca on the back of a Japanese pick-up truck full of Kurdish pilgrims, sunken-faced elderly men, and elderly women dressed in big calico farmdresses to their ankles, with cotton britches underneath. Everyone had just spent hours and hours being processed in the chaotic, pilgrim-filled Jeddah airport and was exhausted. Jihad drooled on Khadra's sleeve, asleep, while she leaned her own sleepy head on her father's shoulder.

Wajdy began leading the *talbiya:* "Here I am, O my Lord, Here I am!"

To which the whole truckload responded, *"Here I am, O my Lord, Here I am!"*

Into the night air they sang, into Mecca they jostled. Past the billboards that said, "Welcome, Guests of the Compassionate One," "Seiko," and "Panasonic." "Give praise to God, the Lord of the Worlds," flashed another highway sign, and beside it, brilliantly lit, a picture of a VCR with the Sony logo.

The hotel room was so tiny you couldn't open the door all the way. It hit the foot of the bed. They all jumbled in somehow. And then somehow Khadra had slept through the night and the next thing she knew there was adhan floating through the air. Such a beautiful sound. Melodies on top of melodies, from mosque after mosque, circled through the living air, clearing sleep from the consciousness. Penetrating the seen and unseen worlds, drawing them together like a magnetic force.

Khadra and her family arrived at the Sanctuary. The Kaba, with her embroidered Black Dress hitched up around her waist for the heavy work days of Haj, welcomed them. She was wonderful beyond the clumsy image of her on the kitschy rug above the faded couch way back in Fallen Timbers. She was the Hostess. Come in, come in. Come into my circle, gracious and kind. For they were guests of God now. Many pilgrims threw themselves into her Lap or *Hijr*, the half-circle on one side where the Kaba used to extend, where Hajar and Ismail slept: where a black woman lay buried in the heart of Islam.

Khadra tried to keep the joyous talbiya in her mind and on her tongue: *Here I am, O my Lord, Here I am! Labbaik, allahumma, labbaik!* But she kept getting it crossed with Phil Collins in her head crooning, *"I can feel it coming in the air tonight, oh Lo-ord . . . I've been waiting for this moment for all my life, oh Lo-ord . . ."*

Everything was ceaseless motion around the Lady of Night, and the Lady was absolutely still. She was *Sakina*, the serenity within the whirl. *Imagine,* Khadra thought, looking at the massive tides of pilgrims around the Kaba, *these circles get bigger and bigger, as people all over Mecca face here to pray, then all over the world, even as far as America, wave after wave of people, in concentric circles going all around the earth, and I am here at the center of all that.* Khadra was a little stunned, and then she was taken up swirling too, and her mother was pleading, "Hold onto Jihad! Hold him tight!" and her father was calling, "Stay with me! Stay with me!" And they were off, part of the sea.

A small elderly man jabbed Khadra in the ribs without being aware of it. He was scrambling to keep up with a litter bearing what looked to be his wife. Suddenly a wall of Arab Gulf men stormed through, elbows locked around their women kin. They shoved everyone aside, barking "We have womenfolk, make way for them! We have women!" What are we, chopped liver? Khadra thought as she was pulled over to the right. A tall black teenaged girl, round-shouldered like Zuhura, got pressed up against her. Despite the discomfort and the fray, her face, up close to Khadra's and meeting her eye, was serene. "Peace," she whispered in Khadra's ear. *"Salamu. Ya salam."* She seemed to surrender herself to the chaos with a sort of trust in its ultimate direction.

After *tawaf,* Khadra waited for an opening to ford the river of people. She found a place to pray and then sat very still, her knees tucked under her chin, contemplating Islam's Lady in Black. Here was the center of the world just as the heart was the center of the body. The massing multitudes about her, flowing like blood through a vein—in the circulatory system of what larger consciousness?

I'm glad God's ways are not your ways,
He does not see as man;
Within His love I know there's room
For those whom others ban.

—Frances E. W. Harper, "A Double Standard"

Stately date palms towered over the adobe wall around the house. An evergreen bush at the door bore creamy yellow flowers. A middle-aged man with a white *ghutra* covering his head answered the door, all smiles through his full beard. A couple of stocky younger men stood beside him.

"Welcome, welcome," Zaid Jafar Tihamy said, extending his hand to Wajdy, Eyad, and little Jihad. He touched his heart in respectful greeting to Khadra and her mother. "My sons, Bandar and Anwar," he said, indicating the young men by his side.

They passed through a courtyard lined with tamarisks and palm trees. The men went left, into the public parlor, and the women went right, where a lovely floral scent grew stronger and appeared to be coming from a compact tree in a soil bed near the door. A large, heavily ornamented woman welcomed them warmly.

"My henna tree," Aunt Saweem said, after greetings. "Isn't it wonderful?" She turned up her plump, braceleted hand to gesture at the tree, displaying the henna arabesques that adorned her palm.

Saweem Shahbandar was Ebtehaj's milk sister. Milk relationships were created by women alone. When a woman breastfed another woman's baby, that child was henceforth considered a sibling to all the children of the woman who'd nursed him or her. In recognition of the milk bond created by Saweem's and Ebtehaj's mothers a generation ago, the Shamys had been invited to stay at Saweem Shahbandar's home for the rest of their Mecca sojourn.

Aunt Saweem had been a teacher at a private lycée in Damascus when she received the proposal from the handsome uncle of one of her Saudi students. Her ensuing life had been spent entirely in her husband's country, and she had assimilated to Saudi customs.

"Why, even your speech is Saudi-ized," Ebtehaj teased.

The two women chatted, catching each other up on their respective lives. Khadra grew drowsy and leaned back on the ornate sofa. Some kind of nature documentary was playing on a television at the far end of the large room. Khadra could hear both narrations, the uppercrust British male voice that reminded her of 16mm films in ninth grade biology class and, layered on top of it, the Arabic dubbing. *To survive in the arid climate of Saudi Arabia's western lowlands, these unexpectedly beautiful flowering plants have developed physical defenses. The forbidding-looking thorns of the acacia trees are an example.*

Such lethal external appearances discourage grazing animals from chewing their foliage . . .

The next morning, Khadra asked the one she thought was the daughter-in-law, "Where's the mosque whose adhan I heard right outside my window?" The call she had heard had thrilled her, bringing pure glory to all her senses. She'd never experienced a real adhan before this trip, the kind that rang out over the rooftops.

"Right next door," Buthayna said.

What Khadra could not explain to this stranger was how the sound had made her feel. She had run to the window, flinging it open, and leaned her head out in the early morning darkness, as if to bring her whole self closer to the call. It was the long-awaited invitation. She was going to the ball.

The next day Khadra awoke to the adhan for fajr as if to the call of love. She beat Buthayna to the bathroom for wudu. Then back in the bedroom, she got dressed and picked up her shoes and tiptoed out.

"Where are you going?" Buthayna asked her guest in the hall.

"To pray fajr," Khadra whispered over her shoulder.

Thirty minutes later, with a tearstreaked face, Khadra was back, escorted by two burly *matawwa* policemen with big round black beards and billy clubs belted over their white caftans.

"Is this one of your womenfolk?" they asked Uncle Zaid, Saweem's husband, his face freshly washed. "We found her trying to get into the mosque." They said it as if she was a vagrant or something.

Uncle Zaid shook his head no, not looking at her bare face. He seemed mortified that the matawwa police were at his door and glanced sideways to see if any neighbors were out.

"But I'm Khadra!—the daughter of Wajdy Shamy and Ebtehaj Qadri-Agha," she cried in a tremulous voice. "Your guests!"

He looked up, startled. "Ah, yes, yes, I'm so sorry—yes, officers—what is the problem?"

"Are you her *mahram*?"

"No."

"Produce her mahram."

Wajdy came to the door. "Khadra! Binti, what's wrong—when did you leave the house, what is this?" He had to produce his passport and travel documents, the whole family's documents.

"How could you leave the house without permission—your parents', your hosts'? Without telling anybody?" Ebtehaj asked in an angry whisper behind closed doors.

"I—just—wanted—to—pray—fajr," Khadra hiccupped between sobs.

"You can pray in the house," Wajdy said.

"But I didn't *want* to pray in the house, Baba. The mosque is so near—the adhan was so beautiful—and it was calling to me, to *me*."

"Well, women are not allowed to pray in the mosque here," her father replied. He was deeply embarrassed by the position Khadra had put him in before his grave-faced host.

"But, Baba, how can women not be allowed?" Khadra had never heard of such a thing. No mosque she had ever encountered hadn't had a place for women. Not even the tiny Kokomo mosque that ran out of a Motel 6. "Then where do they pray?"

"They pray at home."

"But where do they pray when they go to the mosque?" Khadra said, uncomprehending.

"Khadra, you're not listening. Women here don't *go* to the mosque. They don't in most Muslim countries."

Khadra had never heard of such a preposterous thing. It couldn't be right. Being a Muslim *meant* going to the mosque. "*What?* I don't know what you're talking about. It doesn't even make sense. Everyone knows women go to the mosque. Women have always gone to the mosque. It's part of Islam."

"You're used to America, binti," Wajdy said. "In most of the Muslim world, it hasn't been the custom for hundreds of years."

"But you said—*you* said—" she whirled here to include her mother, "you *always* said it was part of Islam. What about Aisha? What about how Omar wished his wife would not go to the mosque for fajr but he couldn't stop her because he knew it was her right? What about the Prophet saying 'You must never prevent the female servants of God from attending the houses of God?' I told the matawwa that hadith and he laughed—he *laughed* at me, and said 'listen to this *woman* quoting scriptures at *us!*'"

Here she started sobbing again. It was like—the tone when he said "this woman"—it was like the police thought she was some kind of bad woman, out in the street at that dark hour, alone, face uncovered, and were going to haul her in for some sort of *vice* crime. None of them believed her or even listened to her. Like she was a joke, like what she said didn't even matter. It was all she could do to get them to bring her to the house.

And then the expression on Uncle Zaid's face when he wouldn't look at her at first and then when he recognized her: it was that look again. For a minute, she actually *felt* like a bad woman, as if she really had done something wrong, and she shuddered, and it frightened her. But then, it made her really angry—angry that they would treat her this way, and angry that she let them get inside her feelings—and she wanted to come out swinging.

I want someone to drive me
Down town

—Memphis Minnie, "Won't You Be My Chauffeur"

Saweem was telling Ebtehaj, in scandalized tones, that her husband's sister, Sheikha, held mixed-gender dinner parties. Ebtehaj tsk-tsked.

"I don't see what's wrong with that, if the women wear hijab," Khadra'd said. She couldn't resist. It was so boring here. And it was bogus of her mother to pretend the Dawah didn't have a mixed-gender work environment.

On the other hand, she couldn't believe her ears when her mother defended Americans later that day. Aunt Saweem had just declared that American women had to be sluts: that much was clear from the way they dressed.

"I used to think so," Ebtehaj said slowly, and her daughter looked up with interest. Her mother had a puzzled frown on her face, as if she were measuring Livvy's tiny halter-tops against the long denim jumpers of Norma Whitcomb. "How they dress depends on their upbringing. We have a neighbor, if you saw her, why, except for the hair uncovered, you'd say she was as modest as you or I." She looked surprised at what she'd just said. It seemed to have come together in her mind at that very moment.

"Really!" Saweem said, with a doubtful look.

"Yes," Ebtehaj said, with a little more certainty. "And also—even the scantily dressed ones—I've found you can't always draw conclusions about them." Under Saweem's questioning, a notion was emerging that hadn't fully formed in her before. "Khadra has an American friend, for example, who—well, to look at the way she dresses, you might think she was a young streetwalker."

"Yee!" Saweem said. "God preserve us."

"No, no—but after you know more, you understand that she is really a very good girl. A *moral* girl. She just doesn't know how to dress."

"Hmmph," Saweem said, not at all convinced that those two things, skimpy dress and good morals, could go together.

"So you really have to pity them, more than condemn," Ebtehaj pressed on, eager now to express the thought. "They don't have the *teachings* of modesty. Their mothers don't teach it to them. And everything else in their culture kills the natural instinct of a woman for modesty, and teaches her instead to expose herself. To please men."

This was an insight Khadra'd never heard her mother articulate before.

* * *

"Want to go visit my Aunt Sheikha?" Afaaf said to Khadra over a ping-pong game in the recreation room.

Khadra lunged to hit back a strong serve. "Does your mother let you go there? She doesn't seem to approve of your aunt."

"She has to—ties of the womb."

Khadra didn't see what was so tempting about going to another house when all she'd done was sit around this one, but it was a change of scene, anyway.

"You're sure it's safe?" Ebtehaj asked Saweem. "To send the girls with a driver?" Ebtehaj wasn't used to servants. Back in Syria, if you had a housekeeper, she was a poor Syrian, not a foreigner—more accountability in that, both ways.

"Aijaz? He's a good Muslim," Saweem assured her, referring to the Gujurati driver.

"And—this sister-in-law of yours—does she have boys?"

"I understand you completely, my dear. Her sons are at camp in Yanbu. And Sheikha may be too liberal for us, but she is a deeply moral woman."

Sheikha greeted them breathlessly. "I'm sorry girls, you're welcome here, but I'll be busy. I've just received word that Raja Alem—the surrealist playwright, surely you know—is in town for a very short time and I must interview her. I've been trying to get her for my Saudi women writers series. And now," she said jubilantly, "I've got her! What a coup!"

"My aunt is a journalist," Afaaf said to Khadra.

"Call Rini in the back when you want dinner," Sheikha said as she threw on her abaya and veil. "You're welcome to use the library but don't disturb the files on my desk." She hurried out to the car and driver the newspaper had sent.

Khadra was interested in the library—she hadn't brought much reading on the trip and glimpsed rows of leatherbound novels on the shelves, *The Remembrance of Things Past, Tess of the D'Urbervilles*—but Afaaf pulled her by the hand to the home theater room instead, where an enormous television center took up an entire wall. She picked a tape out of a well-stocked video library and slipped it in, and soon a shimmering Olivia Newton-John was singing on roller skates, with hordes of roller-skating Americans in her train. This was Afaaf's idea of great entertainment, *Xanadu?*

"This is only a pit-stop," Afaaf said. "Just wait a bit." She picked up a gold-trimmed princess phone and started dialing numbers. Meanwhile, she flipped open a compact and applied mascara, eyeshadow, and blusher, and outlined her lips. "Come on, get your abaya. We're going out!" she said.

Sheikha's driver didn't like being ordered out by Afaaf. The lady of the house had left no such instructions.

"Then we'll take a cab," Afaaf said, pouting.

"No, fine, I'll take you. Better someone keeps an eye on you."

But Afaaf sent him home as soon as he dropped them off at a shiny mall that seemd to be called Prisunic.

"No, not shopping," she hissed, pulling Khadra away from the automatic glass doors. She sauntered around to a side street, pulling her abaya tight against her waist and shapely bottom. A long black limousine with official tags of some sort drew up. To Khadra's consternation, Afaaf got in and pulled Khadra in after her.

The car was full of young Saudis—two cleanshaven guys in white caftans and a girl whose black abaya was crumpled under her Gloria Vanderbilt jeans. *"Like a Virgin,"* a familiar sultry voice pounded out on the stereo system.

"Here she is," Afaaf said to them. "My American cousin."

"Tifham arabi?" one of the guys asked Afaaf. His ghutra was pushed rakishly back on his head.

"Aiwa, bifham," Khadra retorted. She was shocked to see Afaaf throw off her veil and abaya inside the limo. She shook out her short, dark auburn curls. Her lips were full and glossy.

"Oh," the guy said. "So . . . you're not really American? You don't speak Arabic with an accent."

"No. I'm not really American. I'm an Arab, like you."

The girl seemed to think this was funny. Outside the window, the city disappeared. They were speeding down a bare stretch of highway with empty desert on both sides. Khadra felt a pang in her stomach.

"Do you drive?" Afaaf's conversation partner said. He had a wide smile and a funny, kind of broken-looking nose. "I'm Ahmad, by the way," he added, sticking his hand out.

Khadra shook her head. She didn't even shake hands with men in America, just like her mother. She wasn't going to start in the land of the Prophet. During Haj, no less. The strangeness of this whole scene was making her uncomfortable.

"Afaaf's here for her driving lesson," Ahmad said. "Ready?"

"Ready!" Afaaf cried. Ahmad said something to the driver and the car slowed to a stop. Then he pulled off his white headpiece and draped it on Afaaf's head. He and Afaaf climbed into the front seat.

A fat white Mercedes pulled up next to them. "Look, it's

Rasheed," said the guy who'd remained silent until now. He had a John Travolta cleft in his chin.

"And he's got Fawaz and Feisal with him," the girl said, clapping her hands. She buzzed down her automatic window. "PARTY!" she shouted. The young men grinned and waved. One of them mouthed something at her.

The limo jerked forward, Afaaf driving. The fat Mercedes matched its motion. Afaaf darted forward again. The other car kept pace. And suddenly both vehicles were off.

"Wheee!" Afaaf shouted, the wind in her face. Then brakes screeched. The limo whirled in a circle, burning rubber. John Travolta was thrown against Khadra.

"Oh—excuse me," he said, but didn't seem very quick to move from where he had landed on her, rather firmly. Khadra scuttled to her side of the car, hugging the black leather.

"Are you okay?" the girl opposite said. "You look green." The car lurched forward again, then skidded to a stop. "Afaaf, stop!" the girl called. "The American girl is gonna hurl on us."

Khadra closed her eyes. She didn't want to be here. This was supposed to be Haj.

"Here," the girl said. She snapped open a little gold lamé handbag with an Italian label and dumped out an assortment of colored pills. "Try the yellow ones," she suggested, giggling.

Khadra shook her head.

"Suit yourself!" she said, flinging the door open. "I'm going to say hello next door—" and then she was in the Mercedes.

"That's my cousin, Ghalya," the guy left with Khadra said. "I'm Ghazi. So . . . you're American, huh?"

"No," Khadra said. "I'm Arab. I told you, I'm Arab. Just like you." She got out of the car. Where was Afaaf? The limo chauffeur was back in the driver's seat, having a cigarette. A hulking sports utility GMC pulled up alongside them, and a silver Jaguar with a loud, obnoxious engine was arriving. The "party" appeared to be mushrooming.

"What kind of Arab?" Ghazi said, trailing after her.

"The Muslim kind," Khadra flung behind her back.

"I mean, what Arab country? I can't tell from your accent." It was true—her dialect was a mish-mash of Damascene, Palestinian, and Eygptian, all the Arab accents in the Dawah community.

"Syria."

"Ohhh . . . Syria, huh," he grinned. "Syrian girls have a reputation."

Khadra wasn't listening to him. She knocked on the window of the Mercedes. "Afaaf?"

The window rolled down on a cheerful male face. "Hi!" he said in English. Then he said over his shoulder in Arabic, "But she doesn't look American."

"Afaaf?" Khadra called into the car. "Is Afaaf there?" She peered past him into the back seat. There were a couple of open cans of Diet Coke on a polished wooden tabletop between the seats, and something else—a thin line of white powder. Ghalya leaned over it.

"Our house is your house," she said to Khadra, gesturing hospitably.

Khadra recoiled. "Afaaf? Afaaf!" she called, trying to keep the panic out of her voice. The abaya, hanging from her shoulders, spun with her in a dramatic arc. There was utter desert darkness, no streetlights, a full array of stars above her with such clarity as she hadn't seen since the station wagon trip across America. And even though she was in a Muslim country at this moment, and not just any Muslim country but *the* Muslim country, where Islam started, she had never felt so far from home. There was a nip in the air all of a sudden.

"Wait for her in here," Ghazi said, opening the limo door for her. "The desert turns cold on you at night." Khadra shivered and got inside, Ghazi following.

"Surely you don't wear that thing in America," he said, tugging at her veil and pouting boyishly.

What the—? She batted his hand away. A pugnacious look flashed across his face and for a minute he reminded her of—of Brent Lott, of all people. He caught her hand by the wrist. Half-playfully he wrested it down to her side. In the middle of Mecca, this was the last thing she expected.

"Let go," she said.

"Why? No one can see us," he said. Without warning, he was pulling her veil down the back of her head and pushing his other hand up against her breasts and his mouth was grazing her now exposed neck. She was squeezed up against the car door, and then he was pushing himself on top of her, his jeaned thighs taut.

"Get *off*—get *off* of me!" she gasped. And what did he mean by that, "no one can see us"—wasn't the driver of the car right there, and wasn't he looking straight at them in his rearview mirror—only why didn't he do something, why didn't he move? The driver lowered his eyes and tucked his head down and sat very still.

"What *is* it—what is the big *deal*—we're not doing anything you have to worry about," Ghazi said thickly. "—we've got our clothes on—and you grew up in *America*—don't tell me you never do stuff like this in America—"

She fumbled for the door latch and tumbled out when it opened. He fell half out too, and cursed. Khadra pounded her fists on the side of the limo and kicked the back left tire of the Mercedes and shouted at the wan faces that poked out of windows at the commotion. "AFAAF! You get out here! You get out here right now and take me home! Afaaf!"

A disheveled Afaaf stumbled out of one of the two farther cars. "What is your *problem?*" she said, wiping her wet mouth with the back of her hand. "What's the matter, is this not as fun as what you do in America?"

That again. "I'm *not* American!" she yelled in Arabic, kicking dust at Afaaf. Then, because the worst insults she knew in Arabic were what her parents blurted when she or her brothers misbehaved—brat or at worst, churl—she launched into a torrent of English: "I *hate* you—you're a FILTHY girl, with FILTHY friends—you take me home—you take me home RIGHT NOW. You—you—you *goddamn bitch.*"

Ghazi whistled and said, "Listen to her go off in American!" and Ghalya giggled like it was a fine joke.

But Khadra gasped and covered her mouth with her hand because she'd just cussed. In Mecca. On *Haj*. Although she didn't think they were still inside the Holy Precincts. Wait: did that mean she had to do ihram again at the *miqat* before she got back in the city? Had she violated ihram? But what did it all matter—she had done so many wrong things here, was under such wave upon towering wave of darkness, like someone in a crashing night-storm, who can only clap her hands to her ears at every thunderbolt, and see only a handspan before her at every lightning strike—it was hopeless to dream of absolution. So it was all for nothing: she hadn't even finished Haj, and she'd already blown it. She would never emerge pure as a newborn babe.

She went through the rest of the Haj motions feeling hollow, feeling like a hypocrite. On the plane home, she said, "I'm glad we're through with that place."

"Aunt Saweem's?" her mother said.

"Yeah. It creeps me out."

Ebtehaj fixed Khadra with a stare. "She only says things like this to irritate me," she said, turning to her husband.

Khadra was glad to be going home. "Home"—she said, without thinking. She pressed her nose against the airplane window. The lights of Indianapolis spread out on the dark earth beneath the jet. The sweet relief of her own clean bed awaited her there—and only there, of all the earth.

If you were to fill the lamps to overflowing with fat
Their glow would point the way to every acquisition of
knowledge
And if their oil is wanting, their wicks go dry
Where is the light of a thread not immersed?

—Aisha Taymuria, nineteenth-century poet of Egypt

Khadra was elated when she got an acceptance letter from Indiana University, Bloomington. She didn't have to go to IUPUI or community college. Which would have been her fate had she not had a mahram, Eyad, driving to IU every day in a little used Gremlin she could share with him.

Her parents were as excited as they'd been when Eyad started college. Almost too much so: they covered the kitchen table with course catalogs and schedule forms and pored over her distribution requisites and major requirements. Ebtehaj, who'd never had such parental help in her college years, was glad to spend several very efficient late-night sessions mapping out a course plan for all four years and Wajdy, who loved a time-and-logistics management problem, worked out how Khadra could fit in the classes she needed and those she wanted in her first semester, given the parameters of what was offered when.

She was assigned work-study in the entomology department. Damselflies pinned in shadowboxes dotted the wall behind her. And in the top drawer of her worktable, there was a little dish of spare beetle legs. How fine is that, she marveled, a dish of spare legs.

She thought it was cool that instead of a job requiring her to say "Would you like fries with that?" she had one where she could say, "Will that be the *aeshna cyanea* naiads"—those were the nymph stage dragonflies—"or the adult *plathemis lydia?"* Bug taxonomy was so different in each phase—yet the cells of one stage produced the cells of the next, and somehow it was the same creature.

Khadra and Eyad were not a part of the mainstream campus scene of frat houses and tailgate parties. Most of the "practicing" Muslim students stayed away from all that. The CMC (Campus Muslim Council) was the heart of the Muslim scene in Bloomington. CMC had a little ratty cubicle with a file cabinet with the overblown name of office amid the equally tatty offices of other student groups. They met twice a week, once for juma in a carpeted off-campus basement and once in a classroom for organizational stuff. Eyad was vice-president. Of course Khadra joined. The club had a mix of South Asians and Arabs (all engineering and pre-med majors), and increasingly teemed with big-bearded religious male Gulfies, men from the Arab Gulf states. The other Arab men on campus, Palestinians and Egyptians and Iraqis and Algerians, and most of the Arab women foreign students, generally belonged to the more secular Arab Students Club or the African Students Unity Organization, with its pan-African leanings.

If you were a Campus Muslim Council type of student, you wren't the type of Muslim that dated. You could say, as Tayiba had said to Khadra and a gaggle of CMC girls who'd given her the ol' snake-eyes when they caught her walking around easy as you please with Danny Nabolsy, "we had a study group at the library but everyone else left and then we went for coffee but only because we were both thirsty." But you didn't call it dating.

One of the most delicious things about the campus Muslim scene for the earnest young brothers and sisters was the Muslim modesty dance. Its basic move was the lowering of the gaze. Who can lower their gaze more? Who is the modestest one of all? The more attractive a "brother" found a "sister," he more sternly he kept his gaze lowered before her at the Divest from South Africa protest, staring hard at the ground with furrowed brow. I'm a modest guy, his lowered gaze said, and I find you worth showing how modest I am. His lashes trembled on his cheeks with the effort. For if she was some middle-aged auntie, or a mere unripe kid-sister girlchild, why would he bother? Having a male gaze lowered before you said, You are a Woman to me, with a capital W. What a thrill for a woman newly hatched from her egg of girlhood, what a delicious gut-tightening flutter of confusion and power. Her gaze lowered too, and her eyelashes lay down on her flushed cheeks. Or she may on purpose roughen her voice and find some important Islamic point to make or, stepping into the role of girl-next-door Muslim sister, something in the setup of the event that needed brisk tending to, to help her pretend she didn't feel the shimmer in the air between them. And then, in the next round, she may lower her hemline even more, and tighten her headscarf, and make her hijab stricter—lo, she has found someone worth being the queen of modesty for. And how that thrilled the young brothers, for it meant they were not little boys anymore but Men. Watch out then. Danger, sexy danger, Muslim flirtation-via-modesty-games danger, was in the air. It was worth never missing a CMC meeting to be part of this.

Bizarre rumors circulated among the Campus Muslim Council kids about the local Sufis. "They swim naked together in Lake Monroe" was one of them. "Because they think they're so spiritual they're above gender. You know, like Gandhi sleeping with the naked girls!"

"And one of them is gay. The Sufis."

"But he's married."

"But he's gay."

"And he goes to class in his bathrobe."

"It's a kimono."

"It looks like a bathrobe."

The supposedly gay married man in the kimono was actually a Finnish professor and his wife was a Japanese woman who was an adjunct lecturer in thermodynamics and also part of the whole mysterious (to the regular Muslims) Sufi cabal. They were rumored (by the regular Muslims and the general populace) to hold esoteric Sufi rituals in Nashville, Indiana, a nearby artsy-fartsy smudge on the map where yet more Sufis existed among the glassblowers, long-haired sculptors, and budding Georgia O'Keeffes and Jackson Pollocks who congregated there.

"They don't look Muslim to me," Khadra said to a classmate.

"You don't have a 'look' that determines whether you're Muslim," Joy Shelby retorted.

But Khadra knew that you did, no matter what her new friend said.

"So it's *Shalaby*, originally," Eyad said when Khadra mentioned Joy's last name. "Why did she change it to sound more American?"

"She's from Mishawaka."

"Oh," Eyad said. That explained it. The Muslims who lived in that northern Indiana town were the assimilated kind, second- and third-generation Americans descended from turn-of-the-century Arab immigrants. They had failed to preserve their identity—they'd caved.

"Hey—it was a different era when my grandfather came over," Joy said when Khadra mentioned Eyad's comment about her family name. "He was just a farm boy. Immigrants were more afraid back then, okay? Less educated. They did whatever the Ellis Island officer said, okay? If he told you Anglicize your name, you did. Sorry it doesn't meet your standards of ethnic purity."

Joy's family album was part of the American landscape in a way that Khadra did not think it possible for her family ever to be. Her brother and her father, like his father before him, worked in a steel factory, helping to make one of America's basic building blocks.

Khadra and Joy biked to a Kierkegaard study group, Joy in shorts, Khadra in baggy trousers and a long-sleeved tunic top that reached her knees. Dogwoods were in bloom along the avenue. The sun shone on puddles left by the previous night's rain in ruts and chuckholes that splashed as they biked through them, dispersing clusters of midges and gnats. Their destination was a Japanese restaurant where the group was meeting.

Khadra stopped cold outside the restaurant and said, "I can't go in there."

"Why not?" Joy said, her Pat Benatar mullet a little wind-whipped.

"It's a bar."

Joy looked up. The sign read "Japanese Restaurant and Sushi Bar." "It's just a sushi bar, Khadra." She was already threading the lock ring through her front wheel.

"Well I don't know what sushi is, but a bar is a bar. I can't go inside a bar."

"It's not a bar-bar! Like, not a pub or a tavern or a beer house. Sushi is seafood, okay? Christ, I thought I was the hick, coming from Mishawaka," Joy said. She snapped her bike padlock shut. As part of the first generation in her family to go to college, she had enough to deal with, without some little Arab girl from a privileged college-educated family trying to tell her what was acceptable and what was not in the "Islamic lifestyle." As if Islam was a lifestyle. Instead of a faith.

It was moments like this, and things like Joy's casual blasphemous use of "Christ" that made Khadra doubt the whole "it's okay for Islam to adapt to new locales" argument Joy put forth. It seemed to Khadra that her friend was just an assimilated Muslim, plain and simple.

"Do they serve alcohol?" Khadra pressed.

"God, I don't know. Look, we're gonna be late for the study group. I can't believe I'm out here debating this with you. I'm going in." Joy abandoned Khadra to her doubts.

Khadra hoisted her bookbag off her shoulders and squinted up at the sign again. She had a *Fear and Trembling* exam coming up in

Intro to Existential Thought. The material mystified her and she really needed the study group. Whispering a prayer for guidance, she entered the sushi bar.

Khadra resented the way Joy always seemed to assume, as if it were a given, that succumbing to white, middle-class, middle America's norms on all things—proms, birthday parties, eating out, clothing, and a thousand other things—was not only the unavoidable destiny of pathetic newcomers like Khadra and her family, but was somehow morally superior.

"McDonald's Muslim," she once accused Joy hotly.

"What?" Joy said.

"McMuslim" Khadra repeated, sniffing. "It means you believe by default in the typical American lifestyle of self-indulgence, waste, and global oppression." She loved listening to her leftist college professors. They gave her a language to critique America that fit with her parents' stance, or with the social justice part, anyway. This was a revelation, that some of the things she'd learned at home not only stood up to outside scrutiny, but actually coincided with the views of some of her professors. Not the religion part, though.

Say, "He is Lord of the East and of the West and of all that is between the two," if you have intelligence.

—Quran: The Poets, 27

"Why don't you come up and visit?" Joy said one day.

Going up by herself on that far a drive with just some other girl from college was not going to happen. But Khadra persuaded Eyad to come along (he'd get to visit some of his old CMC buddies in the area), making it okay with her parents that she'd be spending the night away from home.

As they drove down Joy's tree-lined street of small white houses with postage-stamp front yards and big porches, someone yelled out her name.

"Your mom said to tell you—she at Im Litfy's."

"Okay, Donnie!" Joy called. "That's our next-door neighbor," she explained to Khadra and her brother.

Khadra was overwhelmed with a sense of home as she entered Im Litfy's kitchen. Maybe it was the garlic and cilantro smell, or maybe it was the scene of kibbeh-making that greeted them. Khalto Im Litfy presided over a Moulinex meat grinder just like the one the Shamys used at home—in fact, Moulinex simply translated as kibbeh machine in Arabic. Here too was the giant bowl of peeled onions, here was the pile of ground lamb meat. Behold, the mountain of bulgur. Into the maw of the Moulinex were poured these three, whose fates would be forever ground together, though they knew not each other before that hour.

A pear-shaped woman came out from around the table with a heavy, comfortable gait. Her short, coarse black hair was partially covered by a snatch of bandanna to keep it out of the meatwork. To Khadra and Eyad she said, "I'm Rose, Joy's mom. I'd shake hands, hon, but as you can see . . . " She was up to her elbows in raw meat and onions. "But I'm glad you're here! You're right on time!"

Im Litfy, gray-haired and jolly, explained, "She means right on time to help out." She had a thick accent in English but a pure native inflection in Arabic.

"Wash your hands! I need stuffers!" Joy's mother said. "Stuff those holla kibbehs for me. Pull up that chair, kiddo," she nodded to Khadra. "You too, slugger," she said to Eyad, who clearly expected to be escorted to the living room to sit with men. And "Slugger?" No Arab woman had ever referred to him with a baseball epithet.

No Arab men turned up to rescue him, either. He and Joy and Khadra were conscripted into hard labor by the Queens of Kibbeh.

For kibbeh was a great and complex task, requiring a whole clan in the kitchen, way beyond the grasp of the lonely nuclear family in America, severed from the web of extended family. Down into the hot oil went the small, football-shaped ovals of stuffed kibbeh, bursting with ground meat and pine nuts. Out they came again fried, shiny and grainy and brown. Into the oven went tray after tray. The pan kibbeh was cut into diamonds, cut into stars.

"For the Arab Pride festival tomorrow," Rose said. "In the morning, we take the food over to Im Litfy's church, St. George's. That's where the parade'll end with a banquet."

You could see Khadra and Eyad do a mental double-take. Church? Im Litfy? Who felt as familiar as their own grandmother, whose kitchen felt like home?

Khadra glanced at their hostess' face, her features so familiarly Syrian, her cadence and voice equally so. What other homes of similar sweetness and joy had they passed by all these years, insisting as they did on their separateness and specialness, then? What a waste. Something started to unravel in Khadra there in the kitchen, bringing her almost to the point of secret tears. Confused, she kept them in.

"We saved some for ya, Baker," Rose said. A guy in a denim jacket suddenly filled the doorway, beefy and big and sloping, with wide hips and slow, heavy movement. He had a shock of coarse black hair and strong black eyebrows from ear to ear. Fresh cold air came in with him, and a smell of woodburning that made Khadra think of crackling logs on a fire and rustling piles of autumn leaves. Two more children appeared when he entered, girls about ten and twelve in soccer uniforms.

"Baker, meet Joy's friends from college," Rose said. "And here's my youngest, Amalie, and this is Im Litfy's granddaughter Lisa."

Baker shook hands with Eyad and then stuck out his hand to Khadra. It was such a big gentle hand; Khadra's little pudgy one instinctively homed into its big clasp and he covered it with his other hand. Eyad flashed her a glance—shaking a man's hand?—but she ignored it. "Hey, welcome to Mishawaka," Baker said. "How's my kid sister?" He ruffled Joy's hair as she ducked her head uselessly.

Later, after tea and baklava, the whole family smoked, except Joy. "Joy's our little crusader for anti-smoking," Rose said proudly, puffing a cigarette out on the Shelby front porch, a generous space cluttered with plants and odd things, like what appeared to be a stuffed king cobra. Khadra started when she found it at her elbow.

"That's Pete Seeger," Joy said, indicating the snake with a nod. "Baker beaned 'im, Dad stuffed 'im, and I named 'im."

The Shalaby father had welcomed them with Arab-style effusions of *"ahlan, ahlan wa sahlan,"* and knew enough old-school ways not to offer his hand to Khadra but to place it on his heart to greet her. He now lit up a pipe. He had a square head, big bushy eyebrows, and thick coarse hair gone to iron gray. "Did you know," he said, puffing out his first cloud of smoke, "that Indiana was once covered so thickly with forest that a squirrel could go the entire state without ever touching the ground?"

"Really?" Eyad said politely. "Just jumping from tree to tree?" He looked such an overly neat college boy in this setting. In any setting, really, but more so here.

Joy nudged Khadra and whispered, grinning,"The long grasses line is next,"

"Incredible, how fertile this land is, Amreeka," Joy's dad went on. "Once upon a time, a long time ago, the Middle East was that rich in greenness. But the kings of the old days—now, I'm talking pre-Islam, pre-Christianity, pre-Roman even, going way back—well, the kings, they cut down the cedar forests to finance war after war, see. And now we have what we have," he finished.

Khadra looked at Joy. She was wrong. Her dad wasn't following the script.

"And the long grass that covered Indiana," Bou-Baker went on, and Joy smiled at Khadra, vindicated. "Why, they were so tall that you couldn't see a rider on a horse come through them at full gallop. *Ey, na'am.* Yes, indeed." Puff, puff-puff. Irongray bushy eyebrows going up and down.

Rose picked up a guitar from the corner of the porch and strummed it as the fireflies of evening came out. Khadra recognized an old Fayruz tune from her father's tapes, a song, she found out in college, which came from a Gibran poem. Something like,

Give me the flute, then, and sing to me
For in song lies the mystery of Being.

The familiarity of it struck a chord in her. She and Eyad had never seen Arab folk like this: women called Rose who mangled Arabic with an American accent and played Arabic music on American guitars, and men who looked like Hoosier farmers in denim overalls but a shade or two darker. All sitting around eating kibbeh nayyeh of an Indiana evening as the midges and moths played in the porch light.

Joy's bedroom was cluttered with Holly Hobbie ornaments, Cesar Chavez posters, stacks of *The Radical Ecologist,* and ratty Green Lantern comic books. The whole house smelled as if it had flooded in 1920 and never recovered from the mildew. As Khadra made her way over the creaky floorboards after using the bathroom to make ablution, she spied, through a door slightly ajar, Joy's father on his prayer rug, his back to her, finishing off a slow-moving rakat. He had made no fuss of "clap-clap-clap, it's prayer time, everyone hop to it." But wasn't it a father's duty to call everyone to prayer?

"Men should be men and women should be women," Rose was saying on the porch. "I don't truck with all this women's lib business. What do we need libbing from? You're with me, right, hon?" she said, looking at Khadra and Eyad. "It goes against religion, am I wrong or am I right?"

Eyad nodded, happy to find common ground. Khadra said, with mild protest, "I think religion allows a little more flexibility than that, Auntie. I mean, the Prophet used to help his wife with the housework, and Sitna Aisha led a battle once."

Rose waved this away. "God created us a certain way and that's the way it's supposed to be. Tradition, hon. It works. You don't mess with what works. Am I wrong or am I right?"

"Wrong or right, Mom, I'd like some more of your wonderful *atayef,*" Baker said with a wink, holding his out plate.

Joy rolled her eyes.

Khadra went home with an itty-bitty crush on Baker. Which she totally wouldn't admit to herself, much less to Joy. All she knew was, she liked to stop by the fireplace lounge of the Union and breathe in that woodburning smell. She nestled into an armchair and put her feet up on her bookbag, and she was riding full gallop through tall grasses right up to the edge of a deep woods, and then she was padding like an old-time Shawnee brave from tree to mossy tree, trying to get a closer glimpse of someone or something that evaded her.

. . . behold! The Shadow has departed! I will be a shield-maiden no longer, nor vie with the great Riders, nor take joy only in the songs of slaying. I will be a healer, and love all things that grow and are not barren.

—Eowyn, in J. R. R. Tolkien, *The Lord of the Rings*

A little while after returning from the Shelbys, Khadra put on a white scarf with tiny flowers like a village meadow in spring, and a pale blue blouse and soft floral skirt. Her broadcloth navy jilbab and plain black scarves she shoved to the back of her closet. Ebtehaj raised an eyebrow at breakfast but said nothing. Her political pamphlets, cassettes of Abdulla Azzam *khutbas,* and modern Muslim revolutionary tracts, Khadra swept into shoeboxes under her bed. Now she raided her parents' downstairs bookshelves for hadith books and Ibn Kathir's tafsir, making Ebtehaj nuts when it was time to prepare for *taleem* and she couldn't find the volume she needed. At the University library, Khadra checked out Muwatta Ibn Malik,

Sahih Muslim, Ibn al-Qayyim al-Jawzia, and *usul al-fiqh* books. The latter, being untranslated, were difficult reading for her. She came home excited one day, dropping her bookbag with a thud.

"What do you have in there, rocks?" Eyad asked.

Khadra took out a huge red brick of a book. "Just came out in translation!" she said. *"Reliance of the Traveler!"*

Her mother, looking over her mending, said "Interesting."

"What does that mean?" Khadra said warily. She already loved the *Reliance* and didn't want her mother to spoil it by having some view about it that would then take up space in her head forever.

"Nothing. It's a good reference. We've had it for years in Arabic and you never took interest."

"Well, this is in English. Translated by an American Muslim. An *American*. A Muslim who is entirely American." Khadra was ripe for this sort of hadith wisdom anthology, steeped as she was since earliest childhood in the words of Quranic and Prophetic traditions.

It was the beginning of her neoclassical phase. She thirsted now to study the traditional Islamic heritage. It seemed to her the answer lay in there somewhere—not in the newfangled Islamic revivalism of her parents and the Dawah, with its odd mixtures of the modern and the Prophetic, and its tendency to come off more like a brisk civic action committee than a spiritual faith. No, not there, but in the direction of the old Quranic and hadith sciences, the various branches of *fiqh* and shariah studies, and the spiritual wisdom that had been handed down with them for centuries—now *there* was something! These things were tried and true; they'd lasted because they *worked.* But how to get them, where? Going to Al-Azhar University in

Cairo, as Eyad had done during his traditional Islam phase, was impossible.

"I'm thinking about changing my major to Islamic studies," she said to her father. He was driving her home from Bloomington one weekend when Eyad was out of town.

"Study Islam as taught by Orientalists?" Wajdy said, frowning into the driving rain on his windshield. "They don't believe in Revelation. They claim hadiths are fabrications. They malign the Prophet. They say Islam was spread by the sword. There is no end to the lies they will teach you—"

"I can see through that stuff," Khadra said airily. "I'll only go for what I want to get out of it. The classical texts."

"It doesn't work that way. They play with your brain." The rain fell in sheets. The wipers couldn't wipe it fast enough. Wajdy slowed down.

"You sound like Mama."

"What do you mean?"

"Paranoid."

Wajdy pulled over, displeased with the ungenerosity toward her mother, and waited for the rain to abate. A neoclassical phase had been part of his own youth, but beginning that path without the guidance of a classically trained teacher was foolhardy. How could you separate the study of texts from the spiritual guidance that a traditional sheikh imparted?

However, next month, again on the drive from Bloomington, he said to Khadra, "I've found something for you. The Terre Haute CMC is sponsoring a Mauritanian sheikh for a year. He'll be imam of their congregation there and offering weekly study. He is a *hafiz,* with *ijazas* in Quran and the Maliki school of jurisprudence."

The flat, featureless landscape of central Indiana stretched out on both sides of the car.

"But—that's in Terre Haute. How does that help me?" God. Soybean fields in winter are the most depressing sight you ever want to see, Khadra thought. She flashed on a Quranic phrase from "The Cave" to describe it—"transformed into dry stubble which the winds do scatter."

"Bear with me, Khadra. '*Sabrun jameel*—patience is beautiful,'" he quoted from the Quran. "You want to seek Islamic knowledge and that is a noble thing. Your mother and I want to support you in this. So I'm willing to drive you down once a week."

Khadra's face shone.

"It's what I think Saeed would have done," her father said. Saeed ibn al-Musayab, of the generation of the *Tabiyun,* the generation after the Prophet, was one of his personal heroes. He would have gone the distance to educate his daughters in Islamic knowledge, Wajdy felt.

The Terre Haute mosque was an apartment in a shabby four-story walk-up. The door number was missing, but you could tell which one it was by the pile of shoes at the threshold. The Mauritanian sheikh, in addition to letting her sit in the back of the men's *tajwid* session, gave over a special session to teach shariah to Khadra.

"He's pretty laid back about mixed-gender interactions," Khadra shared with Tayiba. "He's like, traditional, but that's *part* of the tradition he comes from."

Some of the Terre Haute men at first disapproved of a female presence at the halaqa. Most of them were foreign students from

Musim heartland countries whose wives typically didn't go to the mosque. But the sheikh defended her presence. Maliki thought, the sheikh's school, emphasized the practice of the people of Medina in the early days of Islam, and the sheikh reminded the halaqa that the Prophet had taught women with no curtain between them, and that the first mosques of Islam had no physical barrier between men and women. So mixed-gender meetings, as long as they were circumspect and respectful, were not a newfangled thing in his book, but a continuation of tradition.

And so the treasures of Quran recital were unlocked for Khadra. It began with a diagram of the throat with the Arabic letters charted at their places of origin. Hard palate, soft palate, the root of the tongue, the median sulcus down its middle, the phonemes that belong to each of its side sections. When to soften the t and d and when to harden them. Proper Quran recital was an art form, like opera; Khadra'd had no idea. What a difference the training made. Before, she read the Quran like you'd read a newspaper. Now, she felt it surge through her throat and flow with her breath, and she could fill the room with the mellow sound of it, fill the day and night.

Khadra was in love with it. She practiced constantly. *"Kaf ha ya ayn saad,"* she said in the entomology lab over a branch swarming with ladybugs, *coccinella novemnotata. "And remember Mary in the Book,"* she memorized, over the tsip, tsip-zip of the katydids. *"When she withdrew from her family to a place in the East,"* she said, leaning over whirring blue-green dragonflies.

The Mauritanian sheikh announced that an international tajwid competition would allow him to select one of his students to enter.

Khadra redoubled her recital practice. Tayiba grew used to her holding up her hand indicating that she was in the middle of a verse. *"Thy Sign shall be that thou shalt speak to no man for three nights in a row. So Zachariah came out to his people from his chamber and told them by signs to celebrate God's praises in the morning and the evening,"* she recited between bowling a spare and a strike. In the soundproof study room at the library, she proclaimed, *"Oh Yahya, take hold of the Book with Strength. And we gave him Wisdom even in youth, and tenderness from Us, and Purity, and he was devout. And kind to his parents, not overbearing or rebellious. And Peace be upon him the day he was born, and the day that he dies, and the day he will be resurrected."*

"That's beautiful," Joy said, zipping her backpack. "You ready for Social Justice?" She and Khadra were taking one of the hot history courses on campus, taught by Dr. Turner Mattingly, a charismatic professor whose charm and good looks were quite possibly a factor in the course's brimming enrollments. Khadra's crowd took his classes because he was the only professor on campus who gave the Palestinian cause a fair shake, and even had some positive things to say about the Iranian Revolution. That was as good a reason for the CMC girls to take his classes as for the boys, and if the girls got a little extra flushed when they debated the value of Islamist politics with him after class, well, it was just their hijabs making them a bit sweaty around the neck, in all likelihood.

Her tajwid practice gathered momentum. Every place on campus became associated for Khadra with a cluster of verses. Under the stinky gingko tree was where she found herself setting to heart *"And the pains of childbirth drove her to the trunk of a palm tree. She cried*

Would that I had died before this and been a thing forgotten, long out of memory! But there called to her from underneath her, Grieve not! For thy Lord hath provided a rivulet beneath thee." And in a thundering rainstorm on the path to Lindley Hall, she memorized: *"And shake toward thyself the trunk of the palm tree; it will let fall fresh ripe dates upon thee. So eat, and drink, and cool thine eye."*

In this way, she triumphed, memorizing the whole Maryam sura by the deadline, having perfected the transitions and techniques and tonalities. She recited it for the Mauritanian sheikh and he beamed, saying it was nearly flawless, the best in the class. Now Khadra passed her cassette tape up the row of students to him.

"What's this?" he said, smiling gently.

"My tape. For the contest," she said.

"Ah." He blinked. He opened his mouth to speak, then shut it, then said, "There's been some misunderstanding, dear Sister."

"How do you mean, *Ustaz?*"

"Well—you see—I never meant to imply—the contest, I'm afraid—it is not open to women."

Khadra was crushed. He was apologetic. Nothing wrong with having women in such a contest, he assured her. The sponsoring institution simply had not opened it to women yet. He would be sure to mention it to them for next year. Her reward was with God, in any case, for surely she had been memorizing for God and not for fame in this world?

He gazed, and gazed, and gazed, and gazed
Amazed, amazed, amazed, amazed

—Robert Browning, "Rhymes for a Child Viewing a Naked Venus in a Painting of *The Judgement of Paris*"

Juma al-Tashkenti was a friend of Eyad's, a mechanical engineering grad student from Kuwait. Tall, with a basketball player's build, he was much darker than Eyad in coloring and had dark-rimmed eyes. Like Michael Ansara playing Abu Sufyan, the bad guy in the movie *The Message*. (The character converts to Islam three-quarters of the way through the film, and suddenly he's one of the good guys, just when you were enjoying hating him.) *The Message* had outraged Muslims when it had first come out in '76, with one Black Muslim group threatening that "heads would roll" if it opened in theaters. Later, when people took the time, actually, to watch it, they'd discovered it was not half bad, even ponderously respectful. By the 1980s, it was hailed as a Muslim film classic by people who attended Dawah Center conferences. Khadra had seen it many times at the Campus Muslim Council's annual Ramadan screening.

Juma met her at the point when her black-scarf phase was fading into her neoclassical phase and was impressed, without sharing all her views. When it came down to it, he didn't actually pay close attention to what she said at the podium during Campus Muslim Council meetings, so much as he was wowed by the fact that she got up and said intelligent-sounding things. She had a pure Arabic accent—even though she spoke English with a regular American accent too. She wore perfect hijab, even a little conservatively for his taste, but that was okay, better that she erred on that side than the other way, he thought.

And he'd seen her get passionate about Palestine and other Arab causes. He liked that she had not lost her Arab identity despite being raised entirely in America. Juma didn't know personally any other girls who combined all those qualities. He lowered his gaze diligently before her, which she, without thinking about it consciously, found charming. A scent of sandalwood clung about him.

One afternoon, Khadra picked up the phone. "I was just—is Eyad there?" It was Juma. "I was just calling to see if he's going to the program tonight," he said, using the muted voice proper for a woman not his mahram, the verbal equivalent of that lowered gaze.

"Of course," Khadra said, her tone equally sober. An official from the Reagan State Department was going to explain to the CMC how to expedite trips to Pakistan in aid of the Afghan mujahideen effort against the Soviet Union.

The Afghan jihad was the Muslim cause du jour. Some CMC boys in their first flush of Islamic movement geopolitical awareness had taken to wearing the rolled Afghan caps. Sort of the guy equivalent to the black-scarf thing, Khadra figured. Some even hoped to volunteer at Afghan camps in Peshawar. You could work at refugee hospitals, orphanages, and camp schools. It was the summer trip of choice. It was exciting, and new, and a little strange, to have U.S. State Department validation for such efforts. For similar Jewish causes, there had long been official sanction—like, look at all the government support they got to help free Soviet Jews. The Hillel students all wore those buttons that said "Let My People Go," and now Muslim activists were simply doing the same. Their version.

"Are—I hope I'm not being forward but—are you going?" Juma asked.

Khadra said she was. (And it *had* been forward of him to ask. What business was she of his? But she liked it.)

Of course she was going; she was the one who had reserved the room, designed the flyer, made copies of it, and booked the flight for the speaker, just as she had for the last speaker, on divestment from South Africa, and the one before that, on Hindu terrorism against Muslims in India. That speaker, she'd flown him in from Ontario and arranged his stay in town, down to the meals. Spoke with him on the phone about a dozen times throughout. Yet at the lectern, he thanked the "brothers" of the Campus Muslim Council for hosting him, never once mentioning her.

Eyad said that was her ego speaking. "You're not doing this for honor in the world, right? You're doing it for the Face of God."

"I don't see you turning down the honors of the world," Khadra retorted. Eyad was getting requests from affiliate clubs in Evansville and Terre Haute to speak as a CMC organizer. Eyad's "Islamic work" arc was rising. "What about *your* ego?" she said.

After each lecture, the speaker went out to eat with the brothers. They hung around him asking questions, even having tea in his hotel room. This was inappropriate for the sisters to do, and they did not join such gatherings.

Khadra had opened one of the public events with a reading from the Quran, and Brother Sidky had come up to her afterward. He was the current CMC president.

"That was great Quran recital, Sister Khadra," he said. "Can you open our weekly meetings like that?" Obligingly, Khadra recited at the next meeting, which was on a Friday, choosing the sura called "Friday/Congregation."

On the drive home through the soybean field landscape (they almost didn't see it anymore—it was all they'd ever known), Eyad said to her, "There were some objections to a woman reciting the Quran in front of men. Actually, there was more or less a consensus about it among the guys. Except Sidky. See, we sort of had a discussion. After the meeting broke up."

"You had a discussion, just the guys, and you didn't invite any of us?"

"Yeah. Calm down. We didn't plan it that way. It's just—well, it'd be the first time a Muslim woman did something like that at one of our meetings and so—"

Khadra made an impatient gesture. She'd heard that in the early 1970s, *none* of the Muslim women in the Campus Muslim Council even wore hijab. Zuhura had been the first. The rest were more like Joy Shelby Muslim women. So when he said "the first Muslim woman" Eyad really only meant the first of a certain type.

"It's not that a woman's voice is *awrah* normally," Eyad said. "It's just—well, you have to admit, Khadra, your voice when you're reading Quran with all the tajwid stuff is pretty awesome. I heard some of the guys talking about it. Talking about *you*. It's almost like, if some girl's singing in a sultry voice. You wouldn't want to do that, would you? And I don't want to be put in that position, with guys listening to my sister and getting, well, almost turned *on*. Do *you* want me to have to be in such an uncomfortable position?"

Of course she didn't want to be seen as a vamp. A Quran-reciting vamp. She quit doing the recitation. In fact, she stopped going to CMC meetings altogether for a while, in disgust.

"You should join the Arab Students' Association," Joy said, when Khadra vented to her.

"Why, are they less sexist?" Khadra said.

"Nope."

"Well, then . . . ?"

". . . we just have more fun," her friend said teasingly.

"Den of iniquities," Khadra half-joked. She half meant it: she'd never been around Muslims who drank, as some of those in the Arab club did, and the idea made her uncomfortable. Plus, the Arab students sponsored an annual bellydance performance, a tremendously popular event. They had done this for years, but recently the Campus Muslim Council had begun to object. CMC president Brother Sidky accused the Arab Students Association of promoting the stereotype of the lascivious Arab male. The ASA leaders retorted that the religious group was promoting the stereotype of the "tight-ass Muslim prick."

This was unfair. The Muslims did too know how to have fun. The CMC guys played basketball against the Arab club and African club guys every Saturday morning. The CMC girls bowled in the Union alley every Thursday—although Khadra couldn't always afford to spend money on a game and shoe rental, some nights she joined in. And all the sisters and brothers together had a barbecue in Brown County State Park every semester. "Allahu Akbar and Pass the Ketchup," the flyer advertised.

Juma asked to go home with Eyad and Khadra one day. From where Khadra sat, she had a view of the back of Juma's head, his lush black hair, his deep bronze complexion. Juma's lips as he turned to talk to Eyad were large and exquisitely chiseled, the lower lip wide and curved like a Kuwaiti dhow. The scent of sandalwood subtly invaded her senses.

When it became clear during his visit that he was there to ask her parents and, by their permission, her, to consider a proposal of marriage from him, it was not entirely a surprise, even though he and Khadra had never exchanged a word beyond that phone call without Eyad in the middle.

She considered it. He was up-front about his future being in Kuwait. She didn't mind that prospect. Maybe it was the answer to not belonging in America all these years. Maybe it was the "back" where she was supposed to go.

Meanwhile, Khadra's father and brother swung into action. Their job was to check up on Juma's character and background. Wajdy, through a friend, contacted two of Juma's former professors at Kuwait University. They said Juma had no prior broken engagements or marriages, nor was he known as someone who played around. He was definitely not in the set that drove shiny red Mercedes and cruised for hookers and drugs on the Kuwait City strip. His family was well-liked and well-respected, moderately religious and moderately wealthy. Eyad used his contacts to turn up a cousin of Juma's at the University of Arizona who told him that Juma had an older sister who was a pediatrician. This fact meshed with the family being moderately observant and not among the ultrareligious who barred women working from outside the home. That allayed a worry of Khadra's, because some of the Gulfies she knew were too off-the-deep-end hardcore.

So that was okay.

And then something happened that added to the appeal of Juma's proposal. Wajdy was exploring the prospect of a job in South Bend. So her parents might be moving in a year or two.

The Dawah Center was beginning to change, ever so slightly. A slow, lumbering, generational change toward a substance and style that was by no means progressive, but in the midst of which Ebtehaj and Wajdy seemed too old-school. They had made their contribution, and it was time to step aside. Meanwhile, newer batches of more conservative immigrants needed them, found them not outdated, but just right for their institution-building stage, a perfect balance of American know-how and reassuringly staunch Islamic devotion.

It was one such community that wanted to invite them to South Bend, where Wajdy would serve as the Islamic center director and Ebtehaj would help out at the new full-time Islamic school. Wajdy and Ebtehaj could become in their middle age the wise elders of a youngish newbie community, full of questions about how to raise young children by the waters of Babylon. Because there was no unifying force such as the Dawah Center drawing various ethnicities together, the Muslims in South Bend, as in other cities, clustered in ethnic comfort zones that grew organically in a way that encouraged ethnic sameness—families that were already there drew other families from the same country of origin. Wajdy and Ebtehaj's prospective new mosque was made up mostly of Syrian, Palestinian, Iraqi, and other Arabs.

So, there was a chance that the parental home would soon be folded up and moved. What would Khadra do? Eyad could dorm on campus, but it was not acceptable by the Shamys' highly conservative standards for Khadra, as a young unmarried girl, to live out on her own. How would she finish her degree? She could move with her parents, transferring to a school up there. Go on as before. Or she could get married and stay in Bloomington. She could start a new stage of life, an adventure. A change.

"If you don't marry this one," Ebtehaj said, "you should think about marrying in the next few years, anyway. A girl's window of opportunity narrows after that."

Khadra had radical thoughts on *mahr,* the dowry Juma had to provide. The problem in his home country was that impossibly high mahrs were typically demanded by the bride's side, making mahr an obstacle in the way of many young couples' marriages. Khadra, drawing from the history of the Prophet, came up with a plan to have her mahr be that Juma would memorize a long sura of the Quran for her. She picked "The Table Spread," one of her favorites. However, Khadra's parents insisted that she also take a cash sum, as that would be more protective of her security, and Juma agreed, even insisted, on that, although he was also happy to oblige her by memorizing the sura and was impressed that she wanted him to. His father—who would be paying the mahr, not Juma—insisted, too. They decided on eight thousand dollars, two thousand up front and the rest deferred, due only in case of a (husband-initiated) divorce. It was largely a symbolic deferment, or so every engaged couple tended to feel.

Wonderfully, Téta made an exceptional, and possibly final, trip to America for the wedding.

"Why did you choose to say yes to him?" Téta asked.

It seemed fairly obvious, didn't it? What were the reasons again? "Well, there's Mama and Baba's possible move, and the fact that I want to go to college away from home," she began, ticking off items on her fingers. "And—"

"No, dear, I don't mean, why get married. I hope you're not marrying him just to be married, *te'ebrini.* I mean, what made you choose this one?"

Khadra thought for a moment. "Well, I guess he's as good as any other guy I'd end up marrying, so why not?" She saw Téta's face furrow. She went on hastily, "He's a good Muslim—you know, a *practicing* Muslim—and an active student in CMC, and he's intelligent, and a decent person and all. Everyone says he is."

"What do *you* say?"

"Me? Well, I like the way he talks, his friendliness. And he's handsome, don't you think?"

Téta pondered. "Well. He is that. He has a nice tush, anyway."

Khadra took that as a seal of approval.

"Come, I want to give you your wedding gift," Téta said. She fumbled at her blouse and pulled something out of her impressive cleavage, a silk handkerchief, twisted around something solid. She unknotted the silk. "Here are some earrings for my lovesy Khadra," she said, drawing out a pair of gold linked hoops set with rich blue stones.

"Téta! They're *excellent!*"

"And here is something else," she said. Three fat gold coins lay in her palm. Fat gold coins with mysterious writing, the alphabet neither Arabic nor Latin, nothing Khadra recognized. *"Osmanli liras,"* Téta said. "This is called security, my dear, and we never show it to our husbands. A woman must keep something for herself, in case of circumstances."

"Circumstances?"

"Yes. There are days when things are rosy, and then there may be days when you wake up and feel the future closing in on you, the horizon shrinking. *The world being as we know it, the sad world as we know it . . .* " she drifted off into a song. Then she seemed to remember something and became sober again. "Promise you'll keep the coins to yourself," she said.

"Why?" Khadra said. "I trust him—We—"

"Of course you do, dear. That's lovely. Trust him all you want, but have your own resources, *te'ebrini.*"

Khadra shook her head. "You're so cynical, Téta," she said lightly.

Téta's face clouded as it rarely did when she was with Khadra.

"I'm sorry, Téta," Khadra said immediately. She could see how it hurt her.

"Cynical is not what I am," Téta said heavily. "Turn on the air conditioning, *te'ebrini,* and go now and let me rest."

"Thank you. Thank you for the gift," Khadra said. Téta had already climbed into bed and closed her eyes. Khadra pulled a coverlet gently over her.

After the *katb el-ktaab,* Téta was to chaperone them on a picnic at Eagle Creek. Juma opened the front passenger door of his car for Téta, over her protests that Khadra sit next to him.

"So you can gaze into each other's eyes!" she said, making them both blush.

Khadra agreed with Juma. "More comfortable for your legs, Téta."

"Age before Beauty," Juma said, with just slightly awkward gallantry.

"I'm still Beauty, *yoh!*" Téta harrumphed. She finally took the front seat, muttering that lovers had been smarter in her day.

When they got to Eagle Creek, Téta insisted on their taking out a paddleboat without her. "You must be joking, my old paddlers need a rest," she said. *Now* she was old.

Khadra eased herself into the boat. Juma offered his hand and, unsteadily, she took it. This was the first touch. Immediately there was new grace in both their movements. They lowered themselves into the seats, which were puddled with water.

"My seat's wet." Khadra laughed.

"Mine too."

"How do you work this thing?"

"Well, let's see." Juma reached for a shift in the rack between the seats. "I guess this is the steering. Let's backpedal out of the dock."

They did it too fast, bumping the docking slip. They both reached for the shift at the same time. Second touch. Khadra left her hand there in his, snug as if it was in a pocket. Juma took it up to his mouth and kissed it. "Your hands are pretty," he said.

"No—I've always thought of them as dishpan hands." Her hands made her think of only either prayer or cleaning chores.

"But they are not. They're cashmere." They were stalled in the dock. They worked on pedaling until they got the boat cutting a path out on the lake. Then they leaned back and let it float. Water-skimmers skimmed and dragonflies darted.

"So what do you think?" Khadra said. "Are we going to have a good life, or what?"

"With God's grace," he said. "Hey—" A boat with three children churned past, chopping up the waters. "—how many children do you want?"

"Right away? None," she said, an edge creeping into her voice.

"Okay, okay." He dangled his arm out to the water. A lot of girls talked that way when they first got married; his own sister, for one. Later, they tended to come around. "Fine. Later on. How many?"

"I dunno. I haven't thought that far ahead. How many do you want?" She held her breath, suddenly worried.

"Oh, I don't know exactly. I was hoping somewhere between two . . . and nine."

She sat up. "Nine! Nuh-uh!"

He is laughing at her. "What is this, 'nuh-uh'?"

"Nothing. Just dumb Hoosier talk. Means no. Not nine!"

"Okay."

"No. Say it. *Not nine.*" She was smiling.

He laughed. "*Not nine*. How about eight then?"

"Okay. I see how it is with you." She dipped her fingers into the lake and splashed him. "Let's just go back to shore right now, mister."

"No, no, please. Look, I brought bread for the ducks." Reaching into the little brown paper bag for the bits of stale bread was a nice prospect because it meant their hands got to meet several more times by accident. Every time hers touched his, she now thought, *cashmere, cashmere*. When they went under a cascade of green willow branches, he leaned over to her side and grazed the corner of her mouth with his wide shapely lips.

There was a thrill. The boat got tipsy.

In Islam, it is said "Marriage is half of the faith." In close relationship, the sharpened edges of our nafs (ego-soul) can be little by little smoothed.

—Camille Adams Helminski, *Women of Sufism, Hidden Tresure*

Khadra's wedding was to be held at the Dawah Center—the women's party, that is. The men's party would be at the Community Room at the Fallen Timbers. Nothing was a more natural culmination of Khadra's girlhood than for her to come down the staircase of the blue Victorian house in her wedding white.

Her choice was Butterick #1287, in scads of lace and tulle, sewn by Wajdy at his Singer, beadwork painstakingly added to the bodice and arms by Ebtehaj, who pored over the dress, bead by bead and stitch by stitch. Even Eyad and Jihad helped sew on the last ones, when Ebtehaj was behind in wedding work and panicking.

Regarding herself in the mirror, the bride thought she looked almost pretty, despite the annoying baby-roundness of her face that just would not leave her. She was shortwaisted and plump. Her mother called it "well proportioned." Téta, of course, said she was absolutely gorgeous, but that was just Téta for you.

Joy was exasperated at the separate wedding parties for men and women. "I mean, come on!" she said. "Then how is it a wedding?" She was dating an Assyrian guy nowadays. "Dating" meant double-dating with her brother; her parents had strict boundaries, and Joy was really pretty straitlaced. Not that any of the Shelbys' careful standards mattered to Khadra's circle. The fact that Joy dated at all was enough to put her, in their view, on the slippery slope to promiscuity.

"So he's a Syrian guy?" Khadra'd said when Joy told her about him.

"No, not Syrian. *Assyrian.* It's an ethnic group in the Middle East—they've been around longer than Arabs, longer than anybody." Khadra didn't seem to think it possible that Joy could know something about the Middle East that Khadra didn't already know.

"I've never heard of them. Do they speak Arabic?"

"Yeah but they have their own language, Aramaic. It's, like, the mother tongue of Arabic and Hebrew."

"Well, if they speak Arabic, then they're Arabs."

"No," Joy had said, getting annoyed. "They are *not.* They don't want to be Arabs."

"Are they Muslim?"

"No. Christian."

Khadra had been taken aback.

Joy went on, "They were massacred by Muslims back around 1914. The Assyrians."

"Oh." Khadra's defenses had gone up. Without even knowing the story, she resisted it.

She was sitting in an ornamented chair on the bridal dais now, surrounded by bouquets, and Joy had come up through the throng of wedding guests to greet her.

"Smile," a little kid said, and Khadra and Joy looked up as a camera flashed. Someone had handed one of Aunt Fatma's kids a point-and-shoot and told them to take pictures. That's why all of Khadra's wedding photos showed people in the middle of a bite, their mouths misshapen, or Ebtehaj pointing with her arm stretched out toward something off-camera as she directed the flow of wedding cake.

After the banqueting was done, and several rounds of cake and tea had been served to the women, the Dawah Center front door opened to reveal the crowd of male wedding guests waiting outside, having "brought the groom to his doom," as they said, teasing him. They carried Juma on their shoulders, singing and clapping. Khadra caught a glimpse of him, his head tucked down, sneaking anxious looks into the hall. Behind him were Eyad and Hakim and eleven-year-old Jihad with his tie loose.

There were cries of "shut the door, we're not covered yet!" from the women. The newly "hijabed" little preteen girls, like Aunt Fatma's wild-haired daughter Sabriya, squealed the loudest about their hijab being violated. Eventually, the groom entered, to cheers on both sides of the door. The crowd of male guests outside began to thin as some of the women emerged and families, reunited, headed home.

Juma maneuvered his way up the dais crowded with flower arrangements to sit next to Khadra, marking the family part of the evening. He presented the wedding jewelry sent for her by his parents in a red velvet box. There were "oohs!" and "ahs!" at the appropriate moments. When Téta began belting out a Syrian folk song, "*Girl of my homeland, where are you going, so tender and true,*" Ebtehaj hurried away to the buffet table, no doubt to take care of some important logistical detail.

"Omigosh," Khadra whispered to Tayiba. "I've forgotten something important. Help." And she sent Tayiba to Hook's Drugs before they closed to pick up a refill of her birth control pills, which she'd been taking since her last period.

"Okay, but this is going to look weird." Tayiba smiled, patting her second trimester bulge. She and Danny Nabolsy, who'd married the year before, were expecting their first baby.

More pictures were posed for. And then they made their break. The couple, after a pit stop at Khadra's parents' place in the Fallen Timbers to change their clothes and collect their things, was dispatched in Juma's new black Mercury Capri to their honeymoon weekend. Tayiba pulled into the parking lot beside the Capri just in time and handed Khadra a little white paper sack from the drugstore.

"You're really adamant about that, aren't you?" Juma remarked, looking sideways at her in the car as she broke a pill off the little disk.

In the honeymoon suite, Juma took out a small stone mortar and a little goldfoil package, then unwrapped a nugget from the foil and lit it in the mortar. He tossed a little bit of something like bark on top of it.

"What is that, one of your funky Gulfie things?" Khadra said curiously.

"Aiwa," Juma said. Smoke wafted up from it: Sandalwood.

"Mmm," she said. They lay on top of the polyester bedspread, breathing deeply. He pulled her in to him and she nestled her head in the crook of his shoulder. Exhausted, they fell asleep that way.

And across the sands, from among its lavish gifts,
the Gulf scatters fuming froth and shells

—Badr Shakir al-Sayyab, "The Rain"

High up on a mezzanine in the Kuwait airport, behind a clear fiberglass partition, a great throng of men, women, and children stood waving energetically at Khadra and her husband. Juma waved back. His parents had flown the new couple to Kuwait for a second wedding reception.

"Who's all that?" Khadra said.

Juma shrugged. "Just a few of my relatives."

Khadra grinned. You knew you were an Arab if your ride from the airport was two dozen people.

She and her husband walked out of the air-conditioned airport and it was like stepping into a sauna. The very air was dripping

Married life was bliss. To have a friend always, a built-in friend. To pray fajr beside him in the dark misty dawn and then sleep beside him in your full-sized bed—your very own *man*. To watch him shape his beard and do unfamiliar manly things that bespoke a whole man-world different from the one inhabited by your father and brother. To be beautiful in the mirror of his eyes, a doorway into a whole woman-world for him. To lie in the curve of his body watching TV or falling asleep, his arm slung along your hips, making you feel very feminine and tender. At long last, finding the one place where you could soften like that, and not have to be hard and guarded and defensive and worried. And then to do even more interesting and absorbing things in the curve of his body, the bronze and the olive-colored limbs entwined, belly on belly.

It took her twice the work to get where he got with half the effort. It got easier as they got more experienced together.

"I had no idea it was that much work," Juma said, his hand cupped over her crotch afterward, as she lay breathing hard, her whole heart pounding under his hand. "Mine's like a—what do you call it, the no-brainer camera? A point-and-shoot."

Khadra laughed at that.

She fit the profile of the wife Juma always knew he'd have. An observant Muslim, of course, but also a modern, educated woman, not old-fashioned and boring. Khadra would fit right in with his family when he moved back—she would maybe have to adjust to some Kuwaiti customs, but his mother and sisters could help her learn. Her Arabic was not bad. And being married to a Syrian woman would give him cachet in Kuwaiti society. Plus, he was a breast man

sweat. The crowd of relatives descended upon them, exchanging hugs and welcomes. Besides his parents, there was Johar, the older sister who was a pediatrician, his younger sisters Fowz and Farida, cousins Muhammad, Big Ali, Osman, Omar, Bakr, and Little Ali and—well, assorted others, more than she could keep track of. The entire caliphate of Islam was there, she joked.

The Tashkenti family compound had a main house for the parents, a second house for a married son to live in with his family—that would be Juma and Khadra and their future children ("but we don't have to, we can go out and get a place of our own," Juma assured Khadra)—a guest cabin, servants' quarters, and an extra house in case any unmarried daughters needed to live there in the future. A poor relation of Juma's father had been living there for years; her name was Moza, and she was divorced, with four children.

The courtyard walls spilled over with bright pink bougainvillea. Bird-of-paradise plants were carefully tended and palm trees swayed, yes, Khadra thought, even if swaying palms is a cliché, by golly sway they did with the weight of their high bundles of ripe fruit. Khadra had never tasted fresh-picked balah, or early dates, and found them delicious. She'd never imagined dates could be as juicy as plums. "I did not mean to finish the whole bowl of balah in the refrigerator, forgive me, but they were so cold and so sweet."

Khadra's favorite in-law was Juma's grandfather. He was a leathery old man, small and spry, who spent most of his days at the docks. Family members spoke of him in a protective way that indicated he was a bit senile.

"He used to be a pearl diver," Juma's father said with a sigh, "before oil was discovered. He hates oil." In the fifties, the grandfather had fought—uselessly—the changes the petrol industry wrought in his country. They'd rendered a man with his skills defunct.

The old man refused to sleep in his luxury suite. His preferred space was a tent at the back of the compound with a payload of sand in front of it. The camp was equipped with a campfire and tin cooking gear. Khadra sat out there with him one evening and ate his coal-blackened fish.

"Bless your heart," Juma's mother said when she came in. Her own daughters dodged grandpa-sitting duties as often as they could.

"We hate roughing it," Fowz said. "Mosquitos!"

"We prefer shopping!" her sister added.

Kuwait City was mall after high-rise mall of shopping with Fowz and Farida. Because of Free Trade zone agreements that made the place a capitalist's heaven—and a hell for workers' rights, Khadra knew Joy would've pointed out—the shopping centers overspilled with stuff you never saw in America, the latest appliance brands from Europe and Japan and China, a dizzying smorgasbord. Khadra was uncomfortable with her sisters-in-law's level of spending and felt terrible about the modest amount of it she herself did. That seemed to be what you did in Kuwait: you shopped and shopped.

"What you can't carry, we'll stock in your house," her mother-in-law said.

Khadra realized with a start that she was referring to the house in the family compound that would be Juma's when he returned. *"Ours,* when *we* return," she mentally corrected herself. But she couldn't see herself there.

Any insect that undergoes a complete metamorphosis has several different life stories, ones that describe how it lives in its immature, larval forms, what goes on in its pupal transformation—if it has one—and how it behaves as a mature sexual adult.

—Sue Hubbell, *Broadsides from the Other Orders*

Back in the Tulip Tree apartment tower in Bloomingon, it was too much fun to have a little place of your own with your own little set of pots and pans in a teeny-tiny kitchen. Your own little dinette where you could entertain. With its own dimmer switch on the cute mini-chandelier so you could create "mood." And your own mirrored dresser where you could set up your own jewelry boxes and curvy-curly perfume bottles, and, and, and, your little *things*. To be a married woman of your very own, on equal terms with married women and other real people—in the community, only married people had prime status.

and he could tell from the first time he saw her that she was not flat, even under those boxy jilbabs of hers. He was not disappointed.

"Juma" meant "Friday" in Arabic so Khadra called him "my man Friday," but he didn't get the *Robinson Crusoe* reference. His bookshelf had only engineering manuals and a Quran. And one slim volume of Nabatean poetry because, as he put it, "You can't be an Arab without poetry."

She made him read the Defoe novel. "So what do you think?" she asked, lying on her back on the grass at Brown County State Park.

"His work ethic is very Islamic," Juma said. He was stretched out beside her. A butterfly flittered around the mat, lighting for a moment on his shoulder. It had jaggedy, angular wings.

"A question mark!" she exclaimed.

"What?" Juma pulled himself up on his elbows. The butterfly flew off.

"That butterfly, it's called a question mark. See the cut of its wings?"

They watched it flirt with a ruffle of leaves on a tree branch then float away.

"If you were stranded on a desert island and could only have three items, what would they be?"

"Aw, Khadra. I hate games like this." Juma heard a rustling on the trail that cut around their picnic area and he started to sit up, but relaxed when what surfaced was two American hikers, a guy and a girl in khaki shorts and tank tops.

"What would your three things be?"

He sighed. "A Quran."

"I knew you were going to say that. A Quran and your engineering manual, right?" Khadra snickered.

"You don't want me to bring a Quran? You wouldn't take a Quran?"

"My Quran is in here," she said with a self-satisfied tap on her chest. "I don't need paper and leather. When you memorize it, you own it."

"You're not a hafiza."

"I know. But I've got enough to go on for a few years on a desert island."

"In there, huh." He put his hand on her breast, fondling it through her sweater.

She smacked it lightly away.

"You know, for a Syrian girl, you're not very adventurous," he muttered.

"What the heck is that supposed to mean?" They'd been conversing in Arabic, but she said that in English.

"Nothing." He replied in Arabic.

"No, what is it supposed to mean?"

"Nothing! And sit up! Someone's coming." It was Arab guys this time, people he knew. That meant she had to change her unladylike sprawl to more suitable body posture.

Khadra frowned, but he didn't notice.

One thing her friend Joy found bizarre was Khadra's belief in a woman's right to abortion.

"Wait—you're supposed to be the religious nut in this picture," Joy said. They were biking to the library on a nippy autumn day. The trees that lined the quads of white limestone were offering their last blazes of red and orange turning to rust and brown.

"Yeah, well, Islamic law allows abortion up to four months," Khadra called out, pedaling harder to keep up with Joy. Passersby looked up at the word *abortion,* their faces reflecting the strong and various emotions it stirred. "All the schools of thought allow it. The only thing they differ on is how long it's allowed. Four weeks to four months. That's the range."

"But—but only in case of rape or health reasons, right?" Joy pleaded, slowing down for Khadra.

"No, not just for emergency reasons, actually. Like, al-Ghazali says you can do it if you don't care to lose your figure."

"Oh my God, no," Joy protested. Intellectually, she supported abortion rights, but something in her deeper than politics still found it horrifying.

"But only until the beginning of the fourth month," Khadra said.

"Why the fourth month?"

"That's when ensoulment happens."

"Ensoulment?" Joy called. Khadra had fallen behind again.

"The fetus—the fetus gets—the fetus gets the breath of life blown into it," Khadra panted. "At four—at one hundred and twenty days—four months."

"So you've got it all pinned down to the exact moment that the soul enters the body."

"You betcha."

"Because a whadyacallem, a hadith tells you so."

"You betcha." Green-veined orange leaves whirled up around her.

Joy pedaled away in frustration, crunching brown leaves under her bike tread.

* * *

In the months after the wedding, not a week went by when someone didn't ask Khadra if she was pregnant.

"Why not?" Aunt Fatma said in dismay, when Khadra explained that not only was she not pregnant, but she didn't plan to be just yet. "You're using prevention? Haram!"

"Oh, Fatma, you know it's not haram," Ebtehaj took her daughter's side.

"Well, but it can be harmful, I tell you," Aunt Fatma insisted. She was a little teapot, short and stout. "My aunt took the pills and do you know what?"—Aunt Fatma lowered her voice, her eyes widening—"they made her sterile. I hope you're not using the pills!" She pulled Khadra close and whispered, "The West sends the pills to Egypt and the other Muslim lands to make us all sterile!"

Khadra wished she had never divulged her plans.

Ebtehaj stepped in. "Stop making her worry. When did your aunt take the pills, in the sixties? Horse pills! Big dosages—they tried them out on poor Third World women before deciding what was safe."

"I'm telling you, God doesn't like you trying to prevent life," Fatma pressed. "I'll admit, Abdulla and I tried it once."

Khadra stage-gasped.

"And *that's* when God sent us the twins!" Aunt Fatma blurted.

"Still," her mother told her at home, "you can have babies and finish college too. You can do it all. Look at me: I did."

And her father said, "You have a stable home, and your husband's not poor, even if he is a student. What are you waiting for? Yes, birth control is allowed in shariah, but not indefinitely," he said gravely.

"Maybe you should have just one," Aunt Trish offered. "One, then wait." Her son, Danny, and his wife, Tayiba, had started out with the resolve to postpone children too, but it hadn't taken them long to produce a lovely little granddaughter for her, after all.

Juma's mother, on the weekly phone call from Kuwait, concurred. "Have just one," she cajoled. "At least then you'll know you're able to have them.

What Juma heard was: "Real men don't use condoms," and "I hear spermicide can make you impotent."

"Not impotent, dummy, sterile."

"Bad enough, either way!"

"What's wrong?" Juma asked, when Khadra slid out of his embrace one evening.

"I can't," she said, staring at the ceiling. "It's like they're all here in bed with us, going 'Have babies! Do it, do it!'"

Things came up in their marriage. Little things at first. Like Khadra's bike.

"Where are you going?" Juma said. Khadra threw her leg across the seat. She'd biked to class a couple of times since they'd been married, but he hadn't noticed. Or perhaps he had, but hadn't said anything.

"To Kroger for milk." She'd added a wire basket to the front handlebars. It was all tricked out for cute newlywed couple grocery shopping.

"But—" he looked puzzled. She was an Arab girl, familiar with Arab customs. He hadn't expected her to be doing things that would embarrass him. If he'd wanted to have to explain every limit of proper behavior, he'd have married an American. "But someone might see you."

"Of course someone might see me, honey. It's not a secret or anything."

"No, I mean one of the Arab guys. Please don't do it. Don't do it," he begged. Plus, he leaned in and whispered that he'd make it worth her while to stay home. She felt a tingling where the bicycle seat pressed between her legs. They stayed in all afternoon and didn't even miss the milk and groceries that earlier had seemed so urgently needed.

The same scene was repeated the next week. "It's unIslamic. It displays your body," he objected.

But it was hard for Khadra to resist a bike on a fine spring day.

"Say to the believing women that they should lower their gaze and guard their modesty, that they should not display their beauty and ornaments," he quoted. And this time he didn't throw in any fringe benefits.

The next time they argued over the bike, Juma took a different approach. "You look ridiculous," he told her flatly. "It's idiotic, riding a bicycle in hijab. You look totally stupid and clumsy and clownlike."

Khadra stared at him dully.

It didn't help when her husband moved on to another tactic. One that he thought would be particularly effective with her, as religious as she was.

"Have you examined yourself on this, Khadra, really examined your ego?" he asked. "Is this willfulness of yours pleasing to God?

Or are you following your desires and seeking the pleasures of this world in defiance of God's rulings."

But it wasn't God's rulings. It was just his own sensibilities, the way he'd been raised in Kuwait. So why was he bringing God into it?

She laid a copy of the Quran in front him—their wedding mushaf with the indigo and gilt Moroccan binding, the one they always read from together. "Show me where in the Quran it says women can't ride bikes in public."

"It's not that simple. You know Islamic law is not that simple. And custom is important. Custom is recognized by the Law." His tone was hostile.

Khadra remembered a line from one of Hakim's khutbas, which were circulating on audiocassette and becoming popular already, and he still a grad student at Harvard Divinity. "Show me a couple that reads Quran together and I'll show you a marriage that will never fail." Maybe things were not so cut-and-dried, Khadra thought.

Whenever she biked after that, Juma would get in his black car and roar off. Not tell her he was going. She, who had never spent a night alone in a house, would have to be by herself all weekend in their apartment, sour and crying and waking up with a jolt twenty times in the long darkness, imagining the clink of somebody breaking in. From his cousin's in Terre Haute, Juma would call her, but he only came back when he was ready.

She lay in bed thinking about Zuhura lying in her ditch. Unnamed worries gnawed the bottom of her belly. Turning over on her side, she stared absently at the jewelry box on her dresser. There, under a tangle of necklace chains, were the mysterious Osmanli coins, Téta's gift. What had she said when she gave them to her?

". . . because there may be days when you wake up and feel the future closing in on you, the horizon shrinking." It felt like that now.

Finally, Juma pulled rank. "I forbid you," he said, laying his hand on the bike seat. "As your husband, I forbid you."

Khadra recoiled. She couldn't believe he would out and out say that, even if it was Islamically valid. Her father never said things like that to her mother. It was alien to everything she felt and knew.

But eventually, she put the bike in the resident storage area of their building's basement. Such a little thing, a bike. In the overall picture of a marriage, what was a bike? The gears rusted and the tires lost air. Something inside her rusted a little, too.

Reason stutters famously here, unable to
dance nimbly in leaden clogs.

—Daniel Abdal-Hayy Moore

Khadra took an elective with the German Islamic studies professor, over Juma's protest that it was a waste of time and money. It started out as, "I'm going to sit in on her class to make sure she doesn't distort Islam in her teaching." But as the semester progressed, Khadra began to admit to herself that there were whole areas of Islam that all her Dawah Center upbringing and Masjid Salam weekend lessons hadn't begun to teach her. All the Islam she knew before, she'd looked at from the inside. In Professor Eschenbach's class, she began to see what her belief looked like if you stepped away and observed it from a distance.

"There are three different points of emphasis," Professor Eschenbach said on a shimmering ice-bright day after a snowstorm. Class had not been cancelled but few showed up. She peered at those stalwarts through thick glasses that magnified her eyes. "Those who stressed reason produced Islamic theology. Those who stressed Revelation and hadith produced jurisprudence—the great body of Islamic legal scholarship, or fiqh. Those who stressed seeking a direct personal relationship with God were the Sufis."

Khadra's hand shot up. "So the Sufis reject Revelation?"

"Certainly not," Professor Eschenbach said. "All three accept Revelation. *How* to read and follow it is the question."

"But the Sufis reject shariah, right?"

"That is incorrect."

"But you said—" Khadra looked down at her notes. "'Those who stress personal insight are the Sufis. Those who stress Revelation produce shariah.'"

Professor Eschenbach said, with a hint of reproach, "The Islamic view of shariah is that it is the Divine order of the cosmos. One cannot 'produce' it. It is there. An ideal. What Islamic scholars produce is fiqh. Jurisprudence. A human attempt to manifest the shariah in an evolving body of rulings. And Sufis don't reject it—they just look at it differently."

So the belief system of her parents and their entire circle, including the Dawah Center, was just one point on a whole spectrum of Islamic faith. It wasn't identical to Islam itself, just one little corner of it. What was difficult to accept was that these other paths had always existed beyond the confines of her world, and yet were still Muslim. This Khadra resisted. Heroically resisted.

Particularly all that flaky Rumi business. "No," she said, when the professor showed a film of people in white dresses twirling in circles. "That's ridiculous. I've never heard of that. Dancing is *not* Islam."

"They call it 'turning,'" Professor Eschenbach said serenely. "'Wherever you turn, there is the Face of God,' is the verse they look to in the Quran. Now then," she went on, "from today's reading, people: What are some of the other methods practiced by those seeking to develop personal knowledge of God?"

Tentative hands went up: "Retreat. Spiritual retreat."

"Is it—*dhikr?* Where the person says the name of God a number of times, like a mantra?"

"Concerts, like, um, *sema* ceremonies."

Mantras, concerts, ceremonies other than regular prayer? Khadra checked up on all this bizarre business with Uncle Kuldip.

"Beti, the only way to know God is to obey his Law," he assured her. "But Westerners are obsessed with figures who went outside this way, such as Rumi. Rumi, Hallaj, Ibn al-Arabi—who was a pantheist, be careful. That goes against monotheism," he said to Khadra over his desk. "Westerners like to focus on the heretics and deviants in Islam." Behind him, shelves were lined to the ceiling with books. Maulana Nadvi's *Tafsir*, *Politics and the Islamic State, Fatima is Fatima* by Ali Shariati, Muhammad Iqbal, *The Caravan's Call.*

"Was he a heretic, then? Rumi?"

"Borderline," Uncle Kuldip said. "You see, Westerners are fascinated with Sufism because they cannot stomach the activist Islam that seeks to redress injustices committed against Muslim lands. You find endless Orientalist studies of the crazy heretic Hallaj, for example, who is completely useless and empty, while the real achievements of Islam are ignored."

There were moments during Professor Eschenbach's class in which Khadra felt as if she were standing atop two earth plates grinding as they moved in different directions. The one directly under her was the view of Islam she'd grown up knowing. The other was what she was catching glimpses of. A rift occasionally opened beneath her feet, but she steadied herself against it. Otherwise, suddenly, what she'd always thought was right appeared wrong, and what she'd always known was bad seemed, for an eye-blink moment, good. It was terrifying.

Community life was bracing. There was no dearth of henna parties, baby *aqiqas,* and "Building God-Consciousness" seminars. And, of course, there was activism. Social justice, to right wrongs, to alleviate the condition of the wretched of the earth, these shining projects stretched before her, so she didn't have to think about the rift within her self.

"Faith is work, not obscure metaphysics," the CMC speaker said. He was there "to counter Sufistic myths," the flyer advertised—and he was none other than the Dawah Center's Wajdy Shamy, Khadra's own father. True, his degree was in business management, but he was very well read in Islam, not to mention his life experience with Islamic work. "Faith requires political, social, and economic actualization," he explained. These in turn require the implementation of shariah, which requires the establishment of an Islamic state—which has been absent since the collapse of the Ottoman Caliphate in 1924. Thus, the way to truly manifest faith was to support the Islamic movements in the struggle to reconstitute a rightly guided caliphate, or if that was out of reach, to form Islamic nation-states in as many Muslim lands as possible. In a kuffar land, it meant developing ways to help Muslims live by shariah while being good citizens.

"It is service," Wajdy said. "Others may see it as politicizing religion, but we see Islamic activisim simply as service. Service of humanity, to please God."

Professor Eschenbach turned the attention of the class to an Ibn al-Arabi text on the levels of the self. "Chittock's analysis suggests that the move from the lower ego to the self-examining ego can be a traumatic one," she began. "But that is a first step toward cultivating the higher-ego soul, the 'soul at peace' referred to in *Sura*—"

Khadra raised her hand. "Isn't all this attention to the self selfish? Isn't it just a lot of Western individualism? Islam is focusing on God, not ourselves." She tucked a few stray hairs under her cotton scarf.

"Have you ever heard the saying, He who knows himself, knows his Lord?"

Khadra shook her head. "Who said that, Plato? Descartes?"

"The Prophet," Professor Eschenbach said.

Was this the right farmhouse? The black Capri with Juma's glass-bead *tasbeeha* hanging from the rearview mirror crunched up the ice-crusted driveway. She'd persuaded Juma to let her drive it rather than the Gremlin because she needed the extra power over the ice-patched road. "Can you imagine if I suddenly came face to face with a deer in my headlights? In the Gremlin, we'd both be dead." Driving out of town, alone, in the darkness of night was something Khadra Shamy would rather have avoided altogether. But Juma was busy and so was Eyad; no one had time to come with her during crazy finals week. Her term paper was late and Dr. Eschenbach had granted her the extension on the condition that she deliver it to her home out here in Nashville. Not even Nashville, but turn right after the head shop on the corner and find the rural route and venture out into the snow-thickened rolling farmlands. Out into the John Cougar Mellencamp back roads. And she'd meant to come in the daylight but the typewriter ribbon jammed—of course, it would—at the last minute and it took her forever to install new ribbon and finish typing the darn thing.

If the farmhouse at the end of the gravel drive wasn't Professor Eschenbach's house, Khadra would "have some 'splaining to do" to some irate Hoosier farmer on this dark cold night in December. Not a comforting prospect. *I seek refuge in the Merciful, and ah distinctly, I remember, it was in the bleak December.* Khadra found herself reciting Poe along with prayer as she picked a path over the uneven gravel. The night seemed Poe-ish.

The house was unlit. This made Khadra doubt. When she got closer, she saw that there was a faint light flickering. Closer, it revealed itself to be a lantern in a niche of the porch ledge, giving off a soft glow.

She was late, too late. Professor Eschenbach must have gone out. Maybe she was away on one of her conference trips. Should she leave the paper on the porch? As if in answer, snowflakes began to fall, tiny at first, then fluffier. Khadra looked around the porch for some safe dry spot to leave the manila envelope. She heard a sound, *hoo-hoo-hoo*—an owl? No, it was voices in unison, as of a choir—so the radio was on, or a record—and so the professor must be home.

No doorbell in sight. She opened the screen door gingerly and tried the knocker. No answer. Twice, no answer. The music—of course. The knock wouldn't be heard over the music.

Irresolute, Khadra decided to tap on the living room picture window—but not to peer in or violate the privacy of the house. No answer on the glass, either. Unable to resist a peek, she peered through the pane—and drew back quickly, frightened—the shadowy figure of a hooded person was standing across the room looking right back at her. Oh! it was just a mirror. A mirror on a mantle and Khadra inside it, her paisley wool scarf, her big parka hood over it, everything the same, only murkier.

Back on the front porch, she paused, then tried the doorknob. It opened. Quietly, feeling like a trespasser, she laid the manila envelope atop a stack of papers on a hall table. A little poem hanging on the wall over the table caught her eye, even though she was anxious to slip out quickly:

His Scales of Mercy
love the beautiful
weight of sin

The beautiful weight of sin? That was crazy. What the Sam Hill did that mean?

She was halfway back to the car when another doubt hit her. What if Professor Eschenbach overlooked the paper? She'd call her as soon as she got home to tell her where it was. But wouldn't it be too late then? Or she could turn around while she was still here, and try again to make contact, not give up. She ought to thank her in person for the extension and apologize for slipping into her house without permission to lay the paper down—yes, that was definitely more courteous.

Maybe try knocking on the back door, then? *Enter houses from the front,* the Quran admonished, *seeking permission.* But she wasn't going to enter, was she?

As she tramped around the house toward the back porch, she saw light thrown from a casement window low to the ground. The music seemed to be coming from there. Deep powerful drumming, like an army marching, *Ba-boom, ba-boom, ba-boom!*

God, this is so surreal. The thick gray sky above, the snow falling into my eyes and mouth, me out in the boonies in the dark. What am I doing here? Go home, Khadra.

She stooped at the window, but stayed behind a juniper, unsure if she wanted to be seen. If she caught sight of the professor, she'd—what? Point to the front door and quickly meet her there and apologize for this. Apologize profusely for the intrusion.

Ba-boom, ba-boom, ba-boom! It wasn't a recording—it was live. The lit basement was full of people. Five, ten, more. She could see the tops of heads, men, women, scarves, hair, caps, braids, locks. How odd! They were swaying in time to the rhythm of words weirdly familiar: *All-lahh, All-ahh, All-lahh, All-ahh,* went the chorus. *Ba-boom, ba-boom, ba-boom, ba-boom,* beat the drums.

Then a solo—soprano—in perfect Arabic began: *La ilaha illa allah, laa* . . . and continued in some other language while the chorus went on with *All-lahh, All-ahh* like an undertow.

She didn't know the language but could pick out words: *rahma, rahman, ya ibni Adam*. And then a whole Quranic verse: *And He is with you wherever you Be*. Then the chanting changed and the pace speeded up: *Hey, hey, hey, hey, hey* . . . and then Khadra realized: not "*hey*" but "*Hayy*—Alive."

Was that Professor Eschenbach, her head wrapped in a white prayer scarf like the one folded into the prayer rug at home? The clashing earth plates shifted under Khadra. She steadied herself with one hand against the siding of the house. *Hayy, Hayy, Hayy, Hayy, Hayy*—the chorus was getting hoarse, you could pick out the raspier voices, pushing themselves to the last chord, harder, faster, *Hayy, Hayy, Hayy* the solo no longer separate *Hayy! Hayy! Hayy! Hayy! Hayy!* choppier now *Hayy!* and swifter *Hayy!* swifter the swaying *Hayy! Hayy! Hayy! Hayy! HAYY!* like a SHOUT from the EARTH right under her FEET—Khadra jumped and fell backward into the snow by the juniper.

She fled home, the car wheels slipping and sliding on the country road. Home. Bed. Edgar Allen Poe dreams, a brick cavity inside a house. A niche, a manger. Snow, a green branch in the white. Brick by brick. Mantle. Dismantle. A lamp in the niche, walled up. Oil lamp, yes, or maybe child. Flailing. Flail whale belly of a wail. She would pluck the child out of the wall and save the one who was "Alive." Tracks in the snow like a gazelle. Hold the lamp up high—run! Smoke and mirrors, a monster on the other side. But the child. Let the child be walled or pluck the child out? Smoke and mirrors, snow angels falling landing softly. Lamp child juniper: all evergreen.

I came to see the damage that was done
and the treasures that prevail

—Adrienne Rich, "Diving into the Wreck"

"What's for dinner?" Juma asked. The first time it was cute. Then it got annoying. Finally it made steam come out of Khadra's ears. Like when she'd spent so many hours working on her Western Civ paper that she didn't even know what time it was, what day. She'd left out two whole paragraphs at the beginning of the essay and was frustratedly retyping all eight pages. Then Juma came in, to the papers and books strewn all around, the pencil in her hair, and the wild-eyed look with which she was regarding the blank page in the electric typewriter. "What's for dinner?"

"I don't know. Why're you asking me? Like I'm the one who's supposed to know?" Khadra groused.

"Well, uh," Juma looked around, "let's see: who's the wife in this picture?" Was he trying to be funny? Khadra wasn't sure.

"The Prophet never asked his wives to do anything in the house for him," Khadra snapped. What was the use? It took a Dawah Center man to appreciate that sort of thing. A reg'lar Muslim from the Old Country like Juma wouldn't get it. Seeking knowledge was more important than traditional feminine tasks. She resented the Dawah Center for raising her with false expectations about typical religious Muslims.

"The Prophet wasn't a graduate student. He wasn't studying engineering," Juma retorted.

"Well, I have work-study on top of classes. You don't." Her voice was getting shrill, but she didn't care.

"I'm not a woman—I don't know HOW to cook!" Juma shouted.

"Well, it didn't come with my BOOBS!" Khadra shouted back. "You can LEARN it! Here, I'll show you!" She stomped into the kitchen and slammed an aluminum pan on the counter. She flung open the freezer door, grabbed a package of chicken, and threw it—whole, still wrapped—down in the pan. "Put chicken in pan. Put pan in oven. It's that simple. Okay? Now LEAVE me ALONE!"

Every time she went out in a campus demonstration, Juma complained.

"Does it have you be you?" he asked. "Let somebody else demonstrate. There's no shortage of people. Does it have to be my wife?"

At one rally, he stepped right in front of her. Jim from Student Government had come up to Khadra at a brisk clip, holding a wooden sign upside down.

"Hey, Khadra—it's Khadra, right? I was going to ask if you—" and then Juma stepped between them, putting his wife behind him and facing Jim.

"Excuse me—" Khadra said over Juma's shoulder, standing on tiptoe. She stepped sideways out from behind him. "Excuse me, Juma, I was talking to Jim."

"What did you do that for?" she said that evening, in a fight-picking tone, right after they salam'd from praying *isha*.

"What did he want with you?" Juma demanded. A man rushing up to his wife carrying a stick—of *course* he'd reacted.

"He wanted me to circulate the petition to the Muslim women. We'd talked about it at the planning meeting." Khadra was CMC recording secretary this year. "Anyway, it's none of your business what he wanted—he wanted to speak to *me,* not you."

"It's *always* my business what anyone wants from you," Juma shouted. "What the hell do you mean, none of my business? You're my *wife*."

He went to Terre Haute again. This time he stayed away five whole days.

"I just—I don't know if I can stay married to him, Eyad. I feel like I can't go on in this marriage without killing off the 'me' that I am," Khadra said to her brother.

Pop psychology phrases like "the 'me' that I am" turned Eyad off. "Do you really want to be a twenty-one-year-old divorcée?" he asked. He picked up the big orange snow shovel his sister had propped against the back bumper and started clearing tracks in front of her tires. They were in the parking lot outside her apartment.

"What kind of a thing is that to say?" Khadra said, her voice on the edge of tears. As if it didn't scare her to death. Twenty-one years old and already a failure at one of the biggest things in life. Puffs of frosty air accompanied each of her words.

"Maybe you're being selfish," he said. His eyes had dark circles under them from the stresses of med school. "Divorce is supposed to be a last recourse. Not what you do because you want to ride a bike to class."

He knew about the bike thing. Khadra resented him using it like that. She chipped hard at the solid chunk of ice on the windshield for a while. "I don't think I can stay with Juma without changing who I am. Who I essentially deep-down am."

"Is that so bad? Doesn't everyone change along the way?"

She really didn't know. She prayed an *istikhara* on it, a Consultation Prayer. But she still didn't understand whether Eyad was right or not.

Juma reached the end of his degree. He couldn't extend his visa.

"What about me?" Khadra said. "I've got one year to go." They were driving to Indianapolis.

"You can finish at the University of Kuwait," he said. "It's nice. Really."

"You could apply for U.S. citizenship. You're married to a citizen. They'll let you stay."

"I don't need American citizenship. I'm Kuwaiti, not Palestinian. I don't have a problem getting around with my passport."

"Or—what if—we could live apart for a year. It'd just be one year. You could go on to Kuwait, and I could stay on my own."

Juma laughed. "You're joking, right? Leave my wife in America?"

He swerved to avoid roadkill—a skunk. Its smell invaded the car. Khadra's stomach lurched. She felt queasy all that evening, and the next day too.

Khadra imagined life in Kuwait. Glitzy glass buildings and lots of shopping, and a fairly luxurious standard of living, but there were hidden costs. Was this what marriage amounted to, compromise after compromise, until you'd frittered away all the jewels in your red box? She woke up one morning and felt as if the future were closing in, the horizon shrinking smaller around her. She threw up.

The throwing up didn't go away. It bothered her all week. Then her period was late, and a panicky knot formed in her stomach.

"I can't have a baby now," she whispered to the nurse at the student clinic, sitting on the examination table in shock after the doctor had just told her. Her face was sallow, her eyes puffy. She had never known anything more clearly or more urgently. "I can't."

"You're going to have children sooner or later," Ebtehaj launched at her. "In two or three years, or now, what's the difference?"

"Your life is not in danger," her father said, beginning this line of argument for the fourth time that evening.

Khadra put a sofa pillow on her face to block out the attacks.

"My life *is* in danger," she said to the golden-eyed lacewings in the entomology lab. She stared at one on a twig, about half an inch long, with four pale green wings, antenna the length again of its body, and bulging shiny eyes. It remained motionless, except for the careful survey of its antennae. Khadra dropped right there and prayed another Consultation Prayer on the gritty floor of the specimen room.

She'd really thought her parents would support her, after she told them how much Consultation she'd prayed on the decision. That's why she told them, expecting them to support her against Juma, help him see why this was okay for her to do. Why it was not haram. What about all those teachings where abortion was allowed in shariah? One hundred and twenty days, and all that. It turned out that nothing she'd read described the real Muslim gut reaction to the question of abortion. Imam Ghazali could have an abortion, maybe, but she, Khadra, could not.

Tayiba came over, with her baby girl Nia on her hip. She was, in Ebtehaj and Wajdy's eyes, a voice of reason from Khadra's generation. She was a part-time student, wife, mother, and mosque volunteer.

"It's not so bad? That's what you're here to tell me?" Khadra said. "Be the Muslim Superwoman?" Like Zuhura, she could have added, but didn't.

"Don't put words in my mouth," Tayiba said sharply. "I never said be Superwoman. I never said it was easy." Zuhura's shadow loomed over both of them. Zuhura the martyr.

Khadra's father said, "My mother died having me. They told her it was risky, but she went ahead and had me." He paused. He seemed to lose his train of thought. "She died having me. A woman who dies in childbirth is considered a martyr—goes straight to heaven."

"Well, I don't want to die in childbirth," Khadra said sarcastically.

"I'm not suggesting you do so," he said quietly. "I'm saying, my mother sacrificed everything for a child. Sacrificed her own self."

"Well, I am *not* your mother," Khadra shot back. "I don't want to be your mother."

"I didn't raise you to speak to me in that tone," he snapped, as he rarely ever did.

Yeah, you did, Khadra thought sullenly. You raised me to go out and learn, but deep down you still want me to be just like your mother. So where did you think all these contradictions would lead me if not to this frustration, this tone of voice? But I am not going to kill myself to fit into the life you have all mapped out for me.

The medicine for heart's pain is the death of your tarnished soul

—only this:

the homeopathic cure: a bit of poison

—Attar

Khadra puked a trail to the toilet. It was taking her over, gnawing out her insides, the clot. The bloodclot that glommed to the wall of her womb. The zygote. It was not a fetus yet. Not even an embryo. It certainly was not a baby. It was a growth, invading her body, reaching out its tentacles, even up her throat. It was a possibility, one she could not entertain. It would lock her into a life, a very specific kind of life with Juma, that she was no longer certain she wanted. She knelt on the tiles with a wet rag mopping up the vomit. Seven times, once with Ajax powder.

No. She had been here too many times, kneeling, her face low to the floor, taking dust mites up her raw nose. Hands coarse with scouring powder, scrubbing the filth of two worlds. Scrubbing away some taint she could never escape.

No, enough, no. Her back was up against the wall, the bathroom small, mewing her in. She beat the floor with the Ajax canister over and over with the force of her will, no no no, no no no no, scattering the powder seven times. Where was it, this will of hers, this misshapen self? She needed to know it. *Hello, self. Can we meet at last?* It was not vain-glorious to have a self. It was not the same as selfish individualism, no. You have to have a self to even start on a journey to God. To cultivate your *nafs* whom God invites to enter the Garden at the end of *Surat al-Fajr*. She had not taken even a baby step in that direction. Her self was a meager thing, scuttling behind a toilet, what she hadn't given over of it to Mama, to Juma. Too much, she has given away too much. She will not give the last inches of her body, will not let them fill her up with a life she does not want. Feral, it was not a word but a spasm, the snarl of a fanged thing gnawing at a trap: no. No, no, no, no, no, *no*.

Juma's face looked like it was going to break, just get cracks all over it and crumble. She told him she had prayed Consultation on it three times and was set and determined. And that if it meant divorce, so be it. He went away. Got in the car and screeched away. Went deep into the cave where wounded men go when they walk around not talking to anyone about what's happening to them on the inside. Otherwise known as Terre Haute.

Khadra steeled herself not to worry about Juma. Or the hurt she saw in his face before the shutter went down over his feelings. "He'll go home to Kuwait and his mommy and daddy will find him someone else to marry in a snap. He'll have a zillion kids and live in that family compound and be happy ever after."

Her regular doctor wouldn't perform the abortion. He'd been the one who prescribed the antibiotic when Khadra had strep, but forgot to tell her that antibiotics mess with the effectiveness of the birth control pill. No, he wouldn't do it. Neither would anyone else at the campus clinic, so Khadra had to find one in Indianapolis.

"Why did you come with me?" she asked Joy. Her parents had refused. Eyad, too. "I'm not going to be a party to something I think is *munkar,"* he said.

It was a cold Indiana day in late autumn, when the vibrant foliage was gone, and everything so bare and hopeless that it was hard to believe the world might ever bloom again. Joy had waited out in the hallway reading an Amanda Cross mystery and, when summoned, sat next to Khadra's upholstered recliner in the recovery lounge. Now she was driving her home through the wintry sleet. Home to the broken nest. "You're horrified by abortion, Joy. Even if you're pro-choice. You're the most horrified by abortion pro-choice person I know. So why'd you come?"

"I'm your friend. Friends don't drop you when you do something they disapprove."

Corny Hoosier Joy. Is that what friends did? I wouldn't know, Khadra thought. I've never been a real friend, or had one. I've demanded that my friends conform to what I approve and disapprove. She leaned back in the bucket seat and closed her eyes. "You're a beautiful friend, Joy. You're a teacher of friendship."

"Aw, that's your meds talking," Joy said. She had this exaggerated idea about abortions, like Khadra must be on morphine or something, when all they'd given her was was a little pain reliever.

"Do you know what entomologists call the body of the bug in its different stages of life?" Khadra said. "An instar. Like, they'll go, 'here is the nymph instar of the nine-spotted ladybug' or 'the pupal instar of a blackfly has spiral gills.'"

"I have no idea what you're talking about," Joy said, keeping her eyes on the road.

"Know what they call the adult instar—the mature bug?"

"What?"

"An 'imagine.' Yeah. Like, you and I are the 'imagines' of the human species."

Joy concentrated on getting her home. She was leaving for an ecology internship in New Zealand as soon as the semester was over.

"Joy? Do you think God will punish me by not letting me have babies later, when I want them?" That's what Eyad had said, in his last angry conversation with her before the procedure. Now why did he have to say a thing like that? She needed someone to have her back. *I'm holding out for a hero.*

"God is not such an asshole," Joy said. After a while she added, *"alhamdulilah."*

Khadra had some cramping and bleeding like a heavy period. Not really any more than she usually got. Some lower-back pain the day after she lugged around a chem textbook, her Trapper Keeper, and *The Arab-Israeli Dilemma* in her backpack. Skipped a day of classes but only that one. She had to get through the semester. Just get through.

Her parents would not speak to her. Their throats knotted, and the silence on their end of the phone grew, and they did not come to Khadra. She awoke in the apartment the third night and thought she felt her mother's hand smooth back her hair, stroke her damp forehead. It felt like the old days in Square One. Khadra almost cried. No one was there. She steeled herself. Just get through.

Everyone was talking about her. She felt their whispers feather around her. (Was this how Hanifa had felt?) Was there anyone in the community her parents hadn't told? She felt sure Eyad or Tayiba had told all her old friends and that the awkward glances she was getting on campus from the girls in hijab and the beardy boys were not coincidental. Dawah Center poster girl had fallen.

She offered Juma a *khulu'*, or wife-initiated divorce. That way he wouldn't have to pay her the deferred part of the mahr, the rest of the eight thousand dollars. These were due to her if he initiated divorce. She was well versed on khulu', thanks to Dawah Center seminars. Popular Islam mostly buried khulu', and Muslim women the world over did not know they had this right. Modern Islamists such as the Dawah folk, however, revived many concepts from classical Islam and this was one of them.

Juma's pride was deeply offended by khulu'. *She,* repudiate *him?* He'd never even heard of it. Was Khadra making it up? No matter how many courses with sheikhs she may have taken, she was just a girl in Juma's eyes, a girl who'd grown up in America, to boot, and so couldn't possibly be trusted when it came to shariah matters.

Khadra didn't insist on khulu'. She was relieved, actually. She would have had to sell Téta's Ottoman coins and whatever else she owned to pay him back the front-mahr. And she didn't know what she would have done suddenly to support herself. Eyad was the one who'd worked since high school; other than the entomology lab, she'd never had a job. She wasn't going to ask her parents for money, even if she thought they had it to spare, which she knew they didn't.

It didn't seem fair to take all the after-mahr, since she'd been the one who wanted out. She took only enough to pay the rent and bills. She gave Juma back the wedding gold in its red velvet box.

Just as Khadra's marriage was going through its final twitches, Eyad announced his own intention to find a wife. "I know, I know, I have a few more years of school and residency left. But I'd like to complete half my religion," he said to his parents. "Temptation is everywhere," he complained separately to his father. But he didn't have to, since Wajdy remembered from his college days in Square One what the unmarried brothers went through, being around Americans who had no self-restraint.

Eyad's mother got on the case—a joyful project, but one that required care and circumspection and good planning. She excelled at these. She had contacts in Muslim communities all over the U.S. and Canada and, once a list was compiled, Eyad winnowed it down. They then paid each of the shortlisted girls a visit. This involved road trips to Detroit, Windsor, and Cincinnati over the next few months. In the end, the girl who was the one was right there in Indianapolis, or in the northern suburb of Carmel, anyway.

Omayma Hayyan was the daughter of an Iraqi colon specialist. She was slender, pretty, and expensive. She had wide green eyes, fair skin, a petite nose, and strawberry blonde hair under her exquisite scarves. She shopped at L. S. Ayres and the big malls, not Kmart and Sears, and somehow found ingredients from the racks of high-end lines such as Liz Claiborne and Laura Ashley to put together hijab outfits that set new heights in Islamic fashion. Had a prep school education and went to Butler, drove to classes in a shiny white TransAm, an Eid gift from her doting father and mother. Bought new, of course. Her vanity plates said "WWPMD," which stood for What Would Prophet Muhammad Do?

What was not to like? Eyad was smitten. His brow knotted at the possibility of his sister and her bad choices ruining his outlook with Omayma and the Hayyans. "You just keep a lid on it, Khadra, that's all I'm saying," he said to Khadra at the door of her apartment one afternoon. He was dropping off Jihad to spend a weekend in Bloomington with her. Her little brother came with his Atari box and Pac-Man cartridge, oblivious.

"I'm not advertising it, if that's what you mean, you *jerk,*" Khadra said, quickly converting hurt to anger. "And my recovery is going well, thank you very much for asking. I hate you."

If you go one night
to the mosque,
be sure
you walk with
bright torches
so everyone will note
your piety

—Sanai

Eyad and Omayma's wedding was held in the Indianapolis Marriott, not some apartment complex lounge. Homey little weddings were not for Omayma's social set. Her father trained the hotel staff to understand the separation of the sexes, with the men in one banquet room and the women in another. Waiters matched the gender of the room they were serving. They didn't mind; Dr. Hayyan tipped them well.

When they returned from their honeymoon, Eyad and Omayma set up house in a new garden-apartment complex near Butler, where she was still working on her degree. Eyad commuted.

Khadra's new sister-in-law may have had sequins trimming the edges of her expensive scarves, but she was no less committed to Islam than the Dawah community. "Have you ever heard Dr. Allam speak?" Omayma asked Khadra. "I went to one of his lectures in Paris."

"No. Who's he?" Khadra said, eating another leftover wedding cannoli from a crystal dish on the coffee table. They were in Eyad and Omayma's apartment, in which every stick of furniture was newly purchased. At retail. It wasn't just her sister-in-law, it was Eyad—he seemed to have developed the immigrant child's craving for gleaming new things, after a lifetime on threadbare secondhand couches.

"He's amazing," Omayma went on. Her eyes widened. "He's, like, this religious scholar from Egypt. Oh my God, when he lectured—it was so intense. He turned off all the lights in the auditorium and then he goes, if I were the Angel of Death—if I were Azrael, come to take your lives, right now, how would you meet your Lord? Like, have you lived Islamically, and have you done good, or like, have you wasted your time on earth? And he, like, thundered. I got chills. I am so serious." She wiggled her toes for emphasis.

"Really," Khadra said. Even Omayma's toes were elegant. Not stubby, with flaking cuticles, like Khadra's. Even her toes felt numb, as numb as her heart that short dark season.

"Oh my God, yes," Omayma said. "That's when I totally knew that I had to get good with God and rededicate my life to Islam. And ever since I have," she said, "I've been so blessed—and now your brother has come into my life, so blessed—"

Noticing she was getting a little teary, Khadra handed her a torn-up tissue she dug out of her pocket and, after looking at it, Omayma dabbed a teeny-tiny corner just under her eye. "Always dab, don't wipe, it's better for your skin, dear," she said to Khadra through delicate sniffles.

What's wrong with my skin? thought Khadra. Maybe it was Omayma coming into her life during the raw period after the abortion, or maybe her heart was simply too clenched up just then. She should have liked her. Were they not two very similar Muslim girls of Indianapolis?

" . . . and there's this Muslim restaurant owner, and he, like, serves alcohol. Bottles lined up from here to the ceiling," Omayma said at the meeting to which she persuaded Khadra to come.

"Boycott him?" her friend Maha, the Sudanese doctor's daughter, asked.

"That's it, that's totally what we need to do." Omayma looked around the group with bright earnestness. She and Maha and some friends had recently formed a new sisters' circle called the Nusayba Society. *Très chic* and *très* holy, they were the face of Islamic women's work for a new era. Khadra attended a few meetings to please her sister-in-law, but oh, how she would have despised these Muslim Junior Leaguers in her black-scarf days.

How like Mama she is, Khadra thought to herself while marking up one of the signs for the boycott. How can Eyad stand it? Omayma didn't see herself as being like Ebtehaj at all. She saw her mother-in-law as an old-fashioned innocent, out of style and out of step.

"What an—interesting—jilbab," Omayma said, looking at Ebtehaj's tan double knit with its large, outdated collar.

"Wajdy sewed it for me, thank you," Ebtehaj smiled. "Would you like him to make you one? Then we could have matching mother-in-law/daughter-in-law outfits!"

"Oh—ah—no, it's all right. I really wouldn't want to put Uncle Wajdy out," Omayma said, as Khadra saw her flash a look of "save me" to Eyad. It almost made Khadra want to defend her mother's polyester jilbabs. Almost.

"Have you ever thought about changing the look of the place?" Omayma asked, glancing around at the shabby sofa and the bare white walls, a little smudged around the light switches, and punctuated by "classic Islamic art" such as the black-velvet Kaba and the green prayer rug with the Prophet's mosque. They'd had those ever since Square One. Tacky as they were, Khadra couldn't imagine home without them.

Khadra followed her gaze. And suddenly, although she had vowed never to let country plaid *anything* cross the threshold of her own house, she wanted to smack Omayma's pretty little face. The Shamys (whose South Bend move had been twice postponed) were the last of the old Timbers crowd that still rented there. Everyone else had moved on. But because of the ugly garage-sale furniture, and the rest of the gimcrack décor and the refusals to indulge in things one craved over the years—things of the sort Omayma took for granted—she, Khadra, was able to go to IU. Because of Wajdy and Ebtehaj's extreme mindfulness and annoying diligence in all things.

And they were so vulnerable and fragile, her parents. They could be knocked flat by anyone. But this was a home they'd created, a home. Out of nothing. Out of arriving in America with so little. Intangibles their only treasure—their brains and their values. How dare Omayma? What could she know, just seeing surfaces? The god-awful plaid couch, the ratty black velvet Kaba. *They* didn't tell the whole picture. They didn't tell *anything*.

Khadra gave Ebtehaj a hug when it was time to leave for campus the next morning. Her mother was in her *robe de chambre,* as she still called it, with a vocabulary left over from French colonialism in Syria. Sitting at the kitchen table in the worn old bathrobe and padded slippers, she was getting ready to debone chicken under the cold white glow of the energy-saving neon lights. To pick the slivers of meat even from between the neck-bones, so as to use it in some dish that stretched out small quantities. She was taken by surprise.

"What's all this?" she said. Her cheek smelling softly of Nivea cream. She and her daughter had not been speaking much since the . . . what Khadra had done.

"Nothing." Khadra said. But she clung a moment longer.

"Well. Here's nothing back, then," Ebtehaj said, and hugged her too.

The picket at the restaurant that Omayma organized happened on a cold sludgy day, the kind of day when the Indiana cold has drizzled so deep into your bones that you almost no longer remember what it feels like to be warm in summer. Had it snowed, it would at least have looked picturesque. Instead, the rain beat ugly pocks in dirty piles of shoveled snow. Khadra arrived late. She circled around looking for street parking while Ferdinand Marcos gave up power to

Corazon Aquino in the Philippines and the remains of the U.S. space shuttle *Challenger* bobbed somewhere in the ocean. It was an area of downtown Indianapolis she'd only been to once or twice—she seemed to recall Aunt Hajar Jefferson's salon being around here, near the Projects. And Uncle Taher's restaurant, the one he'd opened with his non-Muslim brother.

Wait a minute. Uncle Taher's restaurant. TJ's. Was it—? Yes, it was. It was indeed the one they were demonstrating against. Khadra's stomach sank. A few passers-by were watching curiously and, inside the restaurant, at the windowside tables, patrons looked out at the line of protesters with their signs. Omayma was keyed up with the thrill of the moment, the collective action, the eyes upon them.

Khadra had to work hard to get her attention, finally practically yanking her out of the line. "Did anyone talk to him before we organized this picket?" she asked her.

"Talk, like, to whom?" Omayma said.

"Uncle Taher."

"Who?"

"Uncle Taher Tijan, that's his *name,* the owner of the restaurant. Did you try to talk to him first, find out *why* he has the bar? Maybe a non-Muslim investor is making him do it?"

"What do you mean? A bar is, like, a bar. A BAR IS A STAIN ON OUR COMMUNITY!" she fell in shouting with the others.

"This isn't your community. You don't live in this neighborhood," Khadra muttered to herself.

A big bulky man with a long, sorrowful face came out of the restaurant toward them. "What's all this about?" he said. He read the first sign, then another. "ALCOHOL IS A SIN IN ISLAM."

"GOOD MUSLIMS DON'T SELL BEER." He shook his head. He spotted Khadra.

"Assalamu alaikum," he said. "Khadra? Is that you? You've changed. What's goin' on here?"

Khadra wished she could drop into a hole and hide. "*Wa alaikum assalam,* Uncle Taher. I'm—I didn't know—I'm sorry—"

"Aah," he said, waving his hand in dismissal. He turned and lumbered back into the restaurant.

"Who was that?" one of the picketers said.

"I think it was the owner," Omayma answered, with satisfaction.

"He was a teacher of mine," Khadra said, kicking a stone on the sidewalk.

When the silverfish is about to molt, he grows quiet, arches his body, and expands and contracts his abdomen until a split appears along his back. Gradually undulating his new body, he pulls himself through the crack headfirst . . . a certain number simply die, unable to escape through the slit in their former backs.

—Sue Hubbell, *Broadsides from the Other Orders*

She drove home and got into bed. It was full of clutter. She pushed to the floor the pile of clothes and books and the empty bowl with bits of milk-softened cereal dried at its bottom. She tipped her heart over like a little boy's toy dump truck. She dumped out Juma and his loving. Sobbing in bed for days. Out, out. Out of my system.

But what was happening to her? It wasn't just about Juma, the fact that her marriage was over finally hitting her. It was more, even, than the days of embryo bleeding out of her in agonizing bits and pieces.

It took her by surprise, the sudden revulsion she felt for everything. For her whole life up till now. She wanted to abort the

Dawah Center and its entire community. Its trim-bearded uncles in middle-management suits, its aunties fussing over her headscarf and her ovaries, its snotty Muslim children competing for brownie points with God.

Twenty-one years of useless head-clutter. It all had to go. All those hard polished surfaces posing as spiritual guidance. All that smug knowledge. Islam is this, Islam is that. Maybe she believed some of it, maybe she didn't—but it needed to be cleared out so she could find out for herself this time. Not as a given. Not ladled on her plate and she had to eat it just because it was there.

These were weeks during which she left the apartment hardly ever. She slept fitfully, ate badly, and puttered around aimlessly. By the light of the flickering TV, which she kept on late into the night for company—for she had never been so alone—the news of the world was too horrible, young Palestinian boys and girls of ten and twelve throwing stones at Israeli soldiers, and the soldiers dragging them and beating them, just pounding those kids with their rifles and boots. It was the first time American television had ever shown Israeli-on-Palestinian violence.

Stupid Connie Chung and stupid American commentators and that all-news channel, CNN, were like, "But Brian, tell us how is this possible, we see Israel doing bad things to the whatcha-callems, how can that be?" and one asshole Zionist "expert" suggested that the violence done to Palestinians was their own fault, because they were not following Gandhian and Martin Luther Kingian nonviolence principles—"a rock is a very violent object!" he actually said. Khadra threw a plastic flip-flop at him and said

"Fuck Gandhi and Martin, and fuck nonviolence, and fuck Israel, and fuck you, CNN!"

It was all so horrible, there was no point watching it, ever. Khadra didn't want to hear another word of news again in her whole life. She switched on Whitney Houston, turned up the music loud-loud, and buried her face in a pillow.

She missed fajr after fajr sleeping through her alarm. It made her feel ill to miss a prayer. It was so drummed into her: the first thing a believer will be asked on the Day of Judgment is prayers. His foot will not move until he has accounted for the five dailies. She made up the late fajrs contritely at first. Then she began to be angry. The rest of the five, duhr, asr, maghreb, isha, she banged out with fierce uncaring roteness, pecking the floor with her forehead. Peck peck peck, one rakat after the other.

There, she said, flinging it at God. Here's what you demanded. Two rakats? Four? Four-three-four? Take it, take them all! Was this what prayer was for, to stave off an exacting bean counter? Ticks on some kind of scorecard He was keeping on her? Fuck it.

She didn't renew the lease on the apartment. Didn't care that the semester was beginning. Didn't care what would happen with her IU degree. *Medical technology?* She couldn't think of anything more meaningless to her. It was all part of some previous life lived by some other Khadra who accepted things she didn't really want, who didn't really know what she wanted and took whatever was foisted on her without examining it. Took whatever crappy unnourishing food for the soul was slopped in front of her and ate it up, becoming its spokesperson and foisting it on others. Ruining friendships for it.

She loathed that girl, that Khadra. Despised her. Blamed her for it all. Wanted to scratch her face, to hurt her, wanted to cut her—she looked dully at a razor, one of Juma's, forgotten in the back of a bathroom drawer. Wanted her dead. Wanted to be dead and gone—what was it Maryam had said when she was all alone in her dark night? *"If only I had died before this and been forgotten, long gone out of memory."* Maryam got an answer, a voice calling out from underneath her miserable butt. But then, *she* had been carrying Christ, the comfort to all the worlds. Khadra was carrying—nothing, by her own wretched—(but she had to, *had* to)—choice. Nothing, nothing. And so no reviving water came for her and no fresh ripe fruit fell upon her.

She stopped watering the maidenhair fern in her little living room and it died. Turned to dry stubble like the garden of the vain man in the Quran's Chapter of the Cave. Its slender green fronds that had once flopped hopefully over the side of the pot now withered yellow and brown. She stood over it thinking dully, my fern is dead. I killed it. She wrapped her arms around the green plastic pot and slid to the floor and lay on her side curled around the fern pot, the black dirt spilling out, rocking and saying, My fern is dead. My fern is dead.

It was rock bottom for Khadra Shamy. "Rock bottom days for Khadra Shaaaaamy, sha-na-na-naah," she air-guitared bitterly, not even knowing what she was saying, just mouthing words that came to her. She was through. She couldn't feel anymore. What else was there to feel?

And finally one day she was done. Exhausted. As if she'd traveled down the seven gates of hell, discarding at every door some breastplate or amulet that used to shore her up. She felt empty. Crumpled and empty, that was her. Like a jilbab you've taken off your body and hung on a nail.

She packed up the apartment. Put Juma's remaining stuff in a cardboard box for one of his pals to pick up: a pocket-sized Quran in a zippered leather binding, an enormous textbook on petroleum extraction with the cover torn off, a Go Big Red sweatshirt, one soccer goalie glove, and a vial of sandalwood oil he used when he took his shower before Friday prayers—and when they went to bed together. The scent made her almost falter. If only their marriage could have gone on the strength of the sex alone. Had she made the right choice after all? Would it have been such a tragedy to have the baby, to travel along the typical wife-and-mother trajectory? She stared at the little golden vial of scented oil, grown warm in her hand. She hesitated—dabbed a dot on her wrist—quickly put it with the other stuff in the box.

And then what? Where do you go when the first part of your life is coming to an end, and you don't know what is yet unborn inside you? Where do you go when you're in a free fall, unmoored, safety net gone, and nothing nothing to anchor you?

Invisible:
How can I see your face
Untouched
Wrapped in yourself?
Who
Will show me the way?
You have no homeland . . .

—Attar

It was time for a retreat. She would betake herself unto an eastern place.

Back where she came from: Syria. Land where her fathers died. Land that made a little boomerang scar on her knee. *Ya maal el-shaam, you were always on my mind. Yellow rose of Damascus. Oh Damascus, don't you cry for me.* She sold Téta's Ottoman coins to a collectibles dealer from Chicago. She used the cash for her ticket.

Her parents were aghast. The Baathists, the mukhabarat, the Asad, the army-police-border-patrol-visa-authorities.

She would risk it. Maybe she had a death wish. She was in a reckless state of mind.

"Speak only English with the Syrian authorities in the airport," Wajdy advised. Her father looked sad and defeated. She had not turned out the way he wanted. He didn't understand why. At the gate, she threw her arms around his neck and hugged him. She had not wanted to disappoint him; it was so hard!

He kissed the top of her head and pressed an envelope into her hands. "You might need this," he mumbled. "Put it away safely in your money belt." This made her cry on the airplane. She pictured her father and mother sitting at that cracked formica table deboning chicken, hands greasy, heads bent, deboning and deboning to stretch out the last sliver.

Syria was blinding, searing sunlight. Where the Indiana sunshine was buttery yellow, its summer palate full of rich brown tree bark and mellow leafy greens, Syria was white light on dried-out, dusty streets, brilliant turquoise sky, scraggly silver-green trees, crumbling stone walls that had been there since the start of time.

In Syria, the shape of things was different: sleep, corner errands, little tea glasses on hammered copper trays, even light switches. Rooms had doors with keyholes you could see through. Doorways had sills you had to step over and the doors were metal and opened with a clang down the middle, like refrigerators, which never opened down the middle in Syria. Neighborhoods meant people leaning out of flung-open windows talking to pedestrians below, dim narrow passageways under ancient stone arches, and people clustered on balconies drinking golden tea as afternoon shadows lengthened. Pulling themselves inward, like a snail retracting, as soldiers passed in their olive drabs. Here the day flowed differently. Asr time in Syria was like fajr in America: things were that quiet, people waking up slowly from the naps of hot noon. Rooftops were where you went of an evening to sit and sing and look up at the stars, like the patio back home.

Somehow all the unfamiliarity seemed familiar to Khadra. "And then we turn here, and there will be a rise in the road, and an arch," her mind said—or no, she wasn't even thinking it with her mind, it was her feet, her body moving itself—and there it was. The rise in the road, the arch. As if her body retained an unconscious imprint, as if the ground remembered her feet and guided them.

She was startled by the gargantuan pictures of the president. His image was the first thing in your face, at the airport, everywhere; you walked under his eyes. It played on her nerves. So did the great rumbling tanks and clusters of soldiers throughout the city.

Through the inherited lenses of her parents' memory, she had thought the city a much smaller place. Since they'd left, the real Damascus had swollen. Whole new neighborhoods had sprung up, and chunks of outlying land had been swallowed by the urban maw. Damascus was full of country folk newly migrated from the villages, and of refugees from neighboring countries. Army garrisons and Palestinian camps surrounded it. Downtown, white-collar women with fluffy shoulder-length hair spilled out of the big concrete buildings on their lunch hour, arm in arm, in neat pleated blouses tucked into short skirts. Men in big handlebar mustaches went about in safari suits—her father's sense of fashion, she realized, had begun and ended here.

Khadra had told no one she was coming. She followed directions to Téta's house. Téta opened the door and gasped.

Khadra said simply, "Here I am."

"Glory be to God who hath taken His servant on a journey throught the night," Téta said, and enfolded her in an embrace. "I have been waiting for you." What did she mean? There had never been any plan for Khadra to come to Syria.

"I can't believe I'm really here," Khadra said. "It's like a dream." Sitting on a low stone ledge in Téta's inner patio, a place open to the sky in the heart of her home. A laurel-scented nest in the scarred land of Syria. There was Téta's tall spindly lilac. There was her walnut tree, and another tree whose branches had white felted undersides. And there was the sweet bay laurel itself. All these she'd heard Téta describe to Mrs. Moore.

"Oh. Mrs. Moore sent this gift for you." It was a homely little gunnysack of cornflour stamped *"Made in Simmonsville, Indiana."* "It's for making cornbread. She said you'd had it at her house and liked it."

She slept in a narrow iron-frame bed—maybe her father's? Or Uncle Shakker's? She was in the old Shamy house in Salihiyeh, the one that used to belong to Téta's brother, Khadra's grandfather. The first night in Syria, Khadra half-woke around—it must have been three o'clock. A faint voice, not Téta's, called her name, or so she sensed as she lay in the dark not knowing who she was anymore. *Khadra. Khadra?* She half-lifted her head off the pillow, listening. Lay her head back in sadness. She felt a withdrawal of love, a pulling away of the kind of love that had been given to her old self automatically, as long as she abided by its conditions. What would she do with the raw hurt left in its wake? She fell asleep listening for the one who was calling her.

Syria was Téta, sitting on a wet wooden crate in the bath with a modesty cloth on her lap. "—O soap my back, *te'ebrini*." Her sloping back, its flesh soft and speckled and old, soaping and soaping it, pouring warm water over it. Happy as a baby in the water, and loving to talk. And Khadra, sitting on a wet wooden crate next to the tub in her calico nightgown, sleeves pulled up to her elbows, soaping her Téta's back, was happy to listen. In the warmth and the vapor, the stories came pouring out.

"—for love, yes, I married for love. This was extraordinary in my day, darling!—and still is, in much of the world. For I am an extraordinary woman. Pish, it's not ego. I'm telling you the truth. You are allowed to know the truth about yourself. Besides, you have to have an ego, *te'ebrini*—of course! You have to have one to live! Who can live without a self? Ego is not the same as ego-monster. You must nurture and guide your ego with care. You must never neglect it. To be unaware of it, how it is working underneath everything you do, to think of yourself as floating high above the normal level of humanity, selfless and pure—why, that is what gets you in the greatest danger. I'm a great philosopher in the bathtub, darling, water gets me started. Are we finished here? My bathrobe please, and the towel for my dripping head, yes and your hand. I am quite old and a slip will do me in, you know. *Te'ebrini*."

Téta's laughter filled the steamy, primitive little tiled room. The bath had been added to the old house when the practice of communal bathing in neighborhood bathhouses had become more or less defunct. One bath a week: she loved her routine. Finite quantity of water, carefully poured into jugs. This was not America of faucets left rushing.

"No, *te'ebrini,* don't drain the bathwater away. I reuse it to water the houseplants. No, the soap won't hurt them—it comes from them, after all." Of course: her laurel soap. "*Ey na'am.* Yes, indeed. It's been a drought for years. Maybe it'll break this year. City of Seven Rivers, no, no more. Barada River only a trickle. You must have heard of it from your parents. Nothing to show you there. Poor Barada. *Te'burni,* Barada."

"—mmm, have I told you I was a telephone operator?" she began, in the next bath session.

"Yes, Téta, of course you have, many times."

"—but I haven't told you what it was *like.* One of the new jobs opening up for women, the very first wave of working women, and I was one of them! *Alô, Centrale? Connect me, please*—and we'd connect them. Strangers, neighbors, wasn't it marvelous! Things were so exciting! We were fighting off the French, an old world was ending, a new one beginning. *Dunya al-ajayeb* like the magical worlds you get when you rub a lamp, all of it opening before our feet. New technology coming to Syria. All the old-fart people hanging back fearfully. They tried to make out that a telephone girl's job was a bad thing, a thing for floozies, imagine! No, but I and my girlfriends laughed in their faces. We wanted to be the New Woman. We didn't know that nothing is new under the sun. All that once was circles back and returns and looks new. But back then, it seemed so hopeful. And we had a little circle of friendship, the three of us—me and Iman and Hayat—you'll meet Hayat soon. We were all *azizahs,* it was our little code word: women who cherish themselves, women who are cherished. So we linked arms and went out into the new day. *Centrale, number please?* I worked as an operator for years and years! O but your Téta was *chic,* my lovesy, *et que j'etais belle!* People used to say I looked like Asmahan, the green-eyed legend.

"More than one fine young man lost his heart to me—don't smirk, darling, I am entitled to preen—but I only gave my heart to one. One heart, one love. *Gazelle, gazeh-eh-elle, now my wound is healed* . . . Hmm? He was Circassian, his grandfather fled the czar and settled in Palestine, and he was in Damascus working with a carriage merchant. My parents were furious when he came to our house to propose. With his older brother and aunt—his parents were far off in Haifa. *Filthy gypsies!*—I don't know, they call anybody who has no settled home a gypsy. Because they were immigrants, you see—his family. My father saw him standing—absolutely crushed, poor gorgeous man—outside my window the next day, went after him with a shotgun. *Nameless nobody!* Hmm? No, they were just typical Damascenes. All Damascenes are snobs. Depend on it, lovesy. Well, I don't know why. Maybe because they live in a heartland, far away from the coast and all new things. They don't trust newcomers. People of Damascus—Shami people—tend to be very satisfied with themselves, I'm afraid. My dear, I don't think you young generation understands how grand a long soothing bath really is, the kind that opens your pores up and restores, ah, so marvelously. . . . Well, we were absolutely in love, there was no telling us no. And then we eloped to Haifa—his parents lived there . . . more lather, lovesy. Like that, yes, that's the way."

"Eloped? *What?* Téta! You never told me this."

"You never asked, lovesy. Circassians do it all the time, elope. Then they pretend to be shocked when their children do it. It was a very respectable elopement."

Khadra giggled.

"Oh, but it was. His old aunt was with us all the time, and as soon as we got to Haifa, we married properly, with witnesses. But it was hard to get there. It was the years of the Palestinian protests against the British, and Syrian protests against the French, all the time raids and soldiers and hiding—only we were hiding from the colonizers like everyone else, and hiding our love, too. People were hard on us. That handsome boy Nizar said it years ago: 'people of my city hate love and hate lovers.' Have you ever heard his poems? Oh yes, I memorized reams and reams of Nizar in my day—bless your heart, Nizar. More water, please. And so my parents said I was dead to them. And what had I done? What was such a crime? Had I gone against God and the Prophet? Not I. They were the ones in violation. They were the ones. Doesn't the Prophet say if you find a good god-loving man, accept him? Does the Prophet say unless he's Circassian? Does the Prophet say he must be from your people? Hardhearted people, using religion—the butt end of it. And my brother, Wajdy's father—only Wajdy wasn't born yet—he didn't dare contact me." She paused, and telescoped what must have been years here. "They came around eventually. People often do, you know, dear. They got over themselves. But it was ages before any of them talked to me again . . . no, it's just a little soap in my eyes, don't mind me."

Khadra had always known Téta with a song in her heart. She had no idea she'd come from such sorrow. Téta turned her eyes—they were closed against getting soap in them while Khadra shampooed her lovingly—to the opaque window high over the tub, sensing the light through her closed eyelids and basking in it.

"We lived in Haifa till '48," Téta went on. "Terrible year, the Nakba. So many were killed in the scattering. My sheikha was killed, the one who was my teacher and friend and guide for years and years. Hmm? Yes of course, dear. Her line of teaching goes way back, all the way back to Lady Nafisa, a great teacher of Love. I used to go to her circles of remembrance, she was of the order that gives constant thanks, my old teacher. The whole order broke up, no more circles. Running for our lives, marching madly for the border, leaving willy-nilly, you grabbed what you could, you strapped your baby to your hip and ran. Because the Yahudi terror squads were at our heels, *te'ebrini*. And that's when I lost him. Killed, shot in the back by one of the Zionist militias. I will never forget those coward Jew terrorists. Never. And then. They wouldn't let me stop, all the other people I was fleeing with. I was like a rag doll, they dragged me along by the armpits, someone held my babies for me. Because you couldn't stop and kneel over the body. The roving Zionist guerrillas would shoot you, or drag you off. You couldn't bury"—here she broke—"couldn't bury him."

It was *not* soap in her eyes, either. Her eyes glittering not with laughter now, but with diamond-bright tears. Turned toward the light filtering through the little block of opaque glass. "Oh, Téta!" Khadra exclaimed, aghast.

"Well, you never asked. You're twenty-one now, time to know things. My sons are there now. They went in '65 to see their father's people—they were grown men by then—and got stuck. Pour me water from that jug, lovesy." And she sat there with her eyes closed in the filtered bathroom sunlight, water running down her head, with its thinning but defiantly black hair.

And then, in next week's bath, another astounding thing:

"Your mother, Ebtehaj. Of course, you know her father married again after your mama's mother died. Married a Turkish woman whom your mother hated. Can you rotate in circles down the middle of my back, *te'ebrini?* Yes, there . . ."

"Why?" Khadra glimpsed a piece of vital knowledge about her mother, long withheld. "Why did she hate her?"

"It was mutual. She was a Kemalist, totally secular, the second wife. Militantly, spitefully secular. Sibelle, her name was. Your mother was seventeen at the time and couldn't stand to see her father go in Sibelle's direction, making light of his prayers, dropping out of his first wife's pious circle, allowing wine at his table. . . .Well, no, he didn't drink, but she and her *copines* did. Made your mother miserable, never gave her a moment's peace in her own home. Yes. Mocked her for wearing hijab. Most of the fashionable people had stopped wearing hijab by then, you see. The city was against it, the tide was against it. Oh, how Sibelle loathed the sight of that hijab. She made fun of it—she tried everything—she'd yank it right off her head. I heard she put it in the pot and shat on it—no, I'm not kidding. She was embarrassed to be seen in public with her stepdaughter in it. Made Ebtehaj walk on the other side of the street. . . . You've stopped scrubbing, *yoh*. Lather up, *te'ebrini*—And that Sibelle yanked her out of that Quran circle she was in for just a few months—her deceased mother's circle. Ebtehaj got interested in it after her mother died.

Well, Sibelle like a good Kemalist thought it was all garbage. Said she wouldn't have anyone in *her* household connected to it. 'Her' household, imagine! As if your mother had no place in her own home anymore! Yanked your mother right out. And then—she's never apologized for any of this, not to this day—Sibelle tried to force your mother into a marriage with a man who drank and whored, just to make her misery lifelong. She had the wool pulled over your grandfather's eyes so well, *yooh*. Men can be a little limited like that, men like your grandfather who enjoy—but never mind that—he and she are in Turkey nowadays, you know—darling I'm getting cold—a little more hot water, please. Your Aunt Razanne, well, her husband Mazen was good friends with Wajdy back then, before their disagreement over politics. Ebtehaj was desperate to get out of that house. Oh yes, it was all Razanne's doing, your parents' marriage. She and Wajdy saved her. Ooh! the water is hot! No, no, dear, that's a *good* thing! But, Khadra, don't think that you need to find out all your mother's secrets and understand her story to go on with your own. Her pain is hers to heal. You are not responsible. Hmm . . . I can feel all my pores open. Thank you, dear. Thank you, Khadra darling. Thank you O thank you O thanks."

I am not among those who left our land
to be torn to pieces by our enemies

. . . . . .

—Anna Akhmatova, "I Am Not Among Those Who Left Our Land"

They studied each other, Reem and Roddy standing before their cousin Khadra in the elevator of their building. The kind with an iron gate you had to pull shut. Outside the dusty lobby with its corridor sounds of flip-flops slapping the floor, the bloated city teemed. Vendors hawked, bicycles tinkled, cars honked, tanks rumbled, buses belched. Heavy construction trucks lumbered up and down the long apartment block. A dwarf fan palm tree grew by their stoop. Huge palmate leaves, a meter across, swayed on delicate stalks over a thick trunk with rough scarred bark.

"So. You're the famous Khadra," Reem said.

"Of the famous 'Eyad and Khadra' duo," Roddy added, grinning.

"The famous?" Khadra asked, baffled.

"Mmm," was all Reem said.

"Our mother was always bragging on you," Roddy explained. "The wonderful, accomplished cousins in America. We could never compare."

Syria, in fact, was sweet relief from the myth of Syria that had hung over her life. Reem was a princess and an airhead. She was the Syrian answer to Marcia Brady. She started brushing her hair, staring demurely at her ivory-skinned reflection in the mirror, her large, gazelle eyes.

"What's that?" Khadra asked, lifting a charm that hung from a gold chain on the nearly sheer stretch of skin between Reem's collarbones.

"A hijab," Reem said.

"Do what?" Khadra didn't understand the word in that context.

"A hijab. A spell, an amulet. You know."

She did not know. "You mean magic?"

Reem nodded. To her, there was nothing at all odd about her answer.

"You—really, you believe in that stuff?" Khadra was incredulous.

Reem held up a hand to request silence. She was counting under her breath and didn't want to lose track. Actually counting brushstrokes.

"I've been put under spells before," Reem told her, when the count was finished. "It was horrible. I'm not going to leave myself without protection again. This one's a specific counter-hex against a woman who envies my beauty and my education." She said it with utter creepy gravity.

For Khadra, Roddy was like having a fun brother her age. It was so refreshing, finally, after Eyad, she thought, with mean satisfaction. ("Gee, an Arab guy with a sense of humor," she said later to Téta, who chuckled.) He was a prankster, and did voices on the telephone. Once he pretended to be an animal-control officer calling to say that a mountain lion was loose in their neighborhood and they had to barricade the doors and remove all fresh meat from the premises. He had the whole street in a panic.

Then there was his petty side. Roddy could, and would, discuss endlessly the price of mangos on the black market and how much it cost to bribe your way to the official document of your choice. Every fifth citizen was an employee of the bureaucracy, and the state did not pay them a liveable salary. Bribes were routine. It was odd when you got an official stamp *without* having to slip money between the forms.

When Khadra asked Roddy what he thought of the Afghan refugee problem in Peshawar and Iran, he said, "What Afghan refugees?" and made a joke out of it. One day, sitting on little round folding stools sipping tea on the balcony, she asked him how students on his campus had reacted to the news of Saddam's massacre of the Kurds in Halabja—had there been there any demonstrations? Aunt Razanne immediately turned up the radio, and Uncle Mazen took Khadra aside, whispering, "No politics. *Ey, na'am.* We don't talk politics in our family. We stay away from that. You see?" He looked over his shoulder.

Uncle Mazen was around the same age as her father, but he looked older, was starting to have an old-man slouch to his frame, kind of a caving in at the gut. His eyes were small and close together. He had the receding chin and mousy blond hair that were the source of Roddy's features. You could see where he'd been handsome in youth, and might have had a haggard older-man handsomeness still, if he'd stand straighter, if his face had strength.

"But Uncle Mazen, we're at home. You're inside your own home."

"There is no home. Walls have ears," he said sharply. "The neighbors, for example."

"But you know them. They're your friends," Khadra said.

"Who knows anyone?" he said, and his nostrils flared suddenly. "Who knows who might report us?"

Khadra was startled. She wondered, a little shaken, if he would ever report *her*.

Later that evening she overheard her aunt and uncle arguing. "What have we ever got behind Wajdy and his Islamic politics but woe?" she heard Uncle Mazen say.

"He hasn't been the same since the heart attack," Aunt Razanne confided to Khadra the next morning at breakfast as they made a large pot of garlicky *kishk* porridge.

"Heart attack?" Khadra asked with genuine concern.

"The day the paratroopers tore off our veils," Aunt Razanne said absently, stirring the pot.

On September 28, 1982, during the height of the troubles in Syria, President Asad's brother Rifat dropped a thousand girl paratroopers over Damascus, with a guy backup soldier behind each one. They blocked off a section of the city. Within it, they grabbed any woman who was wearing hijab. Khadra remembered reading about it in *The Islamic Forerunner* and being outraged. She'd never heard an eyewitness account, though. That kind of thing didn't get out of Syria.

"You could strip off your hijab and jilbab, or get a gun to your head," Aunt Razanne said, tucking a wisp of hair behind her ear. "Well, my Reem was on foot, coming back from the seamstress. She tried to duck into the lobby of an apartment building but it was the buzzer kind and she couldn't get in." Her aunt now looked around to make sure Reem was not in hearing distance. Then she continued, "The paratrooper grabs her by the arm, with a soldier right beside her. She slips off the scarf right away. Why endanger your life for it? But then, the paratrooper barks at her to take off her manteau, too. Well, my Reem is only wearing a cami and half-slip under the manteau that day, as it happens. *Ey, na'am*. I always tell her, wear a proper dress under it, like the rest of us, but she says, "It's hot, Mama." With the soldier prodding her with the rifle, she starts to unbutton. She is mortified. Then that *fucking* paratrooper *bitch*—oh, my goodness—did I just say that? I am so sorry for my filthy language. My word, I don't know what came over me." Aunt Razanne smiled sweetly.

Khadra stared. She began to think they had all gone schizo from living under such a bizarre dictatorship so long.

"Then what happened?" she prompted gently.

"Yes. So the paratrooper can't even wait for Reem to take off her clothes. So she rips off the manteau herself, and holds it up in the air and sets it on fire with a blowtorch."

"A *blowtorch?"*

"Kind of an extra touch. I don't think they used it on everyone."

"And then?"

"Then they moved on. A stranger found Reem huddled in the alley of the apartment building three hours later, disoriented and not speaking, and brought her home off the address on her driver's license. We had been searching for her frantic. That's when your Uncle Mazen had a heart attack, when she was half-carried in the door, hair disheveled and half-undressed with those ugly bruises on her arms."

"How disgusting! How could a government behave like that?"

"Oh no, no, I don't blame them," Aunt Razanne said. "You see, the President was so sorry when he found out. The next day, he sent another set of troops out to the same part of the city with roses. Every woman got a rose. So it's all okay, you see?"

Khadra was flummoxed. "Um, well, whose fault was it, then?"

"Yours," growled Uncle Mazen from behind her, making her start. "Your father and mother. You dissidents. Who politicized hijab but you? Who made life hell for us but you?"

"You see," her aunt said, as if explaining to a child, "if the government hadn't been so anxious over what the dissidents were doing, it wouldn't have been forced to crack down on us so hard."

Wow. "Wouldn't have been *forced to crack down on us?"* Khadra's mind couldn't help but reel at this. At least her parents had stayed true to themselves. Wajdy and Ebtehaj stood taller in her sight. They had not stooped. Had not twisted their minds to fit into a cramped space, had not shrunk themselves like poor Uncle Mazen and Aunt Razanne. Her parents had fled, even if it meant leaving everything, everyone they knew, the life that was made for them, the life they could have lived so easily, without being outcasts in an alien country. All it would have taken was accepting a little suffocation, living on a little less air like Razanne and Mazen. Instead, her parents had flown into new air. Home had been left behind, given up. For the utter unknown. What a bitter and marvelous choice.

Khadra had brought the three younger siblings—Muhsin, Misbah, and Mafaz, ages eleven, thirteen, and fifteen—giant bags of M&Ms from America. She explained that this was the nickname she and Eyad had come up with for them years ago, when they were mere bits of babies with hard-to-remember "m" names. They lay on their stomachs reading *Tintin* and *Osama* comics, popping the candies as they worked a jigsaw puzzle of an American farm landscape she'd picked out for them. She'd given Roddy a farting whoopee cushion, which he loved. To Reem she gave a purse-size pepper spray. She thought it would be a good choice, since the optometry shop where Reem worked was downtown.

"Oh!" Aunt Razanne said, looking at it with interest when Khadra explained its use. "Would that you had brought many of those." Yes, her mother had told her Aunt Razanne would want one. Self-protection devices interested her.

"I did," she beamed, producing another for her aunt.

Muhsin seemed obsessed with the *Tintin* comics. Khadra sat next to him saying, "Tell me about this Tintin." She peered over his shoulder and—oh! That wasn't what he was actually reading. Behind *Tintin and the Treasure of Timbuktu,* she saw the close

Arabic typeface of a badly printed book. "What's that?" she said. He put his fingers to his lips. *Shh.*

"It's Zakaria Tamer," he told her later, when they were alone in the family room.

"Who?"

"A banned Syrian author. He's political!"

She was impressed. "If he's banned, how'd you get him?"

He grinned. "I will not reveal my sources even if you turned me in to the state police and they tortured me unto death," he said, extra-dramatically. He had more gumption than his parents.

"Oh you little devil!" she cried. Mafaz saw the two of them with the *Tintin* between them and winked. So she was in on it too.

"I'm the one who gets the books," Mafaz said. So Muhsin was exposed, the little braggart. His sister tweaked his ear and he ducked, grinning.

At least some members of this family had red blood still left in them.

Say to the fair one in the black headcover
as she appears at the door of the mosque,
"What have you done to a worshipping lover?
He came to pray, then saw you and was lost."

—lyrics sung by Sabah Fakhry ("*Qul lil malihati*")

Peeling an eggplant was like unveiling an ivory-skinned woman dressed all in black. The eggplant in Khadra's hand was plump. She and her aunt sat close to the floor on little wooden crates—the ones the eggplants came in from the vegetable market—working on a tray set on top of another low crate.

"Tell me about my grandma, Auntie." Ebtehaj had spoken of her own mother rarely. There had only been a single photo back in Indiana. It had shown her grandmother with her husband and daughters wearing little set smiles. She had a kindly, concerned face.

"Well. Your grandmother was a sweet soul. Devoted to her children and home. She didn't appreciate Father flitting about with friends, hanging out at the coffeeshop. She was a homebody. And saintly, you know. Neighbors always said of her, 'if there are angels walking the earth, Um Mansur is one of them.' I always remember her sitting on the mat in her bedroom, doing her praise-be's on her beads. And you know she's in heaven, because she lost a child. A mother who buries a child goes straight to heaven, same as a martyr."

"What was her name, Grandma Um Mansur?" All these years, and she didn't even really know her name. Essential things that Khadra needed to know, in her limited time, but her aunt seemed always to get lost in the telling.

"Badriyé. Badriyé Bustanjy. From a very religious family, my grandparents' family, of course. Scholars and sheikhs under the Ottomans. Mother tried to imbue us with all that. But you never know with your children. Some will follow you and some won't. She tried all the time to get Ebtehaj to wear hijab and pray regularly. Begged and pleaded and wept—"

Khadra nearly dropped her eggplant. "*What?* My mother didn't pray from the start?"

Aunt Razanne blinked up, placidly peeling the thick glossy skin. "Hmm, dear? Of course not. *I* was the good girl. Your mother was the rebellious one. I always tried to help and guide her, but . . ." she sighed.

"But *what*?" Khadra's insides were churning. She felt deceived.

"She had to learn the hard way." Her aunt swept a pile of eggplant peelings into the old powdered-milk canister that served as the garbage can. No one in America had a kitchen garbage can that small.

Well? Why was she stringing it out like this? "What hard way?"

Khadra prompted. She tossed a peeled eggplant into a chipped white melamine bowl and picked up another one.

"Well, it was the trip to France." Aunt Razanne sighed.

"So? What happened in France?"

"You mean she's never told you? You've never talked about France?"

Khadra shook her head.

Aunt Razanne bit her lip.

"What happened in France?" Khadra repeated.

"I think I should wait until I can write to your mother first—"

"What happened in France?" Khadra stabbed the eggplant she'd been peeling with the knife and put it down. "Tell me now. Tell me *now.*"

Aunt Razanne, weak of will, was prevailed upon. She took up Khadra's eggplant and set to it herself. "Father called me to come over to the house right away. She'd locked herself in the bathroom for hours. Wouldn't talk to him. Used up all the water in the house bathing. Wit's end, he was . . ."

"From the beginning, Auntie, *please,* from the beginning."

Chopping the stem off another eggplant, Aunt Razanne carefully peeled back the barky petals around the tip. "The whole thing—she wasn't even supposed to go on the France trip. Your grandma didn't want her to go. At the beginning of the school year, she brought the permission slip home and Mother said no. Mother liked us to stay close to home. But, you see, Mother died before the year was out."

She pulled a wooden chopping board from behind the oven. The naked eggplants were stacked high in the chipped bowl. "These need to be chopped in wedges, dear. I'll heat the oil."

Khadra obediently and swiftly took the chopping board. She didn't want to risk distracting her for an instant.

"The whole idea of taking schoolgirls to France is wrong. It was part of the Baathist plan to ruin the morals of the land. To get us out of our homes, out of our veils, make us vulnerable. You see? They succeeded. Aping after the imperialists. You see? *Ey, na'am*. Father let her go. She only had to pout and he'd let her do anything." A bitter look flickered on Aunt Razann's face as she struck a match to light the gas burner, or so Khadra thought. She jumped back as the gas lit. "He was so sad and confused without our mother. For a while—then he started getting interested in that Sibelle woman. So glamorous, so à la mode. She was the daughter of a Turkish diplomat Father met at the athletic club. He had *so* many friends—"

"The France trip," Khadra prompted.

"Ebtehaj was fifteen. Or was she fourteen? Or sixteen? Well, I was nearly nineteen, you see, and married by then, so it didn't affect me as much. Sibelle, I mean. Not Mother dying—of course I was devastated at that. So sudden. Pancreatic cancer. In three or four months it was all over. The doctors said—"

"Aunt Razanne, the France trip." *Yooh!* What was the matter with her? The woman had ADD.

She sighed. "Right. They sailed to Marseilles. Ten or twelve girls and three teachers. You had to have excellent grades to go, and that Ebtehaj had, I'll give her. I was never one for As. No, go larger, Khadra."

"Huh?"

"Chop the pieces larger. This is for ma'lubeh. Upside Down Dish. You don't know how to make that, dear? Your mother never taught you, over there in America?"

Khadra chopped the eggplant into the larger pieces as instructed, waiting for her aunt to continue.

"Saweem Shabandar, she was one of the teachers, or teacher's aide. I think the oil is hot enough. Let me have those chopped eggplants. So you met her in Saudi, you say? She's wonderful, isn't she?" Aunt Razanne held her hand out at arm's length, plunked a handful of eggplant chunks, and jumped back. The oil snarled at her.

"No, not really."

Her aunt was startled and looked away from the violent oil. "You didn't like her? Goodness, why not? She's so—"

"Never mind, I was kidding. I liked her. Please go on?"

"Oh—pull these eggplants out at once, dear, they're almost brown. Here, into the aluminum pot. So. The head teacher, the one in charge of the trip was Sitt Iffat Innaby. The third chaperone was a history teacher named Ustaz Basil. Basil Abul Qushtban. Madame Innaby wanted him to court her daughter. *Ey na'am,* yes, indeed. Mind you, I think our Saweem had her eye on him too," Aunt Razanne chuckled. "Well, he was a catch. I had been hearing about him all year from Ebtehaj and her friends. He was a Nasserite. The young, handsome Nasserite history teacher. How the girls with their budding politics pressed him with questions—just like the girls in that Leila Murad musical, how did it go? It was such a hit. The one with the high school girls following the good-looking tutor around in their smart school uniforms, how did it go? *Abcdefgee-ee, what a handsome teach is he-ee.* Oh, they were very forward girls. It was her own fault, you know. On and on, she would gab in my kitchen, describing him to me. How smart he was. How he told them all about the Nasserite party even though he wasn't supposed to. This was the early '60s—or was it the mid-'60s? Either way, the Baath were in power already. Though they weren't as bad as they are now." She lowered her voice and looked over her shoulder. At the little vent window at the top corner of the kitchen.

The vent window? Her aunt was afraid of what might come through the little *vent* window now? Whew. "So the Nasserite history teacher—?" Khadra said. Aunt Razanne was so damn longwinded.

"Raped her."

Eggplants sizzled in the hot oil.

Did it take long to find me,
I asked the faithful light

—Yusuf Islam, "Moonshadow"

Damascus was the capital city of a deep-set heartland. Full of small-town minds—or, following the axiom "Small minds talk about things, mediocre minds talk about people, great minds talk about ideas," it was full of mediocre minds. Far from the sea and its ports, slow to take in waves of change, suspicious of strangers. Sort of like the Midwest, it occurred to Khadra. Téta kept Khadra's presence secret from this Damascus, buffered her from the tides of Shamy and Qadri-Agha relatives who would have overwhelmed her on a normal visit, wanting to know her business, picking the straws out of her mind like ravens. Khadra didn't know how Téta drew the veil over their eyes. Including the middle-aged Shamy couple, relatives of limited means, who lived in a part of Téta's old house, doing housekeeping and maintenance in exchange for board. They were kindly folk, very curious about America, and could Khadra get them a visa, and could she find them some work there? Somehow his low-level job in the ministry of agriculture posted Cousin Husney to a rotation in Qamishly for the season, and his wife went with him, grumbling about being sent to the provinces.

Téta saw that she got rest. Made a space around her, selecting bits of Damascus for her as she got stronger. For there were many Damascuses. There was the sepia-toned Damascus of Téta's 1940s and 1950s, and today's misshapen city cringing under the giant-sized glances of its president. There was the Damsacus of possibility, you could sense it, even now, under the surface, seeping through lock and key. A Damascus that stirred the imagination, behind the scarred face of the present.

It was was to the mosque of Muhyideen Ibn al-Arabi that Khadra found her steps turning. Not during the crowded prayer times but in between, when she could sit and pull her knees under her chin and rock by herself, untouched by man or *jinn*. The faint rhythms of dhikrs going on in the deep recesses of the mosque filtered through to her. She listened. She looked. She was still. Dark brick, white stone, dark flesh and white side by side, striped the arch-work of the mosque, as it did everywhere in Damascus's traditional architecture.

She found herself framing imaginary camera shots from the first visit, and the second time brought her Pentax and quietly, from the back of the mosque, clicked away in the play of lights and shadows through the colonnade of the mosque interior. She lost herself in these. She clicked to the rhythm of the chanting of dhikr.

A cavernous desire for beauty opened inside her. Rhythm, color, texture, a carefully tended tree, a twirling skater or athlete on television, an afternoon scene she could frame in her head and compose—she ached for beauty, felt like an orphan from it, coming from the pasty bare white walls of poor Indianapolis immigrants with their cheesy half-hearted attempts to decorate, the ugly velvet rug hung with sad thumbtacks, the gilded cardboard Dome of the Rock above the foil-eared TV set. And always that refrain: why should we decorate a temporary abode, and why spend energy on the frivolity of beauty? But beauty was no frivolity. Khadra craved it now like food and water. The arches of the Ibn al-Arabi mosque in the lap of Mount Qasyoon. The strains of Syrian folk songs and Iraqi mawwals she heard on radios through the souk and the neighborhoods. And coming live from oud strings on open balconies in the evenings and pouring out of cafés with *nay* artists and violinists.

"How have I never heard this before?" she asked Téta. "It's the most beautiful music in the world." *Come to beauty, hearken to the mystery, come to the prayer of the reed . . .*

"You have heard it before, *te'ebrini*. All your life. But now you're listening," Téta said gently.

In the fabric alley at the Hamadiya market, Khadra bought a long piece of tissuey silk fabric. "You can pull the whole thing through a ring," said the merchant, for it was that fine—"Bangalore silk," he said, and in a brilliant tangerine color, Téta's favorite. Khadra cut it in half and had the hems finished with a rolled edge at a tailor shop. Two magnificent scarves resulted.

"One for you, one for me," she said to Téta.

"What an unsuitable color for an elderly widow to wear. I love it!" Téta beamed and began dancing with the fabric and riffing Asmahan and Leila Murad. *"Sweet, sweet, sweet, how sweet the wo-orld, full of pretty things for a pretty gi-irl . . ."*

Khadra told her the bit about how you could pass it through a ring and, as she expected, Téta loved that.

"Te'ebrini," Téta said. "That reminds me. I have something to give you." She took a flat screwdriver from the kitchen. "Follow me," she said, and trudged into her bedroom. "Pull my bed back, darling," she said to Khadra. It was an ancient iron bedstead with a thin mattress. "Oof!" Téta said, pulling up a little stool and lowering herself onto it. "Now then. This is where we hid things from the Turks in the olden days," she said, prying first one twelve-inch tile, then another. "My grandfather supported Arab independence—though not by putting his faith in the British, mind you! He said that was out of the frying pan, into the fire. He wanted independence from the Turks *and* the West. Well, his brother was part of the pro-Turk caliphate movement. They quarreled, and the Khalifa movement brother turned in the Arab nationalist brother. Yes, family drama—betrayal—enough for a whole soap opera! They came hunting for him." One tile had been pried up and you could see a dark void beneath. "Khadra, *te'ebrini,* this is too much work for me. My back."

Khadra pried up two more large tiles. A sort of crawl space appeared. "But my grandfather was prepared, you see. This is a secret passage. Hmm? I don't know when it was built. It maybe goes way back, before the Turks. It connects from house to house in the neighborhood—no, not every house. That wouldn't be wise. Select houses. You must select carefully the houses to whom you will connect. Now comes your part," Téta said.

Khadra was mystified. "It's like something out of *The Thousand and One Nights*."

"It is," Téta chuckled. "Now what if I tell you that you are to crawl into it and bring me back what you find?"

"Will it be a lamp with a genie?" Khadra joked.

You had to crawl on your stomach for just a yard or two—"not long, don't worry!" Téta called—and then you got to a little closet-sized space where you could stand. She held her breath, her stomach sliding on the cool slab. She did not like small spaces. Something feathery brushed her arm and she shivered. Bugs are your friends, she said, to calm herself. Instars. Think instars. An instar in a raspberry beret. *"Raaaaspberry beret,"* she sang in the pitch dark.

"What?" Téta called down.

"I can't see a thing down here. Do you have a flashlight?"

"Just feel around," Téta said. That was not a happy prospect. "It's just a trunk, a leather trunk. About the size of a smallish suitcase," she said.

"Found it!" Khadra called. She pushed it out in front of her through the passage and climbed back into Téta's bedroom. "There is *nothing* like this in Indiana," she said.

"Sure there is," Téta said. "Every place has its secret passage. Like the crack in the armor."

From a dresser drawer she pulled a big metal ring clinking with thick iron keys—

"Of course!" Khadra said with glee. "There has to be a keyring with a kajillion keys in the story!"

—and opened the brass latch on the leather trunk. Inside was a wooden mosaic-inlay box, about the size of a tissue box. It contained fat gold coins, same as the ones she had given Khadra as a wedding gift. She knew now how valuable they were. "A treasure that fire cannot eat," Téta said. "My little secret. I've carried them wrapped in a handkerchief in my bosom through some tight places. Not for nothing do Shamy girls have good boobs."

"I don't know, Téta," Khadra said, looking at the pile of coins. "It would take some pretty hefty boobs to hold all that."

"They're yours now."

Khadra gasped. "But Téta—keep them for yourself. How do you live, anyway—surely your pension from the *Centrale* is not enough."

"Khadra, I won't be able to keep these after I die. May you bury my bones—but I don't think you will be here to bury my bones." She lifted up a hand to shush Khadra, who was saying a blessing for long life on Téta's head. That phrase, *te'ebrini,* "may you bury me," always tugged at Khadra's heart.

"There's shariah rules about who gets what. Inheritance laws," Téta went on. "How do we get around them when we need to? We give things away as gifts, before we die. That's how. Take it from me, this will be a load off my heart." Khadra would not take them all, but they came to an agreed-upon division.

The divine face has burning glories. Were it not for the veils, the glories would burn away the cosmos.

—Muhyiddin Ibn al-Arabi

Sitting on Mount Qasyoon looking down on the city of Damascus, you could not possibly hold that one religion had claim to an exclusive truth. Damascus demanded that you see all religions as architectural layers of each other, gave you the tangible sense, real as the crumbling citadel steps beneath your feet, that it all came together somehow in a way that made sense. All the religions spokes on the same wheel. All connected to the hub. All taking their turn in the wheeling of the great azure heavens.

While surveying Damascus from Qasyoon through her camera lens, Khadra came to realize that photography was her thing. "Get the training, learn to make a living at it. There you go," she encouraged herself.

She shifted her angle, and suddenly in her viewfinder she saw: a man, looking plumb at her. He sat on a rock, a writing notebook before him, a cigarette dangling from his lips.

"Don't mind me, keep talking to yourself, my lady," he said in a Damascene drawl. "Qasyoon does that to people." She hadn't realized she'd said anything aloud.

She glanced around behind her. The path was dotted, on this workday, with the usual smattering of mountainside housing residents walking down to the city or up toward their cheap new apartments. She was not in an isolated locale where no one would hear her if she screamed. She approached.

He was older up close than he looked from a distance, with iron-gray hair that was not cut short, Khadra realized with a start as she came near, but tied back in a ponytail. There was a scent about him of musty old woodland. She soon realized it was the cloud of cigarette smoke. Not your usual cigarette smell, yet it seemed oddly familiar to her.

He jotted something into the green notebook. She could see that it was filled with lines of poetry. He was a poet, the type of modernist poet who had been all the rage in Lebanon and Syria throughout the sixties. Khadra didn't understand a bit of his poetry, which he recited to her from reams of Arabic pages. Soon their meetings on Qasyoon developed from random moments into standing appointments.

Goddess, ordinary girl, (he recited in sepulchral tones)
you with the torn jeans and jasmine armpits,
let the slave kill the master in the mirror

The moon dissolves in the knob of your anklebones,
and your kiss begins the world

Jasmine *armpits*? Whatever. She loved listening to the little white pebbles of the familiar-unfamiliar words ring against each other. He spoke half a dozen languages, too, Kurdish and Armenian and Swahili and Aramaic he claimed, as well as others—and all worked their way into his poems.

"My dear chit of a girl, born yesterday," he said—his gravelly voice cut right into her, took her to some other world, made her listen raptly. "Let me tell you something you don't know."

She leaned forward expectantly, and he recited,

The sweetness within, you do not know
Instead, you traipse here and there like a beggar,
Gnawed to pieces by your own hunger
But baby, I am here to tell you:
the baklava is you

She burst out laughing. "The baklava is me?"

"Pay attention. You don't get a poet like me every day, you know," he said.

"And you get a listener, which every poet craves," Khadra teased. She had a sun-burnished strip across her nose and cheeks from her mountain treks by now. Like days in the sun with Hanifa, when they were little girls.

"Wrong, baby," he deadpanned, turning from Khadra and making a notation in his notebook. The iron-gray hair was unbound today, making him look a little like Grizzly Adams. "I get a muse, which every poet craves. In the form of a beautiful woman, no less, which is the perfect form of a muse. *Allahu akbar*." He leaned back and contemplated her.

She basked in the compliment. Even though he was a terrible old sexist. Such a product of his era.

"Ibn al-Arabi said the best meditation for the soul bent on knowing something of Divine Beauty is contemplating the beauty of a woman," he continued, chain-lighting another cigarette. Khadra was sure he was making it up. It didn't sound like something a renowned sheikh such as Ibn al-Arabi would say. He fabricated half of what he said, she was sure. The other day he'd told her he was a sailor once and, on another occasion, he claimed he'd spent years living alone in the desert.

"Hey, wait a minute," she said, putting the Pentax up to her eyes. "Then what does a woman contemplate if *she* wants to know the Divine?"

Without missing a beat, he said, "A poet."

They both laughed. So rich was the timbre of his chuckle it was almost a growl. She clicked away, and caught the light of the setting sun on his creased face. It was a cynical but not jaded look he had. As if he knew the jig was up on the world, yet held onto some small secret hope—one he'd never admit to. His little white cigarette box had a red star and crescent.

"Are those—are those *Islamic* cigarettes?" she asked, laughing at the oxymoron that seemed.

"Oh, absolutely." He handed her the box. "General Directorate of Tobacco, Salt, and Alcohol Products, Government of Turkey," it said. She took out a cigarette. No filter. You could see the bits of shredded tobacco at both ends. She sniffed. Musty, kind of a rich rotten wood smell. Old forest undergrowth. Old rich woodlands.

"Oh my God," she blurted.

"What?" he said. "You are invoking the deity for what purpose?"

"The smell of your cigarettes," she said, half-joking. "It solves a puzzle I've been bothered by all my life."

He lifted an iron-gray eyebrow.

"Indiana," she laughed. "That's the answer. Indiana smells like Turkish cigarettes."

"Why do you spend so much time worrying about what God thinks of you?" the poet asked her once. She was startled at his directness; his low voice seemed to come right out of her own gut. She didn't think she'd shared that much of her state of confusion. "It's the other way around, you know. God is what *you* think of God, you know."

This made no sense and sounded heretical. He must be a leftist, a secularist, maybe what her parents would call a godless communist.

"Oh, no you don't," he said. "Don't try to label me so you can put me away. I am what I am."

At their next meeting, he scoffed, "What's eating you? Begging forgiveness? God should be begging you for forgiveness, you beautiful child."

She was taken aback at this blatant blasphemy, spoken with his characteristic nonchalance.

"You still think of God as some Big Parent in the Sky, don't you?" he demanded. Again she was surprised at how he seemed to be able to speak right into her mind's conversation. "Waiting with a logbook of all your misdeeds to punish or reward you? All those hoary ancient guilt trips and self-flagellations for such a tired notion. Not worth a Syrian dime."

"But then what? Without that, I'm lost," she protested.

"Be lost then. Better lost than false."

Lost to myself,
I am found
in You

She walked home slowly, her camera banging against her hip. Was he sent by God or the devil?

"Your veil is very revealing, you know," the poet said through a haze of tobacco smoke. Just a hint of a mocking tone, was there?

No one touches my veil, buster, she thought, but didn't say.

He sensed her bristle.

"Oh, but veiling is important, definitely" he said, reassuringly. She relaxed. He shook his head mockingly. "You're so easy to bait."

She made her face blank, determined not to show him her reaction.

"Uh-oh—you've gone and veiled your face again!" he yowled.

She couldn't help smiling.

"Your woman-body is loved by God, good and pure. Veiled or not veiled," he said through his teeth, lighting the cigarette hanging out of his mouth.

My body is none of your business, she was thinking.

"Real religion's in here, baby," he went on, "here is your church, here is your mihrab." Instead of placing his hand on his own chest as she expected, he put it on hers. Was he a prophet or just copping a feel? She was ashamed of wondering, immediately the thought came to her. No, she wasn't. She went back and forth.

"Who? You've met—O! But, *chérie*, he's a famous poet!" said Téta's friend Hayat, when Khadra told her and Téta about the man she'd been speaking to on the mountain. "His name is golden—Arabs and poetry, you know, chérie. Give us a poet, we treat him like a conquering hero."

"Mmm," Téta murmured. "A handsome lad, too, this one. *When he arose in all his beauty, in truth, in truth he stunned me,*" she sang.

Damascus was such a small town, the way everybody knew everybody. The poet had wooed one of Téta's cousins in the fifties. It had been the gossip of the land for a good fifteen minutes.

"But if I'd known she had such an exquisite relative, my dear lady . . . " he said with a charming smile full on Téta when Khadra introduced them in the dim lobby of the National Museum. "And that she had such a lovely friend," he went on, turning to Hayat, "I might have lingered in your neighborhood far longer!"

Hayat and Téta smiled then, not like pretty young things, but like the splendid well-lived women they were.

Praise to the emptiness that blanks out existence
Existence: this place made from our love
for that emptiness

—Jalaluddin Rumi

The Jobar *kanees* was only three kilometers from Damascus. It had seen three thousand years of continuous use by the Syrian Jewish community, and locals claimed it was the oldest synagogue in the world still used as a house of worship.

"This was Iman's synagogue," Hayat said, speaking in a low voice because they were inside the prayer hall. To their right, an inscription on a tablet in Hebrew, Arabic, and French told why the kanees was built on this spot: *C'est ici qu'en l'an 3043 de notre ère, le Prophete Elichaa ben Chafat a enterré Eliahou Hanabi.* The Arabic inscription called it *"maqam al-Khidr."*

"Who's Iman?" Khadra asked.

"The three of us were inseparable. Your Téta and I and Iman. We all worked at Centrale together."

Khadra was left to absorb in silence the fact that the third friend had been Jewish. She followed the poet and the two women up the aisle. Now, on a weekday, there were only a few people about, mostly men. One middle-aged woman with a boy by the hand was leaving the rabbi's office.

The rabbi, white-bearded and spry, came out and chatted with Khadra's three companions like an old friend, and when he was told her connection to them, he welcomed her with the same warmth and began to point out some of the features of the ancient kanees.

"Four hundred years old, this lantern," the rabbi said, indicating a great iron lamp that sat in a sort of hearth along one wall. "It cast a magnificent glow in its day, like a living thing." Electric lighting was used now, of course.

He spoke with the deepest Damascene accent Khadra had ever heard, drawling out the last "m" on every word. *"W' intooh keef? Alhamdi'llah, tamam. Ey na'am,"* His voice in those chords was like family to her. Something vibrated in her chest.

"Yes, of course, he speaks like a Damascene, darling—he *is* a Damascene," Téta said, as they emerged, and Khadra felt ashamed for not getting it. Of course, of course; she knew there were Arab Jews. Why should she be like the Marion County librarian who once gushed, "Oh, you can speak the English language! And your accent is so American!"

But this was different, wasn't it? It's just that—all this time, she'd thought of them as *Them,* these people over *There,* not all the same of course, she knew that, but, still not part of *Us*. Never. And even when she grew out of that primitive notion of "There's-us-and-then-there's-them," she grew by accepting, albeit reluctantly, the claims of some of her professors that certain things crosscut religion. Dr. Mattingly used to argue, for example, that class interests could unite working-class Arabs in Israel with working-class Jews.

It had made sense. In her *head*. But not any deeper. She'd kept it there in her head as a plausible idea but did not *know* it with her heart or in her gut. Not the way you know *yaqin*. Not the way you know *mubin*.

And now—when the rabbi said *"ey na'am,"* drawling out the last syllable so you could barely hear the 'mmm' at the end, like such a Damascene, she could suddenly imagine *being* his granddaughter. Blood and soil and home, boiling coffee in the kitchen, puttering about in faded house slippers to find him dozing in his chair, his finger on a word in the holy book in his lap. And then this whole other life opened up in her mind. It sent her whirling in mad agony. This incidental skin, this name she wore like a badge—glance down, check it—what was it again? Had it changed? Was it always changing? Who was she? What was she, what cells of matter, sewn up into this Khadra shape, this instar? Imagine!

It was suddenly too much. She began to gasp. Great gasping sobs poured out and wouldn't stop. Téta and Hayat, full of concern, flanked her, and the poet flagged a *service*. "What's your road?" the cabbie said. "The road to Damascus." When they got home they put her to bed.

She slept and woke. Slept again. Dreamt, cried, and blessed. They came to her, all the people she had once held at bay, as if behind a fiberglass wall. Now the barrier was removed, and they all rushed into her heart, and it hurt: Livvy. Hanifa. Im Litfy. Joy's Assyrian boyfriend, whose holocaust she'd denied. Droves of people, strangers and neighbors. *We are your kin, we are part of you.* Where are those who love one another through my Glory? *Their souls are in the roundness of green birds, roaming freely in paradise.*

She called out for a caller to call to her and listened; she was the caller and the call. *Your Lord delights in a shepherd who, on the peak of a mountain crag, gives the call to prayer and prays. . . .* And if he comes to Me walking, I go to him running. . . . *Let not any one of you belittle herself. . . .* And no soul knows what joy for them has been kept hidden. . . . *I was a hidden treasure . . . and I wished to be known.* O soul made peaceful, return to your Lord, accepted and accepting. Come in among my worshipers, and in my garden, enter. *Come to prayer, come to prayer.*

Khadra came to prayer. She felt as though she were praying now for the first time, as if all that long-ago praying, rakat after rakat, had been only the illusion of prayer, and this—what she began to do now—was the real thing. All that had been lost was returning. All that had been disconnected was connected again—*alô, Centrale?*

The poet called every day. Téta would talk to him and report to Khadra. "Here is what he said today, lovesy, I wrote it down!"

When you do plan to wake up? A blessing on that hour!
Meanwhile, guess Who cradles your head in his lap?

Auntie Hayat, her fine white hair floating about her head like a halo, came in the evenings after the bells of *ramsho* (vespers). On her watch, she took one of the poet's messages: "Today he said, 'baklava!'"

"What?" Khadra said sleepily.

"He said to remind you that you are the baklava, how should I know, chérie? Let me see if I can remember the rest: 'You do not know your own beauty, you struggle in grief, but I, I have seen it all, and I know: You yourself are the secret essence.'"

One day the poet came to the house and said, "*Vámonos*, baby! You haven't seen the Ghuta Orchards. Get up." And he clasped her hand and pulled her up out of bed and into the dazzling sunlight of Syria.

"To the Ghuta, before they cut down the last grove, hurry!" Auntie Hayat and Téta said. The peaches had bloomed and ripened and gone. White cherry flowers in long, pendulous corymbs had blossomed on the dark naked wood, light against dark, like a pale girl in a black man's arms. Fallen petals carpeted the orchards and had melted into the earth and now the cherries, the cherries were in their prime.

In a Ghuta orchard, Khadra and Téta and Hayat and the poet picnicked amid other clusters of picnickers. The sky was the blinding turquoise blue typical of Syrian days. They brought bakery boxes of *ghraibeh,* little O-shaped sugar cookies. And nectar of apricot. It was as if she'd lived on Tang all her life: is this how real juice tastes? Had I known! Sometimes they spread an old blanket on the pebbly ground. From such couches of grace, supplied with such sweetness, they gazed on the city spread below.

After lunch Khadra ran and picked cherries for their dessert, meandering through the colonnade of trees, reaching up through the dappled play of leaf and light and shadow. And the trees bent their fruited branches low for her. She came swinging her bucket, hands and lips dark-stained. Deep pink and orange streaks of light from the sun as it set, like a great lamp in its niche, glowed across the clearing, and across the faces around the little table. Téta and Hayat and the poet were instruments in symphony, their conversation a slow music, variations on themes of friendship and love.

Khadra set the bucket down and scooped out a handful of cherries to set before her beloved Téta. Her scarf, a kelly-green chiffon, was slipping off the crown of her head. She reached to pull it back up. Then she stopped, noticing the wine-red juices running between her fingers, and not wishing to stain the lovely scarf. The poet glanced at her.

Khadra paused, standing there in the fading rays with her palms spread, her hands spiraled upward to the sky like question marks. She was in a position like the first stand of prayer. A yellow butterfly flittered by. The scarf was slipping off. She shrugged. The chiffon fell across her shoulders. She remembered when she'd taken her last swim in the Fallen Timbers pool as a girl. She closed her eyes and let the sun shine through the thin skin of her eyelids, warm her body to the very core of her. She opened her eyes, and she knew deep in the place of yaqin that this was all right, a blessing on her shoulders. *Alhamdu, alhamdulilah.* The sunlight on her head was a gift from God. Gratitude filled her. *Sami allahu liman hamadah.* Here was an exposure, her soul an unmarked sheet shadowing into distinct shapes under the fluids. Fresh film. Her self, developing.

She saw her Téta looking at her. Téta got it. Maybe she'd had such a moment in the Ghuta sunshine herself, ages ago; maybe she knew about *kashf,* the unveiling of light. How veiling and unveiling are part of the same process, the same cycle, how both are necessary; how both light and dark are connected moments in the development of the soul in its darkroom.

Blessed be Ishmael, who taught us how to cover ourselves.
Blessed are you who dress the shivering spirit in a skin.

—Leonard Cohen, *Book of Mercy*

Under the cherry-tree canopy it had felt fine having her scarf slip off. She was safe; she was among friends. Back in the mad soup of the city it was a little different. The first few days without her life-long armor she felt wobbly, like a child on new legs. Her body felt off-balance, carried differently. Gone was the flutter about her, the flutter and sweep of fabric that was so comforting and familiar. Having waist and legs encircled now, being compactly outlined by clothing that fit to the line of her body—that *defined* her body, instead of giving it freedom and space like hijab did—was all so new. At first she felt like a butterfly pinned in a glass case, splayed out and exposed. How to hold herself? Cars whooshed past her as she walked through busy intersections and she'd feel the unfamiliar rush of air at her neck. Reaching up to touch the soft fabric, she'd find nothing, then touch her hair and neck with startled fingers. The cars honked and made her jump.

While strolling with the poet and Téta and Hayat in Medan al-Rawdah, with the vendors' cries (*za'bub! hab'lass!*) in the air around them, Khadra suddenly felt discombobulated. "Where are we?" She misjudged the distance, bumped into an *'irqsus* cart, lost her footing. In a flash the poet realized what had happened. His shoulder behind her head, his arm across her back felt like well-joined iron, like columns of strong poetry.

"I champion you," he said in a low voice, "body and soul." Khadra could never tell if he was being straight or sardonic. "I always champion a woman true to herself," he murmured. He suddenly seemed to Khadra like one of the titans from the old world of gods. He wasn't being ironic. He was solid. He was the real deal. Wasn't he? She shivered.

"Te'ebrini, what's the matter?" Téta cried. "Are you dizzy?"

"Walay hemmek," Aunt Hayat said. "Don't you worry, I've got the thing for the girl." She snapped the clasp of her big clutch and rifled through it. Then, impatient, Hayat dumped its contents out on a ledge. Sewing kit, nail kit, her pearl-inlaid cross that she was taking to get repaired, pictures of grandkids, national I.D. card that every Syrian had to carry—"Here!" she cried. She opened a tiny vial and held it under Khadra's nose. It smelled of eucalyptus, sharp and refreshing.

"I'm whole and sound," Khadra reassured them.

The poet looked at her piercingly. "You are," he said. "Whole and pure. The broken and the holy."

"But how do you know?" Khadra whispered, her heart tight.

She stood, planting her feet moderately apart, her weight evenly distributed, hands down at her sides. *Allahu akbar.* She was coming to find the new, unveiled lightness familiar and comfortable in its own way. Still, hijab had been her comrade through many years. Her body would not forget its caress. Her loose clothes from the days of hijab were old friends. She had no wish to send them packing.

The covered and the uncovered, each mode of being had its moment. She embraced them both. Going out without hijab meant she would have to manifest the quality of modesty in her behavior, she realized one day, with a jolt. It's in how I act, how I move, what I choose, every minute. She had to do it on her own, now, without the jump-start that a jilbab offered. This was a rigorous challenge. Some days she just wanted her old friend hijab standing sentry by her side.

And then, finally, it was time for her to leave Syria. Aunt Razanne pressed a small jar of eggplant jam into her hands. Khadra hugged her cousins. As she pulled away from Reem, she felt as if earring posts she'd worn all her life had just slipped out, and a lightness came unto her.

"Come with me," she said to the poet, half-joking. She wished he would always be there to sift the gold from the dross of her, to rescue her heart from the evil playing of her mind, and to save her again and again from her despair.

"I will, baby," he said drily, and then he was gone, and Aunt Hayat was kissing her cheek.

"Cherish yourself," Téta whispered, "te'ebrini." She held her tightly for a moment.

Khadra turned and waved one last time on the tarmac.

* * *

On the plane, she pulled the tangerine silk out of her handbag. Pulled and pulled, and drew the head-covering out longer and longer in her hands like like an endless handkerchief from a magician's pocket. Before landing in Chicago, she draped the depatta so it hung from the crown of her head. Not tightly, the way Ebtehaj wore it. Loosely, so it moved and slipped about her face and touched her cheek, like the hand of a lover. She wanted them to know at Customs, at the reentry checkpoint, she wanted them to know at O'Hare, that she was coming in under one of the many signs of the heritage. And she wanted her heart to remember, in the dappled ruffle and rustle of veiling and unveiling, *How precious is the heritage!* A treasure fire cannot eat.

She knew by the time she crossed the Atlantic that she was headed home, if there was any home in the world of worlds. She loved the country of her origin, and found that something in the soil there, in the air, in the layout of streets and the architecture of buildings, answered a basic need in her, and corresponded to the deep structure of her taxonomy. She would go back again in a flash if only Syria wasn't so clenched and a path out wasn't so open to her. But she knew at last that it was in the American crucible where her character had been forged, for good or ill. No matter that she had been brought there through no act of her own will. It was too late, it was done, no going back now, no phoning home. She was on her shariah to America. Toto, we're not in Damascus anymore, Khadra whispered, as the wheels hit the ground. Homeland America, *bismillah.*

Come then, here is world upon world, and all that you seek and desire. You yourself are the traveler and the Goal, lover and Beloved. The earth seems a riddle, but you—if you see yourself with Love's eye—are the answer

—Shah Dai Shirazi

But where to go in America? Back to Indiana? There was the new home of her parents in South Bend. Jihad was living at home, still in school. Eyad and his wife still lived in Indianapolis. In "the community." Where you cannot live down anything you have done. Where everyone who knows you knows exactly what you are supposed to become. And where, if you try to become anything else, they laugh and spin your head till you give it up. O you are Ebtehaj Qadri-Agha's daughter? O you are Wajdy Shamy's daughter of the Dawah Center? When are you coming back to carry the banner?

And then Indiana itself, the flat land that felt like a trap. The sweet constancy and modesty of stolid, undemonstrative Indiana white people, of Indianapolis black people with their sights set low. Everyone avoiding extremes, and also avoiding stepping out of the rut of self. Hoosiers in their homes with the gate latched against strangers—who's here? Go away, change. Go away, possibility.

She couldn't bear it, not one more instant, not now, not for a long while. Away. Anywhere but.

And now—with the Ottoman liras—Khadra had a new freedom. What did she want most to do? Not to return to Bloomington and finish a degree she'd never use. Photography, what she'd wanted from the start, but had not even let herself acknowledge she wanted, because it was not in the Dawah program, in the Wajdy and Ebtehaj program.

Now was left only to choose where. She wanted to move to a big city where she knew no one. There, she'd make it on her own, carve out a life that would manifest gratitude and modesty and love. She would throw her beret up in the air in a celebratory way, slow motion. She wanted her own theme song.

But she ended up doing it with help from the community, after all, help from friends of her family, and the families of her friends. One of the aunties had a son who had a friend who'd attended the Art Institute of Philadelphia, and through that channel she learned about its application and financial-aid process. And when she got there, well, one of the uncles had a cousin whose roommate's Muslim sister needed a female roommate and even better if she was a Muslim woman who didn't drink, didn't smoke. In this way, Khadra found a place to live that wouldn't chomp down all her budget. For start-up funds, she could dip into Téta's gift. But she was frugal; it must not be frittered.

Photography school was its own adventure. She opted for the two-year degree for budgetary reasons. No matter; it was a huge amount of work. She met Blu Froehlig when she was at the library, struggling with an assignment in Structure & Form in Composition.

"Blu's short for Bluma—Yiddish," Blu said. She was from Brooklyn, pale, with deep-set eyes and wide cheekbones scattered with freckles.

Khadra and Blu discovered they were both emerging from the shell of a highly observant, orthodox religious upbringing.

"Yeah yeah yeah, a thousand rules for everything, that's *halakha,* too," Blu said, recognizing Islamic fiqh as a parallel structure to Judaic law. "I get it."

Christians in Indiana never, ever got it. Protestants found it so foreign and bizarre to have a religious law, the sort with rituals and specific rules and all. If they knew anything at all about shariah, they equated it with stoning. Death, that's all shariah was to them. Yet it wasn't that way at all. Just like American constitutional law, shariah expanded and evolved, and was meant to protect life, and relationships, and all that was good.

So it was a relief not to have to explain every little thing about that to a friend who was an American. Cool to find an American who was not even a Muslim but *got* it.

"So do you still observe?" Blu asked.

"Sure. Kind of. Depends on what you mean."

"Do you eat pork?"

"No. But I eat meat from the deli slicer," Khadra said.

Blu nodded. Khadra didn't even have to explain the deli slicer controversy.

"So do *you* eat pork? Do you keep kosher?" Khadra asked.

"No pork. And kosher: on the toaster of kosher, I'm medium-light," she said. "Hey—have you been to E. Pluribus Unum yet?"

"No. What is that, another historical landmark? I've been to the Liberty Bell and Independence Hall. And the Quaker church."

"It's a food store. With foods from all over the world."

Blu offered to take her. "But you have that project due in graphic design," Khadra said. "If you want to just give me directions, I'll find it."

"I'm going there anyway. I go all the time. Besides, I'm not too busy for friendship, or it would be a sad day in Philadelphia," Blu said, "City of Brotherly Love, right?" Khadra felt a warmth and a tightening inside. Warmth because of the kindness of the invitation so far she had only acquaintances, no one in Philly whom she saw outside school—and tightness because she had fouled up so many friendships so far in her twenty-odd years. Could she handle a friendship, did she even have the basic human skills?

The store was not huge, just the size of a regular Kroger back in Indiana. But what a difference. In the same number of aisles, it managed to fit a whole world of foods.

"The halal aisle is thataway," Blu said. "The kosher aisle is thisaway."

"No way—they have a halal aisle?" Kosher sections, Khadra was getting used to seeing in Philadelphia grocery stores, but halal sections, never.

"Sure," her friend said. "Here's the Chinese aisle—well, it's also Korean, Vietnamese, Japanese, and Malaysian stuff. Care for some squid?"

Khadra wrinkled her nose.

Blu laughed. "Me neither. Okay, Mexican, Cuban, Puerto Rican, Caribbean, aisle two. Ethiopian we just passed, aisle three. Along with your Sierra Leonian and Nigerian foods. And then there's Persian, Turkish—well, the whole Middle Eastern contingent is aisle four." She was going through the global groceries too fast for Khadra. "Next, you've got your Indian cuisine—look out!"

Khadra, gaping, had nearly sideswiped a pyramid of chutney jars. "It's incredible," she marveled. "You'd never see this in Indiana!"

"Vegetarian, vegan. Whoa—hang on a sec, here's my aisle," Blu said. She scooped heaps of barley into a plastic baggie and took a sticker from the bin.

Halal aisle, they hit next. They found halal pepperoni and—"What the—?" Khadra said—halal bacon bits. "How can bacon bits be halal?"

"Hmm—here you go—it's imitation bacon," Blu read off the label. She made a face. "Doesn't sound very healthy to me."

"Yeah." And then Khadra saw—"Oh my LORD!" she screamed. Right in front of her, gaily packaged in tangerine and yellow. "Look, Blu, LOOK!"

Her friend looked bemused. "Halal candy corn?" she said. "This excites you?"

"Oh! But you don't know, Blu, you don't know—" and she told her the story of the pig in the kindergarten candy corn and her first brush with eternal damnation and the despair that had grown like a malignancy inside her so long after. But now! She would wear red ribbons in her hair again, red and yellow and swing her legs high in the air! She hugged a package to her bosom—hugged two!—she danced, she twirled for joy among the jars of coconut oil and tins of rice dolma.

"This requires a *Shehichyanu*, you know," Blu said. "A blessing for the first taste of a fruit at the beginning of its season." She recited the *b'racha* over it: *"Baruch ata ad-onay, Eloheinu, Melech haolam, shehechiyanu v'kiyemanu, v'higiyanu lazman hazeh. Blessed are you, Hash-em, our G-d, king of the universe, who has kept us alive, and brought us to this season."*

And together they did eat of the candy corn. And it was good.

Where Khadra and Blu repeatedly reached a wall was Israel. Religion was one thing, politics another.

"The Arabs had a chance to share the land peaceably in '48, and they refused," Blu said coolly. "What's with their greed?"

"Right," Khadra said. "So like, if someone came to New York City and told you all at gunpoint to get the hell out of Manhattan, Brooklyn, Queens, Long Island, all the best land and the best access to waterways, because they felt they had a right to own it, and, lookie, they would be generous and give you, ooh, Staten Island and the Bronx, you New Yorkers would just move over and 'share,' right?"

"Don't be ridiculous," Blu said. "It's not like Jews up and came to Palestine. They've been there all along."

"A tiny fraction, and they were Arab Jews, not Europeans with different customs and a contempt for the locals."

"But all Jews long to be there. Love for the land is part of the religion."

"So why is it when Jewish people claim a religious reason for politics, I'm supposed to roll over, but if Muslims do it, it's called fundamentalism?"

That did it. Both were incensed. They didn't speak for weeks. Then they ran into each other again on campus. "Am I speaking to you?" one said ruefully to the other. "I don't know; am I speaking to *you?*" the other said, with equal rue. And they'd start talking about other things, and it would be okay for a while. Khadra went to her first Seder at Blu's apartment. Blu celebrated a Ramadan iftar with Khadra. And it was good. Then a few meetings later, they got into Israel again and a new fight ensued.

"What? You *don't recognize Israel's right to exist?*" Blu stood up. This was beyond bounds.

"What? You mean you actually *expected* me to?" Khadra said, indignant. "Israel was illegally made—by terrorists emptying out villages and forcing a mass exodus of Palestinians."

"I can't listen to this," Blu said, her voice tremulous. "You don't understand: My grandmother died in the Holocaust. My mother grew up saving pennies in her little Land box. You're insulting their lives. Their deaths."

Khadra was taken aback. "I don't mean to be," she said, softer. "I'm sorry about your grandmother. The Holocaust was a horrible, evil thing. And I need to learn more about it, like your grandmother's story—I've never known anyone personally who—I'm so sorry." She took a breath. "But—I don't see how that justifies Israel. How does it follow . . ."

Things blew up right there. Blu said you couldn't follow a statement about the Holocaust with "but." When Khadra got home, she was mad at herself for not having said, "Well *you're* insulting the death of my Téta's husband in '48, and Uncle Omar's parents, and all the other Palestinians who got killed by the *terrorism* that Israel was founded on, so *there.* You don't have a monopoly on suffering, you know!" Why hadn't she said that? She fumed.

All the generosity with which they regarded each other's point of view evaporated when the conversation turned to this issue. Gentleness disappeared and the claws came out. At one point, they made a pact not to bring up Palestine or Israel. But it came up anyway, again and again.

"Yeah well, do *you* recognize the PLO as a legitimate Palestinian government?"

Blu was indignant. "Of course not. They're a terrorist organization."

"Yeah—according to the United States. *Today.* In 1987. But the whole rest of the world recognizes them. Who's gonna be America's pet terrorist twenty years from now, I wonder?"

"They advocate armed struggle against Israel!"

"So? It's called war. Countries do it all the time. You'd do it if your country got taken over. They have a right to fight. Fire with fire. Or did you just expect the Palestinians to lie down and take it?"

"The PLO kills *civilians*—children!—and assassinates *diplomats*."

"If they do, that's different from fighting soldiers—and notice, I said *if* they do. Then I agree, that's immoral, and they should be brought up for it—and so should Israel, 'cause they kill children and diplomats too!"

"They do not! And if they happen to, by mistake, while fighting off Palestinian lawlessness, that's different."

"How is it different?"

They left each other in a huff. Again.

A few weeks later one called the other. A meek voice said, "You talking to me?" Another meek voice answered, "I dunno, you talking to me?"

"Why can't we just be friends?" one of them whined.

"Shut up. We are friends." And they were.

"You know, you really need to go out and get other Arab friends besides me, girl."

"Yeah, honey, and you need to get other Jewish friends besides me."

"Yeah, I can't be your only Arab."

"Me neither, your only Jew."

"Yeah. Puts too much pressure on us."

"Yeah. Sugar?"

"Yeah. Two lumps."

"Yeah."

There was a clink of spoons. They stirred and stirred and sipped.

After Khadra finished her photography degree, there was the search for work and then working, at first-stop, pay-the-rent jobs such as taking evidentiary pictures for insurance companies and shooting for photo stockhouses and even working forensic photography at the city morgue. "You here for the *job* interview?" the assistant coroner looked at her dubiously. "You speak ENGLISH?" he added, raising his voice at her the way people do to foreigners. She wasn't even wearing a scarf that day.

"Oh—I just thought—it seemed to me you had an accent," he fumbled, trying to cover himself after. "Where is your accent from?"

Is he allowed to ask that? Khadra wondered. But all she said was "Indiana."

"India?"

"No, Indi*ana*."

"Oh." Confusion registered on his face. Anyhow, she got the job, alhamdulilah.

She supposed not many people were climbing over each other to work at the morgue. It was a city-government job, meaning the pay was low but the benefits good.

On the side she did weddings and anniversaries, when she could get the work. For this moonlighting, she got the Rabbit, needing to get to the far-flung suburbs of Pennsylvania and New Jersey. It had a spunky power-to-weight ratio, and despite its pansy-ass name was a good little jihad-wager of a car.

She found herself especially sought after by conservative Muslim families holding segregated weddings at which the hijab'd women unveiled and coiffed and ornamented themselves. They relaxed around her once they realized she was from their world, and she'd make *wuzu* and *namaz* side by side with them and get back up out of the prayer line and shoot some more photos and the older ones would beam and nod and heap her plate with food. She took this great shot of one of them holding up an oval platter stacked high with shiny triangle samosas. Auntie's eyeliner was smudged around her eyes, allowing you to see how her smile lines and sorrow lines were deepening. But you could also see the face of the beautiful woman she'd been at thirty, and the hopeful and radiant girl she had been at half that.

Khadra also found the trio of golden-skinned teen boys out on the front steps trying desperately to be sophisticated and "ai'ight," and she saw the pair of tender-faced doe-eyed teen girls sauntering and giggling to be noticed. And it was at these same conservative weddings that Khadra caught on film the religious Muslim men at their sweetest, because they let her in where they would not have let a male photographer, or a woman not of their community. She caught her breath once, because of the unguarded wonder and fragility with which the young man in her viewfinder was gazing at his bride. Because that is one nice thing you can say about religious subcultures, she found herself admitting: Muslim, Christian, or Jewish, they try to cultivate an innocence and gentleness in men that goes against the macho model prevalent in the secular world.

While photographing an Arab bride and groom once, she almost thought she saw Juma through her camera, Juma tall and dark, during those fifteen minutes when she loved him, Juma gazing at *her*. A memory of sandalwood scent came to her. When she looked up from the lens, the illusion passed.

It wasn't all weddings and ghosts from her past. A growing interest of hers was nature photography. She loved photographing insects; she could lose herself in the whirring wings. She'd sent her color work on greenbottle and bluebottle fly larvae ("Ecologists of the Diptera Order: Nature's Recyclers") to Joy Shelby, who now worked for the Center for Environmental Education at the Indiana Dunes National Lakeshore. Joy said her director raved over it. "If you ever want to apply for a job here, you'd have a supporter," Joy told her.

"What kind of job?"

"Documentation of flora and fauna. Managing the Bergendahl Papers—there's tons of slides and photograph of Dunes species."

"Hey, I've heard of him. Norman Bergendahl? From the turn of the century, right? I even have a print of one of his nature sketches—a Dunes trail."

"How'd you come across that?"

"Oh, here and there. I collect Indiana landscapes you know."

"You do not. You hate Indiana landscapes."

The funny thing was, in Philadelphia she felt like a Hoosier. A henna'ed Hoosier, but a Hoosier nonetheless: she wanted people to move a little slower, talk a little less, but stay a little longer.

How to say this: God and I
Will forever cherish
Myself

—Rabia, ninth-century Iraqi poet

"Are you going to the mosque?" Wajdy asked Khadra on the phone. It was so unorthodox, his daughter living so far out from under his wing, neither husband nor brother by her side. There were, of course, other sorts of Arabs, other kinds of Muslims, who would've been quite easy with such a thing. For Khadra's parents, it was new and uneasy ground. Her father wanted her to go to Philadelphia's main Arab/South Asian mosque, where the imam was an old Dawah conference buddy of his, whom he could ask to look out for his daughter.

"I need a break from mosques," she said.

"Are you praying?" Ebtehaj would then ask. And Khadra wanted to answer: "Not five but five hundred times a day," or "By being mindful and grateful with every breath I take," or even "God is not an asshole, alhamdulilah." But she kept quiet about the spiritual nourishment she was learning to give herself. The lack of a mosque was a blessing for her spiritual life. She had to turn inward, for the first time.

Philadelphia, unlike Indianapolis, had a diverse array of mosques to choose from. Besides the one with her father's friend, there was the Black Sunni, the Shia center, the NOI place, student enclaves at each university, and suburban mosques full of immigrant professionals. There was also a radical mosque in a little apartment over a shop on Chestnut Street, where a small colony was congealing around a Libyan sheikh and his Kuwaiti sidekick. There was even a gay/lesbian congregation that met in a secret location that changed every week.

Up in Allentown there was a Circassian community center, which gathered in a lot of Chechnyans, Turks, Bosnians, and Albanians. They held folk dances once a month. In full peasant costume, young men and women linked arms and stepped in time and, their parents hoped, found life partners among their own kind.

Then there was the Sufi lodge—the *dergah*. It sat deep down a dirt road in the Pennsylvania countryside, and the hard winters made the log building hard to get to, surrounded as it often was by great drifting masses of snow. With its Iroquois-longhouse shape, the dergah was the only mosque Khadra had ever seen that looked American. Really American in its style and the way it sat rooted in its physical surroundings, looking like it belonged.

"I'd like to build a Téta-mosque," she said to Jihad on the phone. Except for Téta's unconscious reflection of her country's provincial racist attitudes, which in the fantasy mosque they'd change and make right, of course. "You'd pray, then you'd listen to music and poetry and wisdom from all over the world. You'd go walking arm in arm with your counterpart in every other religion and just relate as humans under the sun. Everyone would be beautiful—there'd be a special sort of lamplight that made you beautiful."

"Divine lamplight. Yeah," Jihad laughed wistfully. He remembered that last phone call from Syria. There was no shouting FINE FINE THANKS BE TO GOD AND YOU? There was only Wajdy talking in a low voice and then slumping in a chair. Téta was dead, and they were all bereft. No, Khadra didn't get to bury her bones. None of them did, for all the hundreds of times she'd begged them to do so. The strong smell of *sabun ghar,* laurel soap, came to Khadra with the sorrowful news. She wished she had a cake of it.

Khadra didn't miss having a regular congregation until it came to Téta dying.

She needed to do something to mourn. Khadra was all by herself in Philadelphia—meaning, there was no one who knew her family, who knew what she had lost. That was when she began to feel that her prized, newfound solitude and the sweet relief of being outside the shell of a tight-knit community had a sliver of loneliness that came with it.

At one mosque, the imam told her that an absentee funeral prayer was not permitted in his school of Islamic law. But another that she tried said it was no problem. "*Janaza* for our sister, Nuwar Abdal-Fattah Shamy of Damascus, Syria, great-aunt of our sister Khadra Shamy," he said, and then raised his hands, *"Allahu akbar."* He did it right after maghreb prayer, so the whole congregation was there to pray for Téta. Such a comfort to Khadra, the sound of their prayer and their breaths, and she didn't even mind that the women prayed on a secluded mezzanine. If you looked over the railing, you saw of the men only a bird's-eye view of the balding pate of the imam and the white prayer kerchiefs of the Indo-Pak men and the leather kufis of a smattering of African-American brothers. She felt the tenderness of being in a space she knew intimately, of hearing the collective "amen," of sharing the loss of her Téta in this prayer language.

Through her business contacts, Khadra was invited to photograph the Philadelphia Muslim Ladies' Luncheon, an annual affair hosted by the Warith Deen community, held in a grand banquet room. She felt a rush when she found herself in the high-ceilinged room filled with the energies of elegant, eloquent black and brown women. I miss this, Khadra thought. A lawyer named Maryam Jameelah Jones spoke at the event, so wittily and intelligently that she couldn't help but feel Téta would have liked her.

"But there was a smile on her face, *chérie,*" Auntie Hayat said when Khadra telephoned her to cry over Téta. "And—Khadra? I went down three months later—" in Syria you "go down" into a tomb, like the Roman catacombs, down a staircase to low, cavelike rooms under the earth where the dead were laid. "I went down there with a cousin of hers, and she was preserved."

"She was what?" Khadra asked, not certain what she'd just been told. Poor Auntie Hayat was fading fast. When she spoke to her on the phone, she worried that she wasn't all there.

"Her body was *fresh*. I saw it. Not decomposing." At the words "body" and "fresh," Khadra flashed on Téta's fleshy back in the steamy bath. Her surrendering body, giving itself up in all its soft flab, to life and now to death.

"And the roots of her hair—they were black. I swear to you, Khadra."

Stories like this circulated all the time in Syria about people who were much loved. Miracle stories. Myths in the composing part of the cycle, starting to take shape.

"What about the poet?" Khadra asked Aunt Hayat. "How did he take the news of Téta's death?"

"What poet?" Hayat said.

If I should die tonight, the self is
all the attempts we made to know . . .
the self is a blue farmhouse on a green hill under a
black sky, three white
horses swish their tails as they graze nearby

—Daniel Abdal-Hayy Moore

Khadra reached for the last copy of Salman Rushdie's *The Satanic Verses.* A beanpole-thin woman wearing a long sweater over stirrup leggings reached for it at the same time.

"You take it," Khadra said. "I wasn't going to buy it, anyway." She'd intended to browse it at the bookstore, just to see what all the fuss was about.

They got to talking, and the woman offered to lend it to her after she'd read it. "I'm Seemi," she said, sticking out her hand. She had quick nervy movements.

Seemi Dost was a recent immigrant from Pakistan, born and

raised in Punjab. She'd originally come to the U.S. to get a doctorate in literature, but now trained horses that provided therapy to autistic and disturbed children.

Khadra found that she enjoyed venting with her about her experiences with conservative religion. Seemi was an agnostic, and hated anything that smacked of what she called Islamic fundamentalism, or "fundies," only she tended to put all of religion into that box. Her parents were both lawyers who butted up against the influence of Jamaati Islami people in the Pakistani courts.

After Khadra had read the book, her new friend invited her to a public reading in support of the author. Khadra turned her down.

"But we have to support him!" Seemi said. "I thought we were on the same page!"

"But I don't like the nasty way he writes about the Prophet," she replied. "And I'm sick of Western publishers getting away with anything they want to put out about Muslims. I'm"—should she admit this to Seemi?—"I'm kind of glad someone's standing up to them—even though I disagree with the extremes they're going to—"

"What?" Seemi didn't appear to hear the last part. "So you support the fatwa on his *life?* You support this—this fundamentalist *shit?"*

"I *don't!"* Khadra said, taken aback at her vehemence. Her progressive friend was being kind of a fascist, she thought. "I'd go if the protest was just against *that.* And I don't want his book burned, either." It was all so confusing. She wasn't against freedom of speech. "But that doesn't mean I want to go out and read it in public. It *offends* me." She'd told Blu of her mixed feelings about the book, and Blu had said, "I'm with you on this one."

"That's bogus!" Seemi snapped. "And it doesn't even make *sense*. You can't have it both ways. You either come out and support him, or you're one of *them*. There's no room here for any other position!"

It was their first fight about religion, but not their last.

Seemi dated Veejay Radhakrishnan, American-born of Hindu parentage, an aspiring actor who lived in Manhattan. He'd been an extra in Peter Brooks's multiethnic production of the great Indian epic *The Mahabharata*. Khadra went over and watched it on video with him and Seemi and their friends. She loved it. She'd never seen anything like it.

"I grew up with South Asian Muslim friends," she explained, "but I never really got exposed to the Hindu part of South Asian culture. The emphasis was on the Muslim identity, you know?"

"See, that's the opposite of me," Seemi said. "My father is this hard-boiled, whisky-drinking atheist, and my mother is a die-hard feminist. They're divorced. But whatever their differences, they both encouraged me and my brother to be totally open-minded about people from other religions."

"Plus, you know, in South Asia, you can't very well ignore Hinduism," Veejay said. "It's part of the shared culture of the land."

"Can we watch my favorite scene again?" Khadra asked. Her friends rolled their eyes and cued *The Mahabharata* tape to the part where Duhasena tries to rip the sari off Draupadi, to humiliate her before the court, and Draupadi prays, and Krishna stands invisible behind her and grants her miles and miles of sari, a never-ending sari to keep her covered. Finally, the evil man, trumped, trips and falls on his rump in the small mountain of yellow silk.

* * *

"That sort of Muslim you're defending would never allow me and Veejay to be together, if they had their way," Seemi said, another day. There was an edge in her voice. She led a gentle brown mare into a stall.

"I'm not defending their *views*. I'm defending their right to have their views. There's a difference." Khadra maneuvered carefully over a pile of horse manure that needed shoveling.

"You're doing more than that."

"Well—I guess so—I'm humanizing them." She could easily picture those in the Dawah Center—her own mother and father, for example—frowning and turning away from Seemi and her family. Shaking their heads and calling them "lost Muslims, led astray by Satan, following their base ego desires instead of God's Law." That sort of phrase came easily to them. But turning into those sneering figures in the news photos Seemi'd pointed out to her, their faces twisted, throwing acid? Khadra could not fathom that. There were several steps between the narrowminded but stable and sane Muslims of her old community, and these—these—what amounted to thugs, really. How did those acid-throwers get what they got from her religion, from the same religion?

"So who's the latest guy your mother's proposing a preposterous arranged marriage with?" Seemi said with a sideways look. Khadra had shared that her single status was an unbearable limbo for her mother, who, with crazymaking regularity, called with ideas for rectifying it.

"Hey!" Khadra stopped short. "Not that there's anything wrong with arranged marriage," she found herself saying, rather hotly.

Seemi seemed amused. "Really? You like it?"

"I'm not saying I like or don't like it," Khadra hedged. "I'm just saying, that in itself is not the problem. It's not this terrible tragic movie-of-the-week thing, okay."

"It works for some people," Seemi conceded.

"Yeah. It does." She hadn't expected Seemi to agree with her just now.

Her eye (I'm very fond of handsome eyes)
Was large and dark, suppressing half its fire
Until she spoke, then through its soft disguise
Flashed an expression more of pride than ire,
And love than either; and there would arise
A something in them that was not desire,
But would have been, perhaps, but for the soul
Which struggled through and chastened down the whole.

—Lord Byron, *Don Juan* I:60

She'd met Chrïf at photography school, and they'd kept in touch as friends, but it wasn't until Saddam invaded Kuwait that they started getting together. On August 2, 1990, a phone call woke her up. "Did you hear?" a man's voice said. "Do you think America is going to let him get away with it? How come Reagan could invade tiny Grenada whenever he wanted, but an Arab can't invade a small country in his own backyard, answer me that?"

Khadra looked at the time. It was six a.m. "Unh," she said. "Who is this?"

Chrïf Benzid was twenty-five like Khadra, stocky, with curly brown hair that fell down around his dimpled chin. Of pale Berber stock from Tunisia. They jogged together in Fairmount Park along the Schuylkill River. A family of Muslims, the classically observant sort with the beards and hijabs, was praying under a tall cottonwood tree.

"Why do these people have to make a spectacle of themselves all the time?" Chrïf said.

"These people? Which people?" she said, panting. Two joggers separated around them, man woman black white, and rejoined up ahead.

"Muslims."

"Uh, you're a Muslim yourself."

"Not like that, man. I'm a secular Muslim. These religious Muslims, they always have to embarrass themselves, on some level. Alls I know is, they give us a bad name. Like, let's make sure the entire world knows we're religious nuts. Look at them, praying in the middle of the park with their rear-ends in the air. Besides being uncouth, it's so arrogant, on some level. *Look at us, we pray.*"

"I pray." Khadra felt it was unfair of him to generalize about their motives, or to assume all religious Muslims were alike.

He only lost his footing for a second. "But you pray in private."

"I prefer to. But sometimes you can't avoid praying in public—if you believe in the prayer times."

"Well, I don't see you over there in line with them."

"I'm on my period," she shrugged, startling him. Oho, thinks he's so progressive, but finds it shocking for a woman to mention her period.

* * *

Chrïf irked her to pieces, but they kept going out. They needed each other because Baghdad was being bombed. "Oh God, oh God." Khadra and Chrïf were out with his friends, a cousin who was a cab-driving civil engineer, and an Algerian couple, when the first greeny night-vision shots of the carpet-bombing of the city of Baghdad were aired. They watched these images as they shone down eerily upon them from the TV set above the bar, seeing the fiery glow dropping from dark sky into dark city. Some guys at a booth shouted "Whoo! Nuke 'em!" and they looked at each other. The Algerian woman pushed her plate away. Her husband opened his billfold, shaking his head. Khadra had her hand on her mouth in horror. Chrïf dropped a tip on the table as the waiter came toward them, tray aloft, and stared bewildered after them as they filed out, faces sad and drawn.

Khadra covered her face when the screen showed shots of a Baghdad street in rubble. "Oh my God, it looks just like Damascus. Oh my God."

What hit Chrïf hardest was when the suspension bridge went down. "The bridge, the beautiful bridge." He'd been there, visited as a kid, remembered the bridge. "Bad enough Algiers is being wiped out by the goddamn fundamentalists," he muttered. Khadra opened her mouth to protest that the ruling *junta* was just as guilty, but decided to leave it alone. "Now we have to watch another Arab capital destroyed," he went on.

From a distance, all Arab cities looked like home. A place you could have been in when the bomb came down. A brown or olive face that could have been your little sister's, your father's, broken in sorrow. Chrïf was outraged at the way the U.S. government twisted the arm of the media throughout the entire operation.

"You can see what they're not showing you," he said, jabbing his finger at the images on the screen. "You can almost see it in your mind's eye, right out of camera range. Why won't they show it?" He was working toward a posting in the Middle East with an international newswire service. He was going to go there and show it.

Omayma said, "I hope Bush takes out Saddam. He's evil."

"Of course he's evil, Omayma," Khadra said to her Iraqi sister-in-law on the phone. You little traitor, she almost added. "Nobody disputes that he's evil. But he's safe in a bunker somewhere and it's the poor ordinary Iraqis who are getting beat down by this. Carpet-bombing a whole city? Can you imagine if they carpet-bombed Indianapolis? Can you imagine if you heard a sound at nine o'clock and it was your dad's practice being flattened, and at ten it was your grocery store, and at eleven it was *your* street in rubble? *That's* carpet-bombing. Water cut off, electricity, roads down, bridges—what that does to hospitals, schools, emergency services? Don't you still have family in Baghdad?"

Dr. Hayyan supported the war even though it made him unpopular in his mosque. His wife, however, who still went every summer to family in Baghdad, went into a depression. When the shelter in the Amiriya neighborhood was smart-bombed, killing five hundred people who had sought refuge in it, Omayma's mother developed migraines and fought a low-key war of nerves with her husband. She refused to take her antidepressants, and started hoarding matchbooks and candles, so many that, whenever her husband opened a cabinet, they'd rain down on his head.

"She knew someone who was reported to have died there," Eyad told Khadra. "Her former dentist. With her five teenaged daughters. The dentist's husband had brought his family to the shelter and gone back outside into the shelling and debris. He survived. They all died."

"Good God," Khadra said.

"They all died," Eyad repeated, in a stunned voice. "His whole family. In one swipe."

New broadcasts spoke of the "video-game precision" of the bombing and the White House Press Office infamously called the casualties among ordinary people "collateral damage."

"Can you imagine living on after losing your wife and all your kids?" Eyad softly asked Khadra over the phone, and she heard his love for Omayma and their brand-new baby in his voice—Coethar, a girl, seven pounds three ounces. This was all he had really ever set his sights on in life. *O upright man, man just and true, patient and kind, content with your lot, rejoicing, not speaking evil.* Simply this: having a family and being able to provide for them, and all of them being able to live as good Muslims, praying their prayers and giving their alms and performing their duties to God in the manner they deemed worthy. Was it not sweetness enough out of life, to ask for this and have it answered? *Cherish the little child that holds your hand, and make your wife happy in your embrace, for this too is the lot of man.*

With the passing of the war, some of the heaviness in their hearts lifted. Now Khadra and Chrïf began to discover their disagreements. "You're so full of contradictions," he said. Out on the broad, rippling Schuylkill.

"Most people are," she said. "Full of contradictions." Chrïf was far more athletic than she and Khadra liked that he pushed her into these outdoorsy activities, like sculling. Chrïf was a skilled sculler. As far as she could tell, a scull was the Philadelphia name for what they called a kayak back in Indiana.

"Well, your contradictions fascinate me, I must admit," Chrïf said. The nose of their scull dispersed pond skimmers, those gangly bugs that live on water, but not in it, preferring to stay on the surface of things. "You're so old school on one level, but then on some other level you're a modern girl. I've never known anyone like you."

A woman loves to be fascinating to a man, and Khadra was a woman—feeling herself so for nearly the first time since her marriage had ended. And so she found herself delighting in Chrïf and things like his curly hair. A damselfly dove beside him, down to the surface of the river and then back up into the blue dimension. Always, in the religious Muslim social scene where her instincts had been honed, you had to dull your awareness of eros. You had to put down that delicious tingling feeling that made you want to be fascinating to men, that made you admit they were fascinating to you. Only for the serious, almost businesslike pursuit of marriage prospects could you allow yourself to look up from lowered gazes. It was a sweet and unfamiliar release to allow herself simply to delight in his tilt of chin, his sexy voice.

Khadra enjoyed the adventure of every conversation with him. An edgy, strange world of avant-garde artists on both sides of the Atlantic, and pan-African travel and friendships and a haunting search for beauty, for getting high on beauty, above all. "And did I mention I love his curly hair?" she said, laughing, to Blu, who remembered him from photography classes. She loved the abundance and abandon of it. The men and boys she grew up around wore their hair trim and tame. Ebtehaj with her buzzing electric clipper had come after Eyad and Jihad if their hair got longer than Beaver Cleaver's. "No Beatles hair in this house!"

He called himself Muslim, in the secular sense of claiming the historical heritage, but he wasn't observant. Then, while they were going out, he started getting into Buddhism. "Alls I know is, I don't like religion, but I like spirituality," he said. They were walking in the city. "On some level," he added, unnecessarily.

Khadra found this glib. "What is religion but spirituality?" She walked a little faster to keep up. She found out when she first moved to Philadelphia that you had to walk fast or people would bump into you and give you dirty looks as if to say, "go back to Indiana, hayseed."

"All the organized shit," he said. The statue of William Penn on City Hall was coming into view ahead of them as they walked.

"Well. Buddhism is a religion too," she said. William Penn held up an unsheathed sword. How odd, for a state founded by Quakers, she thought—weren't they pacifists?

"Is not."

"Yuh huh." He found it ridiculous that she said "yuh huh" like a hick. "My Hoosier girlfriend," he teased when he introduced her to his friends. This, in turn, disconcerted her—his use of the term "girlfriend," that is. She didn't call him "boyfriend."

"It's got temples and priests and monks and nuns," she insisted. "It's a religion."

"Well. You never hear about Buddhists going around killing people in the name of religion," Chrïf said.

"Oh yeah? Ask the Rahingya Muslims who massacred a hundred thousand of them in 1942 and gave their property to Buddhist Burmese, and who raped thousands of women and burned hundreds of mosques and evicted half a million Muslims in '76. Who? Burmese Buddhists, that's who." Wow, Khadra thought to herself, I can still score points thanks to all those years of litanies naming the "persecuted Muslims du jour."

"Oh, don't give me a political lecture. There are assholes everywhere, so? What does that prove? Alls I know is, Buddhism is a philosophy. Get it straight. Not a religion."

"Look, it's both," Khadra contended. No. Huh-uh. She wasn't going to let him get away with that whole "I'm a Buddhist, I'm too cool for religion" pose. He wasn't even a Buddhist. He merely dabbled in Zen. "It's a religion on some level, and a philosophy on some other level." This—the reference to "some level" and "some other level"—was Chrïf's trademark phrase.

"Like any other religion," Khadra continued. "Like Islam."

"No way like Islam. If you believe in Islam you have to believe in cutting off hands and stoning and shit."

"No you don't. Surrender to the oneness of Reality, that's all that makes you a Muslim." From the angle where they were now, the statue of the city's founder with his sword looked a little like a—what was that? Between William Penn's legs? No, it was only his sword sticking out oddly. Khadra averted her eyes. She wasn't going to bring it up.

"Read the fine print before you sign, woman. It's a bait and switch. Believe in One God, or 'Divine Reality' as you put it so fancy? Fine, now you have to believe in the Prophet."

"Peace and blessings be upon him," Khadra interjected, on purpose, just to annoy him.

Chrïf went on as if she'd said nothing. "Believe in the Prophet? Now you have to sign up for hadith and *ulema* and shariah and all that shit, on some level." Khadra winced when he called shariah and hadith "shit." But she knew what he meant. "It's all one package, baby. That's how the scam works. The Islam Scam." It had a catchy ring.

Part of her agreed with him. The part that didn't pressed on, "But shariah law is elastic. It changes. It evolves slowly, like Talmudic law."

"Well, I'm not up for Talmudic law either. Same bullshit," he said.

"There's Sufism."

Chrïf was too cynical for Sufis. He called them snake charmers. Organ-grinder monkey masters with a bag of mystical tricks.

"Okay, there's progressive Islam," Khadra tried.

"Oh, please. There's no such thing as progressive Islam. That is such a crock. What is that, some sheikhs who'll only flog you twenty lashes instead of eighty?"

Khadra sighed. She just wanted to make him admit that being Muslim wasn't such a straitjacket. It was the same argument she had with her mother. She didn't expect Chrïf to be arguing for the same thing as her mother, that Islam was rigid and homogenous. It's like, they both *wanted* Islam to be this monolith, only for her mother it was good, for him bad. She knew it wasn't that simple.

Cultivate tolerance, and enjoin justice, and avoid the fools.

—Quran, The Wall Between Heaven and Hell: 199

Khadra was dealing with a new roommate, one she'd taken out of necessity. She was an Iranian girl named Bitsy Hudnut.

"Excuse me, could you repeat that?" Khadra said.

"Bitsy. Bitsy Hudnut," the young woman with dyed blond hair and brown roots repeated. Her references checked out, and Khadra really needed a roommate. No, what she really needed was a loan so she could buy a place, instead of throwing all her money down the drain on rent. She had gone to a bank once and asked to speak to the loan officer. New territory for Khadra Shamy of the mortgages-are-sinful upbringing, she thought, encouraging herself: You go, girl!

You had to prequalify for a loan before house-hunting, a real estate agent had told her. So she made an appointment, put on her neatly pressed hijab, and sat on a chrome chair in the lobby of the bank. Other people, a white couple and a man with a Sikh turban, also were waiting there amid the skinny trees in square chrome planters. They exchanged mild "we're all in the same boat" glances. The white couple was called. When the Sikh man's turn came, the mortgage officer looked at Khadra, then back in a puzzled way at the man in the turban already walking through the frosted-glass door he held open. The mortgage officer shrugged and followed him inside, letting the door close behind them. Khadra waited and waited after the Sikh guy left, but no one came through the frosted-glass door for her. She got up and inquired at the desk.

"Oh, Mr. Kawalski—the mortgage officer—has gone to lunch, I'm sorry."

"When will he be back?"

The receptionist checked something in front of her and then said, "I'm afraid he won't be back today. He has a closing at a title company across town this afternoon. Tomorrow morning," she said brightly, as if talking to a child.

Noting Khadra's crestfallen look, she said, genuinely puzzled, "But, you know, Mr. Kawalski did come out for you. He met with your husband, didn't he? The man with the, the—turban?" Khadra's face fell. "Mr. Kawalski wondered why you didn't go in with your husband. He assumed you weren't allowed to—"

There was no time in her busy schedule for more of that just then. Back to renting, which was simpler. The landlord of her new building told her she could change the lease to include a roommate if she got one within two weeks. Bitsy must have needed one badly too, because she made it clear after she moved in that Arabs were not her favorite people.

"How did she make it clear?" Seemi asked.

"Well. She said to me, 'I want to make it clear that I normally loathe and despise Arabs and have successfully avoided them all my life.'"

"She actually said that?" Seemi said.

"Actually, factually, said that. Then she goes, 'but at this rent, I am willing to try and live with one.'"

It really was a nice find of an apartment, in an economically challenged neighborhood behind the Art Museum. It was a street of brick row houses that had been converted but not gentrified, with stoops and run-down postage-stamp front yards dignified by shrubs and flowers in window boxes. A racially mixed set of residents lived there, and Khadra was lucky enough to get a first floor one-bedroom. Most importantly, it had a walk-in closet she could convert into a darkroom.

"How generous of her," Seemi said. "And you're letting her stay?" Khadra's apartment also had a slit of a patio, where a porcelain commode served as a planter for bright red geraniums, with just enough room for two beat-up Adirondack chairs next to it. An evergreen holly shrub, glossy and lush, grew in a brick-encased raised bed of dirt. Khadra was going to plant mint at the foot of the holly as soon as her mother sent the mint root.

"Too late to change—I already signed a new lease with both our names on it." Khadra had made the mistake of meeting Bitsy without her hijab. These days, she made sure to wear her it the first time she met anyone. But she'd been in a hurry that day, and it slipped her mind when Bitsy rang the doorbell. Most of Khadra's stuff was still in cartons, like her family pictures and framed photographs of the Ibn al-Arabi mosque. The only things unpacked were *Macrobiotics for Life: The Only Cookbook You'll Ever Need,* a secondhand Anzia Yezierska paperback, *The Collected Works of Daniel Abdal-Hayy Moore*, a Thomas Eakins print, a Clash album, things like that. Nothing telltale about. *The Muslim Feminist's Guide to Shariah Reform* by Dr. Asifa Quraishi was lying cover side down in a crate.

"You could have been Greek," Bitsy pointed out later. But Khadra had known Bitsy was Iranian because the guy behind the desk at the Y, who'd seen Khadra put up her ad for a roommate, had said, "I know this Iranian girl who's looking for a place."

"Why? Why does she hate Arabs?" Seemi asked, looking without much interest at a copy of *The Collected Poems of Mohja Kahf,* Vol. 17, which had been tossed in the remainder bin. They were browsing in Between the Lines, the bookstore where they'd met.

"'Arabs caused the ruination of the once-proud Persian people by corrupting their culture, religion, language, and race,'" Khadra recited. Bitsy didn't answer to *"assalamu alaikum"* because it was Arabic, not Persian, and had been foisted on the once-proud Persian people by the evil empire of the Arabs.

Bitsy left notes on little yellow stickies around the house for Khadra, since their schedules almost never coincided. Sometimes the notes said things like "Electrician coming at ten." Other times, the notes listed reasons why Bitsy hated Arabs, because Khadra had made the mistake of asking. For example, "Reason #5, for conquering once-proud Persian Empire."

Bitsy dated a man she claimed was a descendent of the Hapsburg royal family and boasted about the fancy dinner parties she attended on the Upper East Side of Manhattan, dropping names like Rockefeller and DuPont. "Now *that's* civilization," she said, wrapping tissue around a one-hundred-year-old bottle of brandy he gave her. But if if her true element was the aristocracy, as she seemed to think, then why was she living in Khadra's rinky-dink apartment? Seemi pointed this out.

"No offense," Seemi said.

"None taken; it *is* rinky-dink," Khadra agreed.

Khadra knew better than to discuss the Iranian revolution with Bitsy, who was obviously a Shah loyalist, with a family probably from the ranks of his well-rewarded royal-butt-kissers. Khadra's own enthusiasm for the Islamic Republic had dimmed, of course, a far cry from what it had been in '79. Yet even after her post-fundie transition (as she once flippantly called it in front of Seemi, even though she wouldn't let other people call her family "fundamentalists"), Khadra had a lingering fond spot for revolutionary Iran. Not for its brand of Islam, which Khadra now found distasteful, but the way it stood up to America. Like the people in the south of Lebanon, or the Palestinians who said "fuck you" to America and Israel even though they were getting stomped on. Khadra even had a newfound respect for the human-rights-abusing Hafez Asad,

Syria's president-for-life. For the same reason. Somebody needed to not cave in to the One Great Superpower. Somebody out there needed to be alive and kicking. Saying, hunh—we don't care how you do things over there, we do things our own way. You ain't the Masters of the Universe. You can't come and make us. Wanna piece a this? You had to love them for trying, because it was so obviously a losing battle, after *perestroika* and *glasnost* and, God help us, the impending McDonaldization of the globe.

"Reason #10, for corrupting the Persian language with Arabic words." "Reason #11, for changing the 'p' in Persian to 'f' as in Farsi—why did we have to drop our p's just because Arabs can't say them?" "Reason #3, for making Persians go from white-skinned, green-eyed Aryan people to dark-skinned, brown-eyed part-Semitic mongrels."

Khadra left her a note. "Bitsy, your optometrist called. Your green contact lenses are ready for pick-up. PS, If it helps, I'm so sorry about Arabs turning the green eyes of your people brown."

"Did you know Iranians were Aryans?" Khadra asked Seemi.

"I wonder if Punjabis are too, then."

"Bitsy says Iranians are racially closer to Germans than to Arabs, originally," Khadra said. "I think that was Reason #23."

"Anyway, I don't believe in race. I don't believe in origins," Seemi said flatly. "Origins are myths. And race does not exist."

"Racism exists," Khadra objected. "You can't say racism doesn't exist."

"I didn't say racism doesn't exist. Of course it exists. Races don't.

I mean, the idea that human beings belong to one discrete racial category or another. Like Semitic, Aryan, Slavic, and so on. We're all mixed."

"Okay—but then how can you say . . . " by then Khadra had lost any logical thread. Seemi's definitions dizzied Khadra. She had taken graduate classes in postmodern theory at Temple and said bizarre things all the time, like "the subaltern cannot speak." It was quite unintelligible. Reminded Khadra of the weird stuff the Sufi professors in Bloomington used to say.

To All Brothers: From All Sisters

every nite without you
i give birth to myself

who am i to be touched at random?

—Sonia Sanchez, *Homegirls and Handgrenades*

And then it all came screeching to an end with Chrïf. At the sex crossroads.

"What do you mean, you're not comfortable going any further than that?" he said as she slid his hands from around her waist and gently but firmly held them down at his sides. "Ever?"

". . ." She found nothing to say, amazed at his cheek.

Who did he think he was? She didn't even really *know* who he was. Where was his family, how did he get along with his mother, his father, his sister? Where was her army of kin to probe his history for her, to find out what there was to know? She *wanted* to marshal her family in support of her relationships. Her broadshouldered brothers and fathers and community uncles, where were they when she needed them? If only they could be reprogrammed, her stalwart army of much-maligned Muslim men, if only they could alter their training manuals a little, to reorient its goals around her *actual* needs instead of some handed-down script. It's *Islamic* dating. Hah! Try and imagine saying that to dear old dad, Khadra thought wistfully. Never happen.

Chrïf twisted his palms out of her hands and made to circle her waist again, but, quickly, she interlaced the fingers of both hands in his. Handclasps between her chest and his. *Palm to palm is holy palmers' kiss,* she remembered or misremembered some line from high school Shakespeare. She could feel his heart beating. She had seen to it that they had avoided apartments, his and hers, when they spent time together. Their touching was like lace: the spaces where it wasn't were just as beautiful as where it was, and there was nothing commonplace about it. Interlocking fingers with him still made her tingle. If he whispered something in her ear at the movies, tiny vibrations traveled to all the plush little folds of her body. There were nights when she fell asleep with the echoes of those vibrations still moving inside her. She knew, all right, what it was she was holding back from. Still she made the choice.

Again and again, when the moment came, she rose up up up like a little hummingbird and hovered on the brink, and then chose. And coming down on this side of it was no less delectable. She lifted her chin stubbornly. No less a pleasure than sex, her vibrant, her tender-skinned, her consciously-chosen-despite-the-deep-tug-of-tides chastity, no indeed, not a bit less pleasurable in its own way. Well, okay, a little less.

"Do you know what century it is?" he said, a plaintive note creeping into his voice.

What year it was had nothing to do with it. Why couldn't he keep to his borders and respect hers? Why tear up the lace? Even, Khadra thought with annoyance, even if she was a little confused right now about what those borders were for her—no, *because* she was confused—or maybe confused wasn't the right word—in some kind of transition, the end of which was not yet clear to her—she was not prepared to go that far with her body. Just because she no longer believed the black-and-white certainties of her earlier days, didn't mean that now it was open house for Khadra Shamy. She wanted to keep some inner sanctum to herself. That much she knew.

Again, he released the handclasp and tried to move somewhere else with his hands, hoping in their powers of persuasion.

"Would you please just not?" Khadra said.

He took a step away from her. "Ever? I can understand not being ready just yet. But *ever?*"

"I'm a freak," she said to Blu.

"I know you are," her friend said.

Khadra stuck out her tongue. Then she sighed. "I'm too religious for the secular men, and too lax for the religious ones."

"I know," Blu said. "I'm a freak, too."

It was shocking news: Ramsey Nabolsy was dead. Insaf Haqiqat, who had been out of touch with Khadra for years, phoned from Seattle, where she'd settled after college. She'd been close to Ramsey at one point—his teenaged flirtation with Shiism having been, on some level, a flirtation with her—and she was taking it hard.

It was news, literally. "They have it on MacNeil-Lehrer," Insaf said. "Turn it on."

"Oh my God, no!" Khadra cried when MacNeil said his name: "Ramsey Nabolsy." But there it was. Suicide bombing. Israeli military checkpoint in the West Bank.

He'd been able to get close to the checkpoint because racial profiling made it easy. The Israelis were disarmed by his fair-skinned, redheaded Midwestern looks, his buzz cut and style of dress. He could have been a regular American, or an Ashkenazi Pole. Their Us-versus-Them thinking made them slacken on detecting actual behavior tip-offs.

Insaf wanted to talk. "The last time we spoke, you said you weren't hardcore anymore, like the way we were growing up. I dunno, so when this happened, I thought it would be cool to be able to talk to someone from the community. Who might actually be willing to talk to me." Her voice quavered.

"I'm glad you called me," Khadra said. She held the cordless phone between her shoulder and neck in the darkroom. She was developing photos of Seemi and the horses for the therapeutic ranch's promotional brochure. It looked like there were a few she could use on this contact sheet.

Insaf's coming out as a lesbian had caused a stir in their old community. Her sister, Nilofar, still wasn't speaking to her, going on two years. Khadra had no idea what to make of the strange new territory her old friend had stepped out into, "but I'm still your friend," she'd told her. Insaf had chosen not to contact her, or anyone from the old community, for a while. She said she needed space.

"But now, with this news about Ramsey, I needed to talk to a friend who knew him," she sniffled. "Hold on. I have to answer the other line here," she said abruptly. She worked for a child welfare agency.

She put Khadra on hold with a radio news broadcast. Lebanon was at peace, after fifteen years of civil war. It stayed at peace while the first photo went through the stop bath, the fixer, all the way to the rinse. She hung the first print on the clothesline. It was hard to believe, but it had been a year since the fighting stopped, and it looked like for real this time. On the other hand, civil war was breaking up Yugoslavia.

"I'm back," Insaf said. "Here's the thing: I refuse to believe that God is gonna shut Ramsey outta heaven because he killed himself." Her voice was angry. "I refuse to believe *any* of that so-called Islamic crapola."

"I hear you."

"And I'll tell you what else. I refuse to cheer him for taking an Israeli soldier down with him," Insaf said. "I refuse to cheer." Because that's what the radical Muslims were doing these days, issuing rulings that attempted to define suicide bombers as martyrs. In their black-scarf days, she and Khadra would've rallied around this rationale.

Khadra agreed. "It was stupid, senseless violence that accomplished nothing." Her timer buzzed. She pulled Seemi out of the developer and laid her in the stop bath.

Insaf was silent for a moment, and Khadra could hear her breathing getting jagged. "Ramsey's not a terrorist," she said, crying. "Is he? Is he a terrorist, Khadra?" That was what news was calling him: "Palestinian terrorist bombs West Bank military checkpoint, killing one soldier, wounding another." That was all Ramsey merited, his whole life, the history that brought him to that point, twelve words?

"No. Ramsey is not a terrorist," Khadra said. "If he'd done it at a market, he would be. But he didn't. He didn't go for civilians. He attacked soldiers. Of an army of brutal occupation. Ramsey joined the war. It's sad and I wish he hadn't. But that's what he was, a soldier attacking soldiers. Not a terrorist."

Insaf blew her nose. "And I know the hell he went through with his father. That man took a switch to him too many times—but I gotta go, Khadra. I got more to tell you, but it'll have to wait."

Khadra dunked Seemi and the horse in fixer fluid. The story of the lady and the mare, its subtle shades of gray, its meaning was emerging. If it's true like she read somewhere that it takes your body seven years to renew all its cells, then what was the Seemi-ness of Seemi? Khadra wanted her photographs to find the truth of their subject, to see beyond first appearances. To discern. But what truth can a photo get? How do you see something true and real about a person, any person? Out of all those surfaces like the thousand sides of the eye of a fly? Who had Zuhura been? You thought you knew her, but then as you grew up you figured, well, maybe you had seen only a part of her in your limited vision as a little girl, the part you wanted to see. "This seems to be it." Wasn't that—in the Quran—what the Queen of Sheba had been careful to say when faced with an enigma? Not, "I am certain I know," not the overweening claim, but the more modest, more tentative, "It *seems* to be so."

Who had Zuhura been, really? A martyr? That's what the Dawah Center people had decided. Khadra had bought it for years. But what if she'd been just a regular Muslim girl trying to make her way through the obstacle course—through the impossible, contradictory hopes the Muslim community had for her, and the infuriating, confining assumptions the Americans put on her? A girl looking for a way to be, just *be,* outside that tug-of-war?

And so I passed the night with her
like a thirsty little camel
whose muzzle keeps it from nursing
. . . .
Know then that I am not
one of those beasts gone wild
who take gardens for pastures

—Ibn Faraj, "Chastity"

Chrïf and Khadra came to the same old sex impasse the next time she saw him. "Look, I'm not sure I really know, like, on a deep level what chastity really is," she told him thoughtfully. "I do know, at least, that it's not the simple deal the puritanical set makes it out to be." She wanted him to understand her thought process on this topic.

"Alls I know," he lashed out, before she had even finished explaining, "is that you want to pretend you're some kind of liberated woman on one level, but on another level you're just your typical backward Muslim girl with the old country still in your head. Hiding in your self-righteous *haïk*."

Khadra was quiet until the waiter finished filling her water and Chrïf's wine, silently fuming that he'd been berating her in front of this stranger. "I find you every bit as self-righteous," she said. "Everyone has to accept sex on your terms or get ridiculed and labeled?

"If the shoe fits, baby."

Maybe it was true she was scared at crossing the sex boundaries, but it wasn't out of prudishness. "A prude doesn't like sex. I like sex. At least, what I can recall of it." She tried to make a little joke, but he didn't lighten up.

"You'd rather sleep alone in a cold bed forever than take a lover? Just because some old men back in history made up a rule that you have to be married to have sex?"

"I certainly don't want to sleep alone forever. I would like to get married one day and have sex again. Good sex. Great sex," she said.

"Oho. So you're angling for me to marry you, after all. Typical—just like I said," he snorted. "You can't even hold an Arab woman's hand, before she's all *marry me, marry me.*"

That did it—it felt like bullying and humiliation, and Khadra went cold. She threw down her napkin and got up and left without another word. He didn't even try to come after her. She held back the tears until she made it home to bed and telephone. It was too maudlin to cry over him, but. "Well, I *am* an Arab woman!"

"An Arab-*American* woman," Seemi corrected her, in a mild tone.

"—and I don't need to sit there and take insults for that," Khadra continued, pulling her feet up off the cold floorboards and tucking them under the heavy comforting blanket.

"Good for you for leaving," Seemi said, sane and soothing as a girlfriend should be. "No one should be badgered into sex. Although—can I tell you this—you've got some issues with your mother and how she made you look at your body."

"Besides," Khadra continued, ignoring the last bit, and wanting to parse every word Chrïf had said, "It's not just 'some old men back in history.' Every religion in the world has rules about sex. Including his big-whoop Buddhism that he thinks is so free and feel-goody. Don't you wonder why that's such a constant in all religions?"

"To control women's bodies," Seemi answered promptly. To Khadra, she sounded like a broken feminist record.

"But religion tells men to control their bodies too," she reminded her. "Why do you always have to see it as a conspiracy against women?"

"Because it is. Not to see that is naïve. Because it's never equal. Men always get breaks. Polygymy in Islam ring a bell there, huh? *Please.* Women *always* have to be more pure." Seemi wasn't giving any ground.

"I don't see it that way. I see it as we're all supposed to be careful with what's between our legs. Full of awe and mindfulness and tender care."

There was a pause on the other end. Seemi said, "Tell me, do you see me as immoral, then?" Khadra knew that Seemi and Veejay's relationship included sex.

"No," Khadra protested. "I would never say that about you."

"But you'd think it."

"No. Honest. There was a time when I would have. But I don't now."

"Well, why not then, if you don't believe in sex outside marriage?"

"I—I don't know. Because I know you. I know it's not a casual decision for you either. Because people are human and have different weaknesses, and having a weakness for ego maybe just as much a problem as having a weakness for sex, but people only see the sex one and forget that everyone has something?"

Seemi said nothing.

"Look, I don't know," Khadra went on. "I've never thought it through, okay? I just don't believe in it for me. I don't presume to know you and the path you're on and where this act falls in your relationship with God and the universe. Maybe it just needs to happen in your path, for you to learn from it and get somewhere—how do I know?"

Seemi paused. One of those pauses heavy with unvoiced disagreement. "Well," she said, "getting back to your break-up. Do I need to come over with the tub of raw cookie dough?"

"Nah," Khadra sighed. "I'm gonna be all right."

She fell asleep railing in her mind against Chrïf. That he would think she would just up and—! When she didn't even know his family or, or *anything*. Anything beyond the surfaces he'd presented to her, really.

Why, it had taken her and Juma a month before they really—! And then another six months before they got to the next thing. Nights and nights of patient tendrils curling and growing in the lacework between them. Nesting in their little bed, and Juma wasn't going anywhere, and all of the community around them like branches giving them cushion and support. It had taken all this for her to be able to let go, and let go further, and a little further still. All that takes building up.

Takes a marriage, she thought, as as she drifted off to sleep. *And what have you built up?* a little voice wanted to know. Your mother was married with three children at your age. Your father had begun his life's work. What have you built? Where have you gone? Where are your foundations?

She dreamed of a poet on a mountain. Carrying in his arms a package, a package, a—a child in a bundle. Coming down the mountain into a forest of lights and columns and forms in long caftans floating past the corner of her eye in Ibn al-Arabi's mosque. Arch after arch, and moving between the arches, and through the flutter of light and shadow, someone in pursuit in the light and shadow, pulling her, and pull and push, pull and push and—oh! There! Melting there at the base of the arch in loveliness.

Reason #2, the Iranian Revolution. How the Arabs were to blame for that was unclear to Khadra, but it had to do with them bringing Islam to Iran—excuse me, Persia—fourteen centuries ago, cf. Reason #1, "for bringing Persians Islam, which is one-hundred percent more primitive than Zoroastrianism."

Bitsy had been totally creeped out when she first saw Khadra in hijab. "You're not one of those fanatics, are you?" she said, her voice a little shrill.

"Of course I am," Khadra deadpanned. "I come from a long, proud line of fanatics."

"Don't even joke about that," Bitsy said, her face ashen.

"You should introduce her to your ex-boyfriend, whatsis name," her lawyer friend Maryam Jameela Jones said when Khadra had dinner at Maryam's parents' house. "They both hate Islam."

"Wouldn't work," Khadra said. "You're forgetting, she hates Arabs."

"Didn't you say he was Berber?" Maryam said.

"Yeah, part Berber. Mixed. But still Arab."

Maryam's parents were pillars of the Warith Deen community in Philadelphia. Her father, like Joy Shelby's, had served in the U.S. Army, and his medals hung over the fireplace, like Bou-Baker Shelby's back in Mishawaka. The Joneses were Republican. With Maryam, they believed in the death penalty and strong law-and-order measures.

"Shouldn't you be a prosecutor instead of an assistant public defender, then?" Khadra said.

Maryam shook her head. "They all deserve a good defense, and the innocent deserve to get off, but the guilty? I'm sick of seeing them get slaps on the wrist because the prison system can't handle them. You know the old-time shariah thing, cutting off the hand? I know that's defunct, and I wouldn't want it back—but I almost get it. It's almost less cruel—it's here you go, here's the consequence of what your hand hath wrought, over-and-done-with, now go back and live a new life. Instead of years in prison limbo with your life on hold while we the citizens pay your room and board—and you'll never forget. Never go back to crime. Neither will anyone else who sees your stump." She was, if anything, more conservative than her parents, advocating a reduction in affirmative action, and stricter immigration controls. "It's not an either-or issue, Khadra," she said when her friend gave her a look that said "Hey, I'm an immigrant." She went on, "I believe in equal rights for the immigrants who are here already, but we don't have to have our doors wide open to more people than our systems can handle."

Dinner at the Joneses' home was a formal affair, very different from the chaotic dinner scenes of Khadra's childhood. Here, you sat at a long mahogany table and waited for Maryam's mother to be seated. After she gave the signal, Maryam's father said the blessing. There was a sense of solid tradition at their house, a Muslim American life enduring in this way over the long haul. Yet there were things—the frugality, the family-and-God-centered life, and the ethic of hard and diligent work—that were the same here as back in Indiana.

One of the photos on the mantle was of a man with a delicate face that Khadra recognized as Elijah Muhammad. She was surprised that they kept it, even though they were no longer Nation Muslims but Sunni. There was also a photo of a young man in a bow tie, and a formal wedding picture, with a woman, obviously Maryam's mother, wearing a white satin khimar on her head and a slender white gown. On a cherrywood curio cabinet next to an original edition of Allan D. Austin's *African Muslims in Antebellum America* hung an oil portrait of a grand old woman in a formidable church-lady hat.

Maryam was successful and independent, and had recently become engaged to a schoolteacher named Latif. While they saved up to marry in two or three years, Maryam shared a spacious apartment in a gentrified downtown neighborhood with a white Catholic girl and a gay Latino Muslim man named Raúl/Rasul. She knew him from college; they'd been in the Young Republicans club together or something.

"Wait—Latif doesn't mind that you share personal space with a man?" Khadra asked. The roommate was wearing a dark navy suit when she met him. He didn't act like what she expected a gay man to be like, but then she had rather limited experience other than on TV. He was kind of dour and serious. Kind of—well, straitlaced, frankly.

"I didn't say Latif doesn't *mind,*" Maryam said, shaking out her neat dreads. "But it is what it is, you know? Housing isn't easy to find. This is what works for me, and Rasul is part of the deal, is all." She now gathered her tightly wrapped locks at the nape of her neck into a large jeweled hairclip.

"Plus, he's gay," Khadra murmured. A nineties *Three's Company* scenario, except the roommate here really was gay.

"If anything, the problem in this set-up is Deanna," Maryam said.

"Because she's not Muslim?"

"It would be okay if she wasn't, but knew enough about the culture not to do annoying things. She's—well, I don't mean to be stereotyping, but—she's the poster girl for clueless white insensitivity."

"Like what?"

"Like last week she put bacon bits in the potato salad. You couldn't tell because they looked like the red skin of the potatoes. Rasul had a fit. I didn't flip out—I just stopped eating it. Mid-mouthful. She knows we don't eat pork—she just wasn't thinking. She goes 'Oh! Did I do that?'" Maryam rolled her eyes. "There went the potato salad. I was hungry, too."

"That's nothing you can't work out. Bitsy and I had bacon issues." Her own roommate went out of her way to eat as much bacon as possible, in reaction to the Arab-imposed bacon-ban oppression to which her people had been subjected for centuries.

Once she'd ordered pepperoni on a pizza she and Khadra were splitting, and Khadra had paid up her half in advance with her last cash. This meant she was broke until payday two days later.

"What did you do?" Maryam said.

"I picked the pepperoni off my half and ate the damn pizza for two days."

"The desert island scenario, right? If you're on a desert island and there's no food but pork, and it's eat pork or die: pork becomes halal."

"Or in my case, the drippings, after I picked off the actual pork. My butt was broke! But my parents would have picked death," Khadra grinned. "You know why they won't buy fresh deli meat?"

"The slicer," Maryam said. They laughed simultaneously.

Maryam said, "I'm ready. Shall we go?" She was deeply religious but not a regular mosque-goer. She dropped in on one occasionally. Didn't think it was necessary to attach to a mosque scene at all, didn't find it troubling not to "have" a mosque. She had a *zawiya* at home, a clean, well-lit corner where her prayer rug was spread.

This friend mapped Muslim space in a way new to Khadra. Maryam's thing was service. Service to the poor is service to God. "That's the Sunna," she said. "I don't have to be working only with Muslims or on Muslim issues or Muslim this or Muslim that. By representing impoverished defendants, I'm manifesting Muslim values in my life. We don't need a ghetto mentality."

She argued with her father about this, since his position was that Black people should "Do For Self," following the philosophy of Elijah Mohammed. Patronize each other's businesses, build their own alternate institutions and networks. Not get co-opted by mainstream America.

* * *

"A Hoosier, huh," Latif said, shaking Khadra's hand when Maryam introduced them. "IU?"

"Yeah. For a few years," Khadra said.

"My brother went there."

"Yeah, huh?"

Latif picked up her bummed tone. "My brother didn't like it much either. He had his heart broken down there. The most gorgeous girl in the world, he used to call her. He was gonna bring her up to Philly, meet the folks."

Khadra said, "What happened?" imagining some typical American girlfriend-boyfriend break-up story.

"Oh," Latif said. "She up and dumped him. Her parents wanted her to marry a Kenyan guy or something like that. Someone from the Mother Land, you know."

Something stirred in Khadra's mind. "Kenyan?" she said.

"That's right."

"Are you sure she was from *Kenya?*"

"Yeah. Suddenly Tariq was into all things Kenyan. Put the flag up in his room and everything."

Khadra was silent for a minute, puzzling. How many Kenyan girls could there have been at IU in the mid-seventies? "What else did your brother say about her?"

Latif tried to remember. "Tariq talked about, he used to go out to rallies with her and holler and all that, but mainly just because he wanted to be with her. Tariq's not that political, see."

Khadra's head was spinning. Zuhura, whom I never really knew. Ya Zuhura.

* * *

Bitsy would never say what her Iranian name had been. "We changed it when I got my citizenship," she said.

"Why?" Khadra said, wondering who "we" was.

"Oh," Bitsy shrugged. "So we could do things like, you know, order pizza without the guy on the phone getting all confused, I guess."

There was a pause. You changed your name—your *name*—for the pizza guy? Khadra thought, but didn't say it.

"And job applications and such," her roommate continued. "Makes things just a whole lot easier."

"Why Hudnut?"

Bitsy shrugged. "We picked it out of a phone book at random."

I bet at random, Khadra thought. After you skipped the tries that landed on "Hernandez" and "Nguyen."

"But why 'Bitsy?' Is that short for something? Elizabeth?"

"No," Bitsy said. "Nothing. Just Bitsy."

"What did your name used to be? Basima?"

"No."

"Beetah?"

"No."

"Banafsheh?"

"No."

"Berokh?"

"No."

"Can I borrow your canvas tote bag this afternoon? I'm going to the farmers' market."

"No. Get your own."

* * *

A letter came addressed to Fatima-Zahra Gordafarid.

"My God, Seemi, I think I know Bitsy's real name," Khadra said. "Look at this." The letter had a yellow forwarding label on it. Khadra rummaged through her desk for the lease. It was under a book of prints by *Sebastiao Salgado: Photographer Activist*. The old address on the letter, which you could still partially read under the yellow label, matched the "former place of residence" Bitsy listed on the lease.

"Whew. From a great name like that to Bitsy Hudnut?" Seemi said. "Fatima-Zahra Gordafarid. Whew."

Where are my lovers?
Where are my tall, my lovely princes

—Naomi Long Madgett, "Black Woman"

Khadra was still working at the morgue job. One day she called Seemi from work. A local Muslim university couple, both professors, had been murdered recently and it was in the news—terrible, tragic—and there were Muslims in and out of the morgue. Mosque to morgue and morgue to mosque, to police station—the scene was hopping. Tense.

"What is it? What's wrong? Are you okay?" Seemi said, responding to the urgency in Khadra's voice.

"I'm okay, if I can catch my breath. Oh, my God. You'll never believe who walked in here right past my desk just now."

"Who?"

"I don't know."

"I'm going to come over there and murder you, Khadra," Seemi said.

"I don't know, but he's an African god." *I'm holding out for a poet till the morning light . . .*

"Say an *astaghfirullah* for your blasphemy."

"Astaghfirullah."

"Good girl. Now go on."

"Just this absolute god in a kufi. A tall beautiful man, Seemi. Like—like a column of poetry. Chisled out of onyx with broad shoulders and the Face of Intelligence, radiating energy and power throughout this rinky-dink, sterile place. And I am about to fall over. Just fall over right here between the corpses. Oh. My. God. Help me, in the name of the Almighty."

Seemi was laughing her head off. "Stop hyperventilating. You'll hurt yourself."

"How can I meet him?" Khadra demanded, panicky. "What do I do? I can't let him leave this building and not know his name—what if he never comes back? What if I never see him again?"

"You don't know anything about this man. What if he's married?"

Khadra flashed on fantasies of "second wife"-hood—but only for the barest instant—I've just committed a feminist sin, she thought with chagrin. But if it was the only way to have him, would she consider it? Of *course* not—but then, why did she even go there for a second—*yeee!* Stop!

"What if he's *not?*" she said to Seemi.

"Okay. Girlfriend at work here. What's he there for? Do you know his business? Can you get involved in it in any way? I mean, you *do* work there."

"Okay, okay, that's good. Think, Khadra, think. I don't know what he's here for, but I know who he went in to see. Dr. Pappadapoulus. I think—he could be—I think he's one of the mosque people—the committee people working on the Fayyumi murder."

"Well, what are you waiting for? Get your butt over to Pappadapoulus's office and have something ready to ask him. Take a clipboard. Look professional. Get introduced."

"Okay—okay—good plan—right, right—thank you, and God bless you for ever and ever!"

But he was gone by the time Khadra made it there. The mysterious African god would remain a mystery. "But he's out there, somewhere," she told Maryam and Seemi.

"That's right," Maryam said. She rolled her eyes to Seemi and said, nodding her head at Khadra, "Incurable romantic."

The potential for love, in the City of Brotherly Love, had proved itself only a corner-turn away, Khadra felt. She went out every day with a sense of openness to whatever dazzling niches of light the city would show her next.

Khadra happened to have hijab on when Bitsy came home, a rather formal navy one, because she was getting ready to attend a social function with Maryam. She was beginning to see that, of the covered and uncovered modes, she preferred the covered, after all, and she wore it more often than not. It was a habit—hah, she thought, no pun intended! She was never going back to being a stickler about hijab. But it was something her body felt at home in. She knew this now from letting her body speak to her, from the inside out—rather than having it handed to her as a given.

"Assalamu alaikum wa rahmatullah, Fatima-Zahra Gordafarid! Where have you been?" she said to Bitsy cheerily, holding up the letter with the old name and the yellow forwarding label on it.

She was immediately sorry she had done so. A look of terror came to Bitsy's face and she faltered, almost looked like she was going to faint.

"What's wrong? What's wrong?" Khadra said, helping her sit down on the futon.

Bitsy wrenched away from her grasp. "*Bas!* Leave me alone!" she screamed, and then snapped something else in Farsi, startling Khadra with her vehemence. She pulled her knees to her chin and huddled on the futon.

"I was just teasing," Khadra said quietly, "just taking a guess that that was your name."

"Go away," Bitsy said coldly, but she was shivering. Khadra covered her with an afghan. She almost seemed to be having some sort of episode. Khadra twisted the hijab off her head and threw it on the coatrack, it beginning to sink in that Bitsy seemed to have some had sort of visceral response to seeing her in hijab, something physical and involuntary.

"I'm—I'm so sorry," Khadra said in a subdued voice. "Is there someone I can call for you, a family member?" She rummaged through the desk drawer and found the lease—it listed an aunt and uncle in California, but no parents. "Do you want me to call your aunt and uncle?" she asked, sitting down beside her and touching her hand. Gingerly, in case she recoiled. "Can I call your parents for you?"

"My parents died in '78," Bitsy said dully. "Killed by the Islamic Revolution. I was really little. I remember running through the street, terrified, and being surrounded by women dressed like you are dressed right now, and Islamic phrases ringing out all around me. It was the scariest time of my life."

"I'm so sorry," Khadra whispered. The same revolution she cheered back in high school, and took bruising kicks on her body for. Now here was its dark underside.

"My aunt and uncle brought me to America and raised me. Away from all that."

"I shouldn't have teased you," Khadra said. "About your name, or anything. I'm so sorry about—all of it."

Khadra was still on the lookout for love, after the god who got away.

"At least he showed you how alive you are," Maryam said.

"There's something not right about how, in city single scenes, we meet men apart from the families they come from," Khadra said. "It's too anonymous." She thought of Baker, with his heavy, sloping way of coming into a room, how she met him in the midst of children and raw meat and cilantro in Im Litfy's kitchen, how sweet that was. Tobacco smells, and music, and him, with his wholesome Arab good looks in the middle of all that. She thought about Joy's brother often. About how there'd been a slim window of opportunity to get to know him better, just for a minute, and then she was getting married, and then after her divorce, she'd heard he was getting married.

"Just the way single people tend to segregate themselves by age group throws off the social balance," Maryam agreed. "Bunch of heartless twentysomethings, confused thirtysomethings."

"Yeah. I need to be around people of different ages, around some souls that are a few cycles older in their spiritual life. And around children," Khadra added. "I miss having children in my life. Not talking about having them, I mean—there'll be time for that, I hope. Just being around them."

"Yeah."

"Let's go to the Sufi lodge for potluck."

"Let's."

The head of the Sufi order was an ancient woman from Bangladesh, whom everyone called Mukhtar Bibi. She was such a little shrunken apple, you might almost miss her, sitting and guiding the dhikr serenely. Until she spoke, that is—then you leaned forward to catch every word of her *sohbet.* And Khadra did a double take when she met the imam at the dergah: the Cowboy Imam. Clyde Seymour was a soft-spoken white man with a droopy gray-blond mustache and a cowboy hat, which he hung carefully on a hook when he led the prayer, slipping a white kufi on his head in its place. His wife, Julia Orin, looked like Freya the Norse goddess, with a tall, Scandinavian build and hair of pale yellow turning iron gray tumbling down her shoulders, and rough reddened skin on her face and arms and collarbone skin.

Julia and Clyde had been students of Bibi since 1961—since before Khadra was born. You could tell at once that there was unconditional love and sweetness there, the sort Khadra'd had with Téta. Bibi treated the couple with tender, if occasionally sharp-witted, concern, and they doted on her. Just being around the odd little "family" they formed made Khadra want to do cartwheels across the prayer space of the dergah.

She did it, too, once when she thought the place was empty, five cartwheels in a row, right across the middle. Then, out of nowhere, she heard thin peals of merry laughter, and turned to find Bibi wreathed in smiles, almost not visible in a heap of rugs and cushions in the corner.

"Turn, *beti,* turn," the sheikha said. "Wherever you turn, there is the face of Love."

Khadra was there to learn from Julia some dhikrs with which to ground her city days and nights. Children entered the masallah with their parents and crossed the bay where she and Julia were sitting, each choosing a thick, shaggy sheepskin from a pile by the hearth. Then they picked a spot, threw the rugs down, and lay reading by themselves or talking quietly while their parents prayed. Khadra was reminded of Jihad "floating" in the back of the station wagon when he was little. Talking to God and floating.

Jihad called her often. She picked up when she heard his voice on the machine. She enjoyed hearing about his life, being able to tell him what to expect on the PSAT, and holding his hand when he found out what their parents didn't tell him, either, about Shiism.

"It's nice talking to you. It's kind of like having a parent who isn't clueless," he said when he phoned to complain about their parents disapproving of his band (music was not a serious pursuit, they said, and certainly not a godly one). "A younger—much younger!—parent," he added when she protested.

* * *

"Anger, Avoidance, Rebuilding," the self-help book said. It was called *Recovery for Adult Children of Missionaries in 25 Easy Exercises.* It had been dog-eared and scribbled on by others before it passed into Khadra's hands. She curled up on a sheepskin rug herself, to read. Okay, let's see, where I'm up to: "Avoidance." That explained going off to Syria, Khadra mused, and moving to Philadelphia as soon as she got back, and needing be far away from the old scene of community and family. Just to have the space to think, and God knows she couldn't do that around her mother, bless her heart. Ebtehaj was just so—so Ebtehaj.

The phone calls from her parents during that time, she'd ignored, let her machine pick up. The messages ran along the lines of: "Disobedience of your mother will bar your foot from touching heaven. What's the matter with you? Why you are in defiance of God?" and "When you are coming back to the pale of God? We are worried." And her favorite: "Are you dead or alive? Call soon."

She had a dread of going back to Indianapolis and Simmonsville and Bloomington—the whole central Indiana scene. Tayiba had reported that her daughter Nia was in the same school system now—she herserlf was on a Dawah committee to improve the representation of Islam in schoolbooks—and it was supposedly a whole different world. Teachers were into this new multiculturalism curriculum and words like "celebrating diversity" and "tolerance" tripped off their tongues. Khadra didn't buy it one bit. She didn't believe it could all really change that much. Yeah, right, she thought. If only it were that simple.

"Oh, get over high school already, Khadra," Tayiba said during one of their phone calls. "People do. You're, what, twenty-six now?

Twenty-seven? People grow up." She was content and well adjusted, and didn't understand why everyone couldn't be as reasonable as she.

That was so unfair. "It's not about getting over high school," Khadra protested.

"Listen, Mindy Oberholtzer is a dumpy housewife, pregnant out to here, with a husband who beats her," Tayiba said. "Brent Lott is on probation for meth—Hang on—*Sumaya, stop that! You stop that right now!*—Okay. Where was I?"

"Brent Lott."

"Oh yeah. He's probably sitting around in his undershirt scratching himself like the loser he is. And Curtis Stephenson ran for city council and lost, and now he sells insurance out of a trashy little strip mall. Make you feel better?"

Khadra laughed. "Yes," she said. "But you're still not getting me out to Indiana. What about the other Lott?"

"Oh. Well, he did go to law school. He's a lawyer somewhere. Cleveland, I think."

"Cleveland's good punishment."

"Remember that Allison girl? They called her Allison Bone?"

"Yeah."

"Well, she was being molested by her stepdad the whole time she was growing up. Her and her little sister."

Khadra gasped. No wonder the Bone had run away from home so many times. There were far worse childhoods than her own. A surge of gratitude filled her. For home, for her parents, for the community of aunties and uncles who were like family.

* * *

Actually, Khadra had gone as far into Indiana as South Bend for a visit to her parents one summer. It had been manageable. She'd driven into the state and her gut didn't lurch like it did at the thought of central Indiana. Because South Bend was not really that flat hopeless flatness. The women with the secretary hair, the men with the loose, spotted, white-man jowls, the young good-ol'-boy, football-player-rapist boys—those people in Indiana that wouldn't ever change. No, the north was comfortingly off-kilter. Foreign-born immigrants, Polish and Hungarian and even Arab, built the industrial cities of north Indiana. People with parents who had accents. It was okay.

American culture has not been a blending pot so much as a river Lethe for all its peoples, their languages and arts. Have we baptized our children there only to wonder later to whom they pray?

—Thulani Davis, *The Village Voice*

In the kitchen, Ebtehaj was getting worked up about the Bosnian crisis. "You see, you see, what is happening in Bosnia shows that you can never be true friends with the unbelievers!" she declared. The Shamys' new house had been built in the 1940s, with one of those large kitchens that was its own room, before open floor plans became the way of American architecture. The backsplash tiles were olive green and butter yellow. Mellow afternoon sunshine was filtering in from the backyard through the kitchen window—now her parents had a window over the sink, so you could look out while washing dishes. It was nice to see them in a real kitchen instead of a cramped kitchenette. Of course, even here, Wajdy had installed long fluorescent lights to save energy. Khadra sighed.

Her parents looked so small and vulnerable to her now. Wajdy's hair and beard were grayer, his forehead higher; she could see the worry lines in his forehead under the ugly neon glare. She wished she could smooth them away. Her mother's hair was thinner too. You could see the skin through it, and her cheek with its faint scent of Nivea felt even softer to the touch, like it was going to crumble into powder.

"Those Muslims in Bosnia," her mother went on in a strong voice that caused Khadra to blink out of her woolgathering, "hundreds of years they've lived with the kuffar of their land, taking them for friends and even marrying them, and still the kuffar, in the end, turn on them and murder them. The women are being raped by their own neighbors!" There was no denying that horrible fact, but Khadra didn't like where her mother was going with it. It was pointless to have friendships that crossed lines of religion?

"It goes to show that, in the end, Muslims must become strong again in the world, and get nuclear arms, and depend on themselves. Only they can save themselves from destruction," Ebtehaj said.

Khadra's father was washing a bundle of parsley sprigs. He shooed a fly. "They bite in late spring," he said, "I've never seen a fly that bites. Pests."

"Blackflies. Only the female bites."

"You know about them?" He shook water from the parsley and put the bunch in a small orange colander. He gave it a shake.

"From working in the entomology department."

"Is there a bug spray against them?"

Khadra shrugged. "Just the regular stuff. I remember there was a huge fight between someone in the department who was researching ways to make better sprays to kill the blackfly, and another entomologist who said, we are going about this all wrong. We shouldn't be focused on destroying the blackfly itself, it may have benefits to other animals—we should work on fighting the disease they spread when they bite."

"They spread disease? Yee!" Ebtehaj said, shuddering.

"Buy a nylon shirt, they can't bite through it. Like, bicycle gear," Khadra offered.

"Wajdy, don't garden without protection," Ebtehaj broke in.

Khadra plucked a parsley leaf from the bunch and ate it, bitter and fragrant.

"The parsley is for the tabouleh," her mother said. She had some bulgur soaking in a small bowl.

Wajdy brightened—"Do you know that all these ingredients—parsley, tomatoes, lettuce, cucumbers—are from our own garden in the back? Manna for the wanderers!"

"Praise be to the Provider." Khadra smiled as she gathered parsley together by the stems on the cutting board. She rocked the curved knife back and forth over it, hands wet and flecked with green bits. Parsley should always be the main ingredient in tabouleh, finely chopped. Most people didn't understand how small you must chop parsley, tomatoes, everything for tabouleh: infinitesimally small. But Khadra took pride in her tabouleh skills.

"Our biggest fear was always losing you," Ebtehaj sighed, scraping a small mountain of finely chopped tomatoes into the bowl. "Losing our children to America. Having you not keep Islam one hundred percent."

Khadra rolled her eyes inwardly. She resented her mother assuming that she didn't "keep Islam," or love God just as much, just because she had come to disagree with her parents' idea of Islam. As if Islam belonged to them. Khadra sighed and went around to her mother and kissed her soft Nivea-scented cheek. "I'm not lost," she whispered. "I'm right here." And there she was, hands flecked with parsley.

Ebtehaj looked doubtful. "You're not practicing proper Islam anymore. You're watering it down. That's the first step to losing it." She poured the moist bulgur over the bright green and red mix in the bowl and began adding the final touches—salt, lemon zest, olive oil.

"You know what tabouleh tastes like the way Americans make it?" For tabouleh was a new fad in America. Suddenly it came in boxes at the Kroger's, a sign of the new decade, the 1990s. "It tastes like spew. That's what," Ebtehaj said. "Tasteless, vinegary, ugh. There are *rules* to tabouleh, Khadra. You don't follow the rules, you don't get the taste of Islam."

Late into the night waiting for Eyad and Omayma to arrive up from Indianapolis, they sat on the country-plaid couch set and talked about the old crowd. "Do you keep in touch with Tayiba?" Ebtehaj asked. "She was always a good girl, a good influence for you. Nice stable marriage, three children."

Khadra did not take the bait.

"Her father left his Dawah job, you know," Wajdy put in. "Last year or so. He works for an American firm now—non-Muslim, I mean."

Eyad and Omayma arrived with their children in the old Plymouth Reliant-K, with its "I [heart] Islam" bumper sticker, that was still the family car, Eyad being in his residency and on a budget that was challenging with two children. And Jihad came home from the gig he'd been playing. So the Shamys had a reunion that weekend. They went to Sears and had a family portrait taken: one with Wajdy, Ebtehaj, and the three Shamy kids, and another including Omayma and the babies, and then Eyad and Omayma went ahead and took one of their family. The three photos together would make a nice triptych.

"I appreciate you and Omayma coming up while I'm here," Khadra said to Eyad. "Especially with the babies at this difficult age." The little girl, Coethar, was two and a half and the new baby boy, Khalid, was seven months old.

"Irish twins," Omayma joked.

Khadra was annoyed to see that childbearing hadn't made her sister-in-law dumpy. Yet.

Early the next morning Khadra came down to make coffee and found Eyad giving Coethar a bottle in the gliding rocker.

"Omayma's nursing Khalid," he said with a yawn. "We almost had Coethar weaned off the bottle, but she regressed when the baby was born."

Khadra filled a coffee mug—with its perky "My kitchen is halal!" logo—and sat down to talk to her brother.

The great leaps that had transplanted Eyad, in early childhood, from Syria to America and from Square One to Indiana, had been all the gadding about he could tolerate in his life. He wanted nothing more now than to settle in one place among people who valued him, and to put down roots there. Unlike Hakim, he was not a seeker, not on a quest for anything.

"Nice to see you like this," she said, patting his shoulder.

Eyad smiled down at his daughter's radiant face. "You know, when we first got married, I worried that I might be sterile."

"Huh?" Khadra said.

He leaned his head back on the chair and closed his eyes briefly. "Because—ok—Mom used to tell me that—well, that masturbation makes you sterile."

Khadra hooted.

"Shut up," Eyad said, his ears red.

"Eyad Shamy, you were pre-med. You still believed her by then?"

"I guess she had me convinced it was some obscure fact modern secular science was in denial about. Ah, I dunno!" He shook his head. "The things you believe because they come from your parents."

"They lied to us, Eyad." Khadra said

"No, they didn't. Just because of that? Come on! No, they didn't."

Khadra held the mug up to her mouth and hesitated. Go down this path with Eyad or not? *La ilaha ila allah.* "Are you going to lie to your son, Eyad? About that?"

He opened his mouth in a protesting kind of way.

"Good mo-orning!" Omayma sang out, Khalid on her hip, her feet slap-slapping in their clean slippers on the kitchen floor. "And a morning of glory to Go-od!"

Khadra went with Jihad to a band practice session and hung out with them. Garry was lead guitar, Riley bass guitar, Brig drums, and

Jihad keyboard. Khadra was delighted at the sight of them practicing together and wanted to take pictures. You could Visualize Whirled Peas looking at this group of gangly boys, she thought. How did these peas from such different pods ever get together? They called themselves The Clash of Civilizations. How appropriate. Garry was Nation of Islam, and Riley and Brig Whitcomb were the Mormon brothers who'd lived next door to the Shamys back in Fallen Timbers.

The Whitcombs had ended up moving to South Bend a few years after Wajdy and Ebtehaj. "God wants to keep giving us the best neighbors ever!" Wajdy'd said, clapping John Whitcomb on the shoulder when they'd got back in touch. They were not quite neighbors, but only half an hour's drive distant. After Jihad was done with band practice, the Shamys went to their house for dinner.

It was the first time Khadra could recall seeing her mother sit at a mixed-gender table. Her father had done so, many times, through years of Dawah work. But her mother had been reluctant. These were new horizons. You go, Mom, she thought.

After the meal, Mrs. Whitcomb set out a giant blue-and-orange gelatin mold with cubed fruit floating in it. Ebtehaj's face fell. Had Norma forgotten that they couldn't eat gelatin?

But Norma drew something out of her pocket. "I want to show you this," she said. It was the small box the gelatin powder had come in. "I found a Jell-O you can eat!" She read from the label, *"Contains no animal products,"* and then held the box out to Ebtehaj.

Ebtehaj took it from her. She was floored—and touched. "How—where—how did you find it?"

"From a vegan catalog," Norma said, pleased at her success. "It's from California."

"Vee—veeg—what does this mean?" And the two old friends took their servings of bright bobbing jello and leaned their heads together, poring over the Pure Nourishment catalog and chatting cheerfully.

Jihad caught his sister's eye across the table and grinned. Then he looked at Sariah Whitcomb and she smiled, as if they shared a secret.

No matter how fast you run,
Your shadow more than keeps up
Sometimes, it's in front!

—Jalaluddin Rumi

When the assignment comes up at *Alternative Americas,* Khadra ponders it.

"Going back to Indianapolis might not be so bad," Maryam tells her.

"Yeah. Maybe it will be good for my 'self-actualization,' or whatever the damn phrase is," Khadra says.

"Yoda's phrase?" Maryam says. "I mean, Mukhtar Bibi's?"

Khadra smiles at the *Star Wars* nickname they've affectionately given the small, wrinkled sheikha of the Sufi lodge.

"I think she calls it 'manifesting . . .'" Maryam says.

"Manifesting the divine names in your own self," Khadra finishes off. She is ready for this assignment, she thinks.

A few years before, she'd have only been able to see the dark side of the community she came from, the religious guilt-tripping and world-frowning. And a few years before that, in college, she still would've been gung-ho about conservative Islam, showing only the bright side, the slick PR-campaign side. She'd have criticized anyone who did otherwise as a "cultural traitor," a Salman Rushdie—not deserving death, of course, because she was never that radical—well, maybe in her black-scarf days—but deserving reprimand and protest and boycott, certainly.

Khadra hums one of Téta's tunes to herself. She has been picking up photographic supplies at a shop on Market Street when she sees a poster of a globe in a window that reminds her of something. But what? There's a Korean bodega next door. Two Egyptian women come toward her with plump faces and noses broadened in smiles, pushing baby carriages. *"Assalamu alaikum,"* she offers. They blink, and one of them says *"¿Qué?"* and Khadra realizes they are not Egyptian but Puerto Rican. Then she sees herself reflected in the travel agency window with the globe poster and she remembers—it had been the same globe in the window of the Salam Mosque.

And here she is. Eighteen years distant from that ten-year-old girl terrorized by neighborhood boys shouting "Foreigners go home!" and the girl bewildered by her mother's sobs of "We are not American!" as she scrubbed her clean of American dirt, eleven years away from the girl who cried into her pillow at the defeat the day the U.S. citizenship papers came, caught between homesick parents and a land that didn't want her. Not just didn't want her, but actively hated her, spit her out, made her defiant in her difference, yet at the same time made her unfit to live anywhere else. Going overseas was what enabled her to see that she was irrevocably American, in some way she couldn't pin down. Yet even now, she never thinks of herself as American, not really. When she says "Americans," "Americans do this or think that," she means someone else.

And here she is in the window, and people bustling around her on the street—American people, filling the sidewalk, storefront after storefront, Greek pizza shop next to Afrocentric bookstore, Korean grocery next to Dave's Art and Photo Supply. Here in Philadelphia, America didn't seem so dead-against what Khadra was. The Pennsylvania terrain was hilly, with nooks and crannies in it that held more possibilities than the flat same-everywhere horizon of central Indiana, where a newcomer made an easy target. In Philly, it almost feels as if she, Khadra Shamy, she and her kind, are just the latest in a series of Americans, instead of trespassers on the homestead of the real Americans. Vaguely she recalls a scene from a TV version of *The Martian Chronicles* in which Rock Hudson tricks his kids. They've emigrated to Mars and things have been hard for them and they suddenly want to see Martians, they haven't seen any yet, there seem to be none on Mars. But Rock Hudson takes them to a pond and makes them look down. There, he says, there are the Martians. Real Martians—and they look and, in the mirror of the water, they see—themselves!

She knows something valuable. She knows that faded globe in the window and, also, a piece of history that no one in America has acknowledged yet: a history of the Muslims of Indianapolis,

1970–1985. It sounds like the title of a library book. Or at least a pretty good magazine article.

Khadra has just finished shooting a workshop on "Raising God-Conscious Children: Taqwa Today." It wasn't advertised as a "Sisters' Program"—apparently the new Dawah Center no longer offers parallel women's programs, its new gender integration being a sign of the changing times—but you could sort of tell by the topic that it would be mostly women, and sure enough. So twenty or thirty ladies like the aunties of her youth have just allowed her to shoot their animated, earnest faces while they discuss the challenges of raising spiritual kids in a materialistic world. She works lovingly around them, taking in the large hooked nose and the deep eye hollows of an older woman, Indian by way of two generations in Guyana, and the thin tired face of a white American married to a Sudanese man—she has raised five children in South Carolina—South Carolina?!—yeah, she says *inshalla* with a Southern lilt, Khadra notices.

She thanks them and leaves. Down the hall she finds an empty meeting room. She needs space to sort and repack her stuff, and is immersed in this when she notices the room isn't empty after all. Down at the end of first row a man is sitting alone, his long legs crossed in front of him.

"Hakim?" Him again. "What're you doing all by yourself in here?" she asks, just rhetorically. She is preoccupied with packing up her tripod.

"Thinking," he says quietly.

She glances over at him. "You—you okay, Hakim?"

He stands up and stretches. "Yeah." He walks over to her. "Need help?"

"Um—yeah, sure," she says. She wants him to stay in the room—though she's not sure why. "Could you put this away in that case over there?"

He does, silently.

"What was going on in here, some kinda session?" she says, more to keep conversation going than anything else.

"Yeah."

Something about the way he says it. "What? Did it get ugly?"

He sits down in one of the auditorium folding chairs near her. "You know, Khadra, you tell people what they want to hear and you're a saint. Tell them what they *don't* want, though—"

So he was their fallen star. So that was it. The fallen imam of the 1992 conference. She sits down a few seats away from him.

Hakim leans back. "So how are you, Khadra? I heard that you—well, that you kind of went off the deep end. After Juma."

"Oh? Nah," she says, with a dismissive gesture. She resents that, "off the deep end." What did it even mean? Yeah okay, maybe some of those nights she'd spent in the apartment alone could be described as off the deep end. "I just—I needed to regroup. You know, rethink some things."

"Pulled a Ghazali, did you?"

The eleventh-century theologian and university teacher had dropped out of his very structured Islamic life for a while and left Iraq to wander around seeking enlightenment. Went to Syria, as a matter of fact. Lied and said he was going on Haj but really went to Syria.

"Yeah, I guess so," Khadra says, not going there. "How 'bout you? What've you been up to?"

"Well," Hakim pauses, as if considering whether to tell her. She eyes him encouragingly. "I, uh, been playing trombone. At a club downtown."

"The *trombone?* A *club?*"

"Yeah. It's always been—sort of a thing I like to do. Under the radar. Mahasen didn't like it."

"A trombone, Hakim," she says. She'd love to get some pictures of him playing. "That's a pretty big thing to keep secret."

"I gave it up. For a while. For her."

Khadra thinks about this. "But why couldn't you do both?" She pictures him stepping up to the *minbar* and giving a moving khutba, then turning to a large black case on the floor and picking up a fat brass trombone. Putting it to his lips and sending shivers up and down the spines of a whole floor full of congregants. They start to smile and groove. Never happen.

"It doesn't work that way, Khadra. One thing leads to another. It's not just a trombone, it's a path. And on the other side was my wife and my work in the community and another kind of happiness."

But why couldn't it happen? Why couldn't we have mosques where music and prayer could both happen, both hearten people's souls?

"You sure have changed a lot," she says.

"You too," he says.

"You think?"

"You know, not really. I always thought you had two sides. You, and then you trying to fit the mold."

Khadra thinks about this. "Yeah, that works," she says. "I guess what I've been doing is trying to get to a place where I could reconnect the two, and be a whole person."

"Radical oneness of being," he says, nodding.

"Tell it, Brother Imam," she teases.

He smiles.

"The trombone," Khadra repeats slowly. "Wait—you don't just pick up a trombone and start playing in a jazz club. How'd you learn?"

"I was in marching band in high school."

"Nuh uh, you were not!" Khadra says, disbelieving but delighted. "How come I never heard of it?"

"I kept it quiet. You know why."

"Right. Everyone would have hounded you." Islamic, un-Islamic. Halal, haram. Is it godly? Is it frivolity? No space to breathe. Everyone must have kept secrets from each other about what they really liked, who they really were. How much had any of them really known each other growing up?

Hakim looks incredulous. Like she is trying to pull one on him. "Yeah, everyone. But especially *you*."

"Me? What did you care what I thought?" They'd hardly even spoken in high school. By then it was all boys hang with boys, girls with girls, in their community's teen scene.

"You don't even remember what a bigmouth you were?" Hakim says. "How nosy you were? How you interfered with me, Hanifa, everybody? Tried to root out every nonconformist blip on your little halal-and-haram radar? Felt entitled to mess with everybody's life?"

Khadra is taken aback. Had she been that horrible?

"Do you remember catching me with Kathy by the bleachers?" Hakim goes on.

"I—no—"

"Think about it. Come on."

Khadra gasps. "Kathy Burns." *It's all coming back, it's all coming back to me now.*

"We weren't even doing anything. Just talking kind of close. You narrowed your eyes and hissed at me, 'Hakim al-Deen, I'm going to tell your mother.' And that was just one time. One of many. You don't remember?"

What could account for such a huge gap? "I—I really don't," she stammers. "At George Rogers Clark?"

"No. At the roller rink."

"Oh." She blinks. It is coming back to her. There had been some incident. She has a mental picture of young Hakim straddling the bench behind the roller rink, leaning toward some pretty little American girl. And then there had been a lurching feeling inside her—as if it'd been some kind of personal insult to *her*—now why should she have felt that way? She suddenly remembers that feeling. "I—I told on you, didn't I?" she says heavily. Shit. Why does she have to meet up with her past self like this?

"You did. It spread and got worse with the telling, like backbiting does. The grown-ups cancelled rollerskating after that. It followed me for years. Even Mahasen wouldn't marry me at first because of it."

"Oh God. Hakim—I—I was such a jerk. I owe you an apology." What else can she say? That it all caught up with her one day in

Bloomington—the "I'm so practicing" Muslim self she projected and tried to measure up to, and to make everyone else measure up to? That she fell, and that the person she used to be shattered in the fall, and that ever since then she has been working on putting together a new self, she hopes not as god-awful as that first self must have been? God, she hated herself. Everyone must have hated her.

"Ah," Hakim says, leaning back. She looks like she is about to cry. "I don't know why I even brought it up. What's past is done, anyway."

"Well—but I guess it isn't." No wonder he hesitated to talk to her in the coffeeshop; he didn't know if she could be trusted. He doesn't know who she is. Does *she*? She is beginning to, and it is excruciating. She wonders if there's an exercise for this in that damn self-help book she brought along.

"You were being who you thought you had to be. And please forgive me for any hurt I may have caused you, too," he added.

"You mentioned Hanifa. How is she?" Khadra says, changing the subject. It is getting to be too much, this encounter with her old self. But isn't that, in fact, what she is here for?

"Alhamdulilah."

"Alhamdulilah is not a substitute for an answer." But then, why should he let me in on how his sister really is, she thinks, given my less-than-supportive history with her? Then again, it hadn't just been Khadra. Most of the community had closed ranks on Hanifa for having a baby out of wedlock. And what about Hakim, had he been there for his sister back then?

"She's fine, Khadra. Just fine. Doing well."

"Is it true she's a professional driver?" Eyad had told her this astounding bit of information, and she'd had time to grow accustomed to the idea.

A smile spreads across Hakim's face. "Yeah. Her husband builds her engines."

"Oh? Who'd she marry?"

"Malik Jefferson—Aunt Hajar's boy. Why don't you go see for yourself how she's doing? She lives in Indianapolis, you know. Out in Westgate."

"Really?" Her heart jumps. She'd somehow thought Hanifa was still in Alabama. But why should she have stayed in the same place, anymore than Khadra?

"She's actually been training to drive the Indy."

"Wow! She's really racing in it?" Hanifa al-Deen, in the Indy 500! Now that is something worth coming back to Indiana to see.

"She qualified—just barely—but yeah, she's in!" Hanifa had a hard time getting a sponsor, he tells her—and no sponsor means no car, no crew. "She turned down Coors Beer, on principle," he says, proudly. "The C. J. Walker Company came through in the nick of time for her to train and qualify. Alhamdulilah."

"What kind of car?" Khadra presses. She has other questions: what did she name the baby? Who is Hanifa now, and would she forgive her, could Khadra make amends? But she sticks to the questions she can face.

Hakim grins and looks fourteen again. "Open-wheel, open cockpit, 3.5 liter V8 engine in the back. You know: an Indy car."

"What color chassis?"

"Green, with black and blue markings. Why?"

She smiles. "I just wanna be able to picture her."

"Yeah," he says. "She's the first Muslim woman to—"

"Don't," Khadra says. She puts her hand up. "Don't say it. Don't put that on her. I'm so tired of everyone putting that on us. Every single thing we do has to 'represent' for the community. Zuhura, having to represent this and represent that. Everyone had to put their meaning on her. Just let her be, for God's sake. For the Prophet's sake, just let us *be*." She is surprised at her own vehemence.

Hakim raises his hands in the air as if in surrender.

Am I Esperanza? Yes. And no. And then again, perhaps maybe. One thing I know for certain, you, the reader, are Esperanza. So I should ask, What happened to you? . . . Did you tell anyone about it or did you keep it inside? Did you let it overpower and eat you? . . . Did you give up? Did you get angry? . . . You cannot forget who you are.

—Sandra Cisneros, from the preface to *House on Mango Street*

Khadra makes her way to what had always been her favorite part of the annual Dawah Center conference, the bazaar. In the Quran booths, tajwid tapes play and passersby compare the recital of Al-Menshawi to Abdul-Basit. Khadra like al-Husari best; listening to his deep tones always helped her to memorize the *ayas*. There's the Relief Fund booth for whatever is the dire cause this year. Always there are the donation boxes and photos of starving mangled women and children looking at you helplessly under magic-markered Quranic quotes: *Who is he who will loan to Allah a beautiful loan, which Allah shall double unto his credit and multiply many times?* and *That which you give in Charity, seeking the Face of Allah, it is those who will get a Recompense multiplied.*

"Doesn't the naked manipulation of religion that way make you wince?" Khadra says to Tayiba in front of the graphic photos of privation topped by placards of Scripture. Khadra has found her old friend and sometime-nemesis. Tayiba is hard to catch—she volunteers on half a dozen Dawah committees and is a dynamo of activity during the conference.

"I don't see what's wrong with reminding people to give charity," Tayiba says. She looks very smart and professional in a fitted gray blazer, houndstooth scarf, and long maroon skirt. Sunglasses rest atop her hijab. She was always Ms. Mod Muslim, and Khadra's proud of her for not getting frowzy even with a minivan full of kids. She takes a few shots foregrounding her, making the bazaar scene blur behind her.

Tayiba lets her, at first. Then she says, "All right, enough." Khadra stops shooting.

"You once said on the phone that Muslims are just as messed up as non-Muslims," her friend says. "Been meaning to ask what you meant by that."

"I didn't say that. What I said was that Muslims aren't necessarily better spiritually than people in any other faith. They might be as close or even closer to God and not be Muslims. He hears their prayers too."

"Of course He *hears* them," Tayiba says. "But how can you be close to God except through following the Shariah?"

"Yeah, well." Khadra pauses to examine some books. "Maybe divine law manifests in many ways in the world. Maybe you don't always have to have it set in stone as *the* so-called 'Islamic lifestyle.' Maybe it's all about process."

"If it's like that, then go back to my question: Why be Muslim at all? Why don't I just up and be a Quaker, like Mrs. Moore, or a Hindu, like your nonpracticing friend's boyfriend? Or anything, really? What's to stop me?" There have to be limits to Khadra's posturing, and she is testing them.

"Nothing's to stop you."

This is not the effect Tayiba was going for. "Well—then why are you Muslim? You are still Muslim, aren't you?"

"Of course I am. Come *on!*" She smells sandalwood incense. Mmm. Where is it coming from? "Let's go this way," she says, pulling her friend, following the scent.

"Well, why *are* you Muslim then? If anything else is just as good."

Khadra thinks for a minute. "Love," she says slowly. "Love and attachment. I love the Quran, for example. And the forms and rhythms of salah. I keep coming back to it. It has a resonance for me."

"But you think someone else can pray another way and find a path to God?" Tayiba counters.

"Absolutely."

Tayiba regards her with the look of those who have stayed put toward those who have gone away and returned, full of ideas they think are original, and expecting attention for it. There has been a lot of slow, meaningful work to be done in the community while her friend has been traipsing about the world. Even if it's not as camera-ready as Khadra's angst-filled poses. Who has been doing the real work? She has, that's who. Tayiba, true and steady on her course, through a thousand thankless tasks for her family and community. Alhamdulilah.

"Why do you have to see that as so threatening? Why does it have to be either-or?" Khadra begins. But she stops short at the sight of a giant glossy display poster:

ISLAMIC BATHROOM HYGIENE IN AMERICA AT LAST!
**** The Istinjaa 4000XL****
ORDER NOW!

"Oh my God, check this out!"

"Tired of plastic squirt bottles and other makeshift personal cleanliness methods?" Tayiba reads. She bursts out laughing.

Khadra continues reading aloud, " *'Install the Istinjaa 400XL Personal Cleansing System and appreciate the difference! Affixes to standard plumbing fixtures. Gentle hosing action is respectful to your farj! Fully adjustable nozzle goes from pulsing to streaming spray. Long, flexible metal-coil tubing stretches even to that hard-to-reach najasa.'* " Hard-to-reach *najasa!* Respectful to your *farj!* Oh my God, this is a *hoot!*"

"I don't see why," Tayiba grins. "It's really very needed."

"It *is,* it totally is! I mean, I love it! I love Muslim-American ingenuity! God, the problems this would have solved in my childhood."

"We, um—we actually installed one last year."

"I'm getting one," Khadra says, eyes bright with pleasure. "I'm 'ordering now.' I don't care if I rent. I'll talk my landlord into letting me install it. It's like, the future is here, Tayiba! The American Muslim future is here, and it *is* the Istinjaa 4000XL."

At the Marion County Memorial Gardens, Khadra rummages in her car for one of the henna packets she bought at the bazaar. She and Aunt Ayesha make their way to Zuhura's grave. *Alhamdu lilahi rabil alamin, Arrahmani 'rahim*, they begin. *Praise be to God, Lord of all the worlds, the Merciful, the Compassionate* . . . they recite a Fatiha for Zuhura. Khadra opens the satchel of henna and sprinkles a little bit of the powder into the grass, her tangerine depatta draped loosely over her shoulder and fluttering over Zuhura's gravestone. Aunt Ayesha pulls a few weeds.

"Thanks for coming with me," Khadra says, sitting on a nearby bench. "On my own, I wouldn't have found it."

"I'm glad we could do it together," Aunt Ayesha says, sitting next to her. She wears round glasses now, making her face look softer, but her gaze is no less intense.

"You must be very proud of Tayiba," Khadra says, to fill the awkward silence.

"Yes." She brightens. They've been working together as a mother-daughter team on several committees.

"She turned out the way I was supposed to, I guess," Khadra blurts. She didn't have to say that. She always feels nervous around Aunt Ayesha. "My mother—" she stops there.

Her mother's old friend is quiet for a moment. After a while she says, "We put a lot of weight on your shoulders, didn't we?"

Khadra is caught off guard by the gentleness of her tone.

"Not just you—all our children." She glances toward the headstone. "But especially you girls. You had a lot to measure up to."

She's right, Khadra thinks. It was a lot. It was.

"We were so young when we came, you must know that," Aunt

Ayesha says slowly. Khadra realizes with a start that her parents had been younger than she is now when they moved to Indiana. "Young in a strange land, your mother was, like me. We were both a little jumpy. Afraid of losing something precious. Not only like *that,"* she says, nodding in the direction of the grave. "although that is a terrible part of it. Of being swallowed up by this land, reduced to nothing."

Khadra nods. She knows that fear.

"And we were so idealistic, oof! Full of zeal! But we put it all on you. Too much. Wanting you to carry our vision for us, our identity —our entire identity, on *your* heads, imagine!" She laughs, and Khadra nods, because she's right—"on our heads" is right, she thinks. She's nailed it.

"Forgive us," Aunt Ayesha says abruptly, and then suddenly a sob catches in Khadra's throat—Aunt Ayesha is not the auntie she would have picked to cry in front of, but she can't help it—and now her cheeks are wet. Because she feels like something hard and leaden has just been lifted from her. Because her own mother would never have said that to her.

And Aunt Ayesha, of all people, takes her in her arms, her body so petite under the big, shoulder-padded robe. "But I'm going to get your jilbab dirty," Khadra says, sniffling into the broadcloth. "It's all snotty now."

"Usiwe na wasi-wasi," she murmurs in Swahili, and then translates, "It's all right." And she doesn't even fumble for a tissue out of her pocket to clean where Khadra sniffled on her shoulder. "Never mind all that. It's all right."

Across the frozen Bering Sea is the invisible border
of two warring countries. I am loyal to neither.

—Joy Harjo, "Eagle Poem"

The next day, Khadra pauses at the door of a large room where a panel is taking place on Zionism. "Zionist Agendas and the Islamic Movement in Palestine," "Zionist Media Influence," and "Christian Zionists in Washington" are among the topics announced. She walks down the isle, closer to the speaker. Here is the Islam of fear and defensiveness and political power-staking. It is tiresome. The shouting of the panel members and the rumbings of the audience make her tired. She is still as critical of Zionism as ever, but there are more intelligent ways to protest the injustice of Zionism, she thinks, as she walks down to the front of the hall. She focuses the camera on the current speaker, his mouth contorted with fierce words, nostrils angry. Do I shoot, do I take these pictures? Khadra sighs. Everyone already knows this face of Muslims. That's all they know.

"But it's part of the picture," her photo editor says, when she gets him on the phone, later.

"So many religious Muslims are not like this but full of genuine humility and gentleness," Khadra protests. She has already decided; she will not include the photo of the shouting angry Muslim. Enough already. Space is limited and there are new things to be said.

"Right. The type of nice kindly religious person that will very gently tell you you're going to hell," Ernesto replies. "They're in my diocese, too, believe me."

That's the thing. That's what makes the scene so difficult to figure out, for Khadra, so full of contradictions—the people are good people, in many ways—grounded, kindly. Khadra loves the people. And then at the same time she cannot stand their worldview, can no longer stand to be inside it. It is stifling and untenable *not* because it is Muslim, but in the same way sincere and goodhearted hardcore Christians and Jews are wrong, and hardcore leftists, and militant rightwingers and pulpit pounders of any sort. Even Seemi when she gets up on her progressive soapbox.

"Then help the viewer see all this," Ernesto says. "It's no use censoring yourself, Khadra. That's not how you get at the whole picture."

The whole picture. What did Ernesto know about the whole picture? And what is *Alternative Americas,* anyway? Just another part of the mainstream establishment, poised to take ads from the big corporations, dependent on the marketing of itself like any other for-profit venture, or a genuine class act of the alternative media, an intelligent path to visualizing those whirled peas? Now Khadra finds herself wondering if working at the magazine is enough for her. Where is her life going, what is her task? How is she serving humanity? Okay, that's way overreaching, the ironic undercutter in her protests. That's Dawah thinking. That's the missionary in you, like Exercise 23 in the book showed, remember? All she has to do is keep her inner flame going inside its niche; that one little goal connects her always to all humanity. Fine, she thinks, backing down, nothing grand, then, and returns to the basic question: Is this work something she can do with her whole self? That's the only "whole picture" she has to worry about. Yes, she decides. It is. This assignment is from my whole self, anyway. She will get to the end of it and figure out where to go from there.

She ties her hair back with a faded green bandanna. (She remembers how she and some of the other girls used to wear bandannas for their earliest stabs at hijab, because ordinary Hoosier kids like Allison Bone wore bandannas all the time and the Muslim kids hoped to pass for normal in them.) Khadra goes out in a modest jogging outfit—long cotton drawstring pants and a three-quarter-sleeve T-shirt—and chooses a path on the outskirts of hardcore Islamistan, away from the part of campus overrun by conference Muslims.

God, she knows every inch of this place. It's a part of her. The stinky gingko tree—hers. Her Maryam tree, she called the mulberry—it let fall fresh ripe fruit upon her, like Maryam's tree in the Quran. There's the path where she biked with Joy and shouted about abortion. Here's where she waded in the waist-deep snowdrifts of more than one Indiana winter. This is where the mockingbirds used to swoop down and attack you as you ambled down the path, until somebody taped off a chunk of sidewalk and put up a handwritten sign, *Mockingbirds Nesting, Do Not Disturb!*

She slows to a power walk, cooling down. Rounds a corner and there is Hakim, sitting on a stone bench in the twilight. She waves. He is there when she circles back. They find themselves segueing down the same path toward Lindley Hall. Her sweat is cooling off, but her cheeks are still a little flushed.

"It's maghreb," Hakim observes.

"Mmm hmm," Khadra says absently. She is confused by her sudden heightened awareness of his body. A sensation comes to her, a physical memory of bike riding with him when they were kids, leaning back into his chest, his grip next to hers on the handlebars.

He looks at his watch. "Dang. I haven't prayed."

"Oh—er—" Khadra looks sheepish. "I haven't either. If we hustle back to the Union, we can just about do maghreb in time."

"Maghreb time is short."

She knows that. She also knows that, as a traveler, she can slide over the time limit and pray maghreb when she does the night prayer later. And she knows Hakim knows it.

"Wanna pray together? Here?" Hakim says, gesturing toward the grass.

A warm glow suffuses from her belly. From the jogging. "Sure, why not," she says. They veer off the path to a woodsy spot behind Lindley Hall, away from pedestrians.

"Got wudu?"

"You bet."

She unrolls her bandana and opens it into a little makeshift prayer scarf. She does not stand behind Hakim—he glances around as if to locate her—but beside, leaving a few feet of grass between them.

After salam, they stay sitting on the grass a little while longer, leaning back out of the upright prayer posture into a more relaxed position, each one looking down at his or her finger joints. Hakim gazes at her face as they begin to rise. He leans toward her—she draws back a little—he reaches out and brushes her forehead very lightly with the tips of two fingers.

"Piece of grass," he says, holding out his open palm to show her. Smooth smooth man. They walk back, not talking much, the late afternoon buttering into evening. Butter, too, is his low voice beside her, his gait of smooth restraint.

"Hey—listen," he says, just before they part. "We're all going out to root for Hanifa in the race tomorrow. Me and my folks. Want to come?"

Is—is she being asked on a *date?* A date with the imam? She giggles inwardly. No, she corrects herself quickly, it's a family thing. He's asking me as a friend.

"I'd love to," she says, smiling widely.

She has time for a quick shower before her next shoot. Under the water, she thinks about Hakim. What is happening? *I'm soooo confused,* she could hear herself telling Seemi. She wishes she had a girlfriend here to talk to. It's too much to explain long distance. *What* is too much to explain? Has anything really even happened? Was that a lace moment, praying beside him on the grass? Does he feel it too, or is it just her? Is she imagining it, projecting, ohhhh what what what.

Okay, she says to herself, be your own inner girlfriend, think this through. Say it's real. Say it's lace. Then what? *Hakim?* Does she really want to go back in time to someone from her childhood, from the old mindset? But he isn't, any more than she is. Just because he grew up in it. He's on some kind of journey, he's somewhere betwixt and between, like she is. But he's an imam. Yeah, so? Got anything against imams? Nooo, Khadra doesn't. But what about him being freshly divorced? What is it Americans call that in dating terms—oh yeah: on the rebound. She knows all about that, and that it's potentially dangerous. Getting someone on the rebound is something to avoid. But clearly she is having trouble avoiding Hakim.

Khadra, with two cameras hanging from her shoulder—because she wants both color and black-and-white shots of the concert—heads for the auditorium to get some shots of the curious band her brother is in, The Clash of Civlizations.

The Civ (they go with that for short to avoid confusion with The Clash) does events both in and out of religious enclaves, although the religion people like them because they have a rep as a "straightedge" or "clean" band. No lyrics about the thrills of drugs, drinking, or promiscuous sex. They've been busy practicing for their Dawah conference debut, working out versions of their songs without instruments, to meet the requirement that all entertainment conform to the most conservative of Islamic standards so as not to offend any of its constituency.

She gets there only to find Jihad slumped against a large amp. Garry is packing up. Brig and Riley look glum.

"Man," Brig says, shaking his head. Khadra snaps his expression in grainy black and white as she waves hello.

"What's wrong?"

Just then, an announcement comes over the PA system: "Brothers and sisters, the concert in tonight's Entertainment Program, The Clash of Civilizations, has been cancelled. Repeat, The Clash of Civilizations is cancelled."

"But why?" Khadra says, as she keeps snapping. Their postures are the very picture of boy-band dejection.

"We've been fatwa'd," Garry says. "We've been given the ol' Salman Rushdie."

"Oh my God—you got a death threat?" Khadra says. She stops shooting.

"Not that bad," Jihad hurries to assure her. "The uncles just shut us down," he says, disappointment in his voice.

"But why?" Khadra says again.

"It's not us, it's about some girls who went before us," Brig says, wrapping an orange extension cord. "We weren't even here."

"Somebody explain to me what happened," Khadra says. She knows too well how little support for any kind of arts there is in the Dawah community. Why had she let her hopes rise when she heard they actually tried to put together an arts segment in this year's conference?

"Okay, you know that girl group that performed this afternoon?" Jihad says.

"You mean Hijab Hip Hop with the Nia Girls?" Khadra says. She'd seen the flyers. She loved their name.

"Right," Jihad says. "So okay, there's this rule that girls have to stay behind the podium when performing."

Khadra's jaw drops. But why should I be surprised, she thinks.

"Yeah. I kid you not. Only their head can show above the

podium. 'They are not to dance and not to make their voice suggestive and seductive,' and all that, right?"

"Whew," Garry says.

"So, but it's a rap group, okay?" Jihad goes. "You can't just stand stock still on one X mark on the floor and rap. You move around."

"She moved around, like—like this"—Garry moonwalks to demonstrate—"and they said she was dancing," he says.

Khadra smiles. She would've liked to see it.

"The uncles closed in pretty fast after it got reported up the chain of command," Jihad goes on.

Of course, Khadra thinks. The body of a woman or girl is enough to bring the whole thing to a crashing halt. It's like a lever—what did that Greek guy say? Give me a lever and I can move the whole world? What can transform the self to love? It is beauty. Ibn al-Arabi knew. Back in Syria, the poet knows.

"They had some sort of emergency meeting," Jihad says. "Uncle Kuldip shows up and he, like, sort of apologizes to us but he says they've already heard a lot of complaints from conference-goers about the entertainment segment and the coordinating committee just made a snap decision to cancel the whole thing."

"That sucks," she says.

"He says not to feel discouraged, just that it's too soon to spring it on Islamistan, the conference goers can't take this much change yet, we have to understand. And so on. Give me a break," Jihad harrumphs.

"That really sucks," Khadra says. "Hang on a sec, I have to make a phone call." She finds a pay phone in the hallway. "Uncle Abdulla? . . . Yes, and so I'm coming after all, but is it okay if I invite Jihad along?"

She has to hold the receiver away from her face while Uncle

Abdulla sputters "How can you even think you need to ask such a question, you are like my own children, you must come, you and your brother, I will be very upset if you don't come," etc., etc.

"Great, and also, there's his friends—a Muslim boy named Garry and the Whitcomb twins, remember the Whitcombs from next door to us in the Timbers? Is that okay?"

Uncle Abdulla goes off into another torrent of welcoming phrases and reprimands—how could Khadra question his hospitality? And on the occasion of the aqiqa of his first grandbaby? His door is open, his table is for all. She returns smiling, warmed by his voice; she knew she could count on the kindliness of Uncle Abdulla.

". . . so guys, if you want to come, you've got an open invitation," Khadra says to the members of the band. They look doubtful. She takes Jihad's arm. "Look, I need you to come with me. I'm not driving that evil road to Simmonsville by myself. Come on! I've got room for all of you," she says to Brig and Riley and Garry. "You'll get good food out of it, anyway. At least the evening won't be a total waste."

"It *was* always good food at you guys' house," Brig says.

"Anything that wasn't Mom's endless casseroles with the Campbell's-soup sauce was good food," Riley grins, and Brig punches him in the arm for being a traitor to their mother like that, but he adds, "With the potato chips on top. Don't forget the potato chips."

"I dunno, I kind of liked the potato chips," Jihad says, lifting the amp onto a dolly.

If you'd been loyal to the love we had,
that other girl would not have turned your head
You knew I was the full moon rising,
but went for the cheap Miss Thing instead

—Wallada bint al-Mustakfi, twelfth-century poet of Islamic Spain

In the car, Bette Midler sings "From a Distance" on the station Khadra is tuned to, but the boys are smirking and stifling snickers and finally they blurt, "Aaargh! Enough!" and she lets Jihad tune the radio. After blips of news—*FBI Director Fox revealed that Muslim groups in the United States have been under federal surveillance since 1972—of the UN resolution holding Serbian political leaders personally responsible . . . overt policy . . . systematic mass rape of Bosnian Muslims—calling the Vance-Owen plan grievously inadequate*—he finds a heavy-metal station. She grits her teeth and tries to hear music in the noise of their generation.

She'd been only half-joking when she told Jihad she didn't want to be alone on this stretch of road. Even though she'd trekked all across the country on her own, this is the road where Zuhura died and it still freaked her out. Whenever she sees a group of white men, or even just one white man, who looks small-town or rural or lower-class urban—she admits there is class prejudice in her feeling—in short, whenever she sees Hoosiers of the male persuasion who look like roughnecks, somewhere in the pit of her stomach she freaks out, even if she hides it well. Whether they are paunchy middle-aged men with balding pates or guys her age smooth shaven as Randy Travis, or boys her brother's age, some terrified cell in her lower gut flinches and some buried part of her flashes on Zuhura curled naked in a ditch with her henna'd hands, Zuhura's rapists and killers still out there, never caught: the police didn't care, it could be anyone. Is it them? Coming up behind me in the white pick-up? Then the pick-up passes. Not them. Then another one sidles up next to her, with a rifle rack in the back. Is it them? Who's hunting me? Who is hunting me, who I cannot see? Jihad, and his friends in the back of her little hatchback Rabbit, and the music, even the awful Metallica, keep the terror deep down muffled in her gut where it can't come out.

"It doesn't make sense," Jihad says. "We're going to eat dinner with the people who run the organization that just cancelled our concert."

"Not technically. Uncle Abdulla retired from the Dawah years ago," Khadra says. "He went back to his degree field, electrical engineering."

"Really?"

"Yeah. He had to, to support two wives."

“Two wives?” Brig says incredulously.

Riley says, “You guys really still do that? We're the ones who always take the rap for it!”

“He and Tante Mirvat never had a civil marriage. Just an Islamic one,” Khadra says, keeping an eye out for the turnoff. “I suppose that means in this country they'd be considered having a common whatsit?”

“Common-law marriage,” Garry says. He's pre-law. “No, they wouldn't. Because he's legally married to the first one. The second one'd be his mistress and that's all. She has no legal protection.”

“Oh,” Khadra says. “That's disturbing. No wonder Mirvat has been on Valium since the Reagan era.”

But obviously there is détente now between the two women because they both are there, in the Dawah Center backyard where the aqiqa is being held. The place is strung with Chinese lanterns in the summer night. And there's Sabriya, once a little curly-headed girl who used to climb on her daddy's head during prayer and make the whole congregation wait. Now Sabriya, the new mother, lies on a lounge chair on the women's side of the lawn. In her lap is her one-week-old infant girl, honoree of the day, wearing tiny gold earrings like any Arab baby girl. She basks in a nimbus glow, the spun fabric of a womblike existence. Her will is still undifferentiated, sloshing around gently like yolk in the egg of family life unbroken.

Sabriya's mother, Aunt Fatma, sits sentry in an Adirondack chair next to her. Tante Mirvat keeps her distance at a table over by the towering lilac bushes. Her two lisping little boys run around in white dress shirts and carefully creased pants while everybody else is wearing jeans and sitting on the grass amid the crabapple trees. The bank of tiger lilies is in bloom, obscuring the chain-link fence. The aqiqa crowd is thinner than what it would normally be because of people siphoned off to the conference in Bloomington.

There are two identical buffets (on long folding office tables covered with plastic tablecloths), one for men and one for women. Great chunks of boiled lamb lie atop large platters of rice. A roast leg of lamb centers each table. Kabobs of grilled lamb and vegetables, fried samosas, and rhubarb pie from Mrs. Moore make up the rest.

"Do you think that's right, do you? For one woman to have her own fancy American car and the other woman has no car, is that Islamic? You are supposed to spend exactly the same amount of money on each wife, that is not Islamic!" Aunt Fatma is holding forth.

"What can I do if I married a woman who has her own independent source of wealth?" Uncle Abdulla had told her over and over, when she fumed that Tante Mirvat tooled around town in her own Lincoln Town Car. "I didn't buy it for her, are you kidding, can I afford that kind of car?"

"Khadra!" Aunt Fatma calls, spying her. "Look at you! You've come home at last," she says, pulling her into an embrace. Khadra feels the tug and knows Aunt Fatma wants her to stay on her side of the yard, but she must say hello to Tante Mirvat too; it would not be right. Khadra has taken too many brightly wrapped Eid presents from Uncle Abdulla's second wife not to acknowledge her, and she knows Aunt Fatma knows this and will forgive her.

Sabriya plumps the infant Mona in her arms and, of course, Aunt Fatma says to Khadra, "May you be next, marriage and a baby, and this time, no waiting!"

"I stayed for the children," Aunt Fatma says a little later, in front of Sabriya. "Your mother convinced me. Your mother, bless her heart." And Khadra knows what she's hearing: more bits of Shamy legacy, for good or ill. "I sacrificed my pride, my self. For the children," Aunt Fatima says.

But later in the evening, she pulls Khadra back behind the pussy willow and says, "If I had it to do again? I would leave him. We didn't have an arranged marriage, no matter what people may think. We were in love. We ran to the riverbank to meet each other. We had something most people never have, something like a treasure from God. Now? What's left of that treasure? He's taken it all and given it to that one. I don't hate her. But I do blame him. He didn't know how to treasure love. He let it slip through his fingers. He did not appreciate the worth of my love. It was gold, my love! Pure gold!" she whispers, suddenly fierce, squeezing Khadra's arm so hard she breaks skin. "You don't do that to love. No. No. It hurts. It hurts." Her voice gets throaty and she turns her face toward the lilacs.

Uncle Abdullah clears his throat at the microphone. Ever roly-poly, he is in a stout little safari suit. "Welcome, welcome for the One Week of my gran'dowtar," he says. He takes her from Sabriya into his arms and whispers the call to prayer into her right ear. *There is no god but the God. Come to prayer, hearken to prayer.* Khadra takes several shots of his nut-brown face so near the round face of his baby "gran'dowtar." If her settings are right and the light is not too dim as she prays it is not, they will be lovely. She promises copies.

Baby Mona's father, an awkward, rangy Trinidadian boy named Abdul Rahman from the Terre Haute CMC, takes her gently from Uncle Abdulla. You can tell he is in love with her; he's all elbows, trying to get her comfortable. Khadra takes precious pictures of him cradling the baby, daddy and daughter.

A motor revs up loudly somewhere and Khadra starts and looks instinctively up the street toward where Hubbard used to park.

Sabriya says "I know who you're looking for. Mrs. Moore's brother."

"No," Khadra shakes her head. "I was thinking about that man who used to hate us. He used to park across the street and—"

"I know," Sabriya cuts her off, "that's what I said. Mrs. Moore's brother."

"What on earth are you talking about? He—that wasn't her brother—he *can't* be her brother."

"Ask my father," Sabriya shrugs, like it's old news.

Apparently it is, around here—Khadra asks, and it's true. But to her, it's another astounding disclosure. Her *brother?* The Friend—and the enemy—brother and *sister?*—but suddenly now she can no longer think of Mr. Hubbard with the callous dismissal she used to—he's Mrs. Moore's *brother*—not just an icon for abstract hate—there is another sad and angry family drama there, in the cracks.

She has no time to think about it. The call to isha prayer is made. Mrs. Moore and Brig and Riley and several Dawah women who are not praying sit on the back porch. June bugs clatter around the porch lights and the crickets give the iqama. There are a number of new faces in the crowd Khadra surveys as the prayer lines begin to form, new Dawah officers and their families. The position that used to be Uncle Yusuf's is filled now by a hulking, broad-shouldered Bosnian brother with a blond beard. Sister Peaches from Salam Mosque works as the shipping clerk, Sister Habibaty from Malaysia does secretarial, and Brother Obaidah from Iraq has Wajdy's old liaison job.

Two fourteenish-looking girls lean their heads together and whisper. Khadra recognizes from their faces that one must be Sister Peaches' daughter and the other must be the Iraqi brother's girl. They are clearly the new reigning Dawah princesses. Khadra feels a twinge of jealousy. They're in the place that used to be hers and they don't even know who she is.

Here they are, then, she thinks, during salah. My beloved community. Grass smells pleasant when you put your nose in it, unless you are allergic like someone in the second row who sneezes repeatedly. It really does feel good, your face in the grass in the ripe ripe summer, touching the dark dirt between the flattened blades. I like my lovely community in Philly, too. Even if it's more disparate, not the unified thing going on here. Kind of a relief that it's not, really. All those raggedy knobby parts poking out. I love it. Even Bitsy, hunh.

Khadra rises from the grass with the movements of salah. Bitsy would hate it that I thought of her during prostration, hah. Funny, the strange ways of the heart in its grasp of things, the way Reality unveils itself for an instant and then just when you think you've got a shot at it, the shutter goes down, and the light has evaporated. And all you can do is keep plodding along working it, working it, hoping for another glimpse, and meanwhile working patiently at your little given task, just working at developing the picture, whatever you've been lucky enough to get in that instant.

So here they are. God, she thinks, surveying the rows in salah. My God, they're still pottering along the same way, the same old tired language, the same old restrictive ideas and crabbed beliefs.

Oh sure, some people thought about changing the old mentality. Sure, sure, it was significant, this turn toward becoming more genuinely representative of American Muslims, not the folks Over There. And, of course, the people of Dawah weren't all the same. Some were really quite freethinking, on their own, when it came down to it. But the Dawah as an *institution* still is what it is. Institutions tend to be like that, holding on to systems and perpetuating them. And it's so—limited and cramped and—she sighs—just out-and-out *wrong*. Always stressing the wrong side of religion, the fear-God side instead of love-God. Always stressing the outer forms over the inner light.

Well, now, wait, Khadra pauses, in the last rakat. How arrogant of me. Do I know that for sure? Maybe they're right after all, on some other level I'm not aware of. A right principle wrongly applied, or something. Could be. *Yeah, uh, I don't think so, honey,* an ironic voice inside her says. *Stop making excuses for them.* That's what the poet would say, Khadra thinks drily. Okay. Fine. They're dead wrong. Yeah. They really are. My God. About God and everything. God is not an asshole. Alhamdulilah. I mean, *subhana rabial a'la,* she corrects herself, because she's in sajda.

But *still,* Khadra reflects, after salam. Why not? If all paths lead to God, this one also leads to God. The woman next to her kisses her cheek, sweetly, shyly. An after-salah kiss, her skin wrinkly and soft—papery. There is inner light here, too.

Wrong they may or may not be, but still. I would not have a single one of them harmed. I'd—I'd—here the melodramatic Syrian in Khadra waxes lyrical, I'd give my life to protect any of them, if it came to that! Well, or something. Something pretty close to that.

Wrong and mulish they could be, but dear to her, and maddening and conformist and awful, but full of surprising beauty sometimes, and kindness, and, then, just as full of ugliness and pettiness and, overall, really quite mediocre mostly. But no, some were really quite remarkable, possessed of nobility and courage—yet the pride, the pride of holding themselves *above* the way they do, and thinking they *know.* In the end, then, they were just so very human and vulnerable, like anyone else. Really, so vulnerable, when you think about it. Especially now, Khadra realizes. Especially now.

After salah various people take the mike and make *dua* for the new baby. *May she live a pious life and earn paradise in the hereafter. May she be the apple of your eyes.* Khadra whispers to Jihad, "I wish we were listening to you guys now."

"Way ahead of you, sis. I already asked Uncle Abdulla, and we're on next." He grins at her. "Hey, Khadra?"

"What?"

"Listen, I need to talk to you. There's something I need to tell you."

His guys are calling him—"They're ready for us, Jihad."

"Not now," he whispers. "But later, okay?"

She gives him a corny thumbs-up and he rolls his eyes at her, mouthing "You're so eighties!" as he goes up to join his fellow band members.

Singing a capella, they open with *Hearts of Light,* and then a version of the Islamic traditional *The Moon Has Risen Over Us* and a rendition of *Amazing Grace,* neither of which have verses that are objectionable to any of the religions represented in the yard. They follow with a rousing cover of *If I Had a Hammer.* A few eyebrows rise at the line "love between my brothers and my sisters," but for the most part, the group knows how to play to their audience. At Khadra's request, they do *I Can See into Your Heart, and It's a Beautiful Green Place.* The Clash of Civilizations is a big hit. Both of Uncle Abdulla Awad's wives even agree, from separate, distant parts of the yard. The plump-cheeked young mother, Sabriya, glows contentedly in her reclining chair.

Khadra knows now how to turn down the food she doesn't want and enjoy the food she does want. She doesn't even need an antacid after an Awad dinner anymore. The boys, however, have no such hard-earned wisdom. "I'm so stuffed," Brig groans. "Me too," Jihad moans. They fall asleep as soon as Khadra hits the highway. She switches the radio on—music, some man she doesn't recognize singing *One last cry, before I leave it all behind*—then realizes she is running on empty. She pulls into a gas station off US 31. People stare. She is still in hijab. She pulls the tangerine silk tighter around her head.

The stares only ever make her want to pull it on tighter, not take it off the way Seemi keeps suggesting she do after every Middle Eastern crisis dredges up more American hate. Seemi's mother's car got keyed in Manhattan when 250 Marines were bombed in Beirut, and she doesn't even wear hijab—just looking like you come from a Muslim country is enough.

"It's my connector," Khadra had tried to explain to Seemi once about wearing the scarf through hard times. "It makes me feel connected to the people in my family, my mosque, where I come from. My heritage."

"Don't be ridiculous," Seemi had said. "Take the damn thing off; it's not worth risking your life for."

But it was the other way around. Seemi didn't get it. When you're in danger, you don't strip off your armor. And she couldn't get her progressive, but not very tolerant, friend, to see that hijab was also more than that for her. It was the outer sign of an inner quality she wants to be reminded of, more often than she could manage to remind herself without it. "No matter how much of a feminist you talk me into becoming, Seemi, I won't let go of my hijab," Khadra'd said. And her friend had thrown up her hands.

The radio talk is about the new secret-evidence laws, where the government doesn't even have to tell you the case against you. She blinks at a highway sign, realizing that, without planning to, she has taken the route nearest the gully where they found Zuhura, instead of the shortest, safest, straightest way to Bloomington. A cop pulls up behind her. She quakes. How does she know it's really a cop? Maybe it's one of those men who use flashing blue lights to pull women over and attack them. Well, but I've got Jihad and the boys, she thinks. Be rational. Huh, but how much help would they be? She looks at the four big teenaged lugs with their legs every which way and their heads askew, in seventh snoozeland. But it's really a cop. She fakes calm. He writes her a ticket for speeding.

Back on the rural highway. *Beanblossom Bridge, one mile.* On a sudden impulse she pulls off at the exit. "This is where she was found," Tayiba had told her, driving to Bloomington with her once during college. She parks just before the covered bridge. Jihad stirs when the car stops, but goes back to sleep. The others are snoring. *You're not supposed to stop on the way to Bloomington. You're not supposed to stop on these Indiana white people country roads. The friendly back roads of Indiana, full of friendly Hoosier people yeah right. You're not supposed to be here.*

She walks quietly over to the side of the bridge and peers underneath in the dark damp, her heart beating frantically. What does she expect to see, after all these years? Some orange bead from a macramé bag, some sign of Zuhura? There is nothing here but darkness. Alternating with thin broken moonlight through the slats of the bridge. Crickets clickety-click. A frog slaps the water. It is very late. She should get back, get those boys to Bloomington—there is a crunch of twigs behind her.

"Who's here?" she calls out. Crunch, crack, and no answer. The silhouette of a man. "Who is it? Who's here?" she says, her voice suddenly shrilling.

The heart a sudden rose
flowering rich and deep. Redness darker than sunset,
darkness deeper than
the sea

—Daniel Abdal-Hayy Moore

The moon is backlighting him. She cannot see his face. "Who? Who's out there?" she says, her heart jumping. Panic.

"It's me," a voice says, distorted by a yawn. He takes a step closer, almost upon her. "It's me—" and she flails at him, pummeling, "Go away, stop it, leave me be!" He just stands there in complete surprise and then he's crying out "Khadra, it's me, it's me, it's me!" over and over. "It's your brother, Jihad. JIHAD, *JIHAD!"* he shouts and she begins to calm down. "Khadra?" He shivers, even though it's summer. "What are you doing out here?"

"Oh God," she says. "I'm sorry, Jihad." And she needs to sit down on something, there is nothing here, she sinks down, her knees in the mudbank. "This is where she was killed." We still don't know who killed her, Khadra's mind races. What killed her is still out there. We haven't learned a thing from her death.

"She—" Jihad is about to say, "She who?" But then he remembers —he doesn't really remember the murder or the funeral or anything about Zuhura directly, just that it was a big part of community life growing up, a thing everybody knew. A sign for all to consider. And all these years later, it is making tears run down his sister's face.

Jihad doesn't know what to do, is not good at what to do with girls crying. He gingerly puts his arm around her shoulder.

But she takes his arm and pulls him down into the mud with her and gives a piercing wail. He can't make her stop. She is rocking in his arms, back and forth, and wailing—no words, just an awful keening he wished would stop but knows better than to try to get her to stop. Knows that much, to his credit.

Between wails her mouth is wide-open, lips like the painting of *The Scream* that he's seen a picture of somewhere. She is just this gaping wail, drawing breath drawing drawing then the wail comes again, enormous. And again. Alternating silence and sound, veiling and unveiling, again and again. It has its own rhythm and its own demand for breath. No one has taught her to do this. The body does it with its own will. The body becomes a reed for the sound to blow through. Hearken, hearken to the body's reed. The throat gives it its tone, and the stomach and the diaphragm and the root give it depth.

She has never cried for Zuhura before. Not even at the funeral, the busy busy funeral. Zuhura, and all of the hate and hardness that killed her, and the beating against it that can make you hard too, and the hate and hurt inside that eats us. The men who are hard and the women who are hard, and the waves of hard news that come over the airwaves all the time all the time and now takes the shape of white men in hoods and cops who beat what they call nonhumans and now takes the shape of Muslims who murder not for justice in the end, no matter their claims, but for rage and revenge and despair. There is no Oneness in all that hard separation. *Zuhura, I don't care what you really did or didn't do, who you really were or were trying to be. I'm past holding you to task for anything. It's all right. It's all right. Usiwe na wasi-wasi. You just be. You go ahead and be what you are.* She rocks and rocks. Small sharp pebbles dig into her shins. She feels the creekbank with open hands, palm palm knee knee. She disrupts the home of an entire colony of potato bugs.

The other boys are up of course. Who can sleep through this racket? Not even the sleep-craving lumps that nineteen- and twenty-year-old boys can be. They all appear by the mudbank at the bridge, and are startled and mystified at the sight of their friend and his sister, covered in mud and wailing. Jihad murmurs the deal to them, that this one girl my sister knew was, like, murdered here a long time ago, and it is sufficiently dramatic and urgent a, like, explanation. They stand around awkwardly, Garry with two r's and Brig and Riley and Jihad and at least one frog and several cicada and night crawlers and crawdads in the mudbank under the broken moon at Beanblossom Bridge. Now and then one will offer a hand on her shoulder, just to say "hey now" and "hey there" and other phrases that seem to carry a lot of weight with not-too-talkative young men of the Midwest. And Khadra wails and wails in the midst of The Clash of Civilizations.

And then it is over.

"Okay," Khadra says in a nearly sane voice. "I'm all cried out. *Finito*. Thank you for waiting. Let's move on. Everybody in the car!"

Jihad smiles with relief. Later, in some other night's telling, Khadra might become the nutty sister who cried and screamed at Beanblossom Bridge, but right now he's nice to her. He waves the guys away.

"Khadra? This might not be the best time, but I have to tell you something." He sits down on a rock ledge.

"God," she sighs. She comes over and sits down next to him. "I think I'm covered head to toe in mud. I need a bath."

"That's okay," he says. They sit quietly. The sawyer beetles tssrr-tsssst, tssrr-tssst. "Man, those are some loud crickets," he says.

" '*I love to hear thine earnest voice,*
Wherever thou art hid,
Thou testy little dogmatist,
Thou pretty katydid!' " she recites. "Oliver Wendell Holmes."

"Khadra, I'm in love with Sariah Whitcomb," Jihad blurts.

It is stunning news. "Wow," Khadra breathes.

"We've been in love for two years. No one else knows."

"Wow . . . wait, how old is she?"

"Eighteen." They fell in secret love when she was only sixteen and he eighteen? She feels a twinge of sympathy for the parents, his and hers. Who wouldn't worry about their kids falling in love at that vulnerable age?

"We want to get married," he goes on.

This is huge. "I'm delighted you're in love, Jihad! What a blessing. Alhamdulilah."

"We didn't *want* it to happen. It just sort of—did, you know? Despite our best efforts."

Khadra marvels. She never would've had the courage at his age. It took that, to embrace love that seizes you outside your expectations. She tells him this and he beams.

"I'm *serious*. It was *hard*. We, like, tried to deny we were in love. For a long, long time. Like, *weeks!* I didn't know what was happening to me. It was like, you know in Saturday-morning cartoons, when the Road Runner runs out over the cliff and he's pedaling in the air, right? Then he looks down and realizes there's no ground under him anymore? I didn't *ever* think I'd marry someone outside our religion. Neither did she—she told me. She grew up real religious. Actually, we first bonded over that—how strict our *parental units* are and stuff."

"Just-tell-them-we-are-from-France," Khadra says in her Jane Curtin Conehead imitation. Jihad smiles.

Sariah wants to be a nutritionist, he says proudly. She has a scholarship to DePaul. Jihad is halfway through college. They'd be engaged for three years, giving them both time to graduate. Three years sounds wise.

"We've got a lot of stuff to figure out."

"Yeah."

"Like what about children. We want children, of course. Not right away but someday. What are they they gonna be? I mean, of course they'd be considered Muslim by default because, well, Muslim dad, Muslim kids."

"Yeah?"

"Yeah."

"You're both on the same page with that?"

"Sure," Jihad says confidently. "But even if they are Muslim, what will they *really* wanna be? Because, I mean, they'll get to see both religions up close and like, both positive. Not, like, one is true and the other is false. They'll never have the pure sheltered one-religion experience our parents tried to give us. And, by 'our parents.' I mean mine and Sariah's, both. Because it's not like one of us cares about our religion and the other one doesn't. We both care. A lot. I said that already, right?" He smiles and looks so tender and little boy vulnerable. He has such a huge mountain ahead of him to climb. "So they are gonna hear about religion from me and from her. Won't that confuse them?"

"Why do you suppose the Quran allows Muslim men to marry Christian women and Jewish women?" Khadra asks, in an open-ended tone. "Obviously, mothers are going to influence their children."

"They'll be Mor-lims."

"Mus-mons?"

They are quiet for a while. Then she says, "What about your band?" Chicago to South Bend was at least an hour commute. Puts a crimp in practicing every day.

"Yeah, that's the thing," Jihad says. "When me and Sariah get married, it might break up The Clash of Civilizations. Or it might not. But it's no contest, man."

The kid has his priorities straight.

"So here's the thing, Khadra," he says. "What's your schedule like after the conference? Do you have to get straight back to work, I mean, or—the thing is, could you come up to South Bend? I need you. I need you to be there when I tell Mama and Baba."

"High drama."

"Yeah. Especially Mama. And Sariah's going to be telling her parents at the same time. More drama. Only in her family, it's the dad who's sort of like Mama is in our family."

"He's the neurotic parental unit, then?"

"He's the one. He's all, he wants her to be 'worthy.' They use that word a lot, 'worthy.' So anyway, will you come?"

"Say no more, babe, I'm there," she says. She hugs him. It's going to be fireworks this July, that's for sure, she thinks as she walked back to the car. It's going to take every inner resource we've got to give this love a place to grow. All our families.

Hence vision is through the veil, and inescapably so.

—Ibn al-Arabi

The contact sheets are ready next morning. Good, because she's run into about as much of her past as she can handle. Now all she needs to do is sort the thing out. She spreads everything in front of her and loses herself in the work for a while.

"I don't care," Khadra argues on the phone with her photo editor. "The Awads are like family to me, I don't care if the Chief is excited about the polygamy angle. You said I had creative control."

". . ."

"No, of course I don't agree with polygamy. I think it sucks. But it's their choice and they've figured out a way to make it work for them, and no, I'm *not* going to do an exposé on how many Muslims in America can be found who do it. It's what the mainstream media always does: Pick the most sensational thing and highlight the negative —Am I accusing you of Orientalism? No, Ernesto, I am not accusing you of anything so B-movie as Orientalism. See, the wives thing is just not the core story here. Don't trip on it." She packs her bag as she speaks. "Okay? 'Bye for now."

She addresses the Madonna of the Trail postcard to her parents' home in South Bend. "Dear Mama & Baba," she writes. "Greetings from Muslimland—I'm in the midst of the Dawah! Saw this pioneer lady on the road & thought of you. Love from, Khadra. xxxooo." She'll mail it from Eyad and Omayma's house, where she's going to spend the day after the conference; she's looking forward to seeing how Coethar and Khalid are growing.

The phone rings just as she's at the door to head down for check out.

"Hi. Oh—I mean, *assalamu alaikum wa rahmatullahi wa barakatuh.*" Eyad got all nitpicky when Khadra did not use the full and proper Muslim greeting.

". . ."

"Yes of course I'm putting that in the article, Eyad. . . . Well, I don't care if Omayma and her committee don't want it in. It's an important part of the story."

". . ."

"*La ilaha illa allah.* Because it takes both sides to make a whole picture—the dark and the bright."

". . ."

"Well, I think you're wrong. I think people will see the beauty in it too."

". . ."

"Despite—despite all that. Yeah, even in spite of the Islamophobes and the ignorance out there. I'm counting on the intelligence of the readers—most of them."

". . ."

"I am well aware of that. You don't have to tell me how harsh the scrutiny is that the Muslim community is under. I know all that. We still need to face our darkness too. Negatives and positives. No, for our *own* sake, not to pander to *them*. For the sake of '*studying what our own souls put forth,*' you know?"

". . ."

"Stop it, Eyad. I cannot operate from fear anymore. I cannot operate from fear."

All paths are circular.

—Ibn al-Arabi

"It's about learning to surrender," Hanifa is saying, on the giant screen above the Speedway track. "Every race car driver knows that." It is Khadra's first sight of her since they were fifteen. Later, she'll see her in person, and they'll talk quietly.

"Surrender?" the sportscaster says. "Won't you crash if you do that?"

"You do everything you can to stay on track, of course," Hanifa explains. "You've trained. Your car, your engine, is right, down to the last nut and bolt. But in the end, you surrender—that's the only way you're going to get through the lap, going two hundred miles an hour." Here she gets into the race car, and her eyes sparkle like she's about to cartwheel through a mosque. "So you let go! And you feel your body doing it on its own, and your mind is thinking a thousand things and thinking nothing, and your heart is pounding, and you're connected to everything, to your car, to the air whizzing past, to everyone in the stands, to God. It all becomes one great big living thing." She puts the helmet on and waves.

Khadra is in the stands. She never would've thought she'd be okay going to a place like the Speedway. Coming here is like following the white man into his lair. The sport was founded by bootleggers, for goodness' sake. But here I am, she thinks. I am here!

As if to allay her fears, there is practically a whole Muslim bleacher section. Aunt Khadija and Uncle Jamal are here—she waves at them—and they have Hanifa's daughter, thirteen-year-old Aziza, in tow. More black people and brown have been going to the race in recent years, not only in the stands and the pit, but at the starting line. So, in a lot of ways, it's a new day at the races, Khadra thinks. Maybe.

She looks around at the white people, too—the Americans—no wait, she's American now—the other Americans. Hanifa has a white mechanic in her crew, blond and earnest and solid. Midwesterners —Hoosiers—set in their ways, hardworking, steady, valuing God and family. Suspicious of change. In a funny way, Khadra realizes suddenly, as she surveys the crowd: they're us, and we're them. Hah! My folks are the perfect *Hoosiers!*

Khadra and Hakim go down to the concessions to get pop for Hanifa's daughter and themselves.

"I've been thinking of coming up to Philadelphia," Hakim says, as they take their places in line. He looks at her steadily. "Spending some time up there."

"Yeah?" Khadra says.

"Yeah. Because—I've been thinking—what if—well, what if we get to know each other again, as adults?"

She is caught off guard. What if they did? Her mind races. No, not her mind. It might—it might be nice. He could maybe stay at the dergah. She could introduce him to Mukhtar Bibi. She smiles at the thought of the tall, lanky imam meeting the little wizened sheikha. Wait—you're getting ahead of yourself, she thinks.

"You're smiling. You wouldn't mind?"

"I wouldn't mind," she says carefully. "Just to get to know each other, right?"

"Right."

She's not going to rush anything, this she knows. "For real this time," she says.

"Yeah," he says. After a moment, he adds, "It was for real before. You know—" He pauses, looks at his feet, then meets her eye with a twinkle she has not seen in their encounters all weekend. Hasn't seen since they were little. "Couldn't you tell—don't you know that—well, that I used to kind of have a thing for you? When we were kids?"

She is floored. Then she thinks about it while they buy the soda pop. "You know what?" she says slowly, as they turn toward the stands, balancing trays. "I guess I—I never really let myself think about it, but somewhere along the line, I maybe had a little thing for you, too."

He lets out a whoop and nearly spills the root beer. "I knew it! I *knew* it! *Khadra likes Haki-eem, Khadra likes Haki-eem,*" he teases, and for a moment the years drop away and he is Hakim whose handlebars she rode, whizzing down Tecumseh Street.

"Shut *up,*" she says, giving him a flirty shoulder.

But she is reflective as they hand Aziza her drink and head to their seats some rows up. She is thinking she knows why he never approached her parents.

"All that Muslim-on-Muslim racism," he acknowledges. She appreciates that he is too kind to say, "Your racist parents."

"But you should've told *me,* at least," she says.

"Why?" he says. "You weren't going to go against them. You were very close to them. I *liked* that about you. It was sweet."

"How do you know what I would've done?" Because she did break with their program, in the end. She wondered if she would've done it earlier, if—well, there was no point in wondering. "I know what I'm going to do *now,*" she says, setting down her drink.

"What?" he says, leaning closer to her, but not touching. His face is radiant, a face of intelligence.

"Take some bad-ass pictures!" she says, laughing. She grabs her camera gear and heads down to the press tier, where she shows her pass. She climbs up and gets into position, into focus, legs apart to brace herself, *qad qamat, qad qamat.*

There will be no postponing her task, and no crouching and stooping and restricting her movements for someone else's hang-ups. Not for Hakim or anyone—no surrender in those quarters, anyway.

Because so what if they'd had crushes on each other once—that doesn't settle anything. Whether Hakim is just looking for someone to fit "the wife profile," or really is for real this time remains to be seen. But she's willing to go down the road to find out.

The flag drops and the drivers are off. Click-shee, click-shee! Click-click-click-shee! Khadra is off too, shooting as fast as she can. Her flame is lit, and she will tend and cherish it.

Hanifa is a back marker so far. "But that's okay, that's all right," Uncle Jamal is yelling, up in the stands. "She's *here!* She's in the *race!*"

"Bismillah!" Aunt Khadija screams, covering Aziza's eyes, and Uncle Jamal and Hakim jump up. Hanifa's car has skidded against the wall—there is a terrible screech of metal—will she crash?—*Whoa!—that was a close call for the green and black car—oversteering into the turn—a rookie mistake!*

Is she out of the race? *No!—she's back!* cries the announcer. *She's regrouping*—I'm regrouping too, Khadra thinks with elation, and she is full of gratitude—*she's gathering speed—and there she goes!*—and Khadra and her camera are lockstep with her friend for a cartwheeling second, clicking away, and the crowd cheers as one, and in that shutter-click instant, she knows she is where she belongs, doing what she must do, with intent, with abandon. And it is glorious, it is divine, and Khadra's own work takes her there: into the state of pure surrender.

You claim "I broke
The Idol of Illusion—
I'm liberated!"
But I fear
Your Manifesto is itself
An idol

—Ahmad Jami

Permissions

I would like to acknowledge the following works, cited in this novel. • Quran quotes throughout based on translations by A. Yusuf Ali, Amana Publications, 1997; Ahmed Ali, Princeton University Press, 1993; and Michael Sells's *Approaching the Quran: The Early Revelations*, White Cloud Press, 1999. • Prefatory epigraph from Sue Monk Kidd, *Dance of the Dissident Daughter: A Woman's Journey from the Christian Tradition to the Sacred Feminine*, HarperSanFrancisco, 1996. • Wudu blessing and "salat" definition from Coleman Barks and Michael Green, *The Illuminated Prayer: The Five Times Prayer of the Sufis as Revealed by Jelladudin Rumi & Bawa Muhaiyaddeen*, Ballantine Wellspring, 2000. • Howard H. Peckham, *Indiana: A History*, University of Illinois Press, 2003. • Marvin X, *In the Crazy House Called America*, Black Bird Press, 2003. • Laura Ingalls Wilder, *Little House on the Prairie*, HarperCollins edition, 1971. • Hoda Barakat, trans. Marilyn Booth, *Tiller of Waters*, American University in Cairo Press, 2001. • Diane Wolkstein and Samuel Kramer, *Inanna, Queen of Heaven and Earth*, Harper & Row, 1983. • Libby Roderick, "How Could Anyone," (c) Libby Roderick Music 1988. All rights reserved. From the recordings "How Could Anyone" and "If You See a Dream," Turtle Island Records, P.O. Box 203294, Anchorage, AK 99520, (907) 278-6817, www.libbyroderick.com, libbyroderick@gmail.com. • Leonard Cohen, *Book of Mercy*, McClelland & Stewart, 1986. • James Baldwin, "The Fire Next Time," *Collected Essays*, Library of America, 1998. • Hoyt Axton, "Joy to the World/A Country Anthem (Jeremiah Was a Bullfrog)," Rondor Music Publishing Ltd./Universal Music Publishing Ltd. • James H. Madison, *The Indiana Way: A State History*, Indiana University Press, Indiana Historical Society, 1986. • Michael Wilkerson, "Indiana Origin Stories," in David Hoppe, ed., *Where We Live: • Essays About Indiana*, Indiana University Press, 1989. • Ali ibn Abi Talib, excerpts from *Nahj al-Balagha* (The Peak of Eloquence), trans. Thomas Cleary as *Living and Dying with Grace: Counsels of Hadrat Ali*, Shambhala, 1996. • Middle East Watch, *Syria Unmasked: The Suppression of Human Rights by the Asad Regime*, Yale University Press, 1991. • Martin Buber, *I and Thou*, trans. Walter Kaufmann, Charles Scribner's Sons, 1970. • Thomas Huhti, *The Great Indiana Touring Book: 20 Spectacular Auto Tours*, Black Earth, WI: Trails Books, 2002. • Six lines used as epigraph from *Truth or Dare: Encounters with Power* by Starhawk, Copyright 1987 by Miriam Simos, reprinted by permission of HarperCollins publishers. • James Olney. *Metaphors of Self: the Meaning of Autobiography*, Princeton University Press, 1972. • • Yusuf Islam (formerly Cat Stevens), "Moonshadow" from *Teaser and the Firecat*, A&M Records, 1971. • Marilyn Booth, trans. Aisha Taymuriya, from Miriam Cooke and Margot Badran, *Opening the Gates: A Century of Arab Feminism*, Indiana University Press, 1990. • J. R. R. Tolkien, *The Lord of the Rings*,

Boston: Houghton Mifflin, 1993. • Camille Adams Helminski, *Women of Sufism: A Hidden Treasure*. Shambhala, 2003. • Badr Shakir al-Sayyab, "Ode to the Rain" from Salma Khadra Jayyusi, ed., *Modern Arabic Poetry*, Columbia University Press, 1991. • Sue Hubbell, *Broadsides from the Other Orders: A Book of Bugs*, NY: Random House, 1993. • Daniel Abdal-Hayy Moore, from *Some of the Mysteries of the Self*, Philadelphia, Zilzal Press, 1994, and from "The Question Posed" in *Awake as Never Before*, Zilzal Press, 1984. Now published through www.danielmoorepoetry.com. • Adrienne Rich, "Diving into the Wreck," from *Diving into the Wreck: Poems 1971-1972*. W. W. Norton & Company, Inc., 1973. • Attar, Sanai, Rumi, Shah Dai Shirazi, and Ahmad Jami, trans., Peter Lamborn Wilson and Nasrollah Pourjavady, *The Drunken Universe*, Omega Publications, New Lebanon, NY, 1987. • Anna Akhmatova, *Selected Poems of Anna Akhmatova*, trans. Richard McKane, Bloodaxe Books, 1989. • Naomi Long Madgett, "Black Woman," in Wendy Mulford, ed., *Love Poems by Women: An anthology of poetry from around the world and through the ages*. Ballantine Books/Fawcett Columbine, 1990. • *The Epic of Gilgamesh: An English Version*, by N. K. Sanders, quoted on p. 340. Penguin, revised edition, 1964. • John L. Foster, trans., "The Harper's Song for Inherkhawy," from *Ancient Egyptian Literature: An Anthology*, Copyright (c) 2001. Quoted on p. 340, courtesy of the University of Texas Press. • Sandra Cisneros, "Introduction," *The House on Mango Street*, NY: Alfred A. Knopf, 1994. • Phil Collins, "In the Air Tonight" from the album *Face Value*, 1981, copyright Phillip Collins Ltd., London. • Memphis Minnie, "Me and My Chauffeur Blues," in Wendy Mulford, ed., *Love Poems by Women: An anthology of poetry from around the world and through the ages*. Ballantine Books/Fawcett Columbine, 1990. • "By the Rivers Dark" © Sony/ATV Songs LLC, Robinhill Music. All rights on behalf of Sony/ATV Songs LLC administered by Sony/ATV Music Publishing, 8 Music Square West, Nashville, TN 37203. All rights reserved. Used by Permission. • Translations of Ibn al-Arabi are from William C. Chittick, *The Self-Disclosure of God: Principles of Ibn al-Arabi's Cosmology*, State University of New York Press, 1998. • Excerpts from Hadiths numbers 7, 15, 22, 23, and 27, Ezzeddin Ibrahim and Denys Johnson-Davies, trans., *Forty Hadith Qudsi*, the Holy Koran Publishing House, Beirut and Vienna, 1980. • Translation of lines from poem by Wallada bint al-Mustakfi is by the author, Mohja Kahf. • Rabia excerpts from the Penguin anthology *Love Poems from God*, copyright 2002 Daniel Ladinsky and used by his permission. • Sonia Sanchez, "To All Brothers: From All Sisters" from *Homegirls and Handgrenades*, Thunder's Mouth Press, 1997. • Ibn Faraj, "Chastity" excerpts from Cola Franzen, trans., *Poems of Arab Andalusia*, City Lights Books, 1990. • Thulani Davis, "Don't Worry, Be Buppie: Black Novelists Head for the Mainstream," in Joy Press, ed., *War of the Words: 20 Years of Writing on Contemporary Literature*, Three Rivers Press, 2001. • Trans. by Mohja Kahf of excerpts from "The Palm Reader" by Nizar Kabbani, from the Arabic poem published in *The Complete Works of Nizar Kabbani*, Nizar Kabbani Publications, Beirut, 1973. • Joy Harjo, "Eagle Poem," in John Frederick Nims and David Mason, *Western Wind: An Introduction to Poetry*, McGraw-Hill, 1999.